"Stephen Russell's strong debut pulls you in, and clips along at a fierce pace, with nuanced characters who are hard to leave behind. I can't wait for the next Cooper McKay book to come out."

~ W.H. Watford
Author of Lethal Risk and Mortal Strain

"BLOOD MONEY is edge of the seat reading"

~ Fred Klein
Host, Literary Gumbo TV and
Bantam Books VP (ret)

VISIT STEPHEN ONLINE

Website: www.AuthorStephenRussell.com
Facebook: http://www.facebook.com/stephen.russell.5855

Published in the United States by Blue Jay Media Group
Print ISBN-13: 978-1-936724-41-3
ebook ISBN-13: 978-1-936724-40-6

ACKNOWLEDGEMENTS

Like many novels, I suppose, Blood Money began as an affair of the heart. Unlike most, though, the roots of the Mackie McKay series are anchored in academia.

When I was a young boy of six, still enamored with Star Wars and Legos, my father dedicated a book to my siblings and me entitled Coronary Artery Disease: Recognition and Management. Even as the text of the thick green book remained largely inscrutable, the idea of being an author's son enchanted me. Often during my formative years, I would remove the tome from the shelf and simply hold it, feeling the weighty importance of bound words. Only afterwards would I appreciate the process of producing such a work.

Twenty five years later, in the early-morning hours of infancy, I abandoned the hope of more sleep and began to write. I was no more prepared for the disciplines of authorship than those of parenting, but I pressed forward anyway. I soon realized that my muse would meet me after diaper changes and often stay until sunrise. At the quiet kitchen table in our Cincinnati home, disparate chapters accumulated. By the time our second child was born, I had completed what I thought must be the next great American novel.

Enter the heart again.

An author and cardiology colleague of my father helped me interpret the meaning of a first draft and the importance of revision. At the Santa Barbara Writers Conference, I learned how to polish that first manuscript and where to search for my next next story.

Like so many affairs of the heart, this book is only possible because of the patience and persistence of those who've shared this journey with me. And it all began at home.

Thanks, Dad. This one's for you.

To Richard O. Russell, Jr.

medical mentor, father and friend.

Chapter One

THE HANDCUFFS CUT into Doctor Cooper McKay's wrists each time he shifted in the back seat. He kept his mouth shut, swallowing the pain that ripped through his shoulder.

Nashville Police Officer Lance Pennington glanced in the rearview mirror, a smirk flickering in his gaze. Doctor McKay purposely ignored the man.

McKay's thoughts raced. Fast. Frantic. He struggled to regain his composure and his wits. Don't react, he cautioned himself. Just think. His surgical training had prepared him to stay cool in a crisis. Thirty years in operating rooms had honed those skills, but calm was easier to produce when someone else's family was in crisis.

He continued to ignore Officer Pennington, staring out the window at the hospital entrance instead. On any other Friday morning, the police would still be waiting for him, after being informed that Doctor McKay was halfway through his first surgical case. Last week, all of that had changed with his long-awaited retirement. His heart hammered with anxiety when he considered all that he had left behind. And what remained.

"Has anyone told Reagan?" he asked.

Officer Pennington flicked a glance at the rearview mirror. "Reagan?"

"My daughter." McKay swallowed, mouth dry with dread. "Our daughter. She's in her junior year, but she's studying abroad this semester." He stared, not really seeing the entrance to the hospital. "This is going to kill her."

Pennington cleared his throat. "You are aware, Dr. McKay, that anything you say can and probably will be used against you in a court of law. Until your lawyer arrives, you may want to sit back and shut the hell up."

For the first time since the police had shown up at the hospital, McKay sat back and followed orders. His fly–by to see his pals in the doctor's lounge now seemed ill–advised. But the police would've come to his home next, he guessed, and that had its own set of problems.

He needed to personally break the news to Reagan, but right now that seemed impossible. Italy was an eight-hour flight away once the wheels left the tarmac. Not counting the time it would take to organize the damn trip. And assuming the police would even allow him to leave. The prospects of a face–to–face discussion would also be awkward in so many ways. Between McKay's retirement and divorce, Reagan was all he had left. The only thing permanent that mattered, anyway. Truth be told, he'd lost his relationship with his ex–wife years before the divorce. Like many crumbling marriages, they'd kept up appearances, in part for business purposes. And for their daughter. Christ, he thought, would Reagan even want to see me? She had ignored his emails and phone calls for much of the last year, blaming him for the divorce. And now it looked like others wanted to blame him for her mother's death.

Not the retirement he had expected.

The font passenger door opened. A plain–clothed cop slid into the front seat. "They don't know anything else about the car," she said to Officer Pennington.

To McKay, the words sounded more like *cah.* He studied her profile as she spoke. She hadn't been in the room when Pennington had interrogated him earlier. Her pinned–back black hair exposed wide cheek bones as she focused on Pennington and ignored the cuffed doctor in the back seat. McKay didn't ignore her, though. She looked Asian, maybe Vietnamese, but her accent said northeast. Maybe Boston. Fish out of water in Nashville.

She didn't wait for Pennington to respond. She hooked her elbow over the front seat and pivoted toward the back. "Dr. Cooper McKay," she said, allowing the accent to seep in. Scooping the o's and dropping the r's like his grandmother from Massachusetts. *Coop–uh.* "I'm Detective Libby Pham, Nashville Police Department."

He forced a smile, trying to avoid any further tension. "Mackie McKay," he said.

"Pardon?" It came out *pah-duhn*.

"Mackie McKay," he said. "Nick name."

Detective Pham fixed her gaze on him for a beat, then continued. "When was the last time you talked to your ex-wife?"

Mackie clenched his jaw. "Are these cuffs necessary?"

"Have you calmed down?"

"Enough."

"We'll see." She repeated her question.

Mackie searched Pham's face for compassion, but he saw only her impassive expression. If she was a day over thirty-five, Mackie would be surprised. "We don't speak much," he said, then corrected himself. "Didn't. Stuck to email and texts. More civil that way."

Pham stared at him, a laser-like probing that made him feel uncomfortable and exposed.

"I did see her this week," he finally said. "She came by to pick up some papers that had been sent to my house by mistake. Work related documents."

Mackie did not like being on the receiving end of an interrogation. Most surgeons didn't. "Look, I didn't share the whole truth inside."

"Was that before or after you took a swing at Officer Pennington?"

"He accused me of murdering my ex-wife." Mackie fought to control his tone.

"We found her body in the trunk of your car," Pham countered.

"Which I'd reported stolen the day before," Mackie said.

Pennington chuckled like he'd heard that before, and often. "You're fighting skills suck, Doc."

Mackie ignored him, focusing on Pham instead. "Sarah and I had several mutual interests. Business related, mostly."

Pham nodded. "So even after the divorce, you and your ex kept up civility?" She turned around even more, unencumbered by a seatbelt.

"We owned several joint patents for a synthetic blood product."

"You just said you didn't share the whole truth," Pham said.

He paused. "I saw her last night."

"At home?"

"Where else would I be?"

"That's what I'm trying to find out," she said. "Were you alone?"

Mackie averted his eyes, glancing out the back window of the police cruiser. The blue lights pulsed off the parked cars at the curb.

Patient families gave the cops a wide berth as they walked into the hospital lobby, stealing an occasional glance at the man in the back seat. What was the point of all this? He needed to get out of here and work on contacting his daughter. Mackie preferred not to mention the previous night, but Sarah's death forced his hand. "I was with a friend. An acquaintance, really."

Pham nodded again. "A friend with special privileges?"

"Ah…you've been there."

Pham smiled faintly. Naturally straight teeth, accented by the hint of misalignment in the front. An orthodontist would wring his hands at the subtle imperfection, but it gave her a look of authenticity. Unaltered beauty. "What's her name?"

"Hollie Blanton," he said. "Call the house. She's probably still there. I wasn't supposed to be gone this long."

Pham digested the information. "Did Sarah know about Hollie?"

Mackie held her gaze. "We were long divorced, Detective."

Pham waited.

"Sarah lives—lived—in a downtown condo for the last two years." Mackie's reticence yielded to defensive explanations. "She'd had it during the last year of our marriage, going there for God-knows-what. Closer to her law firm…and her new man at the time."

"She had more than one relationship?"

"I lost track." Mackie took a deep breath before blowing it out. "When she dropped by last night to get those papers, she ran in to Hollie. Suffice it to say, she wasn't happy."

"Why?"

"Jealousy, I'm sure. She had a low tolerance for happiness." Mackie repositioned his body. "These cuffs are killing me."

"Effective, aren't they?"

Officer Pennington, still smirking in the driver's seat, asked, "Did you ask your ex about your car last night?"

Mackie sized up Pennington. Half an hour earlier, he'd hustled a manacled Mackie through the lobby of Nashville Memorial Hospital, all because of a misunderstanding. Now, Pennington pretended to be chummy. Mackie said, "We didn't get around to it."

A tap on the hood of the cruiser interrupted him.

Pham straightened in the front seat. She stepped out of the cruiser to speak to the uniformed officer standing there. They moved to the sidewalk so Mackie couldn't hear.

From Mackie's perspective, cuffed and stuffed in the back seat, Detective's Pham's demeanor shouted new responsibility. Like she didn't want to mess up this interrogation. Probably a new promotion, he guessed. Maybe even her first such encounter as a detective. As he tried to figure his way out of the back seat and on to connecting up with Reagan, Pennington spoke again.

"I once saw a Discovery Channel feature on medical breakthroughs. They covered synthetic blood. It doesn't look like real blood, does it? More like cloudy water or skim milk."

Mackie looked at Pennington. "You wouldn't have struck me as the Discovery Channel type."

"And you wouldn't have struck me as a guy who would swing at a cop."

Mackie didn't respond to that.

"They said, used wrong, synthetic blood can be deadly."

Mackie considered his response. Pennington's role of agreeable cop didn't sit well with him. "It saves lives, Officer. With the proper training, it's as safe a saline."

"To use in the operating room?"

"Or a trauma."

Pennington smiled. "Like a head wound in a brutally-beaten middle-aged woman who's been shoved into the trunk of a car?"

Mackie's ears heated up. Was that where this conversation was heading? To a confession of a crime he hadn't committed? His rebuttal caught in his throat as the front passenger door opened once more. Detective Pham leaned into the car. Her right hand gripped the door frame. "There's something you need to see, Dr. McKay."

Mackie scooted toward the door, trying to stretch his legs and reposition his hands. "Am I being arrested or not?"

"Depends," Detective Pham said. "Right now, all I'm asking for is a little cooperation."

CHAPTER TWO

THIRTY MINUTES LATER, Mackie sat uncuffed in an interrogation room at the Nashville Police Department, processing the photographs in front of him. He waited on his attorney, but he doubted Duel Richardson would change the process much. Just a formality, really. At least in his own mind. Mackie knew he was innocent, and he assumed his cooperation would be his best ticket home.

Pham slid photos across the table towards him. "See anything you recognize?"

Mackie scrutinized the photos. Immediately, he felt sick. Pictures of brown stains on a carpet, probably blood. Close ups of a head wound showing bone chips and glistening grey tissue matted in her hair. He pinched the bridge of his nose, feeling unsteady. "I assume that's the trunk of my car. So that must be Sarah…" He took a breath, fighting for clinical detachment, unsettled by the horrific images of a woman he once loved. A woman who had been a good mother to their daughter. "With all the blood, I don't—it doesn't look like her." He refocused on the close up picture of the wound. Faint white crystals dusted the edge of the wound. "What caused the head trauma?"

"I was hoping you could tell us," she said. "From a surgical perspective, of course."

He rose from his chair, spun the pictures toward Pham, and leaned across the table. He noticed her stiffen slightly. He continued anyway. "If you look at the way the blood pools near the back of the head…uh, you'll see the coagulated lumps…" He cleared his throat, struggling for an objective perspective. Unable to find it, he slumped back in his chair. "How long had she been like that?"

"Hours, at least. Maybe all night."

He shook his head, trying to process the sad reality. "I was home hours ago," he said quietly, more as an afterthought. Then stopped.

Pham raised her eyebrows in the same interrogating expression she had used earlier in the police cruiser. Her brown eyes expanded, dominating her facial features.

Mackie broke eye contact. He glanced at the one-way mirror in the room. He couldn't see anyone, but he felt the press of Officer Pennington's stare from behind the glass. Rubbing his eyes, unexpected grief stabbed at his already shaken composure. Mackie straightened. Pham had shared that she had contacted Hollie, who'd corroborated his alibi for the last twelve hours. "Said she'd been with you since suppertime," Pham told Mackie with a hint of amusement. "Under your watchful gaze…and for much of the night just under you."

Mackie squirmed. While he wouldn't give her high marks for being a reliable witness, right now, Hollie was all he had. "Yes, well, she has her…attributes."

"I'm sure."

Mackie asked, "What other information do you have so far? Besides the photographs?"

Pham took one final look at the images before collecting them and placing them back into the folder marked "Sarah Collins-McKay." She perched on the edge of the table and crossed her arms. "I've got a fifty-two year old woman found dead in her ex-husband's car hours after he last saw her."

"And, who I might add, was with another woman at the time of the murder."

"Apparently." Pham returned to the stoney expression that made her virtually unreadable. "I also have no evidence of resistance, no signs of struggle, no damage to the car, and best I can tell, absolutely no reason for the murder."

"Sounds like we've got some work to do," Mackie concluded.

"I'm not sure where the "we" fits into this investigation, Doctor McKay. Nashville PD is more than capable of handling the investigation without a vigilante crew. Besides, one thin alibi does not exonerate a person of interest."

Someone banged on the door with a disruptive thump. A muffled and rumbling voice with a southern drawl said, "That old guy in the room needs to stay put."

Duel Richardson. Mackie rubbed his eyes.

"Your attorney?" Pham asked.

He nodded.

"You're in more trouble than I realized."

They both chuckled. An odd moment of levity, but these were odd circumstances.

The doorknob unlocked, a metallic *snick* signaling the arrival of Mackie's best legal hope, Duel Richardson. Mackie had known Duel longer than he had known Sarah, more of an acquaintance than friend for much of that time. Repeated casual exposures, though, had changed that. Duel led a full service law firm, Richardson, Quinn & Yanoski. He managed several partners with various specialties, making the firm extremely successful as a one-stop legal shop. Although one of Duel's junior partners specializing in big-ticket divorces initially represented Mackie, Duel took a special interest when he saw it would be amicable and helped finalize the lucrative agreement between him and Sarah. Mackie had forged a peculiar friendship with him, but he never expected to have to call on the firm's expertise in criminal law.

When the door opened, Duel sauntered into the room, his shirt neatly tucked over his protuberant abdomen. Not a pretty sight. In spite of his quirks, or perhaps because of them, Duel's successful law career commanded a sizable income that he poured into cars, clothes, and comfort foods. Right now, Mackie could see two of the three on full display. His jacket and pants possessed the signature of a tailor.

Duel placed both palms on the table and leaned toward Mackie, a master of ceremonies preparing for his opening speech. "Have they read you Miranda?"

"I haven't been arrested," Mackie said.

"Like hell," Duel bellowed. "One of the most common reasons for a mistrial is procedural misconduct, usually beginning with the arrest. Isn't that right, my little geisha?"

"Duel!" Mackie said.

"Shut up," Pham snapped. "Both of you."

Duel straightened and adjusted his blazer. "Uh-oh. Occidentals unite. I've pissed off the Asian cop."

Mackie shook his head in embarrassment.

Pham took one step toward Duel, forcing him to retreat toward the chair. "Sit down. Your client and I were having a civil conversation."

Duel plopped in the chair next to Mackie, pulling out an engraved fountain pen and a leather-bound steno pad. He wrote the date across the blank page. "Last month," Duel said, "when Detective Pham transferred to Nashville, I met this Yankee peach at a get-to-know-your-local-cops gathering between police and trial lawyers. We've crossed paths a few times since."

Mackie hardly relaxed. "I have a confirmed alibi from last night. Hollie is still at the house."

Duel looked up. "The cleaning lady?"

All eyes turned to Mackie. He stared at his hands. "It just sort of happened."

Duel nodded, suppressing a smile. He looked at Pham. "So we're free to go, then?"

Pham shook her head, more in disappointment than disagreement. "You're not off the hook yet, Doctor McKay. You could have faked the stolen car. Left the house after Hollie fell asleep. Seen Sarah one more time before her death. We have a few more issues to resolve."

Duel exhaled, his breath low and resonant from his lungs. "What time's the postmortem? I'd like to share with my client the preliminary results."

"The body's already at the morgue. They'll be getting underway soon," Pham said.

"That's quick," Mackie said. A second, chilling thought followed shortly behind. "Do I have to identify the body?"

He routinely interacted with pathologists at the hospital, and he'd stood in on an occasional autopsy, but almost always in controlled settings where trickles of blood seeped from clean scalpel lines. Others in his profession dealt with the macerated bodies of trauma. The prospect of seeing Sarah as she'd appeared in the photographs rocked him.

"Dental records should help with that, when the offices open." She glanced at her watch.

Mackie saw Duel scratch the words "no hard evidence yet" on the paper. Duel reached in his blazer pocket and handed Pham his card. "Call me when a preliminary report is ready." He placed his hand on Mackie's shoulder. "This man's good name and reputation have taken an inestimable hit today."

Pham met his gaze and smiled. Without the tension in her face, she looked younger still. Almost out of place. Did transferring to Nashville's Police Department represent a rising star looking to establish her reputation? An undercurrent of concern swirled in Mackie's stomach.

She stared at Mackie as she addressed Duel. "Keep your client close by during the preliminary investigation, Counselor. I wouldn't get too comfortable yet."

Chapter Three

MACKIE SAT ON the leather sofa in Duel's law office, waiting for his lawyer-turned-chauffeur to drive him home. Although he sank back into the overstuffed cushions, he could not relax. He absently stroked the slick edge of his uncovered cell phone, staring at the framed prints on the wall. Almost all of the photos showed Duel with his arm slung across the shoulders of politicians and one president. But still no sign of the man himself. Mackie waited.

He glanced at his cell phone. Twice he had called Reagan. Both times an automated voice reminded him she was out of the coverage area. No shit, he thought to himself. She's in Florence, Italy. The recorded voice irritated him and seemed to mock him. Her international call plan provided shoddy service. If he could just get through to voicemail, he thought.

"Are you about ready?" Mackie finally asked.

He waited a beat, then Duel poked his head into the lobby of his office, hand cupped over a wireless phone. "Could you keep your voice down and give me a minute? I'm finishing up a conference call." Duel disappeared.

Mackie pulled himself up from the sofa. He turned on a nearby lamp and scrolled through email on his phone. Nothing of interest. He called Reagan once more, pacing while he waited.

No luck.

Anger soured his stomach. He needed to shower, eat breakfast, and think. How the hell could he tell Reagan what had happened? He needed to tell her, but he couldn't board a plane. He dreaded the call. He also dreaded dealing with all the issues that came with the death of a family member. He didn't even know where to begin. He vaguely remembered conversations they'd had about burial versus cremation. And the murder investigation? That created its own set of problems. When would they release her body? If he was a suspect, would they even release it to him? In other circumstances, Reagan, being the true next of kin, would need to take care of the details.

Mackie knew he should tell Reagan in person, and be there for her to hold on to. He'd practiced the empty platitudes of comfort with families of patients, but he had no personal experience with loss. His father, a military man, had left a legacy of paternal abandonment before his untimely death. Mackie seemed to have learned that lesson well. Going to work early. Coming home late. Making excuses. Until now, he'd not given his behavior a second thought. Like so much else, he assumed he'd have time in retirement to repair his neglected relationships. He knew near the end of his marriage, Sarah felt the same way. Now, Mackie felt mortal, and he didn't like the feeling one damn bit.

Mackie asked his phone to dial the Office of Student Affairs at Vanderbilt. When he called, he was transferred to the voicemail of the woman in charge of overseas education. He left a message.

Duel came into the foyer of his office. "I've got an ass-load of work to do today," he grumbled.

"Any idea what could have happened her?" Mackie asked. "You knew us better than anybody, especially after working on our divorce. Any questionable relationships or business deals?"

Duel chewed on his lower lip, considering the question. "She had a few new clients after you two split. Nothing that would create a risk."

"How many of them did she sleep with?"

Duel laughed, almost nervously. "Jesus, pal. Lose the bitterness and move on." He walked to the corner table and turned off the lamp. "She did the same legal work after the divorce. Offered local representation for international clients. Kept up governmental contracts. Nothing exciting. Of course, she had the H-BOC patent, too, but not much active legal work with that."

Mackie ran his fingers through his hair. "Can we go yet? I'm ready to get home."

Duel stood and walked toward the door, nudging Mackie with his elbow when he walked past. "You got a breakfast date with the cleaning lady?"

"She's not there," Mackie said.

"You got lucky last night."

"Give it a rest, Duel. I'm a grown man, for Christ's sake. In case you haven't noticed, I am moving on."

Duel turned around, looking serious. "That's not what I'm taking about. If you'd spent last night like you usually do, at home with just the dog, you'd be sitting on a metal cot right now, clenching your ass cheeks."

"I didn't kill her."

"You don't have to convince me, although I'm not sure Detective Pham's completely convinced. I'm just saying, the investigation is still wide open. It's a lucky break for you." Duel grabbed a leather satchel and headed out the door.

Mackie didn't say much on the way home. Duel drove, taking the most direct route from his downtown office. As they passed the University, Mackie watched several students amble to class, others jogging the perimeter of the campus. Everywhere he looked reminded him of unfinished work, of words needing to be spoken. The thought of it made him impatient. Edgy. He needed resolution. Where that was not possible, he wanted action.

Duel pulled into Mackie's driveway. "How you gonna get around? This not a walking city, and I'm fairly certain there's a law against driving around in evidence."

"Forensics has my car. Reagan's car is in the garage, though."

Duel waited while Mackie climbed out. "Got dinner plans?"

Mackie shook his head.

"Tell you what. Come by my place tonight. I've got a new turkey fryer and five gallons of peanut oil with your name all over it." He rolled down the window, still talking even as he backed out of the drive. "I'll see you about seven. Call you if I hear any news about Sarah."

Mackie turned and walked toward the house.

Mackie went directly to the bathroom. On the way, he noticed last night's dishes put away and the table wiped clean. Yesterday's paper was no longer on the nightstand. Even his comforter had been straightened and his dirty clothes picked up. Whether she'd felt a guest's obligation to clean up or a professional uneasiness with leaving a mess, he had plenty of evidence of Hollie's activities that morning. Nice touch, especially after a one-night stand.

The landline rang while he stood in the shower. By the time he cut off the water and grabbed a towel, his cell phone buzzed on the nightstand. Both stopped before he could answer. His aging yellow labrador, Jonah, waited for Mackie on the bath mat as usual, but had cowered when Mackie jumped out of the shower. "Hollie got you scared?" Mackie asked the dog while he toweled off. "You won't have to worry about her much longer." Mackie dressed quickly and checked his cell phone. No messages, and he didn't recognize the number, although it looked like a hospital extension. When he dialed back, he heard a busy signal.

He resisted the urge to sleep for a few hours. Nothing would change if he rested. Could he actually rest? Doubtful. The same burdens and zero resolution—with or without sleep.

He sat on the edge of the bed, dialing Reagan's number once more as he glanced at the clock. Mid-afternoon in Florence.

A real phone connection.

Mackie straightened. He heart rate surged. The connection sounded distant, a trilling sound with each ring, static crackling in the background. The ringing continued. A minute passed. Maybe two. Why didn't her voicemail pick up? Mackie looked at the number he'd just dialed even as it kept ringing. Definitely her number. After another moment, he disconnected the call. He scrolled back to the number for Student Affairs and dialed again. A person answered on the second ring.

"Vanderbilt Semester Abroad, how may I help you?" the receptionist chirped.

Mackie explained who he was and that he urgently needed to contact Reagan for a family emergency.

"I hope everything is okay," she said, sounding startled.

Mackie rubbed his temple with his fingers, trying not to snap at the woman on the other end of the line. Innocent words, spoken in ignorance. "It's not." He took a steadying breath while he wrote down the phone number and e-mail address of the University's local contact in Florence. Hanging up without saying goodbye, he dialed the new number. The phone rang five times before it went to voicemail. Mackie left his contact information, then headed for the kitchen. Jonah followed him.

Not only had the dining room table been cleaned, but the kitchen counters sparkled in the morning sun. Mackie grabbed a glass and walked to the refrigerator. Just as he opened the door, he noticed something odd, something out of place. He turned toward the adjoining den. Jonah held back, clearly reluctant.

Mud streaked the carpet on the far side of the room. Not much bigger than a paw print, but against the cleanliness of the kitchen, it stood out. Mackie placed his glass and phone on the counter and stepped closer. At first he saw only the one spot, but as he approached the double doors that led from the den to the back deck, he noticed additional streaks. Clumps of dirt concentrated near the back door, several feet from the print he had first seen. From the kitchen, he wouldn't have even noticed them had it not been for the first mark. Mackie checked the door. Still unlocked from last night.

He studied the dirt. More smudges than prints. He'd been meaning to fix the sprinkler head by the back door forever. This didn't look like Jonah's tracks. A few more smears of mud led down the back hallway. He paused a beat and looked around. Nothing else out of the ordinary. At least, from here. He approached the study and saw a scattered sheaf of papers spilling from the doorway.

Someone besides Hollie had been here.

He stepped into his study, then froze. It was destroyed.

Desk drawers opened and emptied. Filing cabinets disemboweled. Manilla folders strewn across the floor. Papers scattered across his desk and reading chair. His computer sat upside down, resting against the base of a broken lampshade. Sweat broke out and chilled his spine. Like his irrational fear of heights, his body reacted to the unexpected loss of control. Nothing had changed but his perception of safety, yet he couldn't override the sensation. Mackie heard a noise and whipped around. Jonah peered around the corner, his tail uncommonly still.

Mackie exhaled as he squatted down to scratch Jonah's ears and reassure himself. "It's okay, buddy," he said. He wasn't convinced.

Mackie carefully retraced his steps, his senses on alert. Back through the den. Past the kitchen. He stepped into his garage and grabbed a sparkling nine-iron, unused and ready for retirement. With his hand on the grip and the back door still open, he dialed Duel. After explaining the situation, Duel fired off instructions. Don't go searching for the perpetrator. Don't tell anyone else until Duel arrived. And for Christ's sake, don't touch anything. He was on the way.

Mackie hung up. He stepped back inside. Gripping the nine-iron, he moved through the house, turning on lights and opening closet doors. Jonah trailed behind him, barely panting. Mackie heard his own respirations. Then movement in the guest bedroom. He recoiled. Cocked his golf club. No other sounds. Tension in his belly. Fueled by uncertainty. Sparked by anger. He barged into the room, only to find his own reflection in the bureau mirror. Mackie's pulse hammered long after the tension eased. Still, he combed the house, ending up back at the trashed study.

Mackie stood at the threshold to the room. A pencil snapped under his foot. He jumped. Turned full circle. Not even Jonah had followed him back here. He inspected the chaos. Pilfered files. Disrupted order.

He'd long ago practiced an accountant's meticulousness when it came to his office, each manilla folder housed in a precise location. Alphabetized by stuck-on labels, the files contained financial statements and closing documents, paid bills and past taxes. They also contained a slimmed-down version of his professional papers, now culled and collated in his home office. The boxes of papers Sarah had picked up the previous day had freed up an entire cabinet drawer for his own files. Now, scattered across the floor in lost symmetry, those files taunted him. Someone really knew how to find his last nerve.

The drawers to the first file cabinet remained open but undisturbed. Empty sections of the second cabinet marked what was missing. The third and fourth cabinets remained relatively intact. Mackie knew what they'd taken before he reached the cabinet. Between files for First Commercial Bank and Home Equity Loan, he saw an open space for two accordion folders.

Secret documents for the synthetic blood substitute, H-BOC.

"Damn it," Mackie mumbled.

He nudged the papers on the floor with his foot. Staples and clips on the pages stuck to the carpet. He looked at his computer, still leaning against the lampshade. Why? he wondered. The person who'd done this knew what he'd needed, yet he'd been obnoxious and destructive about the theft. Mackie resisted the urge to slam shut the file drawer before he walked back into the kitchen.

Halfway there, he heard Duel walking through the open garage door.

In the time it took for Mackie to explain that he had, in fact, gone looking for the perpetrator and found nothing, Duel already seemed to have a plan. He retraced Mackie's earlier footsteps, scanning each room in the house. He ended his survey at the study. With the golf club still in his grip, Mackie pointed to the debris of the study and explained what he felt was missing. Duel recorded the conversation on his phone, nodding as Mackie outlined the key patent documents that seemed to be missing. When he seemed satisfied with his understanding of the break-in, Duel called the cops.

* * *

It took more than an hour for Pennington and Pham to show up. Hard as it was for Mackie to leave the study undisturbed while he waited, Office Pennington had given Duel specific instructions for his client not to touch or disturb any evidence. Mackie's mind wouldn't slow down while he waited. He flipped through the morning talk shows. Nothing held his interest. When they finally showed up, Pham asked for permission to look around.

Duel stood with his arms folded across his broad chest. "And your search warrant is where?" he asked.

Mackie brushed past Duel to address Pham. "It's okay. I've got nothing to hide."

Officer Pennington just shook his head. "Dumb ass," he mumbled.

Mackie set the golf club down and trailed Pennington and Pham to the study. Papers still littered the floor. The file drawer hung open. In the reflection of the morning sun, discrete fingerprint smudges danced across the polished wood like track marks. Pennington squatted down to inspect the overturned laptop, then lifted it upright to the desk. "Who else comes into your study?" Pennington asked.

Mackie thought for a moment. "Once a week the cleaning lady is here."

"Your alibi?" Pennington asked with a slight smirk. "Hollie?"

Mackie bit back a sarcastic remark. He needed the police to document the break–in and then leave. It would take him the better part of the morning to clean up this mess. A smart mouth would slow down the process. "My daughter would spend time in here before she left for Italy, but that was five months ago."

Pham nodded at his open laptop. "And the computer?"

"No one but me."

She pondered this for moment. "What we're seeing looks less like a random break-in and more like the person who came inside knew you. Or at least knew your habits. There's no forced entry into the house—"

"I didn't lock the back door last night."

Pennington chuckled. "You're kidding, right?"

"—and this is a precision strike," Pham continued. "Looks like once they found what they wanted, they turned over the furniture then left. Out of spite, probably. Anyone you can think of who fits that profile?"

"The only one who comes to mind is already dead."

Pham jotted something in her notepad. "Keep thinking about it. Did they go into any other rooms?"

"Not that I could tell."

"You mind letting me take a look?"

"Not a good idea, Mackie," Duel warned. "The murder investigation is our number one concern."

"They why don't you follow her with your phone to record it all?" Mackie snapped. Turning to Pham, he said, "I'll show you around."

Pham stepped out of the study to follow him. Duel crossed his arms over his chest and leaned against the wall where he could keep an eye on both cops.

"These double doors lead to the hallway, but also to the den and the kitchen. The bedrooms are off the foyer," Mackie said, leading the way. "Bathroom off the kitchen." He stepped over the carpet stain and stood by the back doors. A puddle surrounded the leaking sprinkler head by the back door. Mackie tried to ignore it, focusing instead on Pham's questions. He tried to see the house from her perspective.

Pham crossed to the kitchen then returned to the den. She paused next to the entertainment center. A smile crossed her face as she studied the stacks of alphabetized CD's tucked neatly on the shelves beside the television. "You're an organizer."

"I like to know where everything is," he said.

"Makes it easier to find things. For you and the guys who broke in here." She looked at the two framed pictures atop of the television cabinet. She lifted up the first one, bringing it down to eye level. "Is this Turner Field?"

Mackie walked over to stand beside her. "The first season they opened the ballpark. Right after the Olympics." He looked again at his favorite picture of Reagan. Still a girl. Still enamored with her dad, hugging him around the waist. Pigtails poked out from an Atlanta Braves baseball cap, the hue of blue cotton candy in her grin.

Pham smiled at the picture, handing the frame back to Mackie. "You look younger."

"That's years ago." He wiped the frame with his shirt then set it back atop the entertainment center. "Atlanta's a hell of a place to watch a baseball game."

Pham turned her attention to the adjacent framed photo. A baseball player photographed in mid-stride after hitting a pitch, wearing the powder blue uniform of the Braves from years gone by. A signature scrawled across the middle of the photograph. "What about that one?" she asked.

Mackie removed the photo from its perch. Dust fluttered from the top of the cabinet when he lifted the frame. "Dale Murphy. The greatest Braves player of his time." He smiled at the memory. "We had this signed the same night we took the other photo. He'd retired by then."

"From Colorado," Pham said, offhanded.

Mackie turned toward her. "You've heard of him?"

"Girls like baseball, too, Dr. McKay," she said. "I spent my whole life in Philly before moving down here."

Mackie nodded. "That's right. Atlanta traded him to Philadelphia near the end of his career."

"For two pitchers and a shortstop," she said.

"Worst trade in Braves history. I swore I'd never go to another Braves game when I heard about the trade."

Pham nodded at the other picture. "But there you are, years later with your family."

"Righteous indignation is hard to maintain." He set the autographed photo back in place.

Pennington entered the den, holding a briefcase and a camera.

"That about does it for us." He handed the camera to Pham. "You find anything else of interest?"

She glanced at the photos, then shook her head. "Nothing we can use."

Pennington addressed Mackie. "Call if you think of anything else that may help."

Mackie locked the front door behind them. He turned to talk to Duel, but his lawyer remained leaning against the wall. Duel pressed his thumb over the microphone on phone and said, "The morgue. Calling about the autopsy."

Mackie tried to respond, but Duel returned his attention to the phone. Mackie left Duel in the den and returned to the study. He bent over to grab a pile of papers from the floor, then squatted down to begin the process of reorganizing.

"I've got some bad news for you," Duel said, as he approached from behind.

Mackie knelt on one knee, gathering papers from the floor. "Get in line."

"I don't know how to tell you this." Duel cleared his throat. "There's been a complication with the autopsy."

Mackie turned to look at his lawyer. "What's complicated about a cutting a corpse?"

"It sounds like the person who killed Sarah had second thoughts. Someone tried to revive her after the head wound."

Mackie stood. Too quickly. He steadied himself against his desk. Leave it to a lawyer to screw up the interpretation of an autopsy, he thought. "Did they find broken ribs from chest compressions?"

"Worse than that," Duel said. "The pathologist said she lost so much blood initially, CPR wouldn't have helped. Her killer must have tried to revive her with artificial blood. Her veins were flooded with your synthetic blood product."

Chapter Four

Mackie slumped in the chair in his study, staring at the wall. He had sanitized his house from reminders of Sarah, and until today, his study had remained a refuge from her memory. Now, the relentless refrain echoed in his mind—someone had murdered her and set him up to take the fall. Her death had been choreographed, obviously, and whoever had acquired the synthetic blood had stolen it. Likely from the hospital. Or the manufacturer. He certainly hadn't kept packages of it at home. Pharmacies didn't stock it, and it wasn't readily available on most ambulances. The longer he stared at the wall, the more questions emerged. And one definitive answer: he could no longer rely on someone else to exonerate him.

Duel pushed off his perch on the wall, shoving his hands into his pants pockets. "Total shock for you, huh?"

Mackie didn't respond. Didn't know what to say. His mind wrestled with the implications, but he didn't have enough information to organize his thoughts.

"Let's talk more about this tonight. You should try and get some rest. Maybe take a nap." Duel pulled a keyring from his pocket and headed for the door. "I'll call you when I know anything else."

For ten minutes after Duel left, indecision moored Mackie to his chair. Out of his element and unsure how to get back, Mackie couldn't decide at first where to turn for answers. The unequivocal and logical advice from his lawyer and the police instructed him to let professionals investigate the murder. Any man in his position would comply. So why didn't he feel that he could? He didn't want revenge. Right now, he just wanted answers.

Mackie pushed back his chair. He tossed the cordless phone onto his desk, scattering the few papers already collected from the floor. Ignoring the rest of the clutter, he returned to the den and locked the back door. Screw me once, he thought, but not twice. He glanced at the mud on the carpet. Asking Hollie to oversee the clean up involved explanations he didn't care to tackle right now. Maybe he'd find someone else when he got back.

Mackie grabbed his cell phone off the kitchen counter and a bottle of water from the refrigerator. He opened the cabinet near the sink to get Reagan's car keys. Jonah sat on the carpet of the den, his tail wagging each time Mackie made eye contact. "Be a little more vigilant next time, pal," he said. "At least bark when you hear a noise."

It took less than ten minutes for Mackie to arrive at the doctor's parking lot at Nashville Memorial, and another three to make it to the basement. He used the service entrance, hoping to avoid stares and questions from anyone who'd seen him hauled off in handcuffs earlier that morning.

Mackie shivered when he stepped out of the stairwell. The chill of the morgue and smell of preservatives permeated the basement. He walked forward. Despite the changes and renovations over his thirty year surgical career, the morgue remained insulated from the polish of progress. Most of the employees took pride in the antiquated feel of the place, a pride championed by their senior pathologist.

Mackie approached the intake clerk of the morgue, a man he'd seen more often than his own daughter in recent years. Mackie smiled, hoping word of his earlier involvement with the police hadn't filtered downstairs yet. Past experiences predicted he was safe. "Is Vernon here today?"

The intake clerk smiled, causing his dentures to click and his upper plate to slip. "Been in before the morning paper. Check his office. I know we got some patients waiting."

Patients waiting? Mackie thought. He allowed a measured smile at the respect the staff showed the dead. Most wouldn't consider them patients, but the medical examiner and chief pathologist, Dr. Vern Philpot, professed a different perspective.

"Cops brought one in earlier. They just left 'bout fifteen minutes ago." The old clerk took a sip of his coffee. "Go on to the back. You'll find him."

As Mackie walked through the automatic doors, the soft squish of his shoes amplified in the tile hallway. It felt colder. The smell of bleach intensified. To his left, three unobstructed windows offered a view into the autopsy suite. A steel table, surround by metal carts, awaited the next case. One autopsy assistant hosed blood and body fluids from the stainless steel table while another wiped down the countertops, setting out new instruments. To Mackie's right, a blank wall. Behind it, coolers. And, very likely, Sarah's body. He continued to the end of the hallway and knocked on the office door.

"It's open."

Mackie stepped inside.

A man with a grey pony-tail and clad in scrubs sat at a computer, the only part of the entire basement that appeared fit for the twenty-first century. Dim light from the desk lamp cast shadows on the bank of filing cabinets. Overstuffed bookshelves precariously held journals, skeletal relics, and a few specimens preserved in jars of formaldehyde.

Vern Philphot turned from the computer, a state-of-the-art technical gem that only a true computer guru would own. He grinned when he saw Mackie. "You look pretty good for a guy who's supposed to be in jail. Hell of a way to start your retirement." Vern moved a stack of papers from the other chair in the room and set them on the floor. "Shut the door and have a seat. Tell me what happened."

Mackie sat near his old friend. Most orthopedic cases didn't end up down here, but he and Vern had forged a special bond when they'd joined the faculty at the same time years ago. As a self-proclaimed techno-geek, Vern offered to help Mackie with most of his computer questions over the years. Mackie had reciprocated by not charging Vern for the multiple orthopedic needs of the pathologist's aging mother. During most weekday mornings, Mackie and Dr. Vern Philpot often were the only occupants in the doctor's lounge before sunrise.

"You've seen Sarah?" Mackie asked.

Vern stroked his long goatee. "I'm sorry for your loss, Mackie. I know she meant a lot to you at one point." He averted his eyes. "The cops instructed me not to release my findings to anyone else. There was more of an edge to them than with most homicides. I think they have plans for this one."

"I didn't do it, Vern."

He glanced at Mackie. "You don't have to convince me. But that cop thinks you're guilty."

Mackie shook his head. "Detective Pham?"

Vern grinned again. When he did, his chipped front tooth snuck out from under his mustache. "She's a hottie. That lithe little Asian body of hers. Married?"

"I didn't see a ring."

"She's a piece of work. But she didn't say much during the autopsy. It was the other guy. A real tight ass. Stuck to the script. Paddington?"

"Pennington."

"Right, him. She can do better. He's an ass." Vern scooted back in his chair.

Mackie glanced over Vern's shoulder, seeing Sarah Collins-McKay written on the computer screen. "What'd you find?"

"If I tell you anything, they will hand me my ass. I could lose my job." They both knew that wasn't likely to happen.

Mackie nodded. "Let me tell you what I know, and you can just help me fill in the gaps."

"No promises."

Mackie moved to the edge of his chair. "She died late last night. Head trauma—probably blunt force—the most likely cause of death. The person who did that wanted to frame me, so they stuck a unit or two of the synthetic blood product H-BOC in her veins—"

"More like five or six units," Vern said.

"—and stuffed her in the trunk of my car. Clear cut case of jealous ex-husband going too far then trying to cover his tracks."

"You're good," Vern said. "How'd you get that information?"

"First off, I didn't kill her."

"You mentioned that."

"Detective Pham showed me some of the crime scene images to identify the body. My lawyer told me about the H-BOC," Mackie said. "Besides, I was with someone all last night and the cops corroborated the alibi."

"Word travels fast. We just finished the post twenty minutes ago." Vern scooted his chair toward the row of filing cabinets and opened a drawer. "Give me just a second." He hummed a tune as he thumbed through several folders. He extracted one and opened it. "Take a look at this."

Mackie moved his chair closer. A glossy photo of a dead young woman with blood-caked hair rested atop the other papers in the file. Her head appeared misshaped. Part of her cheek caved in like a dented soda can. Even in death, the bruised and swollen tissue on the side of the trauma caused her eye lid to sag as if it had melted from its proper position. Revolting, but Mackie assumed Vern had a reason for sharing the picture.

"A few years ago," Vern started, "a local college student died while mountain biking. Wasn't watching where she was going and nailed a tree. As you can see, she wasn't wearing a helmet. I did the autopsy. Kept the images, because it's a classic teaching case. Sad, sure, but instructive for my pathology residents." He handed the file to Mackie for a better view. "You can't really tell from this photo, but she cracked her head when she hit the tree. That answers the first question: what caused the injury."

Mackie looked at the photo. "Did you get films of her skull?"

"They're on microfiche in the back of the folder. Depressed skull fracture. That answers question number two: what exactly is the injury."

"Did the autopsy prove the skull fracture killed her?" Mackie asked.

Vern clapped him on the shoulder. "You retired too soon. You've still got skills. That's the third question. And the most important. We know her head's a mess, but is that what killed her? In this case, she had an epidural hematoma. No one's gonna survive that much intracranial blood."

Mackie closed the folder and handed it back to Vern. He nodded toward the rows of filing cabinets. "You have a lot teaching cases."

Vern rolled his chair back to the open drawer and placed the file back inside. "Tons of teaching cases, but also cool shit we find in autopsies. Mostly the kind of stuff you can't scan in the computerized record." He rummaged though another drawer before pulling out a six-inch metal figurine that looked suitable to sit atop a trophy. "A few years ago, I pulled this out of some guy's ass. Perforated his colon, got septic, and died. The family found him days later dead on the floor of the shower. Water turned off. Didn't know what happened until we turned him over. What the hell are you supposed to put on a death certificate in that circumstance?"

"Accidental death due to colorectal trauma?"

"A good thought. Might raise questions with the life insurance company, though."

"Does that factor into your final decisions?"

"We try and be thorough but thoughtful of the family."

Mackie laughed. "And you saved the Anal Trophy?"

"Once you autoclave these things, they're sterile. And this is priceless! I've got cabinets full of metal objects found at autopsy. This just happens to be one of the best. There's some kinky shit out there, Mackie." He returned the figurine to the drawer. "Postmortem metallurgy. A pet project of mine."

Mackie raised his eyebrows. "Fatal sex toys?"

"Fatal metals, man. The human body's a remarkable piece of machinery, but stick some metal inside and weird stuff happens."

Mackie paused a moment to digest that random bit of information, then got back to his purpose for being there. "That girl in the biking accident. Did what happen to her happen to Sarah? Killed by an epidural from a skull fracture?"

Vern nodded. "No question. The blood substitute in her veins was a ruse."

"Not the cause of death," Mackie said.

"Not only not the cause of death, it looks like it was injected into her long after she died." Vern rolled back to his computer. He lifted a note pad on his desk smeared with grease like a hamburger in a brown bag. No matter how careful Vern tried to be during an autopsy, there was no way to get around soiling his note pad with fluids from the deceased. "This is what I wrote down: 'Traumatic puncture neck: right side, angulated. Right jugular vein: coagulated crystals, white. Superior vena cava: crystalline streaks along posterior wall. Right atrium: pooling of white liquid along posterior surface. Coagulated crystals, extended through tricuspid valve. Minimal fluid in right ventricle.' You don't get pooling of blood or any other liquid in the right atrium and ventricle until the heart stops beating."

"She was dead before the H-BOC went into her system," Mackie said.

"Exactly. The fluid circulated south from the neck only because of gravity. It didn't even make it to the left side of her heart." Vern scratched his goatee again.

"Plus, it was crystalized," Mackie said.

Vern looked at Mackie. "Explain that. When I've seen H-BOC at autopsy, it appears different than it would appear in a live patient."

"All of the hemoglobin-based oxygen carriers, the H-BOC class, crystalize at room temperature and liquify around ninety-one degrees," Mackie said. "It's why we refrigerate it. Once the crystals dissolve, its shelf life is limited. Infused into a normal body temperature, it remains a liquid."

"I was gonna look that up." Vern picked up his pen and jotted a note on the stained note pad. "Ninety one. What if you receive the H-BOC and then die?"

"It would circulate through your system."

"But wouldn't crystalize."

"It shouldn't. Unless you're hypothermic. Maybe a drowning victim submerged in cold water would have problems with it, but for the rest of us it's solvent by the time it hits the veins. Then, it's already diffused through your body. No chance to crystalize." Mackie paused. "So her body temperature was already below ninety one degrees when she was found?"

"That's another weird thing. She hadn't been dead that long." He checked his notes. "Her core body temperature was ninety three degrees fahrenheit."

"That doesn't make sense for the H-BOC crystals. Can you estimate her time of death based on that?" Mackie asked.

Vern shook his head. "Not really. Body temperature's not linearly predictable. She had some rigor mortis, some postmortem lividity. Based on that, I'd say she'd been dead just a couple of hours by the time she got to me."

Mackie stood. Something didn't add up, and he suspected it might have been the killer's only mistake so far. "I need to see her body."

"Can't. Officer Tight Ass was very clear in his instructions. No one except them."

"For Christ's sake, Vern. Everything you just said supports the fact that the murderer intended to frame me for this. Nothing you show me is going to change those facts." Mackie turned around to open the door.

"Wait." Vern picked up the phone and dialed. After a moment, someone answered. "Caroline, could you run upstairs and get me a couple units of H–BOC from Central Supply. I'm gonna need it for the Collins–McKay case." He nodded, then replaced the receiver.

"What the hell are you doing?" Mackie asked.

"Buying time," Vern said. "We've got about ten minutes before she gets back."

He stood and grabbed his lab coat from behind the door. When Vern opened it, both men heard the automatic doors close down the hallway, then silence. "Let's go," Vern said.

Mackie followed him across the hall, through a swinging door similar to a restaurant kitchen. A feeling of dread grew inside him. Behind the door, the temperature plummeted. Mackie's breath fogged in front of him. Along both walls, rows of square metal doors stacked atop one another in blocks of three. In this room alone, eighteen coolers faced Mackie, several more in the adjacent room. Mackie's pulse quickened. He shoved his hands into his pockets.

Vern checked over his shoulder before he approached the bank of coolers and paused before one situated near the middle of the wall. Unmarked. "You sure you want to do this?"

"No, but yes."

Mackie heard the seal pop when Vern opened the door. Inside, a metal gurney. And a dark body bag. Mackie briefly closed his eyes, then opened them and approached the body.

Vern slid the gurney out. The position of the body bag indicated the head faced them, but beneath the black zippered tarp, it was hard to distinguish any features. Vern placed his hands on the zipper and glanced at Mackie. "It's not too late to change your mind. You sure you want to see her?"

He nodded.

The low whine of the zipper nauseated Mackie. His first thought when he saw her face was that Detective Pham had deceived him with the pictures from the crime scene. The reality was much worse than he'd expected.

Sarah's face was recognizable, but only partially. On the left side, her check bone and closed eyes, although discolored, looked peaceful. Not quite natural, but easily identifiable. The right side, however, distorted the entire image. Vern had cleaned most of the blood during the autopsy, but he had also made an incision to slip her scalp over her face, standard practice to better assess the brain. Even though the scalp had been repositioned, the underlying damage to the facial bones made it impossible to reconstruct her image. The same image Mackie had seen just yesterday. Her entire cheek and eye socket on the right caved in, similar to the picture of the mountain biking accident. Words caught in his throat as he thought about her. He used to love that face. He could still remember how Sarah's skin used to feel under his fingertips. How she used to quiver when he stroked her cheek. In the still of the morgue, he had trouble remembering all that had gone wrong with them. His stomach lurched. He averted his gaze, focusing on her neck instead.

In contrast to her face, the left side of her neck remained intact, free from bruising or discoloration. A faint scar coursed along her neck lines, evidence of the questionable mole he'd suggested she removed years ago. On the right side of her neck, more maceration. Crops of mottled spots discolored her pallor. Mackie counted at least five puncture wounds, each angled toward the center of her neck. Discrete lumps of swollen tissue distorted her skin. The violation of her neck screamed for attention but had obviously been drowned out by the carnage of her head wound. He felt sick. Put a hand out to steady himself on the table. "They butchered her," Mackie said. "The bastard couldn't even cannulate her neck veins."

Vern stepped back from the body, waiting. After a moment, he turned to Mackie. "Not much else to see. I sampled her organs, looked around inside. The head's where the money is in this investigation."

"You ever cannulate a neck vein?" Mackie asked.

Vern's laugh echoed off the cinderblock walls and metal doors. "How long've you known me, Mackie? I was the only guy in the city for a while who prepared cadavers for the medical school. Each body had to be drained, flushed, and preserved. I did them all through the neck."

"Neck lines used to be my preferred entry point for central lines." Mackie stared at Sarah's body while he spoke. "I quit doing them after a while. Left that to the anesthesiologists. How many times did you do one on the right?"

"Almost never. Sometimes you get a hanging or strangulation and the left side's all mucked up, but it's a hell of a lot more difficult."

Mackie glanced at Vern. "The angle's all wrong for a right-handed person to go on that side. The neck keeps getting in the way of your landmarks. Unless you work from the head of the bed."

"You've reached the same conclusion I did." Vern smiled. "I didn't tell the cops when they were here, but it'll be in my report." He began to zip the body bag.

"Thanks for taking care of her, Vern. I appreciate what you've done."

Vern slid Sarah's body back into the cooler and shut the door. "I'll look out for her."

Mackie nodded.

"You weren't here," Vern said.

"I was not."

"You're lawyer has already put in a request for the autopsy report."

"When will it be ready?"

"I'll have a preliminary report later today. Of course, labs will take weeks to come back." Vern headed toward his office. "Let's get out of here before someone sees you."

Sadness faded, making way for resolve. Mackie reached into his pocket and withdrew his cell phone. No service. Not surprising down here. He scanned the room. "You got a phone I can use?"

"In my office. I'll be there in second."

Mackie walked through the swinging door and across the hall. He entered Vernon Philpot's oasis in the morgue, picked up the phone, and dialed the number for the Nashville PD.

"Homicide," answered Detective Pham.

"I think I know who killed Sarah," Mackie said without preamble.

"Dr. McKay? Where are you?"

"Can you meet me outside the hospital in fifteen minutes?"

She paused a beat. "You're interfering with an investigation, Doc."

"Just give me an hour of your time," Mackie said. "Her killer is left handed, and I'm guessing she has a picture of him at her apartment."

Chapter Five

FOR THE SECOND time that day, Mackie sat in the back seat of a police car. This time, Detective Pham drove her unmarked cruiser. She drove fast, speeding up at each yellow light. Mackie steadied himself with every turn, easier now because he wasn't cuffed. At least she'd given him that courtesy. She still insisted he sit in the back, though. Pham kept the dispatch radio turned up just loud enough to inhibit easy conversation. Mackie stared out the window as they darted through traffic, stealing occasional glances at the back of her neck. Pham kept her eyes on the road.

"This the right building?" she asked as they pulled into the parking lot of the high rise.

Mackie craned his neck. "Yep. Seventh floor. She had one of the best views of the city."

Pham swerved past the entrance and pulled into a handicap parking space. She reached into the glove compartment and removed a blue disability placard, hanging it on the rearview mirror of the unmarked car. She didn't even acknowledge him until he cleared his throat. "What's wrong?"

"Handicap?" Mackie asked.

"Preferred parking. Job perk." She flashed a smile and stepped out.

Unable to open the door from the back seat, Mackie waited. With his hands free, he didn't have to worry about writhing snake-like out of the car this time. He looked up, scanning the balconies of the high rise. "It's been a while."

Pham followed his gaze. "When's the last time you were here?"

"A few weeks ago. Maybe a month."

"Just so you know, we've already searched her apartment. I wouldn't have brought you here otherwise. Honestly, I'm not sure being here is a good idea."

"I won't touch anything."

"I wasn't talking about you."

They made their way inside, crossing the lobby to the elevators.

When they reached the seventh floor, Mackie paused in front of Sarah's apartment door and waited. Pham reached into her pocket and produced a silver key. Before she slid it into the lock, she pulled out her phone. "I'm not taking any chances," she said as she activated the video camera. She pointed it at Mackie. After stating the date, time, and location, she inserted the key and unlocked the door. When she turned the knob, the door opened immediately. She motioned for Mackie to walk ahead of her. "You agree, Dr. McKay, that you are not under arrest, but that anything that happens while you are in this apartment could incriminate you." Dropping the pretense, she added, "Show me what we came here for and don't touch anything. We don't need any more evidence against you."

"I think when we're done, you'll have all the evidence you need to look for the real killer." Mackie winked at Pham. "You're sweet to let me come with you. I certainly don't want you getting in trouble for fraternizing with the accused."

Pham glanced at the camera. "Your ass is on the line, Doc, not mine."

Mackie walked inside. The smell triggered memories first. Nothing specific. Even hard to identify it as uniquely Sarah. Part perfume, part deodorant soap. It used to surround her when she walked into a room, linger when she left. It also alerted Mackie. He preferred to stay in the car when he picked up Reagan from her mom's. When he did enter the condo, the scent raised his suspicion. Even after some of the divorce animosity subsided, the smell of Sarah's place on Reagan's clothes made Mackie uneasy. Reminded him of the last bitter years of their marriage. Only a small part of the scent laced his memories with regret.

Mackie crossed the foyer. Sarah kept the place immaculate, ready to display or entertain at a moment's notice. She insisted on an organized kitchen, the toaster aligned with the counter's edge and the linen napkins stacked precisely in their bin. Yesterday's paper sat on the edge of the kitchen table. More American soldiers dead in the Middle East. More pledges of enhanced U.S. participation in the peace process.

"Those kids getting killed are Reagan's age," Mackie said.

Pham turned around and glanced at the headlines. "They knew what they were signing up for."

Mackie walked to the glass door leading to the balcony. Pham checked it, confirming it was locked. "We searched the two bedrooms."

"The one in the back she used as a study," Mackie said.

Pham kept her distance behind Mackie, but as they passed a small small hallway, she stopped. "Mackie, look at this."

Mackie? His pulse quickened. "I didn't think we were there yet, Detective Pham. You said yourself back at the station—" He stopped when he saw what she mentioned. They took several paces toward the back of the apartment. Spilling into the hallway from the study he saw a flurry of papers. They walked closer, Mackie leading the way. In contrast to the rest of the house, the study was a wreck. Just like at his house, stapled papers and manilla folders littered the floor like confetti. Mackie stared at the empty filing cabinet. "Did you see this earlier?"

"It wasn't like this when we came by."

"They took the H-BOC case notes."

Pham glanced at him. "Don't touch anything in this room."

"It's the one thing we still had in common," he said. "Besides Reagan." He stepped over an upended chair, moving to a wooden credenza pulled out from the wall. Ignoring her instructions, he pushed back one of the drawers and lifted up an overturned picture frame. Sarah and Reagan, smiling in front of the Eiffel Tower last summer. Next to it, the pigtailed Reagan, smiling next to her mom at Turner Field.

"That same night at the ballpark." Pham leaned closer to the picture, letting the phone drop to her side. "They favor one another. She's got your eyes, though."

Mackie turned around and leaned on the credenza. He hadn't seen what he'd hoped for in her den, and glancing around the study, it didn't appear to be here, either. The one difference he could see in this vandalism compared to his own was that they left her desk top alone. Her computer appeared untouched and undamaged. The lamp still lined up perfectly with the edge of the desk. The burglar had made this his second stop, knowing what he needed and where he would likely find it.

"The patent is what they're after?" Pham asked as she panned her phone, recording everything as it happened. "I'm not sure what the big deal is. Doesn't a patent just give you the right to manufacture something? Sort of like having first dibs on inventions and intellectual property?"

"It's more than that," Mackie said. He rested his foot on the overturned chair. "The patent protects its owner from other people, excluding them from making or selling your invention. You can have a patent for twenty years and ignore it. But the key is, as long as you hold the patent for that product, no one else can copy your exact idea unless you give them permission."

Pham considered his explanation. "But it's just a piece of paper on file with the federal government."

"The U.S. Patent and Trademark Office," Mackie said.

"Whatever. It's still public information, accessible to anyone who cares. I'm sure they have a library online to look it all up."

"It's in Arlington, Virginia. We went there after they approved our first patent for H-BOC. Kind of a celebration for the future." Mackie smiled. "You can look up patents dating back to the late seventeen hundreds there."

"They go back that far?"

"Patent protection is a part of the original Constitution," Mackie said.

Pham nodded. "I think I learned that once. But what you just said proves my point. Why go to all the trouble and risk of breaking and entering if you can easily access the information by legal means?"

"Because whoever did this cares about the patent, and what he really wants is the original documentation detailing the dates of the discovery, plus related material for future patents."

"Your theory is that someone is going to try and overturn the patent?"

"Not overturn. More like hijack it. Use the patented information for their own financial gain."

Pham crossed the room and settled into the desk chair. She propped the phone so that the video trained on the both of them. She slid on a pair of latex gloves and then turned on the computer. "That's what was in the files? Additional documentation? And you kept that information at home? Both of you? I'm assuming there were duplicates."

"I emptied my office at the hospital last month. Sarah worked mostly from home. We both had the blueprints of how H-BOC worked."

"Which explains the timing. Wouldn't work to break-in last month, because the information they were after wouldn't be there? At least, not at your place." Pham glanced at the screen. "You know her login and password?"

"Look in the top drawer of the desk. That's where she used to keep it."

Pham glanced inside, then picked up the phone. She recorded herself lifting a taped note card from the drawer. "I'm impressed."

"Look around this place," Mackie said. "She was a slave to habit."

Pham set the phone back on the desk and typed in the password. "Using the obvious personal phrases and dates for your passwords can compromise security."

Mackie leaned forward, studying the login information. She'd changed it. Her maiden name now replaced her married one. The login looked the same. She hadn't changed her password. Predictable. He sat back and watched Pham.

"Is there competition for H-BOC? Another company threatening your product's market share?"

"Yes. And no," Mackie said. "Let's say you've got a lemonade stand, and I've got the world's greatest recipe for lemonade. Patented, of course. I'm an orthopedic surgeon. I love drinking lemonade, but I don't want to sell the stuff. But I can let you sell my recipe, because I know the line for your stand will be wrapped around the block if you do. You'll make a killing, one quarter at a time. But I still own the right to the recipe. For each glass you sell, you pay me a percentage for the right to use my lemonade."

"I'm more of an unsweetened tea girl," Pham said.

"Work with me here. Drink what you want, but you're still loving the money you make selling my lemonade. Now I could sell you the patent for this recipe, but then you'd get to keep all the profits. That's not good for me, unless you fork over big bucks for the patent. The complicating factor in all of this is that my ex-wife has joint ownership of the patent rights for the world's greatest lemonade, but she doesn't like you. Hates you, in fact. Just look in the mirror. What woman wouldn't be threatened by a ballsy, exotic-looking cop?"

Pham scoffed. "Keep going."

"So my ex can do whatever she wants with her part of the patented recipe. She can sell it to Big Dick's Lemonade Stand. Now you have competition."

Pham laughed. "We both do if Big Dick has her recipe."

Mackie smiled. "Joint ownership complicates patents. When we divorced, Sarah and I split the patent rights sixty-forty. She was a co-inventor but it was originally my idea, so I got the bigger share. We had previously licensed the production of H-BOC to a company in Atlanta. A former surgery resident of mine named Singh runs it. There are small companies making other synthetic blood substitutes with other patents, but none as competitive as the product we own. Plus, we had six other variations on the existing product. Patents for other aspects of H-BOC production. One patent for a method of manufacturing that doubled the capacity to carry oxygen. Another for a mechanism to bypass the refrigerated storage."

"Lots of potential profits. Good royalties for you?" Pham asked.

"I retired fifteen years early, didn't I?"

"Must be nice." She turned her attention back to the computer. "So you're not worried about patent violations from this guy who licensed it and now manufactures it?"

"Why would I be? The percentage I retired on is smaller than his monthly salary."

Pham studied Mackie for a moment. "You're thinking like a surgeon. Too trusting and analytical. Look at it from my perspective. If two people hold the patent and they're both out of the way—dead—then your manufacturer gets to keep all of his profits. Score one for Big Dick's Lemonade."

"Sarathi Singh wouldn't do that."

Pham gave him a questioning look. "Your friend in Atlanta? You'd be surprised what a little money will do to otherwise trustworthy people." She turned her attention to the computer. Working from the files on the desktop, she opened random documents. Digital images of Sarah appeared. Many of them showed her smiling in front of notable landscapes and monuments. Others showed her with the new man.

"That's your guy," Mackie said.

"You know him?"

"I've met him."

"And you think he killed Sarah?"

"It fits. First, he's a big guy, so he had the strength. Second, look at where his watch is. On the right. A left-handed trait."

"Why do you say that?"

"Orthopedic surgeon. I notice these thing."

"That doesn't prove your case."

Mackie said, "Think about it. The wounds correlate with the mechanism. If you check him out you'll probably see he has no medical training, which goes along with the hatchet job done to her neck when he tried to inject the H-BOC to frame me."

"What's his motive?"

Mackie shrugged. "That's your job. Greed? Jealousy? Let's call him and find out."

"You said you met him?" Pham asked.

"Once." Mackie crossed his arms, taking his eyes off the screen. "He works at the same company in Atlanta that manufactures our H-BOC. Met Sarah at a Christmas party a few years back while we were still married. I met him that night, too. One of those encounters you hardly remember until later, when you find out what's going on. My memory of that party is stained by all that's happened since."

Pham rested her chin on her hand, interested. She looked toward Mackie. "Once they hooked up, did he move to Nashville?"

Mackie shook his head. "Just visited more often. It began as a relationship of convenience. I guess it continued that way. After a while, I stopped asking."

"You know his name?" she asked.

"Henry Stone. 'Friends call me Hank.' That what he always says." Mackie smiled at the name. "I always thought Hank Stone sounded kind of like a porn star."

Pham laughed and said, "Apparently acts like one, too." Realizing she was being taped as much as he was, she reached for the phone and turned it toward the computer screen. "Let's finish up."

Mackie moved toward the computer. He opened a document entitled "Briefs" and scanned through pages of legal work from the last six months. Cases involving trademark infringements from a local restaurant had occupied much of her time, along with a few new patents on yard tools and outdoor equipment. Finding nothing of interest, he closed the folder and turned his attention to one marked "Financial".

Consistent with Sarah's personality, the file contained clearly marked ledgers of income and expenses. Her budget noted dozens of categories, each with annotations for the actual purchases for the month. The organization of the flow charts didn't surprise him. The total amount of her assets did.

Thirty-two million dollars.

"That's not right," Mackie said. "No way."

Pham studied the ledger. "Click on Income," she said. "Bottom right corner."

Mackie complied. The top category listed her salary from her firm, followed by monthly dividends, then her quarterly bonus. At the bottom of the lists, a deposit from Synthesis Industries. For thirty million dollars.

"She wasn't hurting financially before that, but my God," Pham said. "What's Synthesis Industries?"

Mackie stared at the screen for a long moment before answering. "Synthesis Industries is a biomedical company in Atlanta."

"The one where her boyfriend works?"

Mackie nodded. "She sold that son of a bitch her percentage of the joint ownership for the H-BOC patent."

Chapter Six

LATER THAT AFTERNOON, Mackie sat with his feet on the coffee table at Duel's house, waiting once again for him to finish a phone call. Everywhere he looked, details and decorations spoke of wealth. A hand-carved hearth surrounding a deep fireplace. Floor-to-ceiling bookshelves, stuffed with hardback books above, three-ring binders below. Emblematic of Duel, Mackie thought. Pomp and practicality. Settling back on the sofa, he closed his eyes. Even the smell of wood polish suited Duel's image. Over the years, Duel had cultivated that image, refining it to match his success. He wanted clients and friends to see the tangible rewards of a thriving law practice.

As he sat on the sofa, another smell laced the air. Before he could decipher it, he heard Duel walk toward the study, cocktail in hand. "Turkey fryer's heating up. You ready to see the improvements—" He paused. "What the hell are you doing?"

Mackie opened his eyes, but he didn't move. "I haven't taken a break all day."

Duel approached him, staring at his feet. "You think you could do it without putting your shoes all over my new furniture?"

Mackie smiled, then slowly sat up. He leaned forward, giving an exaggerated consideration of the tabletop. "Aw, crap. There's a slight scratch on the surface. Can't tell if it's caused by the soles of my shoes..."

"Jesus. You act like you were raised in a barn." Duel drained the rest of his cocktail then crunched on a cube of ice. He turned around and headed into the foyer. "The renovation's on schedule."

Mackie stood and joined him. "Kitchen's already done?"

"And the downstairs bathroom." Duel ascended the main staircase. Polished hardwood. Matching bannister. At the top, behind a landing barely big enough for two people, a plywood barricade loomed. Tacked to it, a building permit. And a door.

"Security?" Mackie asked.

"Safety." Duel removed a key from a nail on the door frame and unlocked the door. "Part of the building code. Plus, it's one added layer of insulation." When he opened the door, a blast of cold air slapped Mackie's face.

Both men walked into the construction zone. In contrast to the choreographed appearance of the downstairs, the entire house beyond the barricade displayed the bare studs and bent wires of construction. A patchwork of plywood created a path over the floor joists. Materials and tools lined both walls, without any obvious sign that they had been put to use. All demolition, no reconstruction. At least, not yet.

Duel picked his way across the plywood path. Once he reached the center of the space, he clicked on a bare bulb. "All of this will be the master suite. The builder hedged at first, complaining that it would trash the resale value of the house. He said there's not much of a market for properties with a mega-master suite upstairs. But I ultimately got my way."

"Not surprising." Mackie strolled across the planks, stepped past Duel, and stopped at the far end of the open space. He pushed against the plastic tarp, nailed tight to the floor. "What goes behind here?"

"French doors. Wooden deck. Pool below. It's gonna be nice." Duel craned his neck to inspect the construction zone. "The builder told me he'd be done by summer, but I'm hoping they'll run ahead of schedule. I'm getting cramped camping out downstairs."

Mackie smiled. Duel Richardson, ever the optimist. "Good luck with that time-table."

Mackie walked back to the temporary entrance. Duel let him pass, then followed along. Duel locked the door behind him. Both men headed downstairs.

"What're you drinking tonight?" Duel asked as they entered the kitchen. He set his empty glass on the counter. In the corner of the room, near the kitchen table, steam rose from an aluminum pot on a plugged-in plastic stand. Two jugs of peanut oil sat nearby on stacks of newspapers. The smell of heated grease dominated the room.

Mackie peered over the counter at the turkey fryer. "What do you have to help a headache?"

"Scotch."

"How about a Tylenol?"

Duel shook his head. "Haven't stocked the medicine cabinet yet. But I've got the perfect thing to help your head."

Duel walked to the refrigerator and pulled out three bottles of Lone Star beer. He opened one and took a long slug before setting the bottles on the counter. He reached back inside and removed a platter with a marinated whole chicken. Behind it, he found a plate of desserts. He placed the chicken back in the refrigerator and set the desserts on the counter. Unwrapped Oreo cookies and Twinkies, carefully arranged on the platter as if they deserved the decorative presentation. Duel lifted one of the Twinkies. "This, my friend, is the cure for what ails you." He drank the remaining beer in the first bottle then opened the other two. Handing one to Mackie, Duel balanced the other bottle with the plate of desserts. He walked toward the turkey fryer and put on an apron draped over the chair. "Watch and learn."

Mackie held back at first, then moved closer to the fryer. Duel rested the plate on the kitchen table near two bowls and a plastic canister. Picking up two at a time, he dropped the Twinkies into an egg mixture in the first bowl, then rolled it in the flour mixture of the second bowl. He did the same thing with the cold Oreos.

"Not exactly on the food pyramid," Mackie said.

"If you're worried about your health, I'll eat your portion."

"Home recipe?" Mackie asked, somewhat amused.

"I learned it on YouTube a few years ago. It's not just an appetizer, Mackie. It's a transformative experience."

Duel dropped the desserts into the hot peanut oil. Grease fizzed up from the aluminum pot, but Duel ignored it, concentrating on the bubbling snack cakes instead. "We really should be doing this on the porch," he said, never taking his eyes from the fryer. "This stuff spills or catches fire, and this house is torched. You should see the videos."

"YouTube again?"

"Yep."

Mackie sipped of his beer, mesmerized by the sizzling treats. "You don't have to take a risk on my account."

Duel shook his head as he rubbed his hands together, preparing to remove the snacks from the deep fryer. "It's worth the risk, Mackie. Trust me on this one. If you're still hungry after these, we'll talk about making dinner."

Using a long-handled sieve, Duel removed the food, one at a time, setting them back on their original plate. He picked up a canister and dusted the fried Twinkies with powdered sugar. "Give them just a minute to cool." He fished out the remaining cookies, dusting each one, and continued to talk as he dropped the remaining Oreos into the fryer. "How you holding up?"

"Are you asking as my lawyer or my friend?"

"Yep."

Mackie picked up a fried Twinkie, still too hot to eat. His hand shook visibly as he took a sip of beer. "The hardest part was seeing her body."

Duel remained hunched near the deep fryer, now concentrating on his drink. He glanced over his shoulder. "The police let you in the morgue?"

"I went on my own. They'd already left by then. Figured it was easier to ask for forgiveness than permission."

He stood up straight. "Not in a criminal investigation. That just makes you look more guilty. Stop doing that crap without my permission. I can get access to a lot of areas. Legally." Duel removed the Oreos from the oil. He wiped his hands on his apron when he finished. "You find out anything new?"

Mackie took a bite of the Twinkie. The combination of fried crunch and warm cream surprised him. He closed his eyes, savoring the bite. The taste caressed his tongue. Not too sweet. Not too filling. The perfect comfort food. And to think that under the auspices of good health he'd actually applauded the decision to pull Twinkies off the market when the original company went bankrupt. He took another bite. Maybe not a transformative experience, but damn good. After the last bite, he wiped his mouth with the back of his hand. "I think her boyfriend did it. A guy named Hank Stone."

"Why?"

"The marks on her head and neck are suggestive of a big, left-handed guy. He fits that profile. No signs of struggle seen on the autopsy, so it's likely she knew the guy. Plus his company paid her a fortune last month, which makes me think some twisted motivation of greed or jealousy came into play."

"And the break-ins?"

"A cover up for the real motive."

Duel sipped his beer, modestly this time, then let out a long sigh, his chest emitting a low wheeze of collapsing bellows. "No jury would convict this Stone guy based on that information. Too circumstantial."

"But you think they have a solid case against me?"

"What I said is that it didn't look good for you, finding the H-BOC in her veins. The police always come back to the family in cases like this." Duel pulled out a chair from the table and took a bite of the deep-fried Oreo. Licking his fingers, he said, "The medical examiner's preliminary report says the H-BOC came after her death. It could be argued that the killer wasn't trying to save her at all but was being vindictive."

"Hank meets all the concerns stacked against me, and then some. You remember Synthesis Industries?"

Duel nodded, mouth full. "In Atlanta. They're producing your patented H-BOC. Jointly held. That was a bitch trying to figure out in your divorce."

"He works there." Mackie sipped his beer. "And Synthesis paid her thirty million dollars...I'm assuming for her percentage of the patent."

"Jee-zus!"

Mackie paused. "With all the legal work you did with Sarah, you didn't know about that?"

"No." Duel pushed himself up from the chair, straining against the inertia of his weight. He picked up the plate of fried Oreos and crossed the kitchen. Grabbing a fresh beer, he headed out to the foyer. Mackie hoisted the plate of Twinkies, then followed.

When he reached the study, he found Duel standing near the credenza. Duel stutter stepped, caught himself, then flopped into a chair near the computer. "Xbox on," he said. His words began to slur, but without touching the keyboard, the computer screen flickered to life.

"Voice recognition?" Mackie asked.

"My computer not only hears me, it actually senses me the

moment I walk into the room," Duel said. "State of the art coolness without having to touch a thing."

"Pretty high-tech for a home computer. We still use badge readers for the hospital computers." Mackie pulled the edge of the coffee table toward the computer and sat behind Duel, watching him work. "I didn't bother with the enhanced security on my home computer."

"You should make the investment," Duel advised. "I can access my office's remote desktop from here. I don't leave the security of all of my files to chance."

Mackie glanced above Duel's head. The lower level of bookshelves housed dozens of binders, each with a printed notation on the spine. The titles themselves attested to their contents. Plaintiff versus Defendant. Straightforward. Easy to identify. As he scanned the spines, he found his own file organized among the other cases. Collins versus McKay. "Your binders seem to be the weak link in your security system. I could probably find all the juicy details of my divorce by pulling my files off your shelf."

Duel looked above his computer. He sipped his beer then pointed at the binders. "Those need to be scanned. You won't find any secrets in there, though. It's mostly correspondence. Letters, copies of public documents. Nothing exciting." He turned his attention back to his desktop, asking the computer to open an archive of old e-mails. "I've subpoenaed Sarah's emails for the case," he said as he hunched over the screen, searching through the subject lines. "Choice stuff in there."

"You have them already?" Mackie asked. "She's been dead less than a day."

"The judge owed me a favor." Duel scrolled through another page of documents.

"Anything in those that'll help?"

"I have no idea." Duel gulped his beer. "You said she received a thirty million dollar windfall?"

"Best I can tell. I can't believe she didn't mention it to you. She didn't ask you for help setting up a trust for Reagan with the money?" Mackie asked.

Duel shook his head. "This is the first I'm hearing of it."

"Maybe Hank asked her to keep it quiet."

"New relationships make people do strange things."

Mackie scoffed. "She'd been sleeping with him for years. Even before the divorce."

Duel flinched, then scrolled through more e-mails. "Mostly just chit chat here. Lots of back and forth with Hank. Here's the last message your once-betrothed sent to me. Dated six days ago."

Mackie stood to peer over Duel's shoulder at the emails. No mention of money, trusts, or securities that he could see. "Can I look at those?"

"Hold on." Duel leaned back in his desk chair and said, "Xbox, print file."

Nothing happened.

Duel scooted forward, raising his voice this time. Again, no response to his command. Duel grumbled about the damn printer. He finished his beer while he tried to figure out the voice prompt. Not getting any response, he finally said, "I'll just send you what I've got." Raising his voice, Duel said, "Email attachments to Cooper McKay." Obeying his commands, the computer composed a message to Mackie's email account and asked for confirmation.

Mackie smiled, impressed with the system. "Not bad, when it works. What'd you just send me?"

"Hell if I know." Duel steadied himself as he stood. "I need another drink."

When Duel left the room, Mackie sat in his desk chair. On the screen, a message from Sarah to a group under the subject line of "Holiday Wishes". Somehow, Duel had opened the lone attachment. Mackie saw a drawing of Mickey Mouse, standing in front of a Norman Rockwell-esque table setting, a cornucopia of food behind him. Printed in bold script across the bottom of the page, the words "Happy Holidays".

Duel walked up behind Mackie. He had traded Lone Star for liquor. "Her final words to me. From the grave, as it were. A bit out of character for her, sending this crap."

"I guess even a cold heart gets warmed by the Christmas spirit," Mackie said.

Duel popped the remaining Oreo into his mouth. "So, what's your next step?"

"I've got to get some rest." Mackie scooted back in the chair. He rubbed his temples with his fingertips.

Duel nodded. "Good plan. I know you've got this theory about her boyfriend being the perpetrator, and there may be something to it. But my advice to you is to let this thing play out. You've already overstepped by going to the morgue. You're going to piss off Pham plus jeopardize your claim of innocence if you keep up this parallel investigation."

"You expect me to sit back while someone else takes their time investigating my future?"

"As your lawyer, I expect you to not do anything else stupid," Duel said. "You told me you didn't kill Sarah. I believe you, and we'll work to get others to believe you, too. You've just got to be patient." He clicked off the light and motioned for Mackie to follow. "Don't go snooping around and making yourself look any more guilty than you already do."

Chapter Seven

MACKIE ARRIVED HOME later than he expected that night. His head swam with too much sugar and not enough rest. He kept the windows down on the ride home, radio loud, fighting sleep. Fatigue waterlogged his body, an undertow of exhaustion pulling him to his bed. But his mind fought it, grasping for more information, struggling to make connections between what he knew and what he suspected.

He stopped in the kitchen, popping a Diet Coke and pouring fresh water into the dog bowl. Jonah thumped his tail in acknowledgment from the den, but he didn't get up. Mackie shuffled to his study. Papers still littered the floor. He ignored them. He collapsed into the chair at his desk, then scooted forward to activate his computer. The thugs had tossed aside his laptop en route to his file cabinet, but the old MacBook tolerated the trauma. As he waited for the Internet connection, he heard Jonah amble into the room, circling in one spot over trampled papers before settling down. Mackie scratched behind Jonah's ears with his foot. "Let's see if we can find out what your ex-mama's been up to." Jonah's tailed knocked against the floor in agreement.

Mackie pulled up the e-mail attachment from Duel.

Duel's attachment contained hundreds of emails, each one a separate document in the larger folder labeled "Inbox". Nothing in his quick scan of subject lines caught his attention. He resisted the urge to scan the daily chatter with her colleagues. He noted a flurry of activity that week. Could have been normal since Sarah worked from home. The second batch of documents, still in the attached folder, appeared to be all sent messages. Scores of messages sent to

Henry at Synthesis Industries. He scrolled down the page, finding the holiday greeting she had sent to Duel. When he looked closer, Mackie realized the Mickey Mouse image had originally be sent to Sarah from an account at AFI. Mackie had no idea what AFI meant. The email showed no text or comments. Simply one attachment. Mackie double clicked to open the file, but his computer balked. He dragged the icon to his desktop, but once again, the computer wouldn't allow it.

"What's that all about?" he said to Jonah.

Too tired to care at this point, Mackie leaned back in his chair to scan her sent e-mails. The messages appeared to date back a decade. Easily over a thousand documents. It appeared as if she had never purged her account. Nothing else he found in the subject lines interested him. Still, he found himself reading each message from Hank. Daily banter. Inside jokes. Plans for the next time they'd see one another. The more he read, the more irritated he became. The last batch of documents in the attachment contained the headings "Drafts". Mackie moved the cursor over them.

The first message, most recently updated this week, contained a two-page document, outlining in legalese the sale of her stake in the H-BOC patent. A working copy, edited five days ago. That didn't make sense. Her own financial documents at the apartment indicated she'd made her fortune last month. Why was she still working on the transaction? Mackie moved back to the top of the page, re-reading the document. Key details of cost and ownership had been omitted, while other paragraphs contained unmistakable identifiers referencing the blood substitute. No way this was a generic form. Mackie scraped his fingers through his hair, his concentration slipping. He swilled soda for one last jolt of energy.

Maybe Pham could help him out.

He glanced at the clock. Too late to reach her at the office.

He opened one of the documents near the bottom of the attachment.

A dear-John letter. Without the salutation. Or any specific details to an outside reader. Last edited almost one month ago, the letter contained more ideas than it did specific content. The tone of it seemed apologetic. The timing supported that, coming almost a year after the divorce.

It pains me to write these words to you, but I feel that I have to be as honest with you as I can…I treasure our relationship, both personally and professionally, but I have to follow my heart… Know that I will always treasure the time together…though it may be awkward, we have more than enough financial incentive to maintain a healthy professional relationship.

"That's bullshit." The dog looked up when Mackie spoke. "She was trying to find the right words to kiss my ass. Butter me up, so I wouldn't be angry with her about cashing out."

Unbelievable.

Mackie slammed his laptop shut.

He really needed to talk to Duel about these messages.

The phone rang.

Only Duel would have the audacity to call so late, Mackie thought. He picked up the receiver, hoping to ask him about what he'd discovered in the attachments. "Duel? I've been looking at these emails…"

A pause on the other end. Vacuous. Granular. Then, a thin voice. "Dad?"

Mackie straightened. "Reagan? Are you okay?"

She hesitated, giving a nervous laugh. She sounded exactly like her mother. "I'm fine, but you're the one who called. I've gotten, like, four messages between your calls and everyone else. What's up?"

Mackie's pulse quickened. Words he'd prepared fled his mind. "Is someone there with you?"

"What?"

"Just tell me someone is there," he stammered. "I wanted to fly over and tell you in person, but I can't. I didn't want you to be alone when you heard."

"Dad, you're scaring me."

Mackie paused to regroup. His dry mouth made it hard to swallow, hard to speak. "There's been an accident?"

"Are you hurt?"

"It's your mother." He paused. Considered his words, but nothing he could think of would soften the blow. "She died, honey."

He heard her gasp, almost choke, then a scream of disbelief. "I just spoke to her two days ago." Background noises. Rapid-fire Italian, getting louder. Then a British voice. Male. Consoling. Inquiring.

Mackie pressed on. "Some kind of accident. We're still getting the details."

She sobbed out, "What accident? Are you sure? What—?" She tried to catch her breath but ended up hyperventilating.

The British voice took the phone. "Hello? Mr. McKay?" Deep voice. Authoritative. "This is…I'm Reagan's course director. What has happened?"

Mackie swallowed. He could hear Reagan's hysterics in the background and multiple soothing voices. He should have flown directly to Florence today. Told her in person. He could have been there in twelve hours. "Her mother's been killed in an accident."

"Bloody hell," the man said. A stage whisper. Muted.

Mackie tried to regain control of the conversation. "I'm going to make arrangements for her to fly back to Nashville. Can I speak to her again?"

Reagan sniffled on the other end. "Daddy? Oh… my… God," she choked out.

"You're coming home, sweetheart. I'm buying your ticket for you. Is there someone that can come with you?"

In the next few minutes, Reagan calmed enough to create a plan for getting home. Mackie would buy the first available plane ticket. He spoke to the course director once more. Made sure someone would look out for Reagan. Get her to the airport. Get her on a plane.

Sensing tension, Jonah struggled to stand and moved closer to Mackie. He curled up at his feet, eyes upturned, waiting for instructions.

Mackie finished his conversation and hung up, even more exhausted. Drained from hearing her voice. Edgy from its timing. He had hoped to initiate the call and emotionally prepare himself in the process. He felt like an ass. His daughter, alone in a foreign country, hearing such horrifying news... The weight of the day's events collapsed in on him. He reached to scratch behind Jonah's ear, more heartbroken than he had been in the last three years. As sad as when he'd found out about Sarah's affair. He leaned forward on the desk, buried his face in his arm, and for the first time in as many years, he cried.

For himself.

For Reagan.

And for all that had gone wrong with Sarah.

CHAPTER EIGHT

THE NEXT MORNING, Mackie found himself back in a car. This time, he sat in the driver's seat. He had called Duel to ask for guidance, but his attorney didn't answer the phone. He called the police station, only to be told that Detective Pham would not be in for two more hours. With Reagan expected to arrive early the next day, Mackie had one day to get some answers. He knew that when Duel sobered up, he would rise to the occasion and help. Pham had also reassured him the police would find Sarah's killer, but that could take a while. After scanning through Sarah's emails, Mackie had a lead, and if he acted now, he just might find the answers he sought.

He squinted, adjusting the visor to block the rising sun. Coffee steamed the windshield, making it even harder to see. Not that it mattered. There was only one major turn between Nashville and Atlanta. He drove fast against the traffic at this hour, taking sips of burnt coffee. Mackie pressed the accelerator. With the memory of the previous day trailing behind him, he drove the two hundred mile trip in just over three hours.

He dialed the number as he exited the interstate.

"Mackie?" Sarathi Singh couldn't conceal his surprise. "You're coming when?"

"Ten minutes. Maybe fifteen."

Singh hesitated. "This is unexpected."

Mackie signaled at the end of the exit ramp. He turned right, heading toward the facility. In the years since he had last visited, the once pastoral section of Atlanta, just outside the interstate 285 perimeter, was now paved and zoned for commercial development. "Can I meet you in the lobby in ten minutes?"

Singh acquiesced.

Mackie pulled into the office park shortly after nine a.m. He couldn't see Synthesis Industries from the main road, camouflaged among the asphalt by bright metal and shiny glass. Hidden beautifully by a dozen similar developments. A small sign marked the driveway with a street number. Manicured waist-high boxwoods along the drive whispered "private property, keep out."

The building itself shimmered. In the parking lot, car windshields joined in. The building comprised two circular structures joined by a covered walkway. From the side, they appeared as futuristic silos, foreshortened and made of curved glass. From above, Mackie expected the place would form the shape of a figure eight. He paused to take in the scene. Those windows would be a bitch to clean without a curved squeegee.

Mackie parked his car near a silver BMW bearing a personalized license plate on the back, framed in black plastic with the words "Synthesis Industries" emblazoned across the top. Relentless marketing, he thought. In the short walk to the front door, Mackie began to sweat. Winter in Atlanta. Two hundred miles and one climate zone removed from Nashville. A refrigerated transfer truck rumbled behind him, driving to the side of the complex, disappearing behind the smaller circular building. He stepped inside. The lobby door automatically shut, leaving him with the quiet anxiety of a dental office waiting room. Vaguely familiar from his visit years ago, but updated now.

A boxy-shaped man with his arms crossed leaned against a planter, almost monochromatic with his dark hair, dark skin, and dark blue coveralls. He stood in place for that additional moment that separates hospitality from hostility. Mackie glanced around the room before walking toward the planter.

"Dr. Singh." Mackie smiled, hand extended. "How's my star student?"

"Busy as ever." Singh straightened, a head shorter than Mackie but just as wide. His coveralls bent at the collar from the weight of his photo identification and hexagonal radiation monitor. "I really don't have much time right now."

"Thanks for seeing me." When Singh didn't accept Mackie's proffered hand, he clapped the smaller man on the shoulder. "I had a few business items regarding H-BOC I wanted to talk to you about. Thought, since I'm in the area, I'd come by and see if you had a few minutes."

Singh looked at his one-time mentor. "It's easier to get my undivided attention if you call ahead and schedule with my secretary." He picked at his manicured nails, then shrugged Mackie's hand from his shoulder. "But since you're already here, let's use my office." He turned toward the back of the building.

Mackie followed

The two men crossed the lobby. A bank of elevators were situated behind the security desk in what appeared to be a cylinder in the center of the lobby. A guard took Mackie's name and photograph, issuing him a temporary ID badge. Singh led Mackie past the elevators, toward the smaller building beyond.

"We've changed our layout since you and Sarah were here a few years ago," Singh said. Mackie slowed his stride to match Singh's pace. "Most of the business operations are in the Mother Pod."

Mackie looked directly at Singh. "The Mother Pod?"

Singh offered an embarrassed smile, making him look even more diminutive. "Main building. The architect originally called the two buildings the Mother Pod and Pod Two. Sounds stupid, but the names stuck."

Mackie humored him. "So business operations are now in the Mother Pod. Accounting, legal, marketing. All that?"

Singh walked on. "I don't spend much time up here. Research, development, and production have moved to the back."

Mackie winked. "Pod Two."

"You got it."

They walked to the back of the building. Just like the outside, the walls maintained the curve of the overall structure. Singh swiped his identification badge near the exit. Both doors automatically opened. They made their way through the glass tunnel connecting the pods. Through the walkway's skylights, Mackie saw the first building rise three stories above him, curved windows reaching up until abruptly cut short by the flat roof. Ahead, Pod Two glimmered as a shorter, two-story version.

Singh noted Mackie's interest. "We have more space to market our product than to make it. All of the research takes place in the basement. Production on the ground floor. Top floor is mostly ductwork to cool the facility. A few scattered offices, too. Like mine."

"You got a bum deal, Sarathi. Not much space."

Singh nodded. "Not only did the R&D guys get screwed on the space, we can't increase production unless we expand."

"Demand for H-BOC is up?"

"You have no idea."

"Maybe you could use the basement. Cut back on research, churn out more product."

Singh grinned. He swiped his identification at the far end of the walkway as both men entered Pod Two. Instead of the rising atrium and curved walls of the lobby, the inside of this building looked industrial, practical. Linoleum floors. White walls. Hard edges. No glossy prints adorned the walls. They walked into a small anteroom, low ceilings and lockers.

Singh glanced at Mackie. "Are you gaining weight?"

"You haven't seen me in a while. I'm actually getting skinny."

"Uh-huh."

"I've been running a few days a week." He smiled. "What's your excuse?"

"I come from a fat family in India." Singh handed Mackie an identical set of navy blue coveralls. "Mandatory attire inside."

He waited while Mackie dressed, then the two men left the changing room and stepped onto the production floor. The first thing Mackie noticed was the cold. A blast of air chilled him at the doorway. He breathed into his hands and stepped forward, allowing the door to close behind him. Dozen of stainless steel vats, similar to kettles in a brewery, lined the room in precise formation. Most vats clustered nearer the front of the room. Pipes snaked through the rafters, then extended from the ceiling toward each vat, condensation beading on the exteriors. Workers in hairnets and identical attire circulated around the room. Most wore gloves. Some sat before banks of computers, taking notes, recording data. Others checked the dials on the vats. Mackie expected more noise in a room of this size. No one looked up as both men walked in.

Singh beamed. "This is our production facility. Looks about the same."

"More modern," Mackie said.

"We bought better technology last year. Demand is about ten-fold higher, so we had to increase efficiency. These vats produce the molecular soup that turns out to be H–BOC." He pointed above his head. "All of the substrate is stored above us and feeds into each kettle."

Mackie inspected the production line. "The process is the same, though."

"Up here it is. Same patent, same product. But downstairs is where the future lies."

"Can I see it?"

Singh shook his head. "Any success from the basement will be patented by my company."

"Double check that. We had a pretty broad scope of exclusivity on the original H–BOC patent," Mackie said.

Singh grunted annoyance, then moved to his left, careful to tread the perimeter of the room. Red linoleum squares surrounded the work zone of the building, providing a visual barrier for foot traffic. As they circled the room, Mackie saw that the stainless steel drums only occupied the front half of the building. Near the back, a series of conveyor belts fed into other machines, connected by additional metal pipes positioned overhead. On the far side of the production line, cardboard boxes emerged, frosted and apparently filled. Two workers inspected each box, and once satisfied, taped a shipping label on top. A third person directed the boxes of H–BOC onto distribution pallets.

Mackie crossed the red tiles, heading for the conveyor belt.

Singh grabbed his arm. "Hold on."

"I just want to see the finished product."

"I'll get you one." Singh moved across the threshold to the machine, slipping on a pair of gloves from the counter. He reached inside the machine with his left hand and grabbed a flat bag, the size and shape of a package of frozen vegetables. Condensation beaded on the bag as he carried it back to Mackie. "Nothing special. One unit of H–BOC. Same as it ever was."

"New package?"

"We've updated the label."

Up close, the creamy white contents glistened beneath ice crystals, as if someone had replaced the frozen vegetables with milk and sealed it in thick plastic. Mackie reached for it, but Singh pulled back. "Come on, Sarathi. You think I'm going to spill it? It's the same stuff we stock in the hospital."

"Then you'll know where to find some. If I let you hold this, the bag is considered contaminated and we have to waste it. At a thousand bucks a bag, I think your curiosity can wait."

Singh glided toward the machine with the unit of H–BOC. At the edge of the production line near the conveyor belt, he spoke to a woman inspecting boxes. Her hairnet nodded as he spoke. She glanced at Mackie, then nestled the frozen packet among the others in the box.

Singh joined Mackie at the perimeter. "This is a through–way, not a water cooler. Let's head to my office."

Near the exit, a door led to a stairwell. Several feet beyond them, the red tile curved abruptly, blocking their path as it intersected with the wall. On the other side of the barrier, thick plastic strips hung like curtains, separating the cool of the room from the warmer loading docks. Mackie held back the plastic for an employee as he moved a pallet of boxes toward the door. The employee smiled his thanks. Mackie continued to hold onto the plastic as he poked his head through. A refrigerated transfer truck droned in the loading dock as workers loaded it. Another truck waited outside the curved enclosure of the shipping bay. Workers in the truck's cargo bay secured the newest pallet to the dozens already loaded.

Someone tapped his shoulder.

"You're here to see me, right?" Singh asked.

"This is fascinating, seeing the end result."

Singh motioned for Mackie to follow him. "My office is at the top of the stairs."

"Where's most of the market for Synthesis these days?" Mackie asked as they ascended the stairs.

"Major trauma centers, like you'd expect. L.A. and Houston. We're seeing increasing demand from the Watchtower Building in Brooklyn."

"Jehovah's Witnesses?"

Singh nodded. "It's a growing movement."

"Seems to be a strong orthopedic clientele, at least at Nashville Memorial. Unless that was just an aberration because of me."

Singh reached the top of the stairs and held open the door for Mackie. "H–BOC infusions for joint replacements hold a strong market share for us, same as it ever was."

Mackie laughed. "People go out of their way to avoid blood transfusion for elective procedures."

"AIDS has been great for business. Fear of infections from a tainted blood supply drives the market." He turned to look at Mackie. "For both of us. As long as you hold onto your patent rights, you're going to profit with the growth of Synthesis."

"That's part of what I came to talk to you about."

Singh paused, but he didn't turn around. He walked several paces down the carpeted hallway. The door to his office stood open, lights on. Clearly Mackie had interrupted him with his earlier phone call. Singh pushed open the door, allowing Mackie to walk inside. "I've got to take a piss." Singh said. "Be right back."

Mackie stood in the middle of the office. He unzipped his coverall, beginning to sweat with the temperature change. What struck him most about Singh's office was the impersonal sterility of it. No framed diplomas. No family pictures. No nameplates or recognitions. It could have been any workspace in any of the buildings of this industrial park. His desk signaled business. Open journals. Printed spreadsheets. Coffee-stained napkin under an empty mug. The entire atmosphere telegraphed a far different man than the one Mackie had known several years ago. Singh seemed no less driven than he'd been during his residency days in Nashville. His success seemed to have increased his intensity. Sharpened his edges. But also leached some of the humanity Mackie had enjoyed. Maybe he was having a bad day. Given what he'd intended to say to Singh, he didn't expect the man's mood to improve.

Mackie strolled around the room. On top of the desk, beside the open journals, a stack of shipping labels occupied one corner. He leaned closer and looked. Four separate stacks. Houston and Los Angels on one side. Brooklyn and Frederick, Maryland on the other side. West and East coast distribution centers, Mackie figured. He glanced again at the packing label for Frederick, Maryland. It had been years since he'd thought about that town. Seeing the name printed on a label made him wonder if Synthesis Industries had finally established a contact he'd been unable to achieve. He'd ask Singh about it. After he said what he needed to say.

Mackie glanced at a stack of business cards in a wire mesh holder. He picked one up. Slick Synthesis logo. Singh's name and title emblazoned beneath. Home phone. Cell. E–mail. An unusual degree of access. He slipped a card into his wallet.

Mackie crossed the room, inspecting the bookshelves while he waited. The books offered a roadmap of Singh's education. Heavily weighted with textbooks. Mostly orthopedic surgical resources, but also volumes on pharmacology, trauma surgery, and battlefield medicine. A thin handbook used in residency, now dog-eared, squeezed in among the larger hardbacks. The black spine of Netter's atlas of anatomy punctuated the other books on the bottom shelves. Next to it, another book caught Mackie's attention.

He squatted and pulled Gunther's Joint Replacements off the shelve. A book on metallurgy of synthetic joints slipped out with it, and Mackie pushed it back in. Opening the cover of Gunther's took him back ten years. Maybe fifteen. Mackie treasured the text, not only because he'd used it to teach his own residents, but also because Dr. Gunther had been the one to teach Mackie those same orthopedic principles. On the cover page, the author's scrawled signature, personalized to Dr. Cooper McKay. Below it, Mackie's own note to Sarathi Singh, penned years ago as he'd passed along the treasured text to a new generation of surgical stars.

"Quite a collection, isn't it?" Singh said from the doorway.

Mackie pushed up to his feet, gripping the open book. "You still have Gunther's."

A smile softened Singh's facial expression. "You said it was for good luck when you gave it to me."

"Has it worked?"

"Look around you. We're busier than ever." He walked toward the shelves, toward Mackie.

Mackie flipped through the pages before placing the book back in the bookcase, glancing at the other titles. He pulled two smaller titles from the shelf. "Synthetic joint metallurgy? Battlefield medicine?"

Singh's smile faded. "Market research."

"Which battlefield?"

"The inner city. Urban warfare in our own backyards. Atlanta's gang violence doesn't rival the West Coast, but give a kid a gun and some drugs and you may as well be on a battlefield in the Middle East." Singh took the books from Mackie's hand and restored them to the bottom shelf. After lining up the spines of the various volumes, he stood. "Why are you here, Mackie?"

Mackie studied Singh. Whatever admiration he'd once possessed for his former teacher and mentor had been subsumed by the busyness of success. An unscheduled appointment translated into a diversion from progress. Mackie had been there once, too. "I've got some disturbing news."

"About H-BOC?"

"Sarah's dead."

Singh's eyes widened. "What happened?"

"The police still don't know. Someone murdered her two nights ago. Head wound. Looks like it killed her instantly, but the murderer subsequently transfused her with H-BOC."

"My God." He considered this news a moment. "Second thoughts?"

"That was my question, but the autopsy indicates otherwise."

Singh examined his nails. "I'm sorry for your loss. But you could have called. You have another reason for coming here. What do you need, Mackie?"

"What do you know about Sarah's stake in the patents?"

Singh clicked the manicured tips back and forth. "She was proud of what you two did together for the product."

"Did she ever talk to you about assigning her patent rights to someone else? Or even selling her partial ownership altogether to cash in on her share?"

Singh shook his head. "You're asking the wrong guy. I don't get involved with the business part of our company."

Mackie considered this. "What about Henry Stone?"

"If there's anything that has to do with the finances or market share of Synthesis Industries, Hank would know. You've got a great product, Mackie, but Hank is the one spreading the gospel about H-BOC. As I mentioned, our production increased exponentially a few years ago, and Hank's the one most responsible for that. He's constantly working on emerging markets for the company."

"Would he have paid Sarah for her piece of the action?"

Singh shrugged. "Sounds like something he might do." He collected his mug and slurped down the remaining coffee. "I know talking to him might be kind of awkward right now, but you and Sarah had both moved on since the divorce. It doesn't make much sense to me, paying your fiancée for her share of a patent, but Hank always has a plan for his business decisions."

"Excuse me?" Mackie stared at Singh. "Sarah's fiancée?"

Singh flushed. "Once and future fiancée, I guess. Hank was going to propose to her tomorrow...Dear God."

Mackie's pulse pounded his ears. He felt blindsided, and embarrassed for not knowing. Anger swelled inside his chest. Pushing out. Compressing air. Intensifying with each heartbeat. He stood up, steadying himself on the arm of the chair. "I need to see Hank. Right now."

"He's not here today," Singh said, keeping his seat. "Hank's in Nashville."

Chapter Nine

Mackie wanted to arrive back in Nashville earlier than he did, but traffic delays had kept him mired in Atlanta. Singh had balked at providing any information about Hank Stone's whereabouts, but he ultimately relented. According to Singh, Hank planned to surprise Sarah with an early morning proposal. "Somewhere outside," Singh had said. "Her favorite park or something. He'd been dropping hints to her all week." A convenient cover story, Mackie thought at the time. But it also gave him an idea.

A wreck on Interstate 75 slowed outbound traffic, followed by a back up fifty miles later behind a military convoy. Mackie's anger simmered while traffic moved at a snail's pace, but burned off as he accelerated home. His time stuck behind the wheel allowed him to plan his next move. That's when he had called Pham to ask for her help.

Now he sat in Pham's office late in the afternoon, staring at the unadorned grey walls. "You should hang some pictures," Mackie said as he leaned back in the metal folding chair of her office, rocking on its thin legs. "Personalize the place a bit."

Pham glanced over the top of a manila folder Mackie had brought from home. She looked surprisingly relaxed with her hair pulled back. "I've been here less than a month. There's a box of framed pictures in the corner. If you want to grab a hammer and start hanging them, be my guest." She turned her attention back to the folder containing details of the synthetic blood.

"What do you think?" he asked.

"Gimme a second." She scrutinized the contents, cocked her

head, then closed the folder, placing it on the stack with the others. "What's all this mean? Leucine? Arginine? Lysine? Those are amino acids, but how does that help us?"

Mackie smiled at the inclusive "us." "It's the molecular sequence of H-BOC. The fingerprints of the product found in Sarah's body. Or should be. If you lined that code up next to earlier generations of blood substitutes, you'd find about ninety-five percent concordance."

"But it's that five percent that makes a difference?"

"By about two hundred fifty million dollars."

She glanced at him. "How do you figure that?"

"Basic math. Synthesis charges about a thousand bucks a unit. Their projections estimate that this year the company will sell roughly a quarter million units. Subtract production costs, and you're still talking about some serious cash."

"How much are you making from that?"

"They gave me a fixed sum, not a percentage of the profits."

"That doesn't sound fair," Pham said. "Unless your sum is thirty million dollars."

She moved a newspaper from one of the stacks and picked up another folder. "This was sent to me this morning," she said as she handed the folder to Mackie.

He immediately recognized the autopsy report, in draft form. The same one he'd seen on Vernon Philpot's computer. "I'm not supposed to look at this. I heard your partner gave Dr. Philpot a lecture on chain of evidence and confidentiality."

"I'll never tell. Besides, I'm pretty sure you've already seen it. The medical examiner, he's a friend of yours, right?"

Mackie reached into his pocket and withdrew a pair of reading glasses. As he put them on, Pham cleared her throat. Mackie peered at her over the top of the rims. "Can I help you?"

Pham smiled. "The old man glasses. Kind of softens your rough edges."

"It's a certificate of maturity," he grumbled as looked back at the folder. Inside, pages of text described the state of the body, the extent of the injuries, and the conclusions drawn about cause of death. Philpot omitted the images, making reference to an addendum not yet included. Same with the laboratory data. Mackie skimmed the document before reaching the final section.

He frowned and shook his head as he re-read the concluding paragraph.

"See anything you recognize?" Pham asked.

"Most of it. But I don't see how he could have reached this conclusion." He placed the folder on the desk.

Pham picked it up and read. " '...blunt force trauma to the head with depressed skull fracture and intracranial bleeding...' That's reasonably obvious. What do you make of the other claim, though? '...infusion of a synthetic blood substitute contributing to microscopic destruction of the blood vessels...' That makes H-BOC a contributing cause of death."

Mackie reclaimed the folder from her and read aloud. " 'White coagulated crystals in the superior vena cava with crystalline streaks along the posterior wall, leading to the same pooled liquid in her right atrium along the posterior surface. Minimal circulation of the fluid beyond the right ventricle.' " He looked up as he removed and folded the reading glasses. "I interpret that as postmortem infusion. Her heart couldn't circulate the liquid. Destruction of the blood vessels doesn't make sense, though. I've never seen H-BOC do that to a patient. Or a cadaver, for that matter. Unless we're dealing with an NME."

"A what?"

"New molecular entity. It's what the FDA calls an investigational new drug." He studied her reaction. "You've never heard of this?"

Pham turned both palms up. "I'm a cop, Mackie. This is your area of expertise."

Mackie readjusted in his chair. "Anytime a new drug is being studied in human clinical trials, the FDA has to approve a new molecular entity application before a company can begin research and development for a new compound. It's one of the first steps in ensuring safety."

Pham considered his explanation, then asked, "So it's possible the information Dr. Singh gave you might not match the fluid analysis of Sarah's body?"

"Possible, sure, but the entire application process of new molecular entities—which is essentially the first step in developing new drugs—is a transparent process. It's all public information. I would have heard about a new product in the pipelines." Mackie shifted in his chair again.

"That's not the real reason you went to Atlanta today, is it? You could have gotten most of this with a phone call."

"I was hoping to run into Hank Stone."

"You can't be interviewing witnesses and running a parallel investigation, Mackie."

"He wasn't even at the office. Singh told me Hank spent the last three days here in Nashville."

Pham sat up. "He was here on the night of the murder?"

"Apparently, he's still in town."

"Did Singh say why?"

"He told me Hank came up for a long weekend. Sarah didn't know this. According to Singh, they were going to get engaged in some park tomorrow morning."

Pham let out a slow whistle. "That adds an unexpected twist."

"For both of us."

She picked up a pen, jotting a few words on the first piece of paper she found. "Let's think this through. Hank lives in Atlanta. Sarah in Nashville. He drives up a few days ago to see his friend."

"Friend with special privileges," Mackie said.

She glanced up. "Nothing wrong with that, but it makes this scenario all the more confusing. The only reason you pay someone thirty million dollars for a product is if you anticipate that the payout will be dwarfed by the expected revenues. And even then, if you're married to the patent holder, you would assume you'd share in the future profits. So, why go to all the trouble to purchase the patent in the first place?"

"Unless they've developed a novel product that falls under the protection of one of our other patents. And any new product that is based off of our chemical backbone falls under the patent protection. A new twist on the old H-BOC."

"What are we missing?" Pham asked.

"We need to ask Hank Stone," Mackie said. "That's where I need your help."

Pham scribbled a final note. "Let's go back to the distribution of H-BOC for a minute. Houston and L.A. make sense. Brooklyn for Jehovah's Witnesses. Doubles as a resource for Manhattan. But why Frederick, Maryland? Probably not that much gang violence there. If you're shipping goods to centers that need additional H-BOC for traumas, I'd think you would ship them to larger metropolitan areas. Maybe it's a distribution center for Washington, D.C.," she said. "But wouldn't it be easier to ship it directly to D.C.? Or Baltimore?"

"Could it be a distribution center for an international market?" Mackie asked.

"What do you mean?"

Mackie leaned closer, elbows on his knees. "Singh has always wanted to increase market share of H-BOC. Synthesis has pretty much saturated the U.S. market for blood substitutes, but there's not been much uptake in the major European cities. That's the problem. London, Paris, Frankfurt, and even Florence—where Reagan is studying—are relatively safe cities. The real market for a blood substitute is in troubled areas around the world."

Pham nodded. "Bagdad, Jerusalem, Kandahar. Imagine if they'd had it on the scene at the Boston Marathon."

"That was never intended to be a war zone." Mackie said. "But for the international hot spots, you're not shipping H-BOC directly to those locations. Hospitals there can't afford it."

Pham rested her thumbs under her chin, tapping her fingertips together just in front of her nose. She considered the implications as her eyes brightened. "The U.S. military."

Mackie nodded. "Exactly, which may mean that Frederick, Maryland is the final stop…at least in the United States. There's an army base there, Fort Detrick, which houses the U.S. Army Medical Research Center."

"You've been there?" Pham asked.

"Years ago. Sarah and I tried to negotiate a contract with the military to provide H-BOC. Lots of interest from the army, but ultimately they felt the product was too experimental. Too many restrictions for its use. The biggest impediment was keeping H-BOC cooled. What if Singh has figured out how to bypass that hurdle?"

"Any evidence of that when you toured Synthesis?"

"None."

Mackie and Pham both considered the connection, working out the implications. "Let's assume all of this is true," Pham finally said. "There's got to be a paper trail."

"No doubt. You're dealing with the military. When I was in the Reserves after medical school, you couldn't take a crap without someone wanting you to fill out a form."

Pham rolled her eyes. "Nice image."

Mackie grinned. "It's how it was."

"When did you retire from the Reserves?" she asked.

"After about fifteen years of donating one weekend a month and one week each year. I couldn't keep up with my responsibilities at home and work, plus fulfill my military obligation."

"Did you ever see combat?" she asked.

"Nothing significant. I was a Reserve surgeon. Did mostly check-ups and routine surgical procedures. Lots of suturing. Removed my share of hemorrhoids and cysts. Had a few appendectomies. I did go to Kuwait during the initial deployment of the first Iraqi war. The biggest casualty I saw was when this kid stepped on an old land mine, made mostly of scrap metal and nails. Tore through this boy's right leg. Severed his femoral artery." Mackie shook his head. "A God-awful mess."

Pham listened. "Did you save him?"

"I got him patched up, then shipped him to our base in Germany."

"Did you use H-BOC?"

"Didn't have it yet. It's one of the things that started me thinking about how synthetic blood could work."

Pham considered this. "But if you'd had it, how would the distribution have worked?"

"We would've had a supplier. Triage hospitals would've been stocked with the product. Of course, refrigerated, preferably frozen, which was not a practical consideration in the desert. If we had a blood substitute, though, that kid would have received a transfusion at the time of the injury. Part of the first response in the field to increase on-site tissue perfusion. Probably would have received another unit in the O.R. As it was, I saw him half an hour after the explosion. He'd lost a ton of blood. I think we transfused him eight or ten units of packed red blood cells by the time he was transported to Germany. And he still lost the limb."

"Poor kid."

"That's my question for the military: What's a boy's leg worth?" Mackie asked. "The H-BOC would have cost the army six – maybe eight – thousand dollars, which is not a bad deal. For a leg. When I performed an orthopedic procedure on a hemophiliac in this country, it cost upwards of one hundred thousand dollars to pay for the blood factors alone."

"Not to mention the risk of HIV and hepatitis inherent in the transfusions," Pham said.

"Preach on," Mackie said. "Small, but not negligible."

"Don't think the Ryan White story didn't stick with me as a kid. There are few things worse than getting AIDS from your doctor just because you needed a transfusion."

Mackie sat back. "So you can see the benefits of the military getting involved. Compared to the cost of storing, testing, and processing each unit of blood, H-BOC ends up costing considerably less. Plus, no risk of infection and easy to transport."

"Sounds like a good deal for the military. I would think they would jump at the opportunity. They still have to refrigerate traditional blood products, so I don't see how it's that different."

"We tried that argument, too, but each time we discussed it with the military, their response was the same: H-BOC is an experimental product and they weren't willing to commit money to it unless we could prove it was safe and saved lives."

"You showed them your studies?" Pham asked. "The FDA stamp of approval didn't convince them?"

"We thought of all that," Mackie said. "Just before Sarah and I separated, we worked with the army on a pilot study. Asked them to employ the use of H-BOC in one combat zone for six months. Our plan was to use hard endpoints to evaluate the success or failure—"

"Meaning what?" Pham asked.

"Indisputable events. Death. Cost of treatment. Survival. All stratified according to injury. We figured that with good data, the army would see for themselves the benefit of the project and ultimately invest in the product with a large contract."

"So what happened?"

"Hank happened. Once Sarah and I split, the entire proposal fell apart."

"Ouch. On both accounts," Pham said. "When was that?"

"About two years ago."

"Which coincided with the conclusion of the Middle East military campaigns. Bad timing."

"Exactly," Mackie said. "That was the military's argument. There was no longer an urgent need for H-BOC. We were winning the battles in the Middle East. Uncertainty in the political climate. There was every reason to hope that things would get better."

"But they got worse again." Pham picked up the newspaper. A headline blazed, More Civilian Casualties in Worsening Syrian Conflict.

"That's the modern military. I served during Republican Administrations. Dropping a hundred million dollar contract on an experimental drug or product wouldn't have even been noticed. Political tolerance for that mismanagement has changed. We just happened to approach them at the wrong time."

"Which brings me back to my original question," Pham said. "Did Synthesis end up with a military contract for H–BOC?"

Mackie shrugged. "If I'm reading their annual statement right, it seems like they did."

"Wouldn't you expect that sort of stuff to make headlines?" Pham asked. "The military sometimes announces big ticket contracts, but some things are funded under the table. If those projects are announced, it's because they're a success story, not a cautionary tale."

"You understand the military mind." Mackie considered his own childhood in a military family. Instead of dragging his family around the globe, Mackie's dad had left his mom and his two younger brothers at home, showing up one weekend a month during peacetime. Dad just hadn't been there. By the time Colonel McKay had deployed to Vietnam, Mackie felt lucky to see his father once a year. And that had only happened twice before the Viet Cong killed him.

Pham spoke, jarring Mackie from his memories. "Sorry, I didn't hear you."

"What role did Duel play in all of this? You mentioned that he did most of the legal work for both of you during the divorce. You would think he'd know about any deal between Synthesis and the military."

Mackie shook his head. "I would have known about it."

"But Duel was also Sarah's lawyer. Surely there's some attorney–client privilege involved."

"I'll ask him when I see him." Mackie paused, considering his next step. "I think you and Officer Pennington should track down Hank while he's still in town. Chances are he's staying at a high–end hotel, and there're only a few parks he would choose to propose in."

"If he's at the park, then he didn't kill Sarah. You don't show up for a surprise engagement if you know your future fiancée is dead." Pham stacked the folders together and slid the autopsy report back into its sheath. "Besides, that's not how an investigation works, Mackie. Give me probable cause and we'll decide where to go from there."

As she cleared her desk, she met his gaze. He recognized a busy woman with more on her mind than the work before her. Obviously other cases needed her attention. And by the look of the partially opened boxes in the corner, she hadn't even settled into her new city. Plenty of work would be there long after he left.

She smiled when she caught him staring at her. "When's Reagan coming home?"

"Early tomorrow morning." He glanced at his watch. "She's taking the overnight. Not as quick as either one of us would have liked, but it'll get her here."

"Poor girl," Pham said. "What'll you do once she gets in town?"

"Make funeral arrangements."

She scratched yet another note to herself, speaking as she wrote. "I'll make sure we release the body to the funeral home before her plane arrives. I'll also let you know when when I hear about the H-BOC lab results."

"How long should that take?" Mackie asked.

"If all goes according to plan, I'll have a definitive answer by tomorrow afternoon."

CHAPTER TEN

MACKIE MADE ONE final stop on his way home from Pham's office. With very little food at his house and little interest in cooking, he phoned his to-go order in to a local favorite. Now he leaned against the bar inside the restaurant, waiting for his order. The bartender acknowledged him with a nod while serving another customer, then brought a pint of pale ale to him. "Another ten minutes on the order," the bartender said as he sauntered back to the refrigerator. "If you change your mind and want to eat here, let me know."

Absently nodding, Mackie stared at the Happy Hour crowd. That's when he heard him.

Even amidst the din of the crowd, Duel's distinctive voice and raucous laugh pierced the noise. At the other end of the bar, Mackie saw his lawyer, clearly drunk again, drain his beer before knocking over the glass as he set it on the bar. Two women stood nearby, fawning. Duel said something in reference to the tipped glass. One woman offered an indulgent giggle. He draped his arm around her shoulder and whispered in her ear.

Mackie tried to avoid eye contact. He turned his attention to the television and nursed his beer. He checked his cell phone messages. No calls. He thought of Reagan. She would have spent the day packing, stuffing dirty clothes next to clean ones. Jamming shoes behind an already stressed zipper. She was probably ten minutes late for the airport. He doubted anything about her travel habits had changed in her semester abroad. She wouldn't want to return to Italy after the funeral. Not with the semester almost over. Pham's two-word assessment of the situation echoed in his ear: Poor girl.

Not only for the loss of her mother, but also for having Mackie as a single dad. He'd never felt comfortable acting independently as a father, but he was determined to figure it out. The thought of having to defend his reputation and prove his innocence in front of her not only seemed unnecessary in his mind, it seemed down right unfair. Reagan had already lost one parent. Mackie was determined to make sure she didn't lose the other. And time was running out to clear his name before she returned.

A raucous voice interrupted his thoughts.

"Well, I'll be damned. If it isn't Dr. McKay, making an appearance at Happy Hour." Duel stumbled toward Mackie's end of the bar, beer heavy on his breath. He wiped spittle from the side of his mouth with his monogrammed shirt sleeve. "Where you been all day?"

"Atlanta." Mackie nodded at the co-ed on the other end of the bar. She fluttered her fingers at the two of them. "Who's your friend?"

Duel lowered his voice to a stage whisper. "Check her out. Jee-ee-zus! Met her last week. She's finishing law school in the spring."

Mackie smiled. "Her dad must be excited to meet you."

"Fuck you, Mackie." Duel scooted in beside him at the bar. He staggered onto the barstool, gripping the counter to balance himself. "Whatcha doing in Atlanta?"

"Looking for Hank Stone. Ended up spending the morning, though, with Sarathi Singh."

"He's an asshole." Duel ordered another beer. "You keep playing vigilante investigator, and I can't do my job defending you."

"I'm not a suspect anymore, Duel."

"Says who?"

"Says Detective Pham, for starters."

"She's a babe." Duel muffled his intoxicated laugh, causing it to emerge as a snort. "But don't let her hotness fool you, my friend. She's one tough bitch. Until they catch the guy who killed Sarah, you're going to be her prime suspect. Sorry if that's news to you."

"It would help me if you could stay sober long enough clear my name."

Duel swatted away the criticism with an open hand. "Losing Sarah sucks, pal."

"So while her killer is walking around, you're spending your time looking for him at Happy Hour?"

"All in due time, my friend. All in due time. I know what I'm doing." He took a pull from his glass. "So what'd the esteemed Dr. Singh have to say?"

"Not much. At least, not much that was helpful. He told me Hank's been in Nashville since Wednesday." Mackie sipped his own beer, staring at the television while he talked. "Also said that Hank came to Nashville specifically to ask Sarah to marry him."

"Bastard," Duel said.

Both men stared at the television.

Mackie finally glanced a Duel. "You ever been to Synthesis Industries?"

"Twice. Once when you licensed the patent to them. Another time as part of the divorce proceeding." He belched into his fist.

"State of the art facility," Mackie said. "Did you tour the production floor?"

"First visit. Just about froze my nuts off in that place. By the time I got back to Atlanta for the second visit, we were ass-deep in negotiations. No time for a field trip. They're still going strong, I take it."

"Two thousand units a day. Five days a week," Mackie said. "Singh told me they sell a quarter million units a year now. At a thousand bucks a pop."

"Jesus. I'm going to have to raise my own fees."

The bartender brought Mackie's meal in a bag. He signed the bill, declining a second beer. Duel ordered another round, and sent shots over to his girlfriend on the far side of the room. Mackie turned to leave, but Duel grabbed his sleeve. "I may be drunk, but I'm serious about laying low and leaving Detective Pham out of this."

"She's in charge of the investigation."

Duel nodded. "Of course, she is, but it looks damn awkward when one suspect starts questioning other suspects. I'm talking from a legal standpoint, here. All I'm saying is, let my guy do some of the legwork first. I've got a first-rate private investigator who's working with me on this. We'll get Detective Pham involved when she can really make a difference."

"Whatever, Duel." Mackie's hunger pulled him toward the car. "What do you suggest we do in the meantime?"

Duel wheezed while he considered the question. "My P.I. will track down Hank. Figure out where he was the night Sarah died. See if he's still here."

"And once you find him?"

"We ask him what the hell happened," Duel said. "The answer lies with him."

Mackie left the bar and drove directly home to his darkened house. The neighbor's holiday lights cast shadows across his front porch. When he'd left that morning, he'd expected to return before dusk. Jonah pushed through the front door when Mackie opened it, greeting him just long enough to have his head scratched before heading to the yard. Mackie left the front door open as he turned on lights and placed his dinner and keys on the kitchen counter. He picked up his nine iron, still leaning against the back door, and make a cursory check of his house. Foolish, he knew, but he wanted to be sure. As Jonah's wagging tale had just attested, the house was empty. On the way back to the kitchen, Mackie glanced at the answering machine. No messages. Who was he kidding, anyway? No one used his landline anymore. He should disconnect the service, stick with his cell. Reagan would text him if she needed him.

Mackie stood at the counter while he ate his supper. Once he finished, he went to his study, Jonah still at his heels. He checked for an e-mail from Reagan, but he found nothing. He sent a message to her about his plan to meet her at the airport in the morning. She would probably receive it when she landed in Amsterdam, her one and only stop.

He opened his browser and googled Synthesis Industries, finding addresses for the company's website and several newspaper citations. One mentioned emerging products in health care, quoting Dr. Singh's call for a safer alternative to blood transfusions. Mackie skimmed the article. In another posting six weeks earlier, Synthesis Industries announced the proud partnership with a venture capital firm. The company planned to expand their facilities to meet the growing demand for blood products at home and abroad. Singh had not mentioned the funding to Mackie, and the facility he'd seen that morning had lacked any obvious signs of expansion.

Mackie next googled Frederick, Maryland. Slick websites touting the city's proximity to Washington, D.C. dominated the generated list. Others highlighted Frederick's many outdoor festivals. He clicked on the website for Fort Detrick. Scrolling through it, Mackie noted a typical military polish to the site, providing phone numbers and photos. He saw no significant information in regards to the facilities for medical research. One sidebar mentioned three young soldiers who had returned to Fort Detrick from Iraq with mangled limbs, beneficiaries of emerging medical products from the base. Mackie thought of the surgeries they must have had, as well as the months of physical therapy they would endure to learn a new normal. This was a story of tragedy and triumph posted in newspapers across the country, small town kids returning home, disabled from their service, and learning to live again with their injuries. Three decades of orthopedic surgery had not inured him to the pain these kids experienced. Ten years ago, he might have reacted differently, but these soldiers were now Reagan's age. They could have been her contemporaries, if not her classmates.

Mackie should have turned off his computer then. He'd seen what he considered important. He understood Duel's advice to leave the investigation to the experts, but he couldn't resist asking questions. Not now. Not after what he'd learned. And not after the accusations. If the crime scene investigators hadn't already confiscated Sarah's computer, they would soon. He would ultimately learn about all of her financial documents. Each of her business deals. And someone at the crime lab would scour her e-mails, searching for clues to her killer.

Mackie knew he should listen to his attorney. Let the police do their job. But that wasn't who Mackie had been for most of his adult life. He'd spent his career in charge. Being assertive. Investigating. And, at the end of the process, fixing the problems he found. If Duel didn't sober up to help him, then Mackie would have to find a way to help himself.

He recognized the justification and rationalization of his own thinking. He knew his need to know was a weakness. A liability. He was no longer in the hospital. He no longer needed to be in charge or assertive. In fact, he had a team of professionals working on fixing this problem. He considered all of this knowledge, but couldn't persuade himself to sit back.

Mackie again opened the attachment from Duel of Sarah's e-mail account. He scrolled though her inbox. Randomly selecting messages, he learned about her day through snippets of information that dominated the e-mails. Answers to questions came in two and three line notes. Lunch plans arranged with sentence fragments. He felt pain upon reading this. He felt the senselessness of her death. And he felt stupid for continually reading on.

He scrolled down to the "Drafts" section once more, opening the two-page legal document. As he scrutinized the language, he found more relevance than he had last night. While the cost and ownership details remained as blank spaces, Mackie read a reference to "an interested party in Frederick, Maryland." No mention of names or locations. He also noted, "the facility in Bridgeport, Alabama." Where the hell was that? The final paragraph mentioned that this contract would become effective once all parties were signatory to the terms therein. Maryland. Alabama. Atlanta. An unlikely combination. And an elusive one.

He also re-read the other document in the folder, the Dear John letter. She might not have known Hank intended to propose marriage, but the tone of her words signaled a new beginning. Sarah was finally moving on. She needed him to know that. But was it really for him? The timing seemed off. The content seemed redundant. Curiously, the letter remained undated and unfinished, poised for transmission. Sarah's personality seeped through the screen. Maybe she never intended to send this. Maybe she'd planned to print it and leave it to be discovered. It wouldn't have been the first time she'd left a note in the open, making ambiguous comments, and allowing the recipient to stumble upon what she wanted to say. It was a tactic she'd employed several times during the divorce. Non-confrontational. Passive-aggressive. And ruthlessly effective.

As he finished reading the draft, he saw a final message at the bottom of the attachment. Mackie paused, staring at the inbox. He hadn't noticed it last night. A last message from Henry at Synthesis.

His stomach fluttered as he opened the message. Quick. Familiar. And sent on the night of her death. Mackie read the message:

> *Hey, gorgeous. Looking forward to Saturday morning. Will be a few minutes late to the Parthenon but should be there by nine. Love, H.*

Mackie stared at this screen, mouth agape. He read it again.

He sat in the glow of his computer screen, rubbing his temples with his fingertips. Even as his conscious debated the next steps, the unified message from his lawyer and the police played a continuous loop of their clear warning: let the professionals do their job.

Instead, Mackie picked up his cell phone and placed a call.

CHAPTER ELEVEN

THE PHONE CALL never reached Duel. Mackie had tried his cell, then his office, then his home. At each prompt he left a message, expecting Duel would quickly return the call once he understood the importance. He also sent a text, but again, no response. In spite of Duel's earlier warning, he then called Pham. She answered on the second ring. Mackie explained the new details. The meeting scheduled for Saturday. The location. And the chance to question him. Again, Detective Pham demurred. As before, she advised caution in moving on with this line of inquiry. Mackie went to bed that night thoroughly warned and thoroughly alone.

He awoke the next morning before his alarm. Even though the park was not close to his house, it was a manageable distance for a runner. That Mackie hadn't jogged for more then three miles in months didn't dissuade him, either. With Jonah shuffling reluctantly on the other end of the leash, Mackie set out toward Centennial Park with time to spare. He could be there and back even before he had to leave for the airport. The morning wind bit at his ears. On most Saturday mornings, people flooded the park. Today, only a few pedestrians braved the cold. An elderly couple strolled along the sidewalk near the pond, hand in hand. Nearby, two geese glided across the water, oblivious to the cold weather. Mackie passed the couple, following the path to the Parthenon. A hundred yards in front of him, a dog sat on the brown lawn, waiting for a Frisbee to be thrown. For the first time all morning, Jonah strained against the leash. Mackie kept him close. No one else seemed to be nearby. The enormous columned monument, replicating the original Greek structure, obscured his view. He tried to relax his hands as he jogged, but the chill penetrated his knit gloves. He clenched his fists. A shadow of anxiety followed him, almost overwhelming him. Five minutes before nine. Mackie breathed deeply to steady himself as he jogged on.

The paved path led him toward the building's parking lot. Only three cars so far. He jogged faster. As he approached the building, he looked left. Stone columns encircled the building, a carved facade resting on them in an exact replica of the Greek temple in Athens. On a spring evening, accented with tulips and ground lights, the Parthenon shimmered like a majestic jewel in the self-proclaimed Athens of the South. On a cold winter morning, though, with discarded candy wrappers swirling at the corner columns, the building owned up to its nineteenth century heritage. A relic from an age of World's Fairs and celebrations of a city's centennial. Mackie glanced as he passed in front of the structure. No one waited behind the pillars.

Rather than continue along the path to the parking lot, he doubled back, running near the grass. He lost his footing when he stepped on the lawn, stutter-stepped, then regained his pace. Outside the view of the parking lot, this side of the structures seemed even more deserted. The other dog's owner followed the Frisbee across the open space, away from the Parthenon. Mackie scouted the pillars on this far side of the structure.

That's when he saw him.

At the far corner of the building, someone leaned against a pillar. Even from fifty yards away, the man looked as big as Mackie remembered. Arms crossed. Staring across the lawn. Facing the other way. His features obscured by the winter coat. Mackie closed in, breathing harder than he should have for the pace. Twenty yards. The man cupped his hands over his mouth and coughed, mist seeping through his fingers. Ten yards. He heard Mackie approach and turned his head.

They made eye contact.

"Cooper?"

The sound of his given name startled him. Mackie slowed to a walk. Gripped the leash. Jonah stood at this side, panting. Ten feet ahead of him stood Hank Stone.

Mackie stopped.

They had met only once before, years ago at a party. The time since had etched a bitter image of Hank into Mackie's mind. His weathered face seemed not only recognizable but familiar.

Hank shoved a small box in his hand into his jacket pocket. "Cold day for a run."

Mackie paused to catch his breath. He couldn't read Hank's expression. Surprise, certainly, but also something else. Mackie glanced behind him. Just the two of them. He returned his focus to Hank, still somewhat confused. "What are you doing in Nashville?"

Hank's brow furrowed. "What are you taking about?"

The conversation Mackie had imagined left him, replaced by Pham's earlier conclusion: you don't show up for a surprise engagement if you know your future fiancée is dead. Mackie found himself asking a most obvious question. More of a statement, really. "You don't know about Sarah, do you?"

"Is this some sick joke?" Hank glanced around. "What are you doing here, anyway? Can't you just leave her alone. She left you. There was a reason for that. Why are you still trying to prevent her from moving on with her life? Let her go, Mackie. Get over it." Hank frowned. "Who told you I'd be here?"

"Sarathi Singh told me you've been in Nashville most of the week. Completing the purchase of her patent rights, I guess?"

Hank narrowed his eyes, his face a shadow. "I knew you'd find out sooner or later."

Mackie looked up at Hank, who still squinted in the morning sun. "Singh said you orchestrated the purchase."

A smile seeped across Hank's face. He stepped toward the Parthenon and Mackie. "Of course, he would. At least, to you." He looked around again, obviously still expecting Sarah. "Why am I even having this conversation with you?" He began walking away.

Mackie refused to chase after Hank, but he called out, "Singh also said you arrived in Nashville on Wednesday night."

Hank kept walking. "Go home, Mackie."

"When's the last time you talked to her?"

Hank stopped.

Mackie pressed on, driven by pent-up emotion. "Did you talk to her when you arrived? Did she even know you were here?"

Hank turned and glared at him. "This was supposed to be a surprise today. I called her on the way into town, but she hasn't called me back. She does that sometimes when she's busy. She didn't show up at the hotel for dinner last night, but she warned me earlier that she might not make it. I'm meeting her here this morning. To answer your question," he said sarcastically, "I last spoke to her on Wednesday."

Mackie stepped closer to the pillars. His resolve, along with his bitterness, deflated. "Sarah's not coming."

The morning sun backlit Hank, casting a shadow across his face. He appeared confused. "You know where she is?"

"She's dead, Hank."

"What? No way. Jealous dickhead." Hank drew in a long breath. He exhaled, the sound uneven, before he approached Mackie.

Mackie braced himself. "That's why she didn't get back to you."

Hank studied their surroundings. "What kind of game are you playing?"

"When's the last time you saw her?"

Hank shook his head as if trying to process the new information.

"Someone murdered Sarah two nights ago. Smashed her head. Probably killed her instantly. Shoved her into the trunk of my car, then staged her death to look like an effort had been made to revive her."

Hank froze, his back to the expansive lawn. The sun highlighted his face. His expression disarmed Mackie. Reinforced the mistake in his assumptions.

"My God…you're serious," Hank whispered in a stunned voice.

"She's died instantly…I'm sorry to be the one to tell you."

Mackie stood his ground, but his momentum evaporated. Unsure of what to say, Mackie finally gripped the leash, turned to the right, and began to jog. Toward the far side of the building. Toward home. When he glanced back over his shoulder, he saw Hank. The man lingered near the Parthenon, his head bowed as he examined the small box in his hands.

Chapter Twelve

By THREE O'CLOCK that afternoon, Reagan had texted Mackie twice. A developing weather front first delayed, then canceled, all flights leaving Peretola Airport in Florence. The plane taxied back to the terminal and unloaded disgruntled passengers. Mackie suggested taking a train to another city in hopes of finding open flights, but Reagan assured him no one would fly out of Italy until much later that day, if not Sunday morning. When he finally spoke to her, she sounded pissed off, then tearful. Mackie sat on his sofa and scoured the weather channel for good news. Not finding any, he turned his attention to funeral arrangements. He opened the Saturday paper to find a template for Sarah's obituary. Two hours later, he had a first draft. Now, he needed a woman to proof it for tone before he called the newspaper. Nothing said divorcée like a bitter obituary.

He turned off his computer and picked up the rest of the paper. Jonah thumped his tail while Mackie rubbed the dog's belly with his foot. As he unfolded the front page, he realized the headlines mimicked the ones he'd read all week. More soldiers killed in Middle East guerrilla warfare. Increased injures from shrapnel. More sophisticated improvised explosive devices. Each of those reports commented on escalating tensions, fed by new rounds of American casualties. A side bar of the main article caught his attention. Mackie picked up his glasses to read below the headline:

> A local soldier died this week in an armored vehicle specifically designed to save his life. Matthew L. Jorgensen, a graduate of Montgomery Bell Academy in Nashville, died during an

> attack on his military convoy in Syria. A spokesman for the military reported that insurgents attacked Jorgensen's convoy at seven a.m. local time, only three miles from the military base. According to eye witnesses, a round of rocket propelled grenades forced the convoy off the road toward a roadside bomb, which killed him instantly. Three other soldiers in his armored vehicle survived. The attack follows a string of similar incidents in which questions have been raised about the armored vehicles ability to protect troops riding inside. A spokesman for Armored Forces Industries, a contractor in Bridgeport, Alabama that outfits Humvees with protective armor, declined specific comment on the incident. Company CEO, General Haywood Clark (Ret.) subsequently issued a statement, saying, "American soldiers benefit from the best protection available, and our company continues to find new ways to protect our troops on the battlefield."

Mackie set aside the paper. Bridgeport, Alabama. The name resonated. He had read it in the batch of Sarah's recent e-mails. He returned to his computer and opened up Duel's attachment. For the third time in as many days, he browsed Sarah's email. He found the legal document referencing interested parties in Atlanta, Frederick, and Bridgeport.

Synthesis, Fort Detrick, and Armored Forces Industries.

Mackie studied the screen for a moment. Georgia. Maryland. Alabama. The connection eluded him. Navigating through the documents of her account, he scrolled down to the one sent to Duel. Probably the same one Duel had showed him of Mickey Mouse in a chef's hat. It had arrived in her inbox one day before she'd forwarded it. Sent to her from H Clark with an email address for Armored Forces Industries. That's when Mackie understood it.

Mackie pushed himself off the sofa and hustled to his study. He grabbed a flash drive and brought it back to his laptop. It didn't work as he expected, though. When he tried to save the individual e-mail with the picture on the removable disc, the computer resisted. Mackie then tried to download the information on his desktop, but with a similar results. Unauthorized to save the individual document. He didn't understand why he could view the picture without any problems but not transfer or save it individually.

Finally, he dumped the entire attachment of Sarah's subpoenaed emails onto his flash drive. Duel had shared it with him, but did that give Mackie the right to share it with others? He didn't know the nuances of the law, but he had a feeling that discretion was in order. Besides, Mackie needed technical assistance. And on a Saturday afternoon, he didn't have many options.

Except one.

Mackie slipped on his shoes and walked to the kitchen. He grabbed a Diet Coke from the refrigerator and his keys from the counter. Ten minutes later, he pulled into the doctor's parking lot at Nashville Memorial Hospital.

At this time of the week, only a skeleton crew staffed the hospital, and most of them kept one eye on the clock, waiting for their shift to end. Mackie hurried through the halls, head down. Toward the stairwell. Toward the morgue. Past the empty desk of the clerk. Past the empty autopsy room. Past the entrance to the coolers. When he arrived at Vern Philpot's office, he smiled as he saw a dim shaft of light sneaking through the cracked door. Musical blues rifts echoed in the hallway. Mackie knocked.

"It's open," Dr. Philpot said.

Mackie stepped inside. "Don't you ever go home?"

He saw Vern's shoulder bounce as he laughed, back still turned toward Mackie. "Not until the work's done, my friend, and I'm still doing work for you." He swiveled in his chair. "Your detective's been leaning on me to release Sarah's body. Are you here to plead your case in person?"

Mackie sat down, the stack of journals still beside the chair. "Nothing's going to happen with the funeral until Reagan gets home. And now that's not going to happen until tomorrow night, at the soonest."

"For the record, I finished up with the preliminary evaluation this afternoon. One less thing for you to worry about." Vern rocked back in his chair. "You look strung out. You want a cup of coffee?"

Mackie shook his head. "I'm having a computer issue that I need your help with."

Vern perked up. "You came to the right place."

Mackie held up his flash drive. "I need you to help me download a file and print it off."

"Give it to me. I'll do it right here." He extended his hand as he twisted his body toward the computer.

"That's the thing," Mackie said. "I couldn't transfer it or print it without trouble. Which I infer to mean I'm not supposed to see it."

Vern smiled. "So you need my techno skills, not just my printing skills."

"Sort of."

Vern rolled his chair away from his desk. He stretched both arms above his head, adjusting the band in his ponytail when he did. "Pull up to the keyboard and let's see what I can do to help."

Mackie inserted the flash drive and opened the attachment of Sarah's emails. When he clicked on the specified document, the image of Mickey Mouse filled the screen.

Vern rolled his chair closer. He laughed when he saw it, leaning forward. "Cute picture, Mackie. You want me to print this out in black and white so you can color it? I could call up to the gift shop. See if we could get you some crayons."

"I've got a box at home." Mackie scooted his chair back so Vern could get closer. "Why can't I print this? I can't even e-mail it to my own account. Said the file was too large."

Vern adjusted the image. He couldn't print it either. A similar message of refusal popped up on the screen. He manipulated the image for a moment before turning to Mackie. "Who's the original sender?"

"A military contractor in Alabama. Armored Forces Industries."

"A.F.I.? Hmmm. That's a whole different animal."

"You've heard of them?" Mackie asked.

"Come on. They've only been in the news about once a week over the past year. Haven't you heard their marketing counter-offensive? 'AFI—Keeping busy keeping our troops safe.' They're not too far from here."

"Bridgeport."

Vern studied the screen once more. "That's your problem. You can't manipulate the picture, because you're not supposed to have it. Unless..." Vern adjusted the image, searching the image characteristics before turning to Mackie. A grin punctuated his expression. "Here's your problem. You've got a stego-image."

"Explain."

"A cover image. Something else is embedded in the document. There's no other good explanation for the size of this file." Vern opened another program on his desk top, manipulating the Mickey Mouse image while he did. "This is great stuff. Nothing about this image is visually abnormal. I can zoom in, and the picture stays exactly the same."

Mackie watched him zoom in on the picture. "How is something hidden inside?"

"Redundant bits of information. Once you digitize these images, only a small percentage of the digital information actually encodes the image." Vern hunched over the keyboard of his top-of-the-line computer as he spoke. Exactly as he did during an interesting autopsy. Excited. Animated. Talking while he worked. "If you pack your car and drive to the beach, you're going to have some extra space, no matter how tight you pack the trunk. If I wanted you to carry something of mine with you, you'd throw it in the back and drive on. Maybe you'd have to rearrange a thing or two, but we could find some unused space for my things. No one looking at the exterior of the car would see a difference."

"Kind of like smuggling," Mackie said.

"You got it." Vern dragged the image document to an open window on the desktop and sat back. "Pack your car until nothing else fits. As long as you don't get pulled over, no one's the wiser just by watching you drive. You've stumbled on digital smuggling. It's called steganography. One of the most secure levels of digital deception. If you hadn't tried to download it or save it, you'd probably never even suspect a stego-image."

"What's the smuggled data, then?" Mackie asked.

"Let's see."

Vern scooted forward to the screen. Two view finders appeared on the monitor. In the first, the original Mickey Mouse image. Adjacent to it, a government logo appeared. A cover page. From the U.S. Department of Defense.

"What the hell's the DOD doing teaming up with Mickey Mouse?" Mackie asked.

Vern read from the one-page document. "The following information is intended for private use only. Any unauthorized distribution or dissemination of the pages herein will be subject to prosecution under the fullest extent of the law."

Mackie read over his shoulder. No other images appeared. "Where's the rest of it?"

Vern shook his head. "Can't pull it up. If this wasn't sent to you, you're not supposed to have it. Unless you have a pass code."

"How would I get one of those?" Mackie asked.

"Usually, the sender provides it. In a separate e-mail, of course. Otherwise, what's the use in sending the stego-image if you supply the code along with it?"

Mackie thought about this. Sarah had participated in legal cases involving the Department of Defense before, but that had been years ago. Something didn't add up. She may have had reason to possess this information—whatever it was—but why in such a secretive format? That it had been sent just days before her death concerned Mackie even more.

"Print that out for me," Mackie said. "And then we need to erase any trace of this document from your computer."

Vern looked at him like the novice he was. "You don't want the rest of it?"

"You already said you can't open it," Mackie said.

Vern's grin seemed to poke fun at Mackie's inexperience, highlighting his own geeky computer skills. "Not yet. Give me about twenty-four hours. We'll see if we can't make a key to unlock the rest of this document."

CHAPTER THIRTEEN

BY EARLY SUNDAY morning, Mackie had confirmed Reagan's travel arrangements. Rescheduled on the first flight out that day, she hoped to arrive in Nashville by nightfall. Now he had twelve more hours to fill. He called Detective Pham, banking on the fact that she might finally be able to provide answers to his newest line of questions. His argument was simple, and ultimately persuasive, to spend her day off working on the case. "Consider it a Sunday drive with good company," Mackie said.

An hour after hanging up with her, Mackie rolled and stretched his neck in the front seat of Reagan's car, preparing for the drive ahead. Not much outbound traffic on a mid Sunday morning. Libby Pham reluctantly rode shotgun, still appearing amused by his request. "And you want me to proofread?"

Mackie nodded. "Just for tone. Not content. Make sure I didn't sneak any accusatory verbs or regretful adjectives in there."

"It's an obituary."

"This is new territory for me," Mackie said. "My dad's was written several years before his death. Mom wrote her own. I can't exactly dump that responsibility on Reagan."

"It might be good for her to have some input."

"Maybe."

"When's her flight leave Italy?" she asked.

"Left early this morning," he said. "Which puts her in Nashville late tonight."

They continued south. When Mackie had called Armored Forces Industries earlier that morning, he hadn't expected to get through to a secretary, much less the company's CEO. In Mackie's mind, that alone underscored Sarah's importance to AFI. How she had concealed that relationship from Mackie puzzled him, although it didn't surprise him. Part of a trend, he guessed. Both business and pleasure. What had surprised him was the open invitation for help from the company's honcho, General Haywood Clark. Once Mackie told him of Sarah's death, his response had been prompt and unequivocal: Let us know how we can help. He hoped Pham could help him maximize the invitation. That she had agreed to spend her Sunday afternoon driving two hours to Bridgeport, Alabama sent Mackie a signal. And one hour into the trip, he was still trying to interpret it.

"The first thing I want to know about from General Clark is the Defense Department document," Mackie said.

"Not, you don't," Pham said. "You're thinking like a surgeon. All noise and no nuance. You want to keep that document bombshell concealed. My being with you automatically involves the Nashville Police Department, even if I'm outside of my jurisdiction. You need a more sophisticated and subtle approach to get your information. You want to find out what was sent before revealing that you already have it. See what the company tells you and ask questions from there."

Knowing that neither one of them had the authority to possess the documents made her argument that much more persuasive. Mackie finally agreed. He brought the draft of the obituary instead. At least it made for interesting conversation.

Emboldened by the cop in the front seat, Mackie made the trip in under two hours. Pham never mentioned his speed. He merged off the interstate, heading south with the Tennessee river along a two-lane state road. Pastureland and firework stands dominated the scenery. They passed a military convoy with a full complement of soldiers. Two flatbed trucks in the convoy carried military grade Humvees partially concealed under camouflage tarps. Mackie could see the scorched back wheel well of one of the transported vehicles through the flapping brown tarp.

Pham watched as they passed the second truck. "How did Sarah know General Clark?"

"I'm guessing a connection from her previous job in Washington," Mackie said. "Though she never mentioned him."

"Must be pretty common," Pham said. "Retiring from the

military and moving into civil service."

"Armored Forces is a private company, though," Mackie said. "Cashing in on governmental connections but all private contract work."

He slowed the car as the road narrowed, looking for the entrance to the company. A net of kudzu draped over the roadside trees, obscuring his view. "It's an increase in pay scale. I'm sure he's using the industry to cash in on his rank and access."

"I would." Pham studied the map on her phone. "Two more miles. On the right."

No other cars on the road. Not unusual for Sunday afternoon, Mackie guessed. He braked when the GPS advised him to turn right. Just before he turned, he noticed an opening in the monotony of overgrowth. With kudzu cleared and bramble replaced by boxwoods, a small sign indicated the entrance for Armored Forces Industries. While not deliberately hidden, the driveway appeared unassuming, standing out only due its modest landscaping. Mackie turned right onto a driveway paved as wide as a two lane road. Twenty yards from the turn, a brick guardhouse stood as the lone sentry in front of the complex.

"You'd have missed it without me and the map," Pham said.

Mackie smiled. "I knew I brought you with me for a reason." An armed guard dressed in desert BDU's stepped from the brick hut. Mackie lowered his window.

"Sir, how can I help you this afternoon?" The twenty-something guard rested one hand on a clipboard, the other on his sidearm. He leaned forward, making eye contact but glancing at Pham in the front seat.

"I'm Dr. Cooper McKay. This is Detective Libby Pham. We have a two o'clock meeting with General Clark."

"May I see your IDs, please?" The young guard checked his clipboard, then looked at his watch. "You're early, sir. General Clark will appreciate that. Do you know where you're going?"

Mackie shook his head. "First time here."

"Very well." The guard straightened, pointing ahead. "Down this road, one point six miles, is the AFI administrative building. You can't miss it, but if you get to a left hand turn, you've gone too far. There will be a guard there to remind you if that happens and to head you back in the right direction. I'll radio ahead to let them know you're on the way."

Mackie rolled up the window and edged forward, waiting for the gait to open. Acres of undeveloped pastures flanked the driveway, waist-high grass rimmed with distant pine trees. "You'd think they'd develop this area a bit. At least cut the grass. Give the visitors something to look at."

"Doesn't look like they're accustomed to visitors," Pham said. "Anyone coming here isn't interested in the flora and fauna."

Mackie drove on, the road smooth and well tended. No potholes or cracks. Ahead, a flatbed truck rumbled toward them. Mackie eased toward the right shoulder, but as the truck approached, he realized the width of the road could easily accommodate both vehicles. The tractor trailer lumbered forward. Like the others they'd passed several miles back, this truck hauled two Humvees chained to the bed.

Near the end of the driveway, manicured sod replaced uncut pastures. The paved road widened, fanning into a parking lot on the right and a turn lane to the left. Adjacent to the parking lot sat a two-story building, painted olive drab, appearing more military warehouse than corporate headquarters. Corrugated metal siding, flat tin roof, relatively few windows. Painted near the door, the corporate logo of Armored Forces Industries. Below it, seemingly out of place among it's unpolished surroundings, a slick marketing sign: AFI—Keeping Busy Keeping Our Troops Safe.

Mackie parked in a reserved space in the unexpectedly full parking lot. A chill lingered despite the bright sun as he stepped out of his car. Mackie heard a diesel engine rumble to his left, out of view of the parking lot. He noticed another brick hut at the far end of the pavement. A young sentry stood outside, observing. A truck parked next to them had a "Go Army" bumper sticker along the tailgate. Mackie shook his head. Some people can't leave their military experience behind. That had never been a problem for Mackie, though. Been there. Done that.

"You ready to get some answers?" Pham asked, shutting her door.

They walked toward the building. When they entered the building, a hum of activity greeted them. Employees in civilian clothes strode across the lobby. Phones rang at the front desk while two women wearing headsets checked computers and answered phone calls. Two older men chatted near a bank of elevators. Framed photos of military vehicles, spotless and well lighted, decorated the walls like a dealership's showroom. Pham crossed the lobby to the front desk. Mackie followed in her wake.

The younger of the two women flashed a smile as they approached. "Welcome to AFI. You must be Dr. McKay and Detective Pham."

Mackie and Pham glanced at one another. "We have a two o'clock meeting with General Clark," he said.

"He's expecting you," the receptionist said. "I'm Barrett. Let me get you two checked in, and we'll reach his office right on time." She scanned Mackie's driver's license onto a desktop device that generated a laminated red tag with "Visitor" printed across the top. Doing the same for Pham, the receptionist handed both the licenses and visitor's passes to them. She stepped around the desk.

"Not much rest on Sundays," Mackie said.

Barrett smiled. "No, sir. We operate seven days a week, three shifts each day. It's part of AFI's commitment to the war effort."

"Based on the philosophy that you'll rest when the troops come home?" Pham asked.

"I wish." Barrett's expression dipped. Catching herself, she changed the subject, inflating her smile. "At least we get to sleep in our own beds at night. First time to AFI?"

"I didn't even know it was here until yesterday," Mackie said.

"Obscurity is good for us," Barrett said. "Kind of like a baseball umpire. We do our job and no one recognizes the contribution."

"Which is ironic, given some of the more recent casualties," Mackie said. "I read about AFI in the Nashville newspaper yesterday."

"Yes, sir. We're trying to stay at least one step ahead of the enemy." Barrett swiped her identification at the doors near the elevator. All three entered a carpeted hallway. "I think when you leave, you'll appreciate what General Clark and the rest of the AFI team are doing for national security."

A few paces down the hall, a wreath hung on a wooden door, strikingly out of place when contrasted against the dominant military decor. Barrett opened the door, entering a plush conference room. Leather chairs. Low lights. Three Sunday papers fanned across the boardroom table. Beads of condensation trickled down a carafe of water. "Make yourselves at home," Barrett said. "It's five 'til two. General Clark will be with you momentarily." She left the two of them alone in the room.

Pham sank into one of the leather seats. "Barrett's none too happy about spending her Sunday afternoons at work."

"I don't blame her. This place is a relentless factory. Three shifts, seven days a week. You can't even get away with that in a hospital anymore." Mackie glanced at the headlines of *The New York Times* and the Sunday edition of *The Bridgeport News*.

"There's no money in round-the-clock health care services," Pham said. "You've got medical students and residents to manage overnight crises. It's different in industry. These guys banter about national security, but AFI wouldn't keep the lights on unless they were making money by doing it."

"You woke up on the cynical side of the bed this morning," Mackie said.

"Trust me. It's all about the money."

"Who's making money doing what?" A stentorian voice filled the room.

Mackie turned around. Pham stood up. Strolling through the doorway near the back of the conference room, a man at least a decade older than Mackie approached the table. Pressed khakis. Starched shirt. Cropped grey hair. Even in civilian clothes, his countenance revealed a lifetime of military service. He extended his hand to Mackie. "Haywood Clark," he said. "I'm damn sorry to hear about Sarah. Thank you for calling this morning to tell me."

General Clark shook Pham's hand, then motioned for them to sit. "I want AFI to do whatever we can to help the investigation." He leaned back in his chair, not pausing for a question. "I first met Sarah about six or seven years ago. I was still working in Washington at the time. We had business with her law firm."

"She never mentioned it." Mackie poured a glass of water.

"She was paid not to," Clark said. "I ended my military career at the Pentagon, and one of Sarah's clients had certain military interests. Interests that precluded her from talking about the case. Not just due to attorney-client privilege, mind you, but due to national security interests."

Mackie glanced at Pham, who kept her gaze on General Clark. "Did these national security interests carry over to her more recent work with AFI?"

Clark nodded. "Absolutely. But nothing that would have jeopardized her safety."

Pham leaned forward. "General, I'm leading the murder investigation for the Nashville Police Department, and part of our investigation uncovered something related to AFI that you might be able to help us with."

General Clark shifted in his seat, his eyes on Pham. Mackie listened. This wasn't part of the playbook they'd discussed.

Pham continued. "As we have gone through her papers and electronic documents, we found only one mention of Armored Forces Industries. In an e-mail, sent to her a few days before her death. That e-mail references a document attached, but there is no trace of that document on her computer."

Clark listened, hands folded on the table. He chewed on the corner of his lip while waiting for the next question.

Mackie picked up the conversation. "The unusual part of that, General, is the e-mail referenced more documents to come from AFI. Naturally, that led us to you."

Clark sighed. Interested but irritated. "Information like that should lead you here, but I have to tell you I certainly don't know anything about unsent or missing documents. Sometimes it's hard to know when someone is fabricating information for their own gain. That happens more in industry than I realized before I signed on. Not that I would have changed my plans, but it's been eye-opening. At least in the military, they tell you before you get screwed." He laughed at the analogy, but absent a similar response from Mackie and Pham, he cleared his throat and took a sip of water.

"AFI armors vehicles that are assembled elsewhere?" Mackie asked.

"Exactly." Clark refilled his glass. "We retrofit all sorts of combat vehicles, but the Humvee is our main focus. Our specialty. Makes sense, seeing as it's critical to troop transportation throughout the world. Not long ago, AFI secured a huge governmental contract for a new line of Humvees. After all the shit hit the fan in the first years of the Iraq war, with troops dying from insufficient vehicle armor, the government redefined the needs for troop transportation. That change affected the military ever since. I hired Sarah's legal expertise to help coordinate the aspects of the new contract."

"Why not use a military lawyer?" Pham asked.

"We do. They're a part of the team. By the dozens. But AFI is a privately owned military contractor, so we needed our own representation. Sarah was a natural fit, not only because I knew her from earlier work, but because she has a history of military legal experience."

"And you couldn't find a local lawyer to do the same?" Pham asked.

Clark smiled. "Your accent. Boston?"

"Philly," she said.

"But not Alabama. Not even Tennessee, for that matter. I'm sure you noticed as you drove in, we're in the sticks out here. Not exactly metropolitan Washington, D.C. To get qualified legal representation, we would have to solicit firms in Atlanta or Birmingham. Two hours away, minimum. Why not go with a known entity like Sarah? Most of what we do can be communicated by e-mail and fax, anyway."

Pham maintained her gaze. "But we haven't found any other documentation of your legal relationship yet."

"That validates my decision. We expect discretion as well as expertise," Clark said. "It sounds like I got both."

Pham gave a patronizing smile. "Of course, when you pay for a lawyer, you get all the paperwork that come with it."

A faint siren sounded in the distance, followed by a rumble that rattled the water glasses.

Clark leaned back in his chair. "Field testing," he said. "Sunday afternoon's the perfect time to do that. You may have noticed we're not exactly accessible to the general public. You have to go out of your way to find us. We use all this land to our advantage. It gives us privacy and open space to test the latest armored technology."

"So you ship in Humvees, outfit them with battle-ready armor, then destroy them?" Mackie asked.

"Only retired vehicles. And only occasionally. Our goal is to mimic the conditions in military hotspots across the globe. If the armor can pass our tests, we feel confident sending it overseas to protect a soldier's life."

"Doesn't always work, though," Pham said.

General Clark looked at his hands, bowing his head before answering. "Sadly, it doesn't. The better we can replicate what the enemy is doing, the more we can respond with our technology. Roadside IED's. Insurgent RPG's. We recreate them and bombard the shit out of our vehicles. Worse than anything they'd experience in country. It helps us see where the weak links are and then readjust."

"And when you're finished outfitting the armored vehicles—where do they go?" Mackie asked.

"We ship some to Fort Eustis in Virginia. They train troops on battlefield simulators for the Humvee and other vehicles. The rest of our products go directly into combat." General Clark stood, resting both hands on the table. "Let me show you what AFI is all about. I think it will answer a number of the questions you drove all the way down here to ask me."

Mackie pushed back from the table. Pham closed her notebook and stood.

Clark gestured toward the main door. "I can't guarantee a tour of the restricted areas will answer all your questions, but it will at least give you a sense of what Sarah did when she was not in Nashville."

He followed Mackie and Pham into the hallway, then turned left and led them away from the lobby. As they approached a metal door marked "Restricted", General Clark turned around. "Please stay close to me during the field testing," he said. "AFI can be a dangerous place if you're not careful." He unlocked the door.

As soon as he opened it, an explosion rocked the building.

CHAPTER FOURTEEN

THE CONCUSSION FROM the second explosion rocked Mackie. Pham steadied herself with a hand on the wall. General Clark calmly walked the distance it took to get to the chaos. After a moment, Mackie and Pham followed him. With ear protection snugged into place, they hiked down a wooden walkway that led to a distant observation deck. Dust clouds swirled in a field several hundred yards away. Through the haze, Mackie saw a tow truck hauling a charred vehicle toward the edge of the clearing.

General Clark lifted a pair of binoculars from the railing of the observation deck. He studied the scene for a moment before handing them to Mackie. "We just missed the first test of the LAV's."

Pham raised her eyebrows. "LAV's?"

"Light armored vehicles. Used mostly for forward troop support. That's a Stryker being removed right now. We'll test others later. Up next is a Humvee, I think."

"The Stryker survived the explosion," Mackie said, still peering through the binoculars. "What hit it?"

"It rolled onto a roadside IED before our guys nailed it with a few RPG's." Clark turned to Pham, his smile patronizing. "That's an improvised explosive device and a rocket propelled grenade."

"Cool," she said, clearly impressed.

A crew of men approached the tow truck and walked around the damaged Stryker, inspecting the tires and undercarriage. Apparently satisfied, the tow truck drove forward into the woods, obscured by the rim of trees surrounding the testing grounds. The crew turned their attention back to the field as another vehicle crept forward. Four men in jumpsuits and protective headgear walked behind the new vehicle. Even with the binoculars, Mackie could not see what was happening to the car. He handed them to Pham.

"Who's driving?" Mackie asked. "It looks empty from here."

General Clark laughed. "What kind of company do you think AFI is, Doc? We can't afford to pay anyone that kind of hazardous duty money. During these tests, all the vehicles are remote controlled. Don't be fooled, though. The ammunition is very real. Watch what happens to the Humvee."

The cadre of men surrounding the vehicle finished their assigned tasks and retreated to the sidelines. Each donned protective goggles and ear protection as they stepped behind a transparent partition. A new group of men approached the vehicle from the left side of the field. Dressed in desert BDU's and helmets, they fanned out to one side of the Humvee. Another man lined up behind it. Each soldier set up a weapon in front of him, some with tripods, others with shoulder launchers. Once they were in place, a siren pierced the air. The vehicle crept forward.

As they watched from the observation deck, the scene unfolded like a war re-enactment. With military precision, two men fired their RPG's at the Humvee. The vehicle lurched, propelled by the blast but still upright. Clods of dirt exploded around it. Smoke rose like exhaust from the under the car. The vehicle continued driving.

The other soldiers readied themselves as the Humvee approached. Simultaneous blasts pounded the doors and hood, shoving the vehicle sideways, off course. Concussions from the explosions reached the observations deck moments after the fire flash. One final RPG slammed into the back quarter panel, flipping the armored vehicle onto its side and exposing the undercarriage. Smoke engulfed the battlefield, obscuring the inert Humvee. A light wind swirled the dust. On the test field, silence.

No one on the observation deck said a word.

Pham lowered the binoculars. "Amazing," she said. "All smoke and no flames."

General Clark nodded. "We try and control the chaos."

Mackie took another look through the binoculars. The team of men from the sidelines congregated around the charred vehicle. In spite of being on its side, the armored vehicle appeared relatively intact. He saw the dented scars from each direct hit on the Humvee. The final RPG, though, had taken its toll on the back quarter panel.

Unlike the dented metal on the front of the Humvee, the blast had sheared off the protective shell along the back of the vehicle, peeling it back like a ripped soda can. Beneath the armor, Mackie could see the remains of a deflated tire. Hazy sunlight streamed through the hole. The image reminded him of a more graphic version of the charred Humvee on the back of the military convoy they had passed earlier.

Mackie handed the binoculars to General Clark. "Anyone inside during that attack would be dead," Mackie said.

"Most soldiers survive a flipped vehicle," Clark said. "But most soldiers don't have to endure seven direct hits at point blank range. Like I told you, our experiments not only simulate battlefield conditions, but actually make them worse than the soldiers will encounter."

"Take a look at the back of the truck," Mackie said. "You might as well have not armored it at all."

Clark raised the binoculars. A faint smile spread across his face as he studied the vehicle. "Perfect."

"Not exactly perfect for keeping our troops safe," Mackie said.

Clark turned toward him. "Of course not. But that's an unarmored panel on the back of the vehicle. We compare battle-ready armor to factory-installed siding in order to assess the performance of our products. If you were on the field, you'd see the test panels did exactly what we expected them to do."

Pham squinted as she looked at the charred remains of the vehicle. "You already know what will happen with an unarmed vehicle. Why even waste the time with an unarmored panel?"

"Because it underscores the importance of what we do," Clark said. "You'd be surprised at the number of legislators in Washington who want to cut funding for vital programs like ours. Giving them a taste of reality—or at least a good comparison—can help loosen the purse strings." He began to walk toward a door at the far end of the observation deck. "We'll be studying that back quarter panel this week. Come on back inside and we'll take a look at the production facility."

Pham and Mackie followed him. The observation deck and walkway connected the administrative building of Armored Forces Industries to the production wing. The outside of the building had the same corrugated sheet metal, but stepping inside seemed like stepping into an airplane hanger. Cavernous spaces. Concrete floors. Dozens of armored vehicles cluttered the enclosure in various stages of repair. Twenty yards from the entrance, workers lying on mechanic's gurneys, others wielding acetylene torches, attached armored plates to a Humvee.

"Obviously, the assembly floor," General Clark said. "Each vehicle is fully functional when it arrives here, but some need a higher level of armored protection. That's where AFI fits in. We add bullet-proof glass, fuel tank casings, and armored panels. Each Humvee is custom fit based on future needs."

They made their way to the center of the building. In discrete sections of the room, groups of workers gathered around individual vehicles.

Mackie paused, trying to make sense of it all. "What happened to the assembly line? I thought that was the essence of efficient manufacturing?"

Clark returned to where Mackie stood. "We focus on expertise rather than efficiency. Our production staff is divided into teams which correspond to certain sections of the vehicles. One team just installs windshields and windows. Another does wheel cover protections." He pointed to the first team they had seen. "Those guys protect and secure the fuel tank. Critically important job, as you saw outside."

Pham said, "Let's say that destroyed panel we saw earlier was a faulty design, not an unarmored panel. How do you trouble shoot those kinds of problems?"

Behind them, a pneumatic compressor activated. General Clark raised his voice to be heard. "You both have to understand, what we saw this morning was a test. A demonstration. One part experimental armor, one part mainstream technology. If we had walked outside ten minutes earlier, you'd have noticed a similar pattern on the Stryker. If one of our armored protection panels doesn't perform, we study it to understand why it failed. Nothing we produce leaves these grounds until that model has been tested."

"And passes the test," Mackie said.

"Of course," Clark said. "But consider a hypothetical. You probably read about combat deaths of U.S. soldiers this week. The military will inspect the vehicles involved, and if there is any suggestion of an equipment problem from AFI, we have the vehicle shipped back to us for analysis. We consider everything: the type of ammo used, the angle of attack, even the nature of the soldier's injuries."

"Shrapnel wounds? Blunt force trauma?" Mackie asked.

"Exactly."

"And probably whether the blast killed the soldier instantly or maimed him," Mackie said. "Blood loss and limb destruction. That sort of thing."

General Clark narrowed his gaze. He hesitated. Taking a deep breath, he resumed the tour. "We are a part of the chain of military success abroad. A small part, mind you, but if we are the weak link, the rest of our national defense system can't do its job." Clark motioned for Mackie and Pham to follow him. "If this hanger is the body of AFI's production facility, I want you to see the brains."

They crossed the floor to a metal door at the far side of the room. Clark scanned his identification near the doorknob then entered his code on the keypad. The lock clicked opened. The three entered into a small room. Once the door closed, the silence seemed absolute. Clark led them down a short hallway paralleling the production floor and up a flight of stairs. They stepped into a room the size of a basketball court, its large space separated by cubical workstations, each facing the same direction. Observation windows along the left wall overlooked the production floor. Rows of computers at each work station reminded Mackie of NASA's mission control. All employees working toward the same goal. A visible reminder just beyond the glass.

Two men seated nearby looked up when Clark began to speak. "This is the best vantage point for appreciating what we do at AFI. By standing here for just a few minutes, I can oversee the production of every single vehicle at once. These computers correspond to individual work orders. We have both a craftsman's touch and technological precision with each Humvee or LAV that leaves our plant."

"Total oversight of the plant," Pham confirmed.

"Total transparency," Clark countered. "Nothing to hide. No margin of error. I think the family member of any soldier killed in action could walk through this building and know everything is being done to offer our troops state-of-the-art protection." He turned to Mackie. "I can't tell you how sorry I am to hear about

Sarah. Her work helped pave the way for much of our success. I'm glad you came to see what had been an important part of her professional life for the last few years. If you're looking for clues to who killed her or a connection between AFI and her death, you are wasting your time. We have nothing to hide. But we also have nothing else to share that could help you."

Mackie shrugged off the comment. "We noticed at least three trucks leaving the grounds, hauling away completed Humvees as we drove in this morning. The production floor is filled to capacity. Are you having trouble meeting demand?"

"Combat is good for business," Clark said. "And we're capable of almost doubling our current production. Ten years ago, the military didn't have all it needed in Iraq and Afghanistan. But we responded. As those flames fade, we're setting our sights on Syria. Iran. Wherever the next flare up is. The sad reality is that we profit from other people's misfortune."

"An interesting perspective," Pham said.

Clark crossed his arms and offered a faint smile. "I don't get involved in the political decisions anymore, Detective. I study the situation on the ground and offer a product that directly impacts the troops. If the administration wants to fold up the tents and bring our soldiers home, we'll welcome them back with open arms before moving into a new line of work. But until that happens, we will work seven days a week to offer and supply the best armored protection available." He looked at his watch. "Now, if you don't mind, I'll walk you back to your car."

"One more question," Mackie said.

Clark sighed, shoving his hands into his pockets. "Anything."

"That e-mail I mentioned when we first arrived. The body contained no text. Just a holiday picture. And the promise of an attachment, which we mentioned never arrived. The sender was Clark at AFI, which would lead me to believe you are the one who actually sent it to her. But you're saying you're not aware of it?"

"Christ almighty," Clark said. He glanced at his watch once more. "My secretary sends out one damn holiday greeting to our major clients and support staff and after seeing all of this, that's the only thing you want to discuss?"

Employees in the room tried to shrink from sight, studying their monitors and stealing furtive glances at their boss. One man picked up his coffee mug and left the room.

"It's an inconsistency," Pham observed.

Mackie continued. "You didn't send the message? Because if you did—"

General Clark stepped close to Mackie, cutting him off. Deliberately encroaching into personal space, Clark lowed his voice. "I don't know what the hell you're doing here, but I won't be badgered. I've already answered the question. Let me make this patently clear to you, Doctor McKay. I'm sorry about losing Sarah, but no one here knows anything about who murdered her. Sad as it is, it's not my mess to clean up."

Mackie leaned forward, causing Clark to pull back. "No one's asking you to clean it up, General. But I would appreciate some cooperation if we find any other links in the investigation that lead us back to AFI."

Clark shook his head. "I've got nothing more for you. If you have further questions, contact my secretary." He moved toward the stairwell, speaking as he walked away. "Someone will be back to show you out."

And just like that, the promise to help in any way he could evaporated.

CHAPTER FIFTEEN

PHAM DROVE THE first leg of the trip back to Nashville, faster than Mackie expected. Mackie stared out the passenger window, wrestling with the morning's events. "Something's missing," he finally said.

"I got that feeling, too." Pham craned her neck as she merged into northbound traffic on the interstate. She braked for a minivan, then swerved into the left lane. "The entire operation seemed too staged, even though he took us into restricted areas. The email touched a nerve."

"That's not what bothered me," Mackie said. "AFI's not going to give away trade secrets just because someone asks to walk through the facility. What got me was the testing. His explanation for what we saw just doesn't add up."

"The back quarter panel?" she asked.

"Exactly."

Pham merged right to pass an eighteen wheeler but ended up behind a military transport. She moved back to the left lane. They passed the transporter, hauling two armored Humvees away from AFI. The driver nodded as she accelerated past. "Does it makes sense to test a quarter panel that you know is going to fail?"

"If they knew it would fail, I don't think they'd have tested it," Mackie said. "That's my point. Did they change their testing plans today just for us? Kind of like they do with the politicians. Show us what a great job AFI is doing for the country. The only way that adds up in my mind is if it's a cover for some other activity."

"But what?" Pham asked. "Nothing we saw obviously ties back to Sarah."

Mackie shook his head. "I don't get it."

They drove for another thirty minutes, merging with westbound traffic toward Nashville and into looming storm clouds. Mackie's cell phone rang, but he lost the call as soon as he answered. He didn't recognize the number. He borrowed Pham's phone, but she didn't have service either. The windshield wipers thumped back and forth as they discussed the case. After another fifteen minutes, Pham merged to the right hand lane, slowing for the exit. She turned toward a gas station and got out at the pump. "You want anything from inside?"

"There's a Waffle House across the street if you want to grab a bite," Mackie said.

They both stepped out of the car. She tossed Mackie the keys on her way to the bathroom. "I don't do well driving in the rain. I'd rather not stop longer than we have to."

"Then get me a Diet Coke when you're inside."

Mackie stretched. The gas station's awning protected him from the rain, but a cool mist still greeted him as he filled the tank. He absentmindedly twirled the key ring around his finger while pumping gas. No other cars at this exit. Not even at the Waffle House. When he looked down to check the gas nozzle, the key ring slipped off his finger, spinning under the car. He swore, then bent to pick up the keys. He couldn't reach them. He swore again and straightened. He was going to have to get under the car to retrieve them, and that would ruin his pants. He rummaged through the trunk of Reagan's car and found an old beach towel. Kneeling on the wet concrete, protected by only a thin layer of terry cloth, he leaned under the car. He had to stretch out farther than he expected. As he grabbed them, he spotted something in the back wheel well. What he saw looked out of place. New. A small metal ring fixed to the inside of the wheel well just below the gas tank. He'd grown up watching his dad fix cars and knew enough to know this was not something normal. Gripping his keys, he repositioned himself for a closer look. A small wire extended from the shining metal. Mackie fingered the dime-sized ring, able to move it but not pull it off. He wedged a key underneath, prying it loose.

"Whatcha doing?" Pham crouched down, looking at Mackie under the car. She held two Diet Cokes.

He stood up, pleased he'd found the towel to protect his pants.

Mackie flipped the ring over in his palm, then held it up. "What's this?"

Pham said, "Looks like a GPS tracker. Where'd you get it?"

"Under the car," Mackie said.

She bent down beside him. Pham angled her head to see where the device had been. She ran her fingers over the wheel well, then frowning, stood up and grabbed the device from his hand. "Sophisticated."

"You've seen one before?"

"I've used one before. What's it doing under your car?"

Mackie shrugged. "Not yours, then?"

"No. Although it's a fair question." She turned the device over in the palm of her hand. "You think someone at AFI planted it?" she asked.

"We could drive back to AFI right now and ask," Mackie said. "But there's no telling how long it's been there." He took back the metal ring and the thin wire protruding from the center. "Any way to reverse engineer this and see who's picking up the signal?"

"There's a guy in the department…"

Mackie grasped the wire and pulled, ripping out a small computer chip. "Where the hell did they expect us to go once we left? Downtown Bridgeport? Clark knows I live in Nashville."

"That assumes he's responsible," Pham said. "Whatever. It doesn't belong to you."

Mackie tossed the wire and attached computer chip into the garbage. He set the tiny ring atop the station's gas pump. "Let's go."

They climbed back into the car, Mackie driving this leg. Mist turned into fat drops as the rain intensified. Mackie turned the wipers on high. Traffic increased the closer to Nashville they drove, and what should have been a forty-five minute trip from the last stop turned into an hour and a half. It was dark by the time Mackie saw the lights of downtown. When he pulled into his neighborhood, his phone rang. Vern Philpot. Mackie placed him on speaker phone as he drove.

"I finally opened your files from yesterday," Vern said. "It took a while to hack the pass code."

"What'd you find?" Mackie asked.

"Trouble."

Mackie glanced at Pham, both now riveted on the phone. "More pages behind the DOD cover sheet?"

"Nineteen of them. I printed them out and put the copy on your kitchen counter. You really should move that hide–a–key, pal. It's in the same place you told me about three years ago."

Pham shot Mackie an accusatory glance. He ignored her stares as well as Vern's advice and asked, "So what did you find?"

"Is this line secure?"

"It's that bad?"

"The entire document deals with a High Mobility Multipurpose Wheeled Vehicle."

Mackie steadied both hands on wheel. A Humvee. "Why is that trouble?"

"Because the diagrams in the documents described the specifications for the metal armor of the vehicle...and the ingredients for the exact metallic constituents of that armor." Vern's voice strained against the speaker on the phone. "Man, this looks like some important shit. I'm pretty sure you could go to jail if someone finds out you have this."

"I've got a good lawyer," Mackie said. Pham kept silent.

"I hope so. Each page in this document is clearly marked as classified."

Mackie thanked Vern for his help and hung up. He stared out the windshield, mesmerized by the rhythmic thump of the wipers. The implications of Sarah's involvement pounded his head. Covert military operations. Security clearance for classified documents. Legal counsel for a military contractor two hours from home. Some of it taking place while they were still married, but nothing he saw ever raised his suspicion.

Pham broke the silence. "What had Sarah gotten herself into?"

Mackie shrugged as he pulled into his driveway, parking beside Pham's unmarked car. Rain drops on her hood reflected the floodlights. Sheets of water poured from the corner gutter. One more job to add to his list. Mackie cut the ignition. Both sat in the front seat for a moment. "Before I go, let's take a look at those documents," Pham said. "You have an umbrella?"

"In the garage."

Pham smiled. "I may need a towel, then."

"Meet you on the porch." Mackie ducked his head and ran

toward the door. In the few yards it took to get there, rain soaked his shirt. He ran hunched over to his front porch. His pants stuck to the back of his legs. Pham fared better, but her waterlogged blouse still clung to her body. Water dripped off his nose as Mackie unlocked the front door. They stepped into the foyer.

Jonah greeted them, hesitant at first, sniffing Pham's leg. She bent down to rub his ears, and his tail immediately responded. He folded his body into hers as she scratched him, knocking her back, covering her wet pants with blond fur. Pham reached for Mackie as she righted herself. The dog continued to nudge her leg with his nose. "Long day in the house by himself."

"He's used to it," Mackie said, petting the dog's hindquarters. Jonah wiggled beneath the affection.

Pham looked down. "We're making a mess of your floor."

"I'll get some towels and a sweatshirt for you," Mackie said.

He kicked off his shoes and peeled off each sock, dropping them in a heap next to the door. Pham placed her hand on Mackie's shoulder, steadying herself as she did the same. Her touch surprised him, stopped him, even as his heart rate sped up. His skin tightened under her hand. An electric chill raced down his spine.

Both stepped back, leaving an awkward pause between them.

Mackie walked to his bedroom and grabbed a sweat shirt from the closet for her. He directed her to the nearest bathroom to dry off and then headed for the kitchen counter. She joined him afterwards, still towel drying her hair.

"Soda okay?" he asked as he handed her a glass.

"For starters." She took a sip. "Tell me about Sarah's legal practice."

"Which part?" Mackie leaned against the counter. The thick envelope with the Nashville Memorial Hospital logo sat between them.

Pham glanced at the package from Vern. "I assume Sarah didn't change jobs at the same time you two split. She must have been doing pretty much the same thing as she'd done during the first thirty years of your marriage."

"Twenty-eight."

Pham sat in the chair with her leg tucked beneath her, water stains from her hair darkening the shoulders of her sweatshirt. "Is that a conflict of interest, being a patent lawyer and a co-inventor of a product you submit for patent protection?"

"Strictly speaking? Yes," Mackie said. "But she justified it since her work with the H-BOC patent was a convenience, but it didn't pay the bills. Not at first, anyway."

"But you guys weren't hurting financially."

"We did well for ourselves. Not many expenses. One child. One house. Education loans already paid off."

"So why involve other people in your legal affairs to begin with? You've already said Duel helped out with some of the patent protection for H-BOC."

Mackie laughed. "That was a favor to him, back in the day. He was a chemistry major before law school and was just starting his career. Sarah was already established. She asked him to help with some of the minor legal work, as a way of introducing him to the legal community."

"He's annoys the crap out of me," Pham said, "and I've only known him for three months."

"He grows on you." Mackie took a sip of his drink.

"Doubtful." Pham finally opened the envelope and removed the packet of papers. Mackie pushed off the counter and pulled up a chair beside her. The cover page looked exactly as Mackie had seen it on Vern's computer. The Department of Defense Logo. The warning against unauthorized possession of the document. A legal disclaimer at the bottom. As she flipped through the packet, a red notation across the top of each page marked it as classified. The first page showed a marked up schematic of a Humvee. Dimensions of the vehicle typed in sidebars. Arrows and footnotes annotating the page. The remaining eighteen pages focused exclusively on the fuel tank. Descriptions, drawings, and dimensions of the back panel included exquisite detail that would be helpful only to a manufacturer. On companion pages, a listing of the metallic composition of the car's armor, as well as details of how the armor attached to the vehicle. Pham thumbed through the pages once more before handing them to Mackie.

"You're sure she received this from AFI?"

"The original was sent to her e-mail account," Mackie said.

"And you know this how?" Pham could not hide her skepticism.

"Duel subpoenaed her emails.

"Interesting."

"She was just one of three who received this attachment from Clark at AFI."

"Who were the others?"

"Duel Richardson and Sarathi Singh."

Pham flipped through the pages once more, reconsidering them with this new information.

Mackie stood up and returned to the refrigerator. "You want something else to drink? Something stronger?"

"I've got to head out," she said, still scrutinizing the DOD pages while spoke.

"Got to unpack more boxes?"

Pham smiled. "Something like that."

With a full glass, Mackie hoisted himself onto the counter, sitting atop the granite countertops Sarah had insisted they install so many years ago. His legs dangled, slowly moving back and forth. "I'm still trying to figure you out, Detective Pham. Why Nashville? Of all the places you could live, why here?"

Pham didn't answer for a long moment. She appeared to be reading the document, but soon she began to twirl her hair with her fingers. Nervous habit, Mackie supposed. "I wanted something different," Pham said. "Something that allowed me to do what I trained for, but not remind me every day of what I once had."

Mackie waited. "A guy?"

"A husband." She took a drink, but realizing the glass was already empty, sucked on an ice cube instead. "Married three years in July. We just missed our anniversary."

"What happened?"

Pham repositioned her legs in the chair. Her eyes tensed then relaxed, pushing back the memory. "David was a cop, too. Your typical boy meets girl at the firing range kind of story. He'd been called out to a domestic dispute that afternoon. Not uncommon in Philadelphia. Anywhere, for that matter. The call came in about four-thirty. Late enough to where he could have sent another crew to respond. In fact, there was already a squad car in the area. He liked the action, though. Always said he didn't want to miss a chance to do good."

"Were you with him?"

Pham shook her head. "Day off. We had friends coming over that night." She gave a bitter laugh. "My first response when the chief called was to be pissed off, sure that David had volunteered for something at work he didn't want me to know about. He knew the one thing that bothered me most was when he worked later than necessary. Used to have his partner call me to tell me he was running late."

Mackie stopped swinging his legs. "But his partner didn't call. The chief did. You're too good of a cop not to have suspected something."

Pham shook her head. "It's probably the same with doctors. When you're looking at someone else's problems, it's easy to be objective. It's the emotional bullshit that comes along with loving someone that clouds your judgment. Makes you deny what's in front of your face."

"Was he shot?" he asked.

Pham tightened her eyes once more. It didn't work. Tears collected along her eyelid, the light of the kitchen magnifying them. She brushed them aside with the back of her hand. Angry at what had happened. Angry at how it still affected her. "The guy was coked up. Came home and started beating on his girlfriend. Neighbors called nine-one-one when the screaming started. Baby wailing in the background. It was a fucking mess. David called for back up, but he rushed the house when he heard gunshots. He didn't make it through the front door. Point blank shot to his face. Another to the chest after he'd fallen." She wiped her eyes.

Mackie waited, listened. Pham didn't say anything else. She didn't try to change the subject either. Outside, thunder rumbled as the rain intensified. Jonah wandered into the room to investigate, placing his nose in her lap. Pham reached out to scratch the dog's head.

"Did you stay for the trial?" Mackie asked.

She shook her head. "There wasn't one. David's partner killed the guy once he stepped onto the porch. One shot to the head. Twenty yards out. The video camera in the front of the cruiser caught it all on tape. There wasn't even much of an investigation afterwards." She sat up, pulling both knees to her chest as she stared at the fanned out pages of Vern's printed document. "Long answer to a tough question."

"So what brought you here? Tonight?" he asked.

She smiled. "Dale Murphy."

"That's the first time that's worked."

Pham laughed. "David was a huge baseball fan. Probably a bigger fan of the game itself than any individual team."

"He pulled for the Phillies?" Mackie asked.

"Eventually. Actually grew up in the Bronx, pulling for the Yankees before his dad took a manufacturing job in Pennsylvania." She twirled her index finger through her hair as she talked, smiling. "The Braves went to the World Series the year after they traded Dale Murphy to the Phillies. The Phillies went to the World Series during the last year of Murphy's career, but by then he'd been traded to Colorado. That one of the game's best players missed a chance to play in the World Series not once but twice really aggravated David." She chuckled at the thought. "He used to say that Murphy's career represented the plight of the blue collar worker. Alway one step away from making it to the top. Always missing the opportunity at the last minute."

Mackie shook his head. "Murphy was a two-time MVP and seven-time All-Star."

"It never was a perfect analogy." Pham turned her attention back to Mackie. "You piqued my curiosity during the investigation after the break-in. And when I saw that autographed picture on your entertainment center, I saw a different side of you that I didn't expect." She wiped her eyes. "You reminded me of David. And your loss of Sarah reminded me of what I went through."

Mackie started to say something. He wanted to hop down from the counter, go to her. But before he could make up his mind, his cell phone rang. He looked at Pham, then at the kitchen clock. Ten-thirty.

"You expecting anyone?" Pham asked. "Maybe Hollie calling for a night cap?"

"She usually doesn't call 'til eleven." He winked at Pham when he said it.

"Smart ass." Pham stood and stretched.

Mackie answered the phone.

"Dad?"

He looked at Pham, then back at his mobile phone. "Hey, Reagan. Where are you, sweetheart? I thought your you'd be in mid-air right now. Have you already arrived in Atlanta?"

"My plans changed again. I tried to call before we left," she said. "Can you pick me up? We just landed in Nashville."

CHAPTER SIXTEEN

BY THE TIME Mackie saw Reagan standing at the curb, he had already circled the terminal once. Raindrops danced against other car headlights, blurring his view of the arriving passengers. He spotted her just beyond baggage claim. Beside her, a suitcase bulged, a red strap fashioned around the middle. She wore a fleece pullover and faded jeans. Hair pulled back. Birkenstocks. Exactly like her mother would have looked thirty years ago. Mackie parked, left the car running, and stepped out. In one hand, she held a cardboard tube. In the other, an oversized carry-on. She dropped both, darted in front of the car, and hurled herself into his arms, holding tight.

Her body crumpled into his. Her smile vanished. She buried her face in his shoulder and burst into tears. Between chest-heaving sobs, she said, "I miss…her…so much."

Mackie hugged her. Didn't know what to say. Platitudes would worsen her loss. Or worse, sound disingenuous. He embraced her for another minute, maybe more, before she finally eased free. Her face sagged, her eyes wet and red. The tension that had maintained her smile on the curb now gone. Twenty-four hours of travel and two days of lonesome hell had sapped her energy. She had nothing left.

"Let's get you home," Mackie said. "Jonah's waiting for you." Taking her by the arm, he opened the passenger door and helped her into the front seat. He returned to the curb to fetch her bags, placing the largest one in the trunk.

"Can you hand me that tube?" She sniffled and wiped her tears on her shirtsleeve. "I've lugged a semester's worth of projects across Europe this weekend. I'm not ready to let them go yet."

"Is that all you have?"

She nodded. "My checked bag, my carry-on, and the tube."

The rain continued to pound the protective awning as he shut the trunk. Streams of drainage water cascaded over the side, splattering the ground. He shut the driver's door, fastened his seatbelt, and pulled into traffic. Several cars drove ahead of them toward the interstate. Others continued to load passengers. Mackie signaled to merge into the flow of traffic.

Reagan spoke to him. "Just before you drove up, I saw—"

A pick-up truck blared its horn, interrupting her, and accelerated past them on the left.

"Slow down," Mackie barked.

"Don't, Dad." Reagan peered over her shoulder as he merged again. "You pulled in front of him."

"I had my signal on," he mumbled.

Reagan stared out the windshield, crossing her arms. "With Mom...what happened?"

"We don't know for sure." He took a deep breath, searching for the right words. "I've spoken with the lead detective and the pathologist. They're piecing it all together right now. No one knows why yet." He studied the road through a thousand wet prisms.

"Did she suffer?"

Mackie glanced at his daughter, who still stared straight ahead as if searching for the answer just beyond the headlights. "She died quickly, honey. Head traumas are usually like that."

"Was it a robbery?"

"Probably."

"Damn it, Dad, either they know or they don't! All you can tell me is probably this and maybe that. Either she suffered, or she didn't. Someone either killed her during a robbery, or they didn't. I don't see why it's so hard to get some fricking answers." She gripped the cardboard tube with one hand, swiping at her tears with the other.

He had considered how much to tell her. Much of this she would find our eventually, but how could he explain what he'd seen, what he suspected. She needed some version of the truth, but Mackie wasn't even sure what that was. He decided to change the subject. "Her obituary runs tomorrow in *The Tennesseean.*"

Reagan let that statement hang for a minute, not responding as she continued to avoid his gaze. Finally, she asked, "Have you made arrangements yet?"

"Some. I was thinking a graveside service in a few days. A memorial at the church afterwards. Maybe gifts and donations to the United Way in her memory."

Reagan nodded.

Much of the responsibility could have fallen to her as Sarah's lone surviving relative, but Mackie wanted her to avoid the pain of making funeral arrangements when she hadn't yet processed Sarah's death. He'd done it for Reagan's sake. In spite of the animosity from their divorce, Sarah would have done the same if Mackie had been killed. Even in the darkest days of their separation, Sarah found a way to work with Mackie for Reagan's benefit. He just hadn't expected to do the same so soon. Or under these circumstances.

"Slow down, dad. There's a line of cars ahead."

Mackie followed the taillights toward the interstate. Break lights brightened as cars stopped, then dimmed as traffic moved forward. Mackie misjudged the distance. When he depressed the break pedal, the back of the car fishtailed before gripping the pavement.

"Are you okay to drive?" Reagan asked.

"I'm just tired. We'll be home in a few minutes." He put both hands on the wheel as he concentrated. Traffic cleared as it accelerated. Mackie sped up. He didn't see the pickup truck until it pulled up beside them.

Reagan screamed.

Mackie jerked the wheel to the right to avoid a collision. The truck grazed the trunk, anyway. Gravel skidded from under the car. His tires hydroplaned on the slick roadway. Rather than cut away from Mackie's car, the pickup veered even closer to the driver's side. With a hideous crunch, the truck slammed into Mackie's door, driving them onto the shoulder. He saw the concrete barrier, but he couldn't avoid it. The car flipped. Dark sky followed by roadway lights. Metal groaned when the car landed right-side up. For a brief moment, Mackie thought they'd avoided complete disaster. Then his body lurched forward. Glass broke. Wood splintered. A shower of tree bark pelted the windshield. Mackie felt the cold before the rain. A bright light.

Then, darkness.

* * *

Sirens wailed in the background. Distant, then closer. Steady.

He opened his eyes but they stung each time his eyelids separated. Pain seared his arm when he moved. A cold, slick film stuck to his chest. His lungs throbbed with each breath. He reached out and felt the airbag deflating, its hot air gusting across his face. He grabbed the steering wheel to reposition himself, but his seatbelt pinned him. Mackie slid his hand down to his hip and depressed the buckle. His body lurched forward, slamming against the deflated airbag on the steering wheel, knocking the breath out of him. It took him a moment to be able to move again. When he did, pain electrified both arms, chilling his spine. Mackie looked down. Blood pooled on the airbag, now draped over the steering wheel. Rain seeped into the car, dripping on his head.

Mackie reached under the steering column to yank the keys from the ignition. Silence ensued. He listened.

"Down there," a distant voice said. "I think the driver's moving."

He turned his head to check on Reagan.

The passenger seat was empty.

"Reagan," he said. Then again, louder. "Reagan? Where are you?"

The angle of the car skewed his perspective. With his body now pressed against the dashboard, and the passenger window pressed against the ground. Mackie knew the car had flipped, but he didn't remember it. He searched the front seat, but the strobe of red lights distorted the images of the empty passenger seat. He yelled her name once more.

A man approached from the driver's side. "Sir, can you hear me?"

Mackie turned his head, frantic. "Where's Reagan?"

"Is there someone else in the car with you?"

Mackie struggled to get out. He pushed against the door. "My daughter," Mackie called out. "She was in the passenger seat. I can't find her."

"We've got a team of people on the way right now," the man said.

Mackie still couldn't see him. "Help me out." He twisted his body, both arms free but limited from the pain. "Open the door. I've got to get to Reagan."

More voices approached. "Hold tight, sir. We'll need some assistance to get you out. The door is jammed shut."

Rain dripped onto his face, running down his nose. He pushed off the console, against the door. Pain from his arm seared the right side of his body, overwhelming him. Nausea crashed down. He felt faint. Mackie yelled, but couldn't hear his own voice.

His vision began to fade.

He fought to stay awake, but pain overtook him. Before he passed out, he heard another man's voice, nearby but receding into the background. "I need a light down here in the grass," the voice called out. "I think I've found a body."

CHAPTER SEVENTEEN

MACKIE LOOKED UP and saw a familiar scene from a new perspective. Bright procedure lights hung from a white paneled ceiling. Stainless steel carts draped in blue cloths sat near his gurney. A monitor beeped nearby. Hushed voices murmured from a distance. His arms felt heavy when he tried to sit up. Plastic tubing and paper tape tethered him to the bed. The lights and acoustics around him suggested a trauma bay, not an exam room. Mackie became lightheaded when he sat up. He lay back, trying to remember what had happened.

Images returned with haunting clarity. The dizzying swirl of his car flipping. The groan of a metal door scraping against concrete. The swirl of blood and rain on his face. And the airport. He had picked up Reagan, but he couldn't remember seeing her at the crash site. Someone had called for help. Someone asked for a flashlight. A body?

Where's Reagan? His head throbbed, offering some clarity through the pain. Mackie again attempted to sit up. He kept his eyes closed as he propped up on one side, using his elbow for support. When the dizziness passed, he opened his eyes. Through a glass partition he saw two nurses working with their backs to him, one plump and busy, the other wiry and bored. Beyond them, the familiar face of an aging custodian mopping the floor. Thank God, he thought. Nashville Memorial. Mackie turned toward a noise in the corner of the trauma bay.

Not far from the gurney, Libby Pham nodded off in a chair. She looked very professional in a business suite. Mackie scooted up in the gurney. His right arm still felt numb. "Where's Reagan?" he asked.

Pham opened her eyes and smiled. "They said you'd be awake before too long." She stood and walked to his bedside. "I heard about the crash on the police scanner. I'd just gotten home. I called the officer at the scene and found out it was you. Said you'd flipped your car merging onto the interstate." She placed her hand on his arm. "Didn't I tell you that hanging out with me could be dangerous?"

"Where is Reagan?" Mackie snapped, rubbing his sore arm.

"In the operating room," Pham said. "Something about a spleen."

"But she's okay?"

"They wouldn't tell me."

Mackie leaned back on the gurney. "Give me someone who can." A splenic rupture was manageable. Not optimal. She'd be sore as hell and have a scar, but she would live. Christ almighty, he thought. What a mess. He remembered a pick-up truck. Remembered fishtailing on the wet pavement. He now assumed he'd driven too fast. He thought he had been hit on the left side. Probably some idiot trying to pass on the entrance ramp.

Mackie lay still for a few more minutes, then he made an effort to stand. He felt every jarring movement, first in his arm, then in his back. He swung his legs off the side of the bed, his feet feeling heavier than they should.

"The nurse is coming," Pham said, stepping back into the room. "You should lay down."

"Lie down," Mackie corrected, hardly paying attention. "Intransitive verb."

Pham smiled. "Either way, smart ass, you don't look too good."

"I'm fine." Mackie glanced at the nurses through the glass partition. No one paid attention to him. He yanked free the wires leading from his chest to a heart monitor. Pain ripped down his chest wall, but he could freely move. As he did, monitors blared and alarms screamed. Through the glass he could see one nurse whirl around in her chair. The other darted for the doors to the trauma bay. A frantic voice called over the intercom. "Code blue! Trauma bay one. Code blue!"

The doors burst open. Both nurses stopped short, blocking a stream of blue scrubs and crash carts behind them. Just beyond the crowd, a tall doctor cruised down the hallway, white coat billowing behind him. Clearly put off by the interruption.

Mackie stood by the gurney, half naked. He steadied himself. "Where's my daughter, damn it? Where's Reagan?"

The plump nurse emerged from the crowd. "Sit back down, Doctor Mac. She's being taken care of upstairs. Let's get you reconnected to that monitor."

As the reality of the false alarm set in, the crowd turned around and oozed back into other areas of the emergency department. The wiry nurse from behind the partition approached the bed. "You're feeling better," she said, her observation more of an accusation than a compliment.

Mackie pushed off the bed, swaying but managing to stay upright on his own. He took an unsteady step forward. "I need to see her."

The tall doctor passed between two medical students. A surgical mask hung partially untied on his scrubs like a bib. "Damn, Mackie, haven't you had enough of this place?" Marc Greenfield asked as he shook his hand. "You look like hell."

"Reagan's in the OR?" Mackie asked.

Greenfield nodded. "Splenectomy. She's stable right now."

He breathed a sigh of relief that seemed to deflate his entire body. She definitely could survive that. "When can I see her?"

"She's fine. We're taking good care of her." Greenfield looked at the sutures along Mackie's right arm. "The med student did a pretty good job on you."

Pham introduced herself, shaking Dr. Greenfield's hand.

"You came from the scene?" he asked.

"No, but I've got a team there, working on extricating the car."

The plump nurse continued to fuss over Mackie's monitor. "Come on now, Dr. Mac, let's get these leads back on you—"

Mackie stilled her hand with his own. "I need to see my daughter. If I could just get a shirt..." He stumbled as he stepped forward, grabbing Pham's shoulder for support.

Greenfield nodded to the nurse, who stepped out of the room. She returned moments later with a fresh scrub top in her hands. "Don't want you getting chilled while you wait."

"Give us a few minutes. Go grab a wheelchair for us," Greenfield said to the nurse, who placed the scrub top on the bed and backed out of the trauma bay.

Mackie pulled the shirt over his head, struggling to ignore the pain in his shoulders. Once he adjusted the shirt, he turned to Pham. "Don't leave. I'll need a ride."

"Do you need help walking?" she asked.

Mackie shook his head. "Wait down here."

Greenfield and Mackie exited the trauma bay through the double doors, past the waiting room and toward the staff elevators. When they stepped aboard, Mackie saw in his reflection what everyone had commented about. A black left eye. Abrasions across his forehead, but no lacerations on his face, cheeks or chin. Nose intact. Blood caked along his hairline. He needed a shower.

"Prepare yourself, Mackie. It's hard to see a family member in the O.R.," Greenfield reminded him.

"She couldn't look any worse than I do."

"You didn't bleed into your abdomen."

The elevator doors opened. At this hour, the surgical suite opened only for emergencies. Quiet halls. Low lights. One sleepy technician surfed the Internet at the nurses station. The white board behind the desk already contained the Monday morning cases, which would start in several hours. For now, only one operating room was in use. Greenfield strode down the hallway. A swinging door led them into the scrub room for that suite. Three metal sinks with gooseneck faucets and foot pedals, still wet from recent use, sat adjacent to the observation window. In the next room, a surgical team. And Reagan, inert on the table.

From behind the window, Mackie could see her face, but just barely. A cloth partition separated her head, attended by the anesthesiologist, from the rest of her body, attended by the surgeons. Had she not already been identified, Mackie wasn't sure if he would have recognized her. A plastic endotracheal tube protruded from her mouth. Her cheeks appeared swollen, eyes shut. Behind the partition, blood stained the surgeon's gloves and her pink abdominal contents glistened under the spotlight. A bag of white liquid fed into her IV.

Greenfield followed his eyes. "Her hematocrit is stable, but she lost a bunch of blood at the scene. No more than expected for a ruptured spleen, but enough."

"How much has she been transfused?" Mackie asked.

"We've got packed red cells standing by if we need them. So far, she's only received four units of H-BOC."

Mackie turned away from the window. "In the field?"

"Two units. The ambulance that responded to the wreck was part of the study protocol. Looks like your H-BOC for first responders paid off. Her vitals are solid, Mackie. She's going to be just fine." Greenfield walked to the sink and activated the faucet with a bump of his knee. He ripped into a scrub sponge and began to wash his hands.

H-BOC saved her life. In all the planning he and Sarah had done years ago for this product, he never could have envisioned this—saving his own daughter's life. "How much longer until I can see her?"

"Give us an hour to finish in here, then time to get her stabilized in recovery." A rich lather of soap dripped from his arms as he scrubbed. "They've already got a bed in the SICU once she's stable. Go clean up and then come back. We'll take good care of her."

Mackie took one final look at Reagan. She would be in the ICU for a minimum of twenty-four hours, probably more, then on the surgical floor for another few days. Now was the best chance for him to leave. Once she woke up, he wanted to be with her. And hope to God she didn't remember the accident. Mackie shuffled down the hallway to the elevators. He felt somewhat stronger. At least he could walk without dizziness, which he counted as a positive sign. Mackie rode the elevator back to the ground floor and found Pham seated in the waiting room.

"How's she look?" Pham asked.

"Better than I do."

"I should hope so." Pham handed him a cup of coffee and a bagel. "The nurse wants you to come back to the room."

Mackie took a sip. The hot liquid rejuvenated him. He continued to stand as he drank, unwilling to put his body through the pain of getting up again. At least, not yet. He took a bite of bagel, but chewing hurt his jaw. Mackie returned to the coffee, draining it after a few minutes. He needed a shower and a nap. Right now, only one seemed practical.

"Give me a few more minutes," Mackie said as he handed Pham the empty coffee cup. "I'm going to shower in the Doctor's Lounge and grab a fresh pair of scrubs."

Pham raised her eyebrows. "They haven't discharged you yet."

"I'd like to leave," Mackie said.

"It would be against medical advice," Pham said.

"Not against mine."

"Save the 'doctors make the worst patients' cliché, Mackie. You're not doing yourself any favors by skipping out when your daughter needs you most."

Mackie whirled around on Pham. "Is that what this looks like to you? Skipping out? Did you even consider that for the next two hours Reagan will be either intubated in the operating room or doped up in the recovery room? Two hours is about all I have to figure out what the hell happened coming home from the airport."

Pham held her ground. "And how do your propose to do that, doc?"

"By going to find my car."

Mackie headed down the hallway, back to the Doctor's Lounge where he had met the Nashville Police just four days ago. Or was it five? So much had happened since then he'd lost track of time. Even earlier this evening he couldn't imagine things getting any worse. He tried not to think about the implications of recent events. Tried to ignore all that he needed to do, not just for Sarah's case now but also for Reagan's recovery. The shower washed away the roadside filth, but a residue of dread and uncertainty lingered. He rejoined Pham in the lobby fifteen minutes later, hoping she could at least help him identify the parts of the investigation that he could control.

She greeted him with another cup of coffee. "Your best bet is to meet me at the car," she said. "That heavy-set nurse just sent the med student up to the O.R. to find you. They're planning to admit you for twenty-four hour observation."

"Right." Mackie took a few more sips of coffee to fuel his escape. "I'll leave by the side door and meet you outside," he said. "Can you help me find my car?"

"I'm two steps ahead of you," Pham said. "They just towed your car to our forensics lot downtown near the station. Let's see if we can figure out who ran you off the road."

They pulled out of the parking lot in Pham's unmarked cruiser, streets still slick with rain. The rain smeared his view of the city through the windshield. He closed his eyes as Pham drove. Resting didn't last long. Within a few minutes, she slowed the car and took a left. Mackie opened his eyes to the sight of fading streetlights and crumbling sidewalks.

"The compound is a few blocks from the station," she said. "Your car is already there."

"That was quick," Mackie said.

She pulled the cruiser onto the lot, pausing at the chain-link gate while it rolled slowly back. Razor-wire coils atop the fence reflected the cruiser's headlights. Pham pulled forward. Dozens of cars in various states of destruction parked in the lot. Rain pooled on dented hoods.

Mackie peered through the windshield. "All impounded cars?"

"Mostly. Some abandoned. Others ticketed and towed." She parked in front of a cinderblock building with two large painted garage doors to their left. It looked more like a self-storage facility than police property. A flood light illuminated the garage door, casting shadows from the cars parked nearby. "Most of them just sit here until they're sold for scrap metal. We'll hold on to all of them for at least thirty days. The tows are usually gone before that. The abandons rarely get picked up."

A man emerged from the building wearing a yellow rain slicker and galoshes. He held open the door, motioning them inside. Mackie climbed out of the car, every movement reminding him of the accident. He walked through the rain and stepped inside, too tired to care about his drenched clothes. Pham followed.

The man with the rain slicker and galoshes locked the door behind them, hung his jacket nearby, and gestured to the television in the corner of the room. "It's gonna get worse before it gets better. Radar says more's on the way." He handed Pham a towel and extended his other hand toward Mackie. "Bernie Graham. Please to meet ya."

Pham combed her fingers through her hair, dried her face, then handed the damp towel to Mackie. "When'd the car get here?"

"Less than an hour ago," Bernie said. "Cleaned up the scene pretty quick, from what they told me. One car. Two injuries. No pedestrians. Not much to see in the dark, anyway."

Pham glanced at Mackie, then turned back to Bernie. "This is Dr. McKay from Nashville Memorial. He was driving his daughter home when their car wrecked."

Bernie shook his head, letting out a slow whistle. "Who'd you piss off?"

"Excuse me?"

"I'm just impressed to see you walking around, after what that red car did to you."

"I don't quite follow you," Mackie said.

"I'll show you in a second," Bernie said. "Your daughter. She's okay?"

"She's alive," Mackie said. "Busted spleen and broken bones, but she's going to make it."

"Thank God for little miracles," Bernie commented.

Bernie led the two of them to a glass door at the far side of the lobby nearest the garage. Mackie and Pham entered a cavernous room. Darkness engulfed Bernie as he moved forward. A rim of light slid under the two garage doors, marking them but doing nothing to illuminate the room. They stepped forward onto a concrete floor. The room smelled of wet tires and motor oil.

"Give 'em just a second," Bernie's voice called out from the right.

An electric hum above, followed by stuttering overhead lights. Mackie squinted. The light's intensity increased, along with the pitch of the hum. As his eyes adjusted, Mackie noticed that the room looked even more cavernous. Work benches and tool chests lined the wall opposite the garage doors. Two cranes reached from the roof, jaws open, waiting. In the far bay, a few yards from the garage door, he saw his car.

Or what was left of it.

"Christ almighty," Pham said. Her voice echoed in the room.

"See what I mean," Bernie said.

Mackie limped to the car, more compressed from the head-on impact with the tree. Overhead lights revealed every scrape and tear in the metal. Approaching from the passenger side, he saw shattered glass in the front seat. Blood stains on the dashboard above the glove compartment. Fabric hung limply from the jagged glass of the window. The right front wheel jutted out from its housing as if put on sideways. Mackie circled the front of the car to the driver's side. The hood collapsed back, pushing the steering wheel toward the driver's seat. He saw the deflated airbag dangling from the steering column. "What hit us?"

"First, a concrete barrier," Pham said. "Ultimately a tree." She inspected the hood before walking to the driver's side.

"Is this what you were talking about?" Mackie knelt down and rubbed his hand across the back door. Grey paint flecks from his own car fluttered to the floor. Streaks of red etched both doors on that side, as well as the trunk.

Bernie shuffled over. "Either one of these streaks could have been an accident. A bump by someone driving too fast. Maybe a car passing in a single lane."

"But not both of them," Mackie said.

"Not accidentally." Bernie rested his hand on the dented trunk. "Those two separate impact marks tell me the red car didn't finish the job the first time. Looks like the driver intentionally ran you off the road, Doc."

CHAPTER EIGHTEEN

REAGAN'S CHEST MOVED with mechanical precision. The ventilator droned beside her, its green lights and plastic tubes controlling her breathing. Mackie slumped in the vinyl chair at her bedside, trying to sleep. Every time he nodded off, a new alarm would startle him awake. Often a nurse would enter to check Reagan's vitals, interrupting his dozing. In the few hours since her surgery, she was the only one able to rest, and that was due to the anesthesia. Mackie repositioned himself in the chair, folded his arms, and stared at his daughter while he waited for her attending physician to arrive.

Seeing Reagan lying in the intensive care unit caused a balloon of emotion to swell in his chest, causing more discomfort than any injury could have. His baby, lying broken before him, still showed signs of road rash on her face and arms. She seemed tethered to the bed with monitor wires and clear plastic tubing. He studied the settings on the ventilator, the position of the endotracheal tube, and the rhythmic rise and fall of her chest. Surely these professional observations were his mind's way of giving him some distance from the overwhelming emotion of seeing her like this. Simmering just below his sadness about Reagan, though, in areas where professional distance could not reach, was a protective paternal instinct, fueled by anger at the person responsible for the accident. Irrational as it seemed, he wondered if he should ask hospital security to post a guard outside of her room.

In the early hours of the morning, Mackie and Pham had left Bernie with the remnants of his car. An investigational team would inspect it today and try to glean snippets of information from the wreckage. Pham had accompanied Mackie to the recovery room, only to discover that Reagan had already been transported to the surgical intensive care unit. For the last three hours, Mackie had waited at her side. Nurses updated him on her condition, allowing him to rest in the corner of her room rather than in the family waiting room. He appreciated their consideration, but the price of proximity was interrupted sleep.

Mackie startled when a nurse entered the room. Regaining his composure, he looked outside the window. Clouds fought off the sunrise as a fine mist still shrouded downtown. Mackie wanted to inspect the crash site that morning, then wanted to go home and sleep. "How's she looking?" he asked.

The nurse straightened a fresh sheet over Reagan, tucking it into the mattress. She turned her attention to Reagan's IV pump. "Just fine," she said as she attached a new bag of fluids. "Dr. Greenfield's written an order for us to wean her off the ventilator this morning. She's not needing much sedation, so I think she'll be ready."

Mackie studied Reagan's swollen face, which glistened with antibiotic ointment over the sutures in her cheeks. "What time's he coming by?"

"Rounds have already started," the nurse said. "Shouldn't be too long." She adjusted Reagan's tubing once more before stepping out of the room.

A few minutes later, Mackie heard the scuff of shoe covers on linoleum outside the door. Beneath the drawn curtain, two sets of surgical booties and greens scrub pants paused. Mackie heard two men talking.

"Twenty-one year old passenger in an MVC now post-op day one from an ex-lap with splenectomy, stable vent settings and I's and O's. Left-sided chest tube to water suction. Right radial head fracture. Unremarkable exam, minimal output from the drains. Plans for extubation later this morning, and if she does okay, move her out to the floor tonight." The young voice encapsulated the last six hours in thirty seconds. The curtain separated, and Marc Greenfield breezed in, his surgical resident in tow.

"You came back," Greenfield said. He wore new scrubs and a clean shave. "That ER nurse just about called the police when you didn't return to the trauma bay."

"I left with a cop," Mackie said.

"Always thinking two steps ahead of the rest of us. That's what I like about you, Mackie. No worries. All's well that ends well, I guess." He walked to Reagan's ventilator and began to change the settings. "How's she doing?"

"She's not breathing over the vent, which has me concerned. Otherwise, she looks okay." Mackie stood to approach the bedside. He stumbled from the lightheadedness of standing up. With a surreptitious hand he gripped the back of the chair for balance. Marc Greenfield noticed even as the surgical resident remained near the doorway.

"You're not gonna like this, Mackie, but when we're done here, I'm going to examine you myself. More for the nurses's benefit than yours, really. They're worried about you."

Mackie managed a smile that came out more like a grimace. "Buttering up the nurses?"

"Can't do my job well without them."

Greenfield approached the bed. He listened to Reagan's chest with his stethoscope. "Still sedated from the splenectomy. She'll perk up as soon as the anesthesia wears off. I'm thinking one more night in the SICU then move her to the floor tomorrow. You need to go home and get some rest. You're not going to be much help to her once she gets home if you're too exhausted from your bedside vigil."

Mackie nodded. "I didn't want to miss rounds."

Greenfield had Mackie sit in the bedside chair. He took a few moments to inspect Mackie's wounds, listen to his chest, and perform a cursory neurologic exam. When he finished, he said, "Good enough. Leave your contact numbers with the charge nurse. We'll call you if there's any news." Greenfield shook Mackie's hand before he glided toward the next patient's room, receiving a report from his resident on the way.

Mackie walked to the bed. He brushed Reagan's hair away from her face and kissed her forehead. She continued to sleep, peaceful but unresponsive to his presence. He picked up his cell phone and stepped to the window. Traffic already backed up leading into downtown. He called Duel to let him know about the accident. He left a voicemail message, then dialed Pham. She answered on the second ring.

"Did you get any sleep?" she asked.

"Interrupted," he said. "What time are you driving to the crash site?"

"An hour or so."

"Could you pick me up on the way? I'm still at the hospital with Reagan."

"You're comfortable leaving her?"

"As long as she's stable."

"Hang on, then," Pham said. "I'll be there in thirty minutes."

* * *

Pham merged onto the interstate. Her tires hissed as she accelerated. Even though the rain had stopped, she turned on her wipers to clean the road spray from the windshield. She took the far left lane and set the cruise control on eighty. Mackie nursed a cup of coffee in the front seat. He needed about two more hours of consciousness before he surrendered to his fatigue. He intended to spend the rest of the day in bed. At least, until Reagan awoke.

Pham's police radio crackled in the background. Reports of accidents. Locations of officers. Mention of a robbery downtown. She lowered the volume. "Any problems going through life without a spleen?"

"Not at her age," Mackie said.

Pham thought about this. "It's just a big bag of blood, right? Trouble if you bleed from it, but not really a critical organ."

"Depends," Mackie said. "It filters damaged red cells, sequesters rogue bacteria. Does a lot of general maintenance in your blood stream. But people can live perfectly productive lives without one."

"You can lose a ton of blood if it ruptures, right?"

"Reagan could have died," Mackie said. "Bled out in her abdomen and no one would have known until it was too late. Which is why we were so damn lucky the ambulance that responded stocked H-BOC."

"How long has that protocol been going on?" she asked.

Mackie adjusted in the front seat. "Last year, ten ambulances packed coolers with a half dozen units each of H-BOC. Now, I think there are twenty five trucks—maybe thirty—stocking it. It's a hassle to lug around the city, primarily because the coolers take up precious space in the back of the ambulance. Dispatchers know which trucks carry it, so the plan is to preferentially assign ambulances with H-BOC to the trauma. Gun shot wounds and car wrecks, mostly." He took a sip of his coffee, considering the implications of a first responder without transfusion capabilities.

"Ironic, isn't it? That your product saved your daughter's life?"

"True. But there's a part of me that wonders if a tainted batch of H-BOC may be part of the reason she's still in the ICU."

Pham let that comment linger. Signs for the airport loomed ahead. She signaled and eased the car into the right lane. "It should be just up here," she said.

Mackie peered through the windshield. "I don't think so. We were coming inbound from the airport. The site is on the other side of the road."

Pham pulled onto the shoulder and parked. "That's why we're taking a look from over here first. Get some perspective."

Mackie opened his door. The morning air felt warmer than he'd expected. More humid. The smell of diesel fuel followed each passing tractor trailer, and Mackie forced himself not to flinch when cars tore past them at seventy miles an hour. A concrete barrier bisected the highway. Across the road, a similar barrier lined the shoulder.

Pham walked in front of the car to get a better view ahead. "Look about fifty yards up and to the left." She pointed in that general direction.

"The smashed concrete?" Mackie asked.

"That's it. Your car almost made it to the end of the ramp."

Mackie squinted, but he couldn't see any more detail from this distance. "I've had enough perspective from here. Let's take a closer look."

They climbed into the car, easing along the shoulder toward the exit ramp. Other cars passed nearby, signaling for the exit. One man blared his horn at Pham's driving on the shoulder. She ignored him, continuing in the emergency lane until the gravel turned to pavement at the exit. She eased the car onto the road and turned left at the top of the ramp. Crossing the overpass, she turned once again into the flow of inbound traffic. Pham hugged the shoulder, inching down the road with her hazard lights flashing.

Mackie leaned forward. His back pulled with the movement, but a steady ache had replaced the sharp pains from the previous night.

Peering through the windshield, he noticed typical skid marks on the concrete, but nothing that appeared fresh. "I don't seen anything on this side."

"Look out my side," Pham said.

Mackie craned his neck to the left. Then, he saw it. Arising like shadows from the mist, black tire marks jutted toward the concrete. Small marks. His car. Paralleling them, another slash of rubber on the road. Marks twice as wide as his. Ahead, shards of reflective red taillights sprinkled along the base of the wall, mingling with pieces of plastic and gravel. Pham pulled the car close to the barrier and parked. She left the hazard lights engaged. "You have enough room to get out on your side?" she asked.

"Just," Mackie said. He slid out of the car, pinned between the metal door and the protective wall. Crumbled concrete littered the shoulder ahead. He squeezed forward.

"A red car?" Pham asked.

"Pick-up truck. A big one." Mackie lifted a strip of rubber from the side of the road. "It first passed me as I pulled out from the airport. It must have pulled off and waited for me to turn down here." He closed his eyes, trying to remember the details. His memory before the accident seemed fuzzy. He still had trouble recalling the crash scene. He shook his head and opened his eyes. "I can't place the details."

Pham stepped onto the wet grass through a car-sized hole in the barrier. Concrete rubble at her feet. The blunt force of the truck, combined with the slick road, had catapulted his car into the grass. Puddles formed in the deep furrows caused by the flipping car. Twenty yards from the shoulder, a pine tree splintered at the base and leaned forward. Grey paint tattooed the trunk.

Mackie moved through the barrier and into the grass, the heavy dew causing his pants to stick to his legs. He struggled for his balance as he walked down the hill. Shards of rocks shifted under his feet. "Where did she land?"

"Over here." Pham knelt down several paces from the tree.

As Mackie approached Pham, the pulverized concrete dissipated, replaced instead by splintered wood and flattened grass. Depressions from what appeared to be a stretcher etched four marks into the ground. Medical supply wrappers smeared with mud had been trampled into the ground, forgotten in the rush of the rescue. Several feet away, behind the apparent scene of Reagan's resuscitation, Mackie saw a cylindrical object poking up from the grass. He bent over and picked up Reagan's cardboard carry-on. The contents of her projects felt remarkably dry. Mackie tucked the tube under his arms.

He stood amid the destruction, concentrating on the events surrounding the crash, but his memory locked up. Probably better that way, he thought. Nature's way of sparing him the haunting memory of what had actually happened. He hoped Reagan would be so lucky. A noise from the roadway interrupted his thoughts.

A car pulled up.

Pham looked at Mackie. "You expecting company?"

"Not here." He walked up the hill. Even the gentle incline tugged at his back muscles, shooting bolts of pain down his legs. "Sonofabitch," he mumbled.

A voice rumbled from the top of the hill. "Jesus Christ. Isn't one night in a roadside ditch enough for you?" Duel Richardson peered over the barrier, careful not to let his tie touch the wall. With his hair slicked back and clad in an expensive suit, Duel looked out of place.

"You want to come down here and give us a hand?" Mackie called out.

Duel shook his head. "Are you kiddin'? These are Italian leather shoes. I'll wait up here."

Mackie stumbled his way back up the hill, stopping just before the broken wall. "How'd you find us?" he asked, panting from the exertion.

"You called me this morning."

"I didn't tell you we'd be driving out here."

Duel paused. "Where else would you be?" He brushed dirt off his shoes with the back of his hand.

"At the hospital."

"Already checked there. Knowing you have a tendency to go where the action is, this was the next most likely spot." Duel peered over the damaged wall along the shoulder, inspecting the tree line. "Y'all got beat up in the wreck."

"Side-swiped by a truck, then flipped the car," he said. Mackie picked his way across the refuse at his feet to reach the shoulder.

Pham had already returned to the car. She removed her camera from the front seat and snapped several shots of the scene.

Duel hitched his pants. "Your voicemail message said you got banged up at the scene, but I didn't expect this."

"You should have seen it last night," Mackie said.

"Jesus," Duel said. "How you feeling?"

"Shitty."

"You look terrible. How about Reagan?"

"Had surgery last night. She's stable now," Mackie said. "I've got to give credit to the SICU nurses at the hospital. They've gone out of their way to take good care of her."

Duel grinned. "No one wants to piss off their old boss. They're probably scared to death the medical error of the month is going to happen on their watch and to your family. Count yourself lucky, my friend. On many fronts."

Mackie shook his head. "I don't feel lucky."

"You have no idea," Duel said.

A tractor trailer surged past them in the nearby lane, kicking up roadside mist and drenching their conversation with traffic noise.

Duel turned to Pham, raising his voice above the traffic. "Any idea who's responsible?"

She shook her head. "Doubt we'll know. This kind of thing doesn't leave much evidence. We'll trace the paint from the truck back to the manufacturer. Probably even get a make and model. That's about all we have to go on so far."

Duel picked at his back tooth with a finger, flicking the results in the grass. "Y'all call me with any developments." He glanced at Mackie. "You need a ride?"

"Got one."

"Be careful."

Duel climbed into his car and eased back onto the interstate. Pham finished taking photographs of the barrier, then moved back down the hill. "Just a few more minutes," she said.

"I'll wait for you in the car."

Mackie looked at the skid marks on the road once more. If he was interpreting them correctly, Pham had parked almost directly over the point of impact. Ten yards farther, the road appeared normal. But those ten yards made all the difference to Mackie. When he pressed himself against the wall to open the passenger door, he noticed broken plastic on the road just under Pham's cruiser. She'd pulled so close to the wall, Mackie had not seen it earlier. Not that it would have drawn his attention. With so much litter along the shoulder, it almost blended in with the rest of the detritus. But for the events of the last twenty-four hours, he probably would not have even noticed it. Except for the letters on the plastic.

He couldn't stoop down in the tight space, so he reached out for it. Straight black plastic, broken at both ends, angled in the center. He picked it up. Its weight, unsubstantial. The consequences, however, monumental. It must have snapped off the back of the truck on impact. He turned it over, shocked at the words emblazoned on a partial license plate frame. *Synthesis Industries.*

CHAPTER NINETEEN

SOMETHING STARTLED MACKIE awake. He bolted upright and stared at the wall in his bedroom. Six-twenty glowed in green from the bedside clock. Fatigue froze his memory. Glancing through his window, he saw nothing but darkness, which made it impossible to distinguish night from day this time of year. At the foot of his bed, Jonah thumped his tail in response to Mackie's stirring. Must still be night, he concluded, or else Jonah would have already waked him up to be let out.

Memories melted from his mind in reverse order: Pham dropping him off at his house after helping him secure a rental car, the plastic license plate frame with "Synthesis Industries" inscribed on it, the accident scene, and Reagan still intubated in the ICU.

His heart accelerated. He should have already received an update about her.

Mackie clicked on the lamp and reached for his cell phone. Jonah wobbled to the bedside, investigating with a wet nose. Mackie checked his phone. No missed calls. He yawned and dialed the hospital. The operator transferred him to the SICU.

"Dr. Mac?" the charge nurse said, urgency in her tone. "We've been trying to reach you."

"When did you call?" His heart slammed against his chest as he stumbled out of bed and into the den. Jonah followed. A red light flashed on his answering machine. Two messages. He had not heard either call. "What's wrong?"

"Reagan's awake. She came off the ventilator a few hours ago," the nurse. "She's been asking for you."

Mackie hurried back into his bedroom, almost tripping over

Jonah. He grabbed a pair of chinos and a knit shirt from his closet. "Let me speak to Greenfield," he said as he sat on the bed and pulled on his socks.

"He's with another patient right now," the nurse said. "Hold on. I'll transfer you to Reagan's room."

Mackie waited less than thirty seconds before she answered.

"Dad?" she rasped, her voice weak.

"I'm on my way, sweetheart. How you feeling?" Stupid question, he thought. She's been intubated for the last day and has a pink scar slashed across her abdomen. The phone magnified her labored breathing. He automatically switched into doctor mode. "It helps if you take a deep breath through your nose…then blow out through your mouth."

She coughed. Her breath whistled as she tried to inhale through her nose. "The car…" She paused. Took a breath. "What happened to the car?"

"It's taken care of. I brought your things home with me from the accident." She probably didn't even realize the extent of the damage. There would be plenty of time for that. "Do you remember what happened?"

"I don't understand," she said, her breathing sounding more shallow than before. "He told me to watch out."

Mackie paused. "Who did, sweetie? Who told you to watch out?" He waited for her to answer. Her breathing sounded more distant, almost like the phone had fallen from her grip.

"My chest," she said. "It hurts to breathe."

"Reagan? Talk to me, honey. Are you okay?"

One of her monitors went off, frantically beeping. He heard scuffling in the background, A woman called out, "Can I get some help in here?" A click. The line went dead. He immediately redialed the number. Busy signal.

Mackie panicked.

He shoved his phone into his pocket. He grabbed his keys from the counter, knocking the package of classified documents to the floor. Mackie left them there. He jumped into his rental car and screeched out of the driveway. He arrived at the hospital sooner than expected, double parked in the doctor's lot, and darted up the stairs two at a time toward the ICU. He burst through the automatic doors into the unit, but froze at the site he encountered.

A medical team crowded the entrance to Reagan's room. The crash cart waited just behind them, red drawers partially open, torn packaging scattered on the floor. The relentless pulse of a cardiac monitor sounded, faster than it should have, rising above the baseline cacophony of the monitors from other rooms.

Mackie sprinted to Reagan's bedside.

He pushed his way through the crowd toward her bed. More discarded wrappers littered the floor. The overhead light, usually reserved for procedures and emergencies, illuminated the bed. Some of the staff in the room parted when he approached. Greenfield looked up, making eye contact with Mackie even as he continued CPR. Reagan's body rocked with each chest compression. A firm endotracheal tube protruded from her mouth. No spontaneous movements. Lifeless.

"What the hell happened?" Mackie yelled. He moved to the head of her bed. Nurses stepped out of the way, but they continued their resuscitation efforts.

Mackie looked at the heart monitor. The oscilloscope spiked with each chest compression, then plummeted to a chaotic baseline, fibrillating but not pumping. Greenfield noticed the same thing.

"I need paddles on her now, please." Greenfield spoke with authority, his voice steady. Nurses immediately moved. The crash cart appeared at the bedside. One nurse ripped the covering off the electrodes and handed the paddles to Greenfield. The surgical resident stepped in to continue chest compressions. Greenfield grabbed the paddles, barking rapid-fire orders to the team. The resuscitation effort had its own rhythm, frantic but structured.

He approached her with the paddles, depressing them on Reagan's chest. "Stand back. Two hundred joules." He waited. "All clear."

Mackie watched in horror. The team surrounding the bed stepped back as one. An electronic siren screeched. Mackie heard a thump. Simultaneously, Reagan's chest thrust into the air, her arms and legs limp below her, as if someone had picked her up by a belt and dropped her back onto the bed. All eyes turned to the monitor.

More chaotic squiggles.

"Two fifty joules, please." Greenfield gripped the paddles as he waited, then relaxed. "All clear."

Again, the team eased back in unison. The second shock thrust her body up, more violently this time. Again, the heart monitor spiked but returned to its ineffective baseline. The surgical resident resumed chest compressions.

Fear paralyzed Mackie. He felt the urge to do something to help the team, but indecision anchored him to the floor. He couldn't step forward, much less think about how he could help. He reached out and gripped Reagan's hand. And waited.

"Come on, goddammit," Greenfield murmured. He checked the monitor. Looked at the clock. Peered at Reagan's face. "Let's go to three hundred joules," he finally said.

In concert, the team shifted back. A nurse placed her hand on Mackie's shoulder. "Dr. Mac. You need to step away for just a moment."

Mackie couldn't. Reagan's clammy hand represented a suspended state. Not dead, but not fully alive. The nurse squeezed his shoulder. "Let's let Dr. Greenfield do his job."

Greenfield glanced at the team. "Clear." Louder this time. More authoritative. Chest compressions stopped. The siren sounded. The monitor paused. Then, the shock.

With a force of three hundred joules, Reagan's body lurched up. Her arms, initially limp beside her, flew outward with the surge of electricity, giving her the appearance of a rag doll tossed on the bed. Her legs folded under her when she landed, causing her body to sit sideways on the bed. All eyes turned toward the monitor.

A spontaneous pulse.

Greenfield pressed his fingers to her neck, confirming the heart beat. Once verified, he started to bark orders. Loudly. Forcefully. In charge. "I need crash labs sent stat. Start an epi drip at zero point two mics per kilo. Set her vent for pressure support. Get me the x-ray technician—"

"Right here, sir." A woman emerged from the crowd.

"Check her ET tube placement."

With the efficiency of a pit crew, the nurses and technicians swarmed around Reagan's bed, restarting medications, cleaning up the mess. Greenfield listened to Reagan's chest. Apparently satisfied, he turned toward Mackie. "Close call."

Mackie sat on the edge of her bed. He squeezed her hand, sweaty but warmer. As he cradled her wrist with his palm, her pulse tapped against his fingertips. "What the hell?"

Greenfield shrugged. "Who knows. Pulmonary embolus, probably."

"She's twenty-one years old."

"With broken bones and immobilization. She's a set up for a blood clot." Greenfield scratched his scrub cap as he examined the surgical site on her abdomen. "She did great right after we extubated her this afternoon. Whatever happened, she's stable now. We're looking into it."

The crowd receded from Reagan's room as the intensity of the code subsided. Medical staff returned to other patients, excitedly murmuring about what they had just witnessed.

Mackie stayed with Reagan, gripping her hand. In less than a week, his world had collapsed around him. He felt entirely helpless, terrified of what would come next.

CHAPTER TWENTY

THREE DAYS LATER, Mackie settled into his plane seat after most passengers had already boarded. Without any checked bags and only a small carry on, the entire process of purchasing a ticket from Nashville to Atlanta was seamless. Not so for Pham. Between declaring her sidearm and producing proper identification, she arrived in her seat as the airplane door closed. An early morning commuter to their right scowled at the woman who'd caused the delay. She flashed a smile at him, then her badge. He retreated back to his newspaper. Pham shoved the hard case under the seat in front of her, then propped her feet on the luggage. A few minutes later, the plane took off.

"You're sure we're going to save time this way?" Mackie asked. "Last week, I drove door to door in three hours."

"We'll arrive in under two. No checked bags." Pham reached into her billfold and produced a gold card. "This is the key. Preferred rental status, thank to the Nashville PD. We'll have a car waiting for us just outside the gates, heater running."

"It's going to be seventy degrees in Atlanta today."

Pham shook her head. "When does winter arrive down there?"

"I think we missed it already."

"You nervous about leaving Reagan so soon?" she asked. "It's only been a couple of days since she woke up. I didn't think you'd be ready."

"I never said I was ready," Mackie responded. Left unsaid, though, was his knowledge that once Reagan was discharged from the hospital, he would't want to step away from her at all. With blood thinners administered and her breathing back to normal, she had made the tenuous transition to convalescence. She was almost out of the ICU, and he knew at the hospital, she was in good hands. Safe hands. For now.

Mackie closed his eyes as the plane ascended, but he couldn't relax. Long nights in the SICU, followed by restless sleep at home, had left him grumpy and sore. Pham had called late yesterday, suggesting the day trip to Atlanta. Unannounced. Questions for Hank, plus the broken plastic frame on the roadside, gave enough probable cause to return to Synthesis. She suggested they arrive before lunch and see what happens. Mackie agreed. Tired as he was from the last several days, the thought of calling Hank—or even Singh—to account for the accident energized him. Drove him. God forbid, even nourished the rage within him. That he found sustenance from revenge gave him pause, which Pham seemed to recognize. Rash actions on his part would only complicate the investigation, she said. Still, she wanted him there when she investigated Synthesis.

Her logic grounded Mackie. They would take their chance that an unannounced visit might cause them to miss Hank. Worse case scenario, a quick search of the building could reveal additional clues about the accident. And about Sarah's murder. Just as Mackie drifted to sleep, the stewardess woke him to ask about drink choices. Rest would wait. He ordered a coffee. Mackie looked over at Pham, her attention glued to a People magazine. "Do you have a Plan B if things get ugly at Synthesis?" he asked.

"I've got a badge and a gun," she said. "What else do you think we'll need?"

The inconvenienced passenger to their right looked up. Mackie leaned closer to Pham and lowered his voice. "Even though I think he's a philandering prick, I doubt Hank's willing to kill someone to protect his investment."

"Your point's well taken," she said. "But what if Hank knows who's involved? People who commit crimes of revenge or greed usually do so because they think they can get away with it. They're often brash enough to brag about it to someone else, too. Having a cop with you and the element of surprise alters the equation. For Hank and for us. I've never met him, so the key is to obtain as much information as we can before he summons help."

"And by then, we're gone."

"You should be sleeping in your own bed tonight."

"Or at Reagan's bedside." Mackie sipped his coffee. "I won't be resting well regardless."

Pham returned her attention to the magazine. For the remainder of the flight, Mackie stared out the window, trying to link the disparate pieces of recent events into a coherent narrative. So far, he couldn't tie Synthesis Industries to AFI. Couldn't connect the robbery in his house and the roadside attack on his family. Not only could he not connect the events, he couldn't imagine that the blame rested solely with one person. Maybe Pham would have better luck with Hank.

As promised, a four door sedan waited for them just outside the terminal. It still took fifteen minutes to negotiate the Atlanta airport, even bypassing baggage claim and the car rental counter. Mackie checked his watch. "Let's hope that traffic is in our favor," he said as he climbed into the passenger's seat. "We'll be cutting it close on your two hour time–frame."

"I'm driving. We'll make it." Pham shoved her gun case into the back seat.

She pulled into morning traffic, leaving the airport and heading for the 285 perimeter. They found the exit easily, and wound around until they spotted the all–glass building complex. She eased the rental car into the parking lot, every bit as crowded as the previous week.

Pham shielded her eyes. "It's a bit over the top. What's wrong with brick and mortar?"

"Too twentieth century. That would never fly in Atlanta." They parked and stepped out of the car. Even at ten a.m., the day felt unseasonably warm. Every bit of seventy degrees, and then some. Interstate traffic hummed in the background, less than a mile away. Nearby, a diesel truck rumbled, unseen at first, then emerging from behind the smaller of the two glass silos. Pod Two. The vehicle looked like a large shipping truck. Looked almost like a UPS carrier, but the brown was all wrong. Dustier. Almost tan. Plus it sported a refrigeration unit, adding to the noise of the vehicle. As the truck approached the entrance to the property, another one trailed behind it. The first truck waited at the entrance for the second one to catch up. Then, both pulled into traffic, toward the interstate.

Mackie waited for Pham to get what she needed from her carry–

on. Last week he'd walked into this building, looking for answers to question he couldn't even articulate, his judgment anesthetized by the shock of Sarah's murder. Now, specific questions emerged as the shock faded. His mind offered accusations, suggested only confrontation. Perhaps Pham could channel those emotions into productive questions. Mackie swallowed against the dread of what he might discover. Knowing that Hank could be nearby just pissed him off. He was ready, he realized, for however this foray played out.

Pham adjusted her blazer to conceal her weapon as she walked to the building's entrance. Mackie followed her to the Mother Pod. He decided not to mention the name to her. When they stepped inside the air conditioned circular lobby, only one person sat inside. The receptionist looked up when the door sucked shut behind them, offering an obligatory smile.

"Welcome to Synthesis," said the woman, apparently remembering she was supposed to be more inviting.

Mackie approached the curved desk, introducing himself. "We're here to see Sarathi Singh."

The woman's expression sagged. She looked skeptical as she checked a clipboard on her desk. "It's McKay? I don't see any mention of your name. Not surprising, though, because Dr. Singh is away from the office today. He's taking a much needed day for himself." She offered a smug grin as she spoke.

Mackie paused briefly, tamping down his natural inclination to challenge her. "He's expecting us," he began. "I was just here on Friday—"

"I heard."

"—and we made arrangements for a follow-up meeting this week."

The woman sighed. "Dr. Singh is not here, and he won't be back until tomorrow."

Pham reached inside her blazer and showed the receptionist her badge. "Perhaps we can speak to Henry Stone, then." She exaggerated her own smile. "If you don't mind."

The woman's expression tightened, clearly not accustomed to being pushed around on her own turf. Equally clear, however, was that Synthesis was, in fact, her turf. She leaned forward to study Pham's identification. "Detective Libby Pham," she said as she recorded her name. "I'll be certain to tell Mr. Stone that you came by."

Pham stood her ground. "I'll wait while you do."

"Perhaps I'm not making myself clear. Dr. Singh is not here. You're too early for Mr. Stone—he won't be back until later today."

"From Nashville?" Mackie asked.

The receptionist blinked several times, startled that Mackie appeared to know Stone's location. While they waited, she called Hank's office. "Voicemail," she said as the recorded voice chirped on the other end. She left a brief message, informing him that a doctor and a detective were in the lobby, eager to talk to him. Pham handed over a card, asking the receptionist to call if either Mr. Stone or Dr. Singh returned sooner than expected. They turned around and headed toward the entrance.

"So much for Plan B," Pham said when they stepped out into the escalating Georgia heat. "What next?"

Mackie stood near the doorway, glancing around the parking lot. In the distance, the tree-lined horizon shimmered under the morning smog of downtown. A low rumble emerged from the side of the building. More transport trucks.

"They're churning out H-BOC today," Pham said, following Mackie's gaze. "That's the third—"

Mackie stopped listening, not because of the noise of the approaching truck, but because of the truck itself. It also appeared UPS-like, but with one notable difference. More than just an oversight, he thought. His mind raced with the implications. In the time it would take to explain this to Pham, he might lose his opportunity. The truck gathered speed as it rounded the smaller building to the parking lot. He turned to Pham. "Give me your badge."

"What for?"

The truck approached them. Fully visible. Accelerating.

"I'll explain later." Mackie snatched her billfold and jogged down the sidewalk toward the parking lot. The truck turned as Mackie dashed into its path. The driver didn't see him at first. The fifty yards between them shrank. The engine roared. Mackie stood his ground. The crescendo of the diesel engine halted. Air brakes hissed. The truck lurched to a stop less than ten yards from Mackie. He took a steadying breath to slow his heart rate.

The driver leaned out the window. "Damn, buddy, you could'a been killed, standing there in the road like that."

Mackie stepped to the side of the vehicle, holding out the badge as he approached the lowered window. He slid two fingers over the picture on the identification. "Detective Pham," he announced to the driver, holding out the credentials only long enough to establish authenticity and authority. "Where're you headed?"

The driver adjusted his Atlanta Braves baseball cap, squinting into the midmorning sun. Mackie could have displayed the entire badge without a lick of anxiety, courtesy of the glare. Advantage Mackie.

"Over to interstate 95, then north to Maryland," the driver said. "Our usual Tuesday route."

"Our?" Mackie asked.

The driver nodded behind the truck. "Travel in groups of two. The other truck's loading right now."

Mackie peered behind them. No sign of another truck yet. If he acted quickly, he could finish this without anyone else asking questions. He peered into the cab, which did not connect to the truck's cargo bay. Definitely not UPS. "Let me see your manifest," Mackie said.

The driver picked up a clipboard and handed it to Mackie. "This is all they give us."

Mackie studied the shipping manifest. Beneath the logo of Synthesis Industries, Mackie found lot numbers for a product known as "H-BOC MG-70" lined up with stickers from packaging labels, the quantities of each product being shipped, and the destination of the shipment. Mackie didn't need a ledger to interpret the code F-MD. Frederick, Maryland. Fort Detrick. Not a complete surprise. Mackie had even seen the labels while he'd waited in Singh's office on Friday. What shocked him, though, was the method of shipment.

"Let's take a look in the back." Mackie glanced over his shoulder. Still no sign of the other truck.

The driver hesitated. "Something wrong?"

"That's what we're fixing to find out," he said, matching the driver's southern accent. Holding on to the shipping manifest, Mackie stepped back from the cab door, giving the driver room to get out. "We'll have you back on schedule in no time."

The driver climbed out of the cab clutching a separate keychain. He kept the motor running as the two of them walked to the rear of the vehicle. Unlocking the padlock at the base of the cargo door, the driver yanked back the bolt from its latch. The lever jammed. The driver banged the bolt with the padlock, sliding it forward then pulling back once more. Once disengaged, the cargo door slid up the tracks. It clattered as it retracted into the ceiling of the cargo bay. "Take a look," the driver said. "Nothin' but blood."

Mackie climbed into the cargo bay. Cardboard boxes lined the walls of the van, two rows deep on either side. With shelves built into each wall, the boxes almost touched the ceiling with stacked boxes eight rows high. Mackie strode the length of the cargo bay. Ten rows. A total of three hundred twenty boxes. He wiped the sweat from his brow as he bent down to read the packaging label of one box. Sweat dripped onto the box. Add ten degrees to the exterior temperature, he thought as he scrutinized the label in the hazy light from the translucent ceiling. Fancy company logo. Detailed lot number. The notation "H–BOC MG–70: ten units."

Mackie surveyed the contents of the truck. Over three thousand units of H–BOC in this truck alone, with another one to follow shortly. All headed to Fort Detrick. He stood, his knees groaning in protest as he walked to the end of the truck. A faint breeze cooled him as he hopped down.

"You find what you need in there, buddy?"

"How many trucks leave from here each day?" Mackie asked.

The man shrugged. "I just load the trucks and drive them."

"How many routes will you do a week?"

The driver said, "Depends. Usually 'bout five trips out a month, but they got us doubling that for a while. This week, we ship out Tuesday and Thursday. Next week, we do Monday, Wednesday, Friday. Ten trips total this month."

"You drive for anyone else?" Mackie asked.

The man laughed as he closed the door. "Wanted to. You know, at least bring something other than an empty truck back from the East Coast. But we got a tight schedule. Don't really matter, though. They make it worth my while." He secured the padlock, then tugged on the door to be certain it was secure. He looked behind him at the sound of an approaching truck. "Anything else, Detective, 'fore we go?"

"That's it." Mackie stepped back as an identical truck pulled in behind the first. Once the driver climbed back into his cab, both trucks moved forward. Mackie crossed the parking lot to the sidewalk as both trucks disappeared from sight.

Pham sat on the curb, having observed Mackie's performance. She smiled at him. "What'd you find?"

"Trouble," Mackie said as he helped her to her feet. "Singh's solved the cold storage problem. He's producing military grade H-BOC, and he's shipping it to Fort Detrick."

CHAPTER TWENTY-ONE

THAT SINGH HAD kept secret the newest generation of H-BOC only marginally surprised Mackie, especially since he'd probably violated Mackie's various patent protections in developing the new product. The volume of production of this new generation of H-BOC stunned him. Over three thousand units shipped in each truck. Two trucks at a time. Ten times this month alone. Even if the military paid below market price for the synthetic blood, Singh's company made at least thirty million dollars a month on the military grade product. Probably much more.

"Here's what I don't get," Pham said. "You've got a synthetic blood substitute. Why go through the refrigeration process at all? Don't you obviate the need for preservation when you make your own blood?"

Mackie scrapped the toe of his shoe across the parking lot pavement of Synthesis Industries while he thought about that. "The theory and the technology don't…didn't…match up. In order to create a synthetic product, you need to use real blood."

Pham stared at him for a long moment. "You lost me."

"What's H-BOC stand for?"

"We've been over this," she said. "Hemoglobin-based oxygen carrier."

"Hemoglobin based. That's the key. Hemoglobin grabs onto oxygen in the lungs and spins it off in the tissues. Basic physiology. Red blood cells house four hemoglobin molecules at a time. They also house immune cells that can carry all the bad stuff people hate about blood transfusions. HIV. Hepatitis. Bad actors like that. To make H-BOC, you've got to release the four hemoglobin molecules.

Kind of like sucking the center out of a jelly doughnut and throwing away the doughnut itself."

"Now you're making me hungry," she said. "If you extract a bowl full of jelly and have a mound of discarded doughnut shells, haven't you gotten rid of the biologically active part of the blood?"

"Thirty years ago, that's what we thought," Mackie said. "But it doesn't work that way. If these naked hemoglobin molecules don't remain cold, they fall apart. The jelly turns to juice, microscopically, and the entire product is useless."

"Keep it cold, and it carries oxygen," Pham concluded. "Complicated stuff."

"Right. The hemoglobin jelly is actually made of those four fibers I mentioned, wound together like a hair braid—"

"Disgusting," she said.

Mackie smiled. "Work with me here. You keep the naked hemoglobin cold, add a bunch of chemical preservatives, and you've got a product that won't spoil on the shelf. Works just as well as blood at carrying oxygen. Maybe even better, in some instances." He glanced at Pham. "Let me preempt your next question. The braid of four hemoglobin molecules don't unwind all at once when heated. Just like the jelly won't turn to juice immediately when left out. And in that window between the reheating and the depolymerization—"

"De- what?"

"The unwinding of the molecules. In that moment when the H-BOC is infused, it gets chemically activated in the body and you've got your blood substitute, coursing through a patient's veins, carrying oxygen to starving tissues."

"How did Singh bypass that process to make a heat-stable braid of hemoglobin?" Pham asked.

Mackie nudged her with his elbow. "That's what we're getting ready to find out. Plan C. Come with me."

He guided her along the sidewalk. It ended near the edge of the first building, so they stepped onto asphalt and continued around the perimeter of the property. Toward Pod Two. Following the road toward the loading dock. At this point in the morning, no one loitered outside the building. Mackie watched their reflection in the circular window panes of Pod Two. They were clearly out of place. Mackie pressed on. As they approached the back of the building, a transport truck generated a low rumble from inside the loading dock, coming from an opening wide enough for two trucks in the continuous curve of the building. The pavement fanned into a turnabout so that one truck could wait while the other loaded. The two could pass one another with plenty of space. Efficient and well designed. A passenger van, the same dusty brown as the larger UPS–type trucks, was parked at the far end of the pavement. Empty. They walked down an incline into the loading dock.

Pham slowed her footsteps just before they crossed the threshold of the curved entrance, forcing Mackie to slow down, too. "You know where you're going?" she asked.

"Roughly. I may need your help getting there, though."

No one paid attention to them inside the loading dock. Backed against the building, a refrigerated transport truck similar to the first one Mackie had seen idled as its driver leaned against the front bumper, smoking a cigarette. Two workers in blue coveralls and hairnetsrolled an empty pallet from the cargo bay of the truck back through the thick plastic curtain he'd seen on his first visit. Mackie moved forward, catching the attention of the driver. Pham stepped to the far side of the truck, waiting out of view.

"Dr. Singh wanted me to ask you what time you're leaving?" Mackie called out above the noise.

The man looked at his watch. "Don't have to be out of here for another half hour."

Mackie stepped closer, shaking the man's hand but not introducing himself. "Where's your partner?"

The man dropped his cigarette, crushing the butt under his heel. "Whatcha mean?"

"You guys travel in groups of two, don't you?"

"Not today. I'm heading to the airport. This load gets drop–shipped to Los Angeles this afternoon. I got some time, but I also gotta do two more loads by three o'clock."

Mackie nodded. "You ever drive the East Coast route?"

"Used to, but it's over eight hundred miles. Cheaper to ship it all on cooled cargo planes." He looked at Mackie. "What's Dr. Singh doing sending someone to ask about me?"

Mackie clapped the man on the shoulder. "Quality assurance. I won't mention the cigarette, but keep it away from the loading dock. We've got flammable materials just beyond that door." He left the man leaning against the bumper. He rounded the truck, looking for Pham.

She stood alone at the base of the loading platform. "Get what you need?"

"Almost. What's going on back here?"

"Nothing yet."

Above them, the strips of the plastic partition fluttered at the base of the curtain. Mackie felt cold air seep from the partition into the heat of the loading bay. A row of coveralls hung to the right of the doorway. Mackie glanced at them, then at Pham. "Let's take a quick look inside." He hoisted himself onto the loading dock, pulled Pham up to his side, and grabbed two coveralls similar to the one he'd worn during his tour with Singh. They hurriedly donned the outfits.

"We're stepping off the reservation here, legally," Pham said.

"If anyone asks, Sarathi Singh invited us to his office. We'll work out the details later. Just don't show them your badge."

Mackie glanced into the cargo bay of the truck. No one there. It looked exactly like the one he'd seen out front, except refrigerated. The bottom two shelves had already been filled. Boxes secured. They turned to the entrance of the building, pushing through the plastic barrier. A blast of cold air greeted them.

Workers outfitted in coveralls manned their stations, just as before. No one seemed to notice Mackie and Pham. Mackie crossed the red-tile threshold, leading Pham to the stairwell. "See those kettles at the far side of the room? That's where the hemoglobin is extracted and purified." He pointed to the pipes flowing to additional kettles. "Chemicals are added to stabilize the hemoglobin tetramers."

"The what?"

"The four piece braid of hemoglobin. You've got to put a chemical rubber band on the end of the four hemoglobin molecules to keep them together. Otherwise, they'll fly apart when infused in the patient, regardless of the temperature."

She leaned close, whispering in the relative hush of the production floor. "What happens if the braid comes unraveled?"

"Blood vessel spasm. Kidney failure. Heart attacks. Sometimes death. Stuff that's generally bad for business."

"Gotta have the rubber bands, then." She surveyed the facility, nodding when one of the workers packing boxes looked at them. "I think we're loitering."

"Let's go see if Singh is really gone," Mackie said. He opened the door to the stairwell, heading upstairs. No one greeted them when they arrived on the second floor. They walked down the desolate hallway. Doors closed. Shades drawn. Mackie knocked on Singh's door and jiggled the knob. No response.

"Is it worth looking around inside his office?" Pham asked.

Mackie shook his head. "I've been in there once. There's nothing worth breaking and entering to see again." He paused for a moment to survey the halls, then turned around and headed for the stairs again. Pham followed.

"Research and development is in the basement," he said as they descended the stairwell, his voice echoing off the concrete walls. They passed the ground floor entrance. At the bottom of the staircase, they found a linoleum hallway to their left. Florescent lights buzzed overhead. Mackie followed the hallway, Pham close behind. Within ten yards, they saw a door with a single glass window at eye level. Mackie peered through it, then stepped out of the way to allow Pham a look.

"Similar to upstairs," she said.

"That's what I was afraid of." Mackie pushed on the door, which opened immediately. They walked inside.

Similar to the main floor, large steel kettles and snaking ceiling pipes filled about half the area. Mackie saw two workers clad in protective white jumpsuits, plastic gloves and face masks designed for protection, not insulation. The room felt comfortably warm, even hot. Steam rose from a large metal canister in the rear. Mackie began to sweat in his coverall. Thin sleeves of flat plastic emerged from the far end of the production line, the packaging similar, although flatter and without the condensation he expected from a unit of H-BOC.

"More development than research down here," Pham said.

"I'll be damned," Mackie said. "That son of a bitch figured it out." He inspected the machinery from the entrance. Whatever Singh's epiphany in the development of this new generation of H-BOC, Mackie couldn't discern the answer from inspecting the process itself. If Singh had synthesized the hemoglobin molecules rather than extracting them, Mackie would have expected a different manufacturing layout. Certainly a new additive could have prevented unwinding without cooling, which might explain the similarities. However, it didn't make biologic sense. Mackie needed more information. His forward movement attracted the attention of the worker seated fifteen yards ahead. The man paused at first, obviously unsure of their identity. He spoke to his colleague before getting up from his work station to approach Mackie and Pham. "This is a restricted area, folks. Can I help you?"

Mackie glanced at Pham, then at the man. "Is Mr. Stone here yet?"

"You're not going to find him down here in the basement, sir."

Mackie scratched his head. "Not what he told me. We're from Fort Detrick. Stone said he'd meet us in the production facility. We already checked upstairs."

"You'll need to go back, then," the worker said. "I'll call ahead and have him meet you in the lobby." He reached inside his coverall and withdrew a radio.

"No need. We'll find it on our own." Mackie glanced around, talking fast. "You've finally got the process down. We were wondering when the output here at Synthesis would catch up with our demand. Now that you don't have to worry about keeping everything cool, it looks like your production time is shorter."

The man followed Mackie's gaze. "So far the dehydration doesn't save us any time. In fact, it's the longest part. But that's getting quicker."

Mackie's heart quickened upon hearing the man's words. Choosing his words carefully, he said, "We just take what you give us and get it to the right place." Mackie pointed to far side of the room. "You think this way's easier than the purification?"

The worker chuckled. "They really don't tell you military folks much, do they? The purification's exactly the same. It's the processing afterwards that's different. And a lot easier to ship. You take a unit of H-BOC in powdered form. Not only is it easier to store, you can reconstitute it in the field. Preferably with saline, but we've had good results with purified water. Just got to be careful the water's clear, or else you're gonna strip the veins when it's infused."

Images of Sarah at autopsy flashed in Mackie's mind. Crystalline powder on the skin. Pooling of H-BOC in the heart. Destruction of the jugular vein. His thoughts raced. The autopsy report. Hank's serendipitous arrival in Nashville. The automobile accident. The roadside plastic frame with the Synthesis logo. All tying back to the product directly in front of him. His product. Bastardized and stripped from its patent protection. Sold to the military for millions a month. Anger choked him, squeezed his chest with its unrelenting grip. The worst part, among many bad parts, was that Mackie couldn't stop it. Not here. Not now. And perhaps not at all.

He headed for the end of the production line. "Let me see a unit."

The worker stepped in front of Mackie. "You can't be down here. Y'all head back upstairs. I'll have someone meet—"

Mackie pushed past him, bumping his shoulder. The man stumbled, stunned for a moment. Long enough for Mackie to advance several paces. His head pounded with the reality around him. He heard the crackle of a radio, but he didn't process its significance. He heard Pham call him back, but he neither heeded her words nor stopped his own forward movement. It wasn't until a familiar voice bellowed his name that Mackie snapped out of his trance.

"Cooper, what the hell are you doing down here?"

Mackie froze. Pham turned, clearly not registering the identity of the man. Mackie knew him, though. For the second time that week, and for the third time in as many years, the sound of that voice enraged Mackie. Not just for what he'd done, or for what he represented. Instead, because Mackie felt powerless to stop Hank Stone's wholesale destruction of his life.

The worker hurried forward. "I don't know what to tell you, Mr. Stone. He said he came downstairs to look for you."

Chapter Twenty-Two

"JUST SHUT UP and let me do the talking," Pham said to Mackie as they sat in front of the desk in Hank Stone's office. "He had every right to call the police. We're damn lucky he didn't."

Mackie sipped a bottle of water given to him earlier by Hank's secretary. A circle of steam surrounded Pham's styrofoam cup as it sat on the glass-topped desk. Mackie stared at the steam, not making eye contact with Pham. "I asked you not to show your badge."

"I'm accustomed to asserting my authority when people act like assholes," she said.

"The answer to this entire case was twenty feet in front of me."

"For Christ's sake, Mackie, we were trespassing in the basement. My badge is the only thing that saved you from yourself down there. All I'm asking of you now is that you shut up and let me do my job." She paused, picked up her cup, and blew on the black liquid. She said quietly, "We're on the same team. If your theory is right, the team at Synthesis will be taken care of. Just let the process work."

They sat in silence for the next few minutes. Unlike Singh's cramped office in the upstairs hallway of Pod Two, Hank's office embodied the opulence of the Mother Pod. Sleek curved widows overlooked the second building. Oiled leather furniture. Plush carpeting. His desk, a marble slab polished to an impossible shine, reflected the recessed lights overhead. No stacks of journals or crammed bookshelves. A computer and a cup of pens sat atop the desk. On the credenza, a cordless phone perched near a fax machine. If the office had recently been used for business, all traces of that activity had been wiped clean. This was a space designed to impress.

Hank Stone stepped into his office, immaculately dressed in black slacks and a charcoal shirt that could have been sold as a matching set with the office furniture. Compared to his appearance in Nashville, he was now composed and confident. His jaw muscles clenched as he walked around the desk.

Pham rocked forward in her chair, preparing to stand. Mackie balled his fists in his lap.

"Sit, sit. Both of you." He circled his desk and leaned against the credenza, arms crossed. "The usual process for seeing me in the office is to schedule a meeting with my secretary, Detective Pham. Not trespassing."

"We tried that. The secretary in the lobby brushed us off," Pham said. "Not a very nice woman, by the way."

"Being rude doesn't give you the right to break the law," Hank commented.

"Just like the potential for profits doesn't give a company the right to kill a woman," Pham countered, holding his gaze until he looked away.

A pang of emotion flickered behind Hank's gaze. He started to respond but moved to his desk chair instead. Recomposing himself, he said, "I didn't realize anything had happened until Cooper told me at the park on Saturday." He swallowed hard, turning his attention to Mackie. "This has been devastating for all of us."

Pham set her styrofoam cup on the desktop. "You were in Nashville on the night of the murder," she began, leading him to say more.

Hank shook his head. "I left Atlanta on Wednesday. Met with a client that day and arrived in Nashville on Thursday morning."

"Who was the client?" Pham asked.

Hank pressed his lips together, drawing in air through his nose. "That's not germane to this conversation."

Mackie leaned forward, placing both hands on the desk. "You don't get to decide what is and what is not germane to this investigation, Hank. Answer the damn question."

Hank glared at him for a beat, then looked at Pham. "We have clients across the Southeastern U.S. Across the country, really. And as you discovered this morning, we have an exclusive contract with the U.S. military. Classified, in fact."

"The contract or the product?" Pham asked.

"Both," Hank said. "Your discovery complicates that, but it shouldn't be a surprise to anyone who's followed our progress over the years. I spoke to a military contact on Wednesday, then had a meeting with a hospital administrator on Thursday once I arrived in Nashville."

Pham continued with her investigative agenda. "When did you last talk to Sarah?"

"Wednesday morning. Called her on the drive up. I e-mailed her at the end of the week." He turned back to Mackie while still speaking to Pham. "Apparently after her death, but I didn't know that at the time."

"What did you talk about?" Pham asked.

Hank sat up. "Am I going to need my lawyer?"

"Your choice," Pham said, maintaining her smile. "Cooperate now and save yourself questions later. Or we can press charges, bring you back to Nashville for questioning, and see where it all leads. Either way, until we find the person responsible for the death of Sarah Collins-McKay, you're simply a person of interest. You were the most intimate contact she had."

This time, Mackie winced at the comment, but he didn't speak.

Pham continued. "Your company's synthetic blood product was found in her system. You were not in Atlanta, but apparently not in Nashville, on the night of the murder. The autopsy report indicates that the H-BOC recovered from her body was not a traditional product. The pathologist mentioned some kind of powdered crystals."

Hank took a steadying breath. "Military grade. That's the classified part you discovered. A product similar to the traditional blood substitute but dehydrated into a powder during production. That's where the white crystals originate. Won't spoil. Doesn't have to be refrigerated. It's an advance on an already solid product."

"One that I have patented rights on," Mackie said.

Hank shook his head. "Not this product, Cooper. You may have thought of the idea, but the technology is different." He turned back to Pham. "In order to use the military grade H-BOC, it has to be reconstituted at the scene with saline. I image that if someone got a hold of a unit or two and didn't know what they were doing, it could cause problems with the vessels you've described."

"Who has access?" Pham asked.

Hank shrugged and glanced at Mackie. "Anyone who has contacts in the military. Anyone who has contacts at Synthesis. As you both demonstrated this morning, our security is not as tight as it could be."

"Why the secrecy? There's no real competition in your field, and you've already acknowledged the process," Pham said.

"It's a national security issue," Hank said. "And it has nothing to do with Sarah's death."

"Maybe, maybe not." Pham sat back in her chair. "What did you and Sarah talk about on the day of her death?"

"Excuse me?"

"You mentioned that you talked to her on Wednesday. What did you talk about?"

"The usual stuff," Hank said. "Everything. Nothing. I told her I'd be in town later that week, but she mentioned she had another engagement on Thursday night."

"Did she say what she was doing?" Pham asked. "Not much would trump the arrival of one's future fiancée."

"Cooper told you about that, too." Hank closed his eyes and rubbed his temples with his fingertips. He wiped the corner of his eye with his thumb, before looking at Pham. "She didn't know about the ring. I had planned to surprise her at the park on Saturday morning."

Pham persisted. "Did she say why she couldn't meet with you sooner? Forty-eight hours is a long time to sit in a hotel and wait, isn't it?"

"She had work responsibilities. We both did. That she couldn't meet me for dinner didn't seem unusual. We'd just spent the previous weekend together, taking part in strategic planning for the new product."

"Was Sarathi Singh involved?" Mackie asked.

Hank slowly shook his head at Mackie, a patronizing gesture showing amusement at his persistence. "In spite of what you think, Cooper, that's company business and not relevant to this discussion. Your ex-wife had a professional interest in Synthesis Industries and much of her time in Atlanta directly related to that. There are things Sarah did in Atlanta that had nothing to do with me."

"Like getting paid thirty million dollars for her stake in the H-BOC patents," Mackie snapped.

Hank clenched his jaw, but he remained silent.

Pham softened her approach. "What we're trying to figure out is if Sarah's murder had anything to do with her business interests in Synthesis. Unless you have something to hide, I suggest you let us decide what is relevant or not."

Hank stood. His size eclipsed the sun streaming through the window as he paused to glance at his watch. "We need to wrap this up. I've got a meeting in twenty minutes." He walked around the desk, gesturing for them to follow him toward the door.

Mackie pushed back his chair. Nothing he had heard exonerated Hank, but his admission about the military grade H-BOC stunned him as much as the sheer volume of the new product that Synthesis produced and shipped on a daily basis. He doubted Hank would offer any more details of his time in Nashville the previous weekend, but one questions still nagged at him. "How much contact do you have with Armored Forces Industries?"

Hank stopped. Slowly turning to face Mackie, he dipped his chin to make eye contact with him. "I have no idea what you're talking about."

"They're a major defense contractor in Northern Alabama, less than two hours from here. You're not aware of them?"

"Of course, I've heard of them," Hank said, his words measured. "But AFI has nothing to do with Synthesis Industries."

"You don't remember getting an e-mail from Sarah last week, forwarded from Clark at AFI? Something with a Mickey Mouse attachment?" Mackie asked.

Hank froze. "You're reading her e-mails?"

"Don't pretend to be naive. This is a murder investigation. Law enforcement has had access to her emails since the day she died. What I can't figure out, though, is why AFI would be sending out encrypted holiday greetings in the first place."

Hank forced a laugh. "You're amazing, Cooper. Just because your ex-wife, who happened to be my girlfriend at the time of her death, is mysteriously murdered, doesn't give you the right to know shit about me or my business. If I want to send a picture of Minnie Mouse getting gang-banged by Goofy and his pals, it's none of your damn business." He pointed at Pham. "The two of you have no right to barge in here and sling accusations, fabricating bullshit stories to trash my reputation for no other reason than to deflect attention from yourself." Hank stepped forward, overshadowing Mackie. "I want you off my property in the next five minutes. And rest assured, the next time you set foot in this building, you will need more than Detective Pham's badge to keep you from being hauled out of here by the police."

His secretary poked her head into the office. "Is everything alright?"

Hank stepped back, pressing the palm of his hand against the wrinkles in his shirt. "Please escort Detective Pham and Dr. McKay to the lobby. When you get back, call Dr. Singh and let him know I'll be a few minutes late."

CHAPTER TWENTY-THREE

LEAVING THE GROUNDS, Pham let Mackie drive. After he pulled out of the Synthesis parking lot, he eased the car to the side of the road. He placed the car in park, turned on the hazard lights, and drummed his fingers on the dashboard. The confrontation with Hank had energized him. "I forgot to ask him about the red truck."

Pham said, "I looked while you were playing cop with the shipping truck. Only one parking lot. Plenty of trucks, none red."

"Behind the building?"

"Not there, either."

Mackie's fingers kept pace with his racing thoughts.

Pham finally asked, "What's on your mind?"

"What time does our plane leave?"

"Four-thirty. Eastern time."

Mackie glanced at the dashboard clock. "We've got four hours."

"Three. We can't just breeze through security like we did on the way down." She looked out the window and back at the building. "I wanted to see Singh. I had some questions for him."

Mackie nodded, half listening as he scrolled through the possibilities in his mind. Singh. Hank. Sarah. An unlikely combination to begin with, all tied together by her access to the H-BOC case files and Synthesis's desire to create a superior product. Link that with a classified military contact and thirty million dollars in Sarah's bank account and Mackie concluded that someone had paid her for the patent and then killed her for what she knew. But what did she know? Mackie still didn't understand the reason for the financial transaction. If they intended to kill Sarah, then why pay her the money? They couldn't recover it later. Technically, the money was now a part of Sarah's estate, which meant that it would go to Reagan. And where did AFI fit in? Sarah provided the common thread again, first providing legal work to General Clark in Washington, then shifting that relationship to AFI. After the last two encounters, neither Hank nor Clark would voluntarily answer Mackie's questions. Which left only Singh. A tenuous hope, at best.

Mackie turned to Pham. "Let me see your phone."

She swiped her finger across the touch screen and tapped her password on it. "Decent reception. What do you need?"

Mackie fished Singh's card out of his wallet. Home phone. Cell. And e-mail. "Pull up your Google app and type this in." He read off the home phone number.

Pham entered the information, smiling when she read the screen. "Clever. Where'd you learn that?"

"It's a reverse phone book. Rather than looking up the name to get the home phone and address, if you enter in the number, you get the rest of the information. Unless the person opts out. Obviously, Sarathi didn't."

"This doesn't look that far from here," Pham said. "I'll navigate. You drive."

Mackie turned off the hazards and pulled away from the curve. According to the phone map, Singh lived only ten miles from the office park, but with the traffic lights, turns, and one errant command from Siri, they arrived twenty minutes later. As they entered Singh's neighborhood, pastures replaced pavement.

At the entrance to his street, the road forked. To the left, a gravel road led up a steep incline, apparently leading to a ridge which overlooked the houses. To the right, smooth blacktop and sidewalks. Mackie turned right. The houses spoke of new construction built on large lots. Fenced front lawns and long driveways offered privacy. To their left, a wooded hillside with occasional rock faces gave the feel of a rural community even though Mackie could see the haze of the city over the distant horizon. Half a mile down the road, the map indicated Singh's house. Mackie paused at the driveway entrance.

"Family money?" Pham asked.

"More likely profits from H-BOC." Mackie craned his neck to look at the property. "Sarathi lived in Nashville for five years of his surgical residency. His parents still lived in India at that time. If he came from money, it certainly didn't spill over into his lifestyle then."

"I doubt he'll appreciate a surprise visit," Pham said as she handed her phone to Mackie. "Give him a call before we go barging in."

Mackie dialed the home number. No answer, no machine. He then dialed the cell, which immediately went to voicemail. He didn't leave a message. "Let's take a look around, anyway," he said as he pulled the car into the driveway.

The house sat almost a hundred yards off the road, nestled among a tended lawn and azalea bushes. Adjacent to the wide front porch, the driveway doubled in width, providing ample room for cars to pull forward and turn around. An old silver sports car was parked near the back of the blacktop, across from the double doors of the garage. Mackie positioned their rental next to the older car. He stepped out and inspected its interior. "The last vestige from his Nashville days."

Pham joined him, adjusting the gun in her holster. "First car I bought on my own was a Beamer. Different model, though."

"This is a two-double-oh-two series. Mid-seventies." He smiled at the memory. "Singh bought it during his second year of residency. Financed most of it with moonlighting money then spent his spare time tending to it." Buffed chrome on the bumper sparkled. The leather seats looked recently oiled. Mackie slid his hand across the waxed hood. "It's not like him to leave it out in the open."

"Sounds like he's changed since you worked with him," Pham said. "Front or back door?"

"Front," Mackie said. "The back door route didn't work so well at Synthesis."

They walked to the front porch. Mackie's senses went on alert. Bills and catalogs spilled out of the mailbox. A week's worth of newspapers sprawled around the steps. He bent over and gathered up a few of them. Stepping onto the porch, he rang the doorbell. Like the neighborhood, the house was quiet. Almost abandoned. He waited, his gaze traveling from the expansive front yard to the wooded hillside across the street. Three huge boulders jutted out from the tree line less than a quarter mile away. "Hell of view of Atlanta from up there," he said. "I'm sure it's only a matter of time before someone starts a new development on the hill." Mackie turned his attention back to the door. He rang the bell again.

"You spoke to him last week?" Pham asked.

"Friday." Mackie knocked. No answer. He dropped the newspapers on the welcome mat. Leaning forward to an adjacent window, he saw no movement or lights on when he peered inside. He knocked a final time. No response.

Pham tried the door handle. Locked. No surprise there. "You have a Plan D?"

"Not yet." Mackie descended the porch stairs, traipsing across the lawn to the far side of the house. He weaved between azaleas to get to the front windows, but interior blinds prevented him from seeing inside. Mackie negotiated the remainder of the planter to the edge of the house, but drawn blinds blocked his view in each window. He stepped onto the grass and returned to the front walkway. He stopped when he saw Pham standing in the driveway. "What's wrong?"

"We've got a problem," she said.

Mackie looked around, expecting to see someone else.

Pham motioned for him to join her. "Take a look."

He followed her around the corner. Two wide garage doors separated by a single walkthrough door. He cupped his hands around his eyes and pressed them against the glass of the second garage door. Even in the darkness of the carport, he saw enough detail. His stomach clenched and nausea swirled. The taste of bile lingered even after he swallowed. "That son of a bitch!"

"Does that match what you saw?" Pham asked.

He nodded, too enraged to speak as he stared at the gouge in the passenger side of the truck, streaks of bare metal scarring the red paint.

He stepped back, leaning against the door. His heart galloped as adrenalin surged. He heard the sound of the crash, Reagan screaming, and he felt the warm blood on his forehead. Mackie fought his visceral response. Tried to redirect his raging emotions. Needing action. Seeking a means by which to exact penance.

He inhaled, deeply, then pushed off the garage door. "I need a closer look."

Pham pulled out her phone. "Let me call for back up first."

Mackie didn't wait. He jiggled the doorknob. The handle was

locked but not the deadbolt. The door moved slightly back and forth as he jerked on it. Mackie slammed his shoulder into the door. Pain shot through his arm but the door didn't open.

"What the hell are you doing?"

Mackie again drove his shoulder against the door. Wood splintered. The handle gave way. The door opened.

"That's breaking and entering," Pham said.

"Do you have jurisdiction in Atlanta?" he asked.

"I've got probable cause for a search warrant. It can be arranged," she said.

"And by the time you get what you need, Singh will be home and the truck will be gone." Mackie ran his fingers across the doorjamb, flattening the splintered wood with his thumb. He reached around to unlock the handle, then he closed the door. The knob still lined up with the door frame. Mackie turned the handle and opened the door. "Looks like it's unlocked. Simple trespassing. I think that's a lesser charge." He stormed in the garage. Pham shoved her phone in her pocket and followed him.

The interior could accommodate two cars, but one bay sat empty. Mackie clicked on the overhead light and approached the truck. The hood showed a dent above the front wheel, probably from the first hit. Streaks of grey from Reagan's car etched along the front fender. The second impact had crushed the passenger door, jamming it into the doorframe. Jagged black plastic jutted from the passenger door where the side mirror had been. As he walked to the back of the car, he saw the bent license plate surrounded by a partial plastic frame. Mackie seethed as he turned around.

The rest of the garage looked unremarkable. Yard tools lined the back walls next to a small work bench. An improbably clean shovel hung on the wall beside a rake with the manufacturer's tag still attached, like forgotten house warming gifts. An old refrigerator hummed in the corner. Mackie opened its door. Inside sat a six-pack of Bud Lite longnecks. A half gallon of milk, expired. A plastic butter tub. He peeked inside the freezer, finding two frozen pizzas.

Pham peered over Mackie's shoulder. "Lives alone?"

"Probably." Mackie closed the freezer door. The longer he stared at the red truck, the faster his heart thrummed. Mackie had to adjust his breathing to slow it. "I don't get it."

"The motivation?"

Mackie shook his head. "The betrayal. What the hell did I ever do to him to deserve this?"

"Owned a part of something that he wanted and couldn't get. You guys were friends, but that was a long time ago. More often than not, greed trumps loyalty."

"It just pisses me off." Mackie glowered as he walked to the back door of the house. The full sized truck didn't leave much space to maneuver, but he squeezed past the front bumper. He tried the doorknob. It turned, but the door wouldn't open. No way he could smash his way through a deadbolted door.

"Wipe your prints off that handle, then let's go eat," Pham said. "I can arrange for a warrant while you drive."

"Hold on." Mackie looked under the doormat. Nothing. Turning to the workbench, he inspected it for any small container that appeared to be out of place. Nothing. He rummaged through the tool chest as Pham watched him. Yet again, nothing. Mackie scanned the entire garage before heading back to the refrigerator. He opened the freezer compartment. Same old pizza boxes. He reopened the refrigerator side and picked up the butter tub. Lighter than it should have been. Something rattled inside when he shook it. "Bingo."

Inside the butter container, he found, wadded up in a paper towel, a single key. Mackie returned to the back door, inserting the key into the deadbolt. Perfect. He unlocked the door. Just before he opened it, Pham grabbed his arm.

"Two issues here," she said. "Number one, it's trespassing."

Mackie released the knob. "Easily explainable. A close friend is missing. That friend's concerned neighbor happens upon the key and decides to check on him. Legally, I think we're good on number one."

"Possibly. But that doesn't change number two." She looked above him to the top of the door.

A small black box no larger than a crayon was fastened to the door frame. A thin wire protruded into the molding of the door.

"Where's the keypad to disarm it?" he asked.

"Probably inside. When you open the door, you'll break the circuit, activating the timer. Standard security systems give you about thirty seconds to enter your code. Afterwards, the alarm activates and the police are called."

Mackie studied the circuit. "What are the chances he didn't activate the alarm?"

Pham shrugged. "Fifty-fifty." She reached into her wallet and removed a thin piece of metal from behind her license. One side shiny, the other side dark. Reaching up to the top of the door, she slipped the metal sheet between the groove in the circuit and the door. Holding the metal with one hand, she turned the door knob with the other. It opened. No alarm. A black cat scurried outside and into the garage. The metal hung from the small box, maintaining the circuit.

"Nice! Okay, five minutes," he said to her.

Pham hesitated. She glanced at the red truck, then back at Mackie. "Not a minute more," she cautioned.

"Set your watch. Tell me when my time's up, and we're gone." He crossed the threshold into the house.

A mud room greeted them. Dirty boots and a torn windbreaker crumpled in the corner. A washer and dryer to one side. Next to it, a basket of unfolded laundry. Mackie turned right into the kitchen. Bare formica counters. Black appliances. Empty red walls. At the base of the refrigerator, a scratch on the hardwood floors. Mackie wondered if Singh ever used this room. They moved into the adjoining den. Functional furniture faced a mounted flat screen. It looked like Singh had opened up a magazine and ordered it all to fit the space, ignoring the accents and accoutrements of the display. The room felt empty. No personality. Nothing to identify the space as uniquely his.

Pham ran her hand across the leather chair as she inspected the room. "Not much for decorating, is he?"

"He's married to his job," Mackie said. "I doubt he does more than sleep here."

"I'm going to check out the front rooms," she said.

Mackie approached the windows. Off the deck, pool water rippled under the afternoon breeze. Like the rest of the house, it appeared well kept by lack of use. He found few, if any, answers as he studied the lay-out. About ready to leave, he heard Pham shout.

Mackie ran in the direction of her voice. Down a small hallway. On one side, a dining room. Empty. Mackie crossed the foyer. Pham stood in a shadow-darkened room. She stared at what appeared to be a table full of body parts.

"What in God's name are these?" she asked.

Mackie squinted, allowing his eyes to adjust to the dim lighting. Arranged along two sides of the study, banquet tables displayed a series of metal joints. Along one wall, five models of a synthetic knee were propped against individual display stands, as though taken from an orthopedic trade show. The other table displayed six additional prostheses. Artificial hips. Mackie moved closer. He noticed a specific arrangement of the joints. To one side, the prosthetic components shined with stainless steel and ceramic. In subsequent joints, the appearance of the metal changed. Mackie smiled as he looked at the arrangement.

"What's so amusing?" Pham asked. "This reminds me of tokens from a serial murderer."

"Singh's first love," Mackie said. He clicked on the desk lamp, lifted one of the prosthetic knee joints, and showed Pham. "Part of his training at Nashville Memorial involved joint replacements. Standard practice for all orthopedic residents. Singh had a gift for understanding the possibilities of synthetic joints. He spent the first part of his career in the O.R., mostly replacing hips. Gave all of that up to work for Synthesis, but looks like he never abandoned his fascination with the technology."

Pham surveyed the display of joints. "This is some kind of a timeline then?"

"It shows the changing technology of joint replacements over several decades. Ceramic. Stainless steel. Metal alloys. They've all been tried at one time or another, until a newer version comes along." Mackie set the prosthetic knee back in its place and picked up another one. "He actually invested in this one. I did, too. Indirectly." He held it up for Pham to see.

"Why indirectly?" she asked.

"I gave him the time to do it. Near the end of his residency, he participated in clinical trials for a prosthetic joint company. New Horizon Prosthetics, or something like that. One of the faculty members in the Division of Orthopedic Surgery agreed to participate in a clinical trial, using New Horizon's joint replacements. He brought Singh on as a co-investigator. He was supposed to be working with me during that last six-month block of his training, but I allowed him to switch his schedule to participate in the trial," Mackie said. "The company ultimately filed for bankruptcy. Some safety concern with the joints. But by then, Singh had graduated and moved his part of the clinical trails to Atlanta with him." He set the prosthetic joint back on the table, slowly shaking his head. "A lot's changed since then."

"Look at this." Pham handed him a paper from Singh's desk. Printed on it, a map of the Nashville airport. Written in Singh's hand on the bottom of the page, a flight number and time. "Reagan's flight?"

Mackie heart rate accelerated again, his stomach knotting. He paced like a marathoner before a race. Pent up energy. No release. Mackie wanted to act, but all he could do was stare at evidence and speculate about what happened. He grumbled to himself, "That damn son of a... How would he know that? Her flight changed three times."

The sound of a car pulling into the driveway cut him off.

Both he and Pham looked at each other. "Did you shut the back door?"

"Shit." Pham darted into the foyer.

Mackie shoved the airport map into his pocket, then clicked off the desk lamp.

Pham peered through the front door window. "I can't see the car from here," she said, her voice tight, pressured.

Mackie crossed the foyer into the darkened dining room. Shades drawn. He strained to hear voices, but no one spoke. All he heard was the muffled sound of a slamming car door.

CHAPTER TWENTY-FOUR

MACKIE LEANED CLOSER to the blinds that shielded him from the car, concentrating on the sounds in the driveway. He resisted the impulse to crack the shutters, fearing he might expose his position inside. As if their rental car and the open back door wouldn't expose them anyway. He thought of Pham's metal contraption bypassing the security system. No way to easily explain away that. At this point, he hoped the unexpected arrival represented another guest who wouldn't know their rental car seemed out of place. Singh home early from lunch? He hoped not.

Pham glided into the dining room. She peered out the front window, then shook her head in frustration. Neither one of them could see what they most needed to know.

Mackie motioned to Pham that he would walk into the kitchen to close the door. At least he remembered closing the garage door behind him the second time he opened it, which should buy him enough time to lock up and hunker down in the mud room.

Pham stepped beside Mackie, whispering in his ear. "I'm going out the front door. Lock it behind me, then go to the kitchen and wait. Party line is this: I was walking around the house when they arrived, whoever they are. Alone. If they ask, I had probable cause to search outside based on the truck. Wait for me to come back inside through the garage." She gripped his shoulder. "Let me handle this."

When they turned to walk out of the dining room, Mackie heard voices. More than one. Getting closer. Pham paused before entering the foyer. Two men with southern accents laughing about something as they walked along the front path. Directly in front of the dining room. Mackie placed a hand on Pham's waist, shoving her out of view.

"Let me—" she began. She didn't finish.

Footsteps ascended the front porch steps.

"Down," Mackie whispered.

He slid along the dining room wall adjacent to the front windows. Pham squeezed in next to him. She unclipped her pistol, gripping it in her right hand. She whispered to Mackie, "If they come inside, I do the talking."

Mackie listened. One set of footsteps on the porch. He couldn't hear the other man, but he didn't risk peeking through the shutters. The man on the front porch stepped forward. Four quick raps on the door. Mackie's heart pounded in his throat.

"You seen anything?" a muffled voice called out from the front yard.

"Too dark to see much," the first man said. He sounded like he was in the next room. The door knob rattled. The thump of his footsteps grew louder as he crossed the porch directly in front of them.

Another set of footstep on the front porch. "Don't make no sense. I swear to you there was a light on when we got here."

"Maybe it's on a timer."

Pham squeezed Mackie's arm, simultaneously stroking the grip of her gun with her thumb.

The door handle jiggled once more.

"Ain't nobody inside," the first man said. "I already tried the door. It's locked."

"Dr. Singh said there'd be one car in the driveway and one in the garage. Where'd that other one come from?"

The first man laughed derisively. The sound receded along with his shadow as he walked away from the window and down the front steps. "Not my problem. I get paid to load the trucks and make deliveries. Let's unload this stuff in the garage and leave before everybody else gets here."

The door shook once more before the second man grunted and descended the stairwell.

Mackie darted through the small hallway. He could see into the kitchen. The door stood wide open. He sprinted across the floor, grabbing the doorknob with both hands and easing it shut. Mackie squatted below the window of the back door, then scooted out of view and back to the front of the house. Pham stood in the hallway, her gun drawn. "Back door's closed," Mackie said. "I'm going out the front. Same plan."

"Don't."

"We're running out of time."

Pham shook her head. "Let them finish whatever they came here to do."

"And stand by while a crime is being committed?" He reached for the door knob.

"What crime are these two guys committing?"

"They're involved in..." He paused.

"My point exactly. Involved in what? The only two people on the property committing a crime right now is us." Pham lowered her voice as she edged into the dining room. "I want to find out what's going on as much as you do. Getting these two guys involved is only going to slow that process down."

They heard the low groan of a motor outside, followed by the clacking of the metal garage door. Mackie glanced at Pham. "They have a key?"

"Sounds like it," she said.

They both crept across the dining room, toward the side windows that overlooked the driveway. Mackie pressed his ear to the drawn shutter, listening. He heard footsteps. Then, silence. Neither man spoke.

Mackie squatted down at the base of the window, concentrating on the sounds outside. He heard the rhythmic pace of the two men walking back and forth, unloading something. Mackie inched apart the bottom two slats of the blinds. In the driveway sat a dusty brown cargo van, backed toward the house with its doors open. Probably the same van he had seen parked in the back of Synthesis earlier that day. Behind the van, Singh's silver BMW. And their rental car.

One of the men came into view, walking out of the garage empty-handed. He reached inside the bay of the van, pulled out a box, and hauled it out of sight. Presumably into the garage. Moments later, the second man did the same.

Mackie watched them hurry to unload their cargo. He studied their faces, but neither man looked familiar.

Pham squatted next to him, eyebrows raised. Mackie leaned

back, holding the blinds slightly open. She looked for a moment, then leaned back, too. "H-BOC?" she whispered.

"Probably." Mackie slid the slat back into place and stood up. "It's almost time to go."

He crept back to the kitchen, hearing the automatic garage door close. Moments later, the van doors slammed shut. Pham walked in the kitchen just as the engine started. Mackie waited for it to pull down the driveway before opening the back door. He looked up at the metal affixed to the alarm system, hanging from the top of the door like a black credit card.

Mackie stepped into the garage, Pham right behind him. A stack of boxes filled the once-empty carport beside the red truck. Like the boxes he had seen earlier, each displayed the Synthesis Industries logo stenciled on the side. He squeezed around the fender of the truck to take a closer look. Instead of a shipping label attached to the top, each bore the letters: A-F-I.

Pham asked, "Any reason a military contractor would need a supply of H-BOC?"

Mackie didn't answer. He picked up one of the boxes. Just a couple of pounds. Lighter than he would have expected, even for the powdered military grade H-BOC. He slid a box from the top of the stack. Shook it. Something rustled inside. Mackie reached into his wallet, withdrew a credit card, and slid it under the edge of the tape, then down the center of the box. It split open along the taped seam. He pulled back the box and stared inside at bricks of one hundred dollar bills. "Not H-BOC," he said.

Stuffed around the side of the box, Mackie found wadded up newspaper supporting the bricks of money. He lifted individual bundles of bills, counting ten in all. He glanced at Pham. "A hundred thousand dollars."

"Times ten boxes from Synthesis." Pham gazed at the money. "What did AFI do to receive a million dollar kickback—in cash—from Synthesis?"

"We'll find out soon." Mackie crammed the bundled cash back inside, placed the box in the middle of the stack, and slid another box over it to conceal the split tape. "You ready to go?"

"We've got to lock up," Pham said.

Mackie looked at the back door, still ajar with the black metal card maintaining the circuit. "Go start the car, and I'll be right out."

"Make sure the door is fully shut before you remove the metal," Pham said. "Otherwise, you'll set off the alarm."

Mackie smiled. "I've got it under control."

Pham left the garage while Mackie walked around the red truck. He waited, listening for Pham to start the car. As soon as she did, Mackie held the inside door knob with his shirt tail covering it, wiping off prints. Once finished, he repeated the process for the outside knob. He then grabbed the metal card above the doorframe. With coordinated precision, he jerked on the metal, breaking the circuit. He heard the beep of the alarm. Smiling, he shut the door behind him and locked it. Thirty more seconds, he thought, then the fun begins.

Mackie hurried out of the garage and into the waiting car.

Chapter Twenty-Five

PHAM SPED DOWN the driveway. "You did what?"

"I just called for backup. Indirectly," Mackie said from the passenger seat. "Take a left up here, then a hard right at the entrance to the subdivision. There's a gravel road that should take us to the hillside that overlooks the neighborhood."

With no other cars on the street in sight near Singh's house, Pham accelerated. She tapped the brakes at end of the street, then jerked the steering wheel right and onto the unpaved road. Gravel pinged off the undercarriage of the rental car. "How far?"

"About a half a mile. Give or take." Mackie leaned forward. The tree canopy, along with the overgrowth along the side of the road, cast shadows ahead of them. Mackie pictured the three rock faces jutting from the hillside that he'd seen from Singh's front porch. If they could reach one of them, they should be able to observe any activity at Singh's house from a safe distance. He would love to be able to see Singh's expression when the police started asking questions about the truck. And the money.

Pham gripped the steering wheel as she negotiated the uneven grade of the road. Packed dirt replaced gravel. Glancing at the odometer, she slowed the car, looking for any landmarks.

"What's in your carry-on bag?" Mackie asked. "Besides your gun."

"Change of clothes. Pair of binoculars. Extra bullets and a tooth brush." Pham cut her gaze to the dashboard clock, then back to the road. "Our flight leaves in two hours."

"I brought a book for the plane and a camera with a telephoto lens," he said. "I should've taken it into Singh's house."

Pham eased the car to the side of the road. "I wouldn't have done it this way, but if your stunt works, we probably won't need any photographs. We may have enough evidence to get a search warrant with what we've seen and the police discover. Photos would have been nice, but they'd pose a number of tough questions. At least, for me."

Pine straw covered the edge of the road, dipping into a gully. Pham killed the engine. Reaching into the back seat, she opened her gun case. She pulled out two extra clips of bullets and her binoculars. She checked her gun, holstered it, and shoved the clips into her pants pocket.

"Probably leave the toothbrush in the car." Mackie climbed out onto the shoulder, opening the back door to get to his bag. He turned on the camera, checked the battery life, then slung the strap around his neck. The weight of the telephoto lens caused the camera to hang awkwardly to his side when he bent over to retie his shoes. He pointed to a dirt path that led directly into a bramble thicket. "Should be straight this way."

They walked for several minutes, stepping over stumps and around fallen trees. Thorny vines grabbed at his pants. Mackie jerked his leg free, ripping the hem. Pham walked closely behind him. Mackie shivered under a cool breeze. Too hot for a jacket in the sun, too cool to be without one in the shade. They navigated the edge of the hillside. About twenty yards from the clearing, the dirt path curved right. Mackie paused to re-orient himself. When he did, he heard sirens in the distance. He smiled.

"Can you see it yet?" Pham asked.

Mackie shook his head, then turned left off the path. "Should be this way." The sirens grew louder. He took high steps over the debris of the forest, blazing a new trail. Using the light of the clearing as a guide, Mackie maintained a straight line through the underbrush. Thirty yards ahead, he saw it.

Pham came up beside him. "That boulder looks smaller from up here."

"There was more than one." Mackie picked his way forward. At the edge of the clearing, a slab of rock the size of kitchen table jutted out from the hillside. Mackie squatted down. His knees ached, so he shifted onto his stomach and stretched out across the rock.

Situated above the subdivision, they could see most of the

houses in Singh's neighborhood, each built facing the hill with expansive back yards beyond. Singh's property appeared even more impressive from afar, although at an awkward angle. He saw the front porch and the right side of the house near the study. The rock, positioned at the entrance to the subdivision, obscured any view of the garage or Singh's BMW. Mackie watched with satisfaction as two police cars, lights flashing, drove down the driveway.

Pham reached for her binoculars. Mackie craned his neck for an improved view, but all he saw was the trunk of the second unit. "Any one else there?" he asked.

Pham shook her head. "Can't see much from this angle?"

Mackie pushed up from his position, studying the terrain. Not far to his left, he noticed another rock sticking out of the hillside. Bigger. Better angle. He stood. "We didn't go far enough," he said. "I'm going over to the next one."

Mackie picked his way through the underbrush, Pham close on his heels. He tried to walk along the ridge, but brambles and boulders diverted him. The next ledge was close enough to hit with a thrown rock, but it took them several minutes to reach it. At one point, they dipped back into the trees, away from the edge. A small ravine split the hillside with a fallen log as the only clear path to the other side.

Pham waited while Mackie traversed the log, balancing himself as he gripped his camera in one hand. He tried not to look down, but couldn't help himself. Even with the shadows of the tree canopy, he could clearly see jagged rocks at the base of the ravine. He eased forward ten feet before reaching the other side. He looked ahead. A straight shot to their destination.

Pham gave him a thumbs-up. "See if you've got a good view before I break my neck following you."

Mackie approached the ledge, squatted down, and stretched out on his belly. He felt less exposed now. And he had an unobstructed view of Singh's house. Police officers strolled about the property. One peered though the garage window. A car slowed on the road, turning into the driveway. Probably Singh. Mackie needed the binoculars. "Come on over," he whispered to Pham, gesturing with his arm. "The view's perfect."

Mackie lifted camera to take a closer look though the telephoto lens. Just as he removed the strap from around his neck, he heard

Pham gasp. Mackie whirled around, bounded up from his position, and raced back to the log. Pham squatted in the middle of the log, her entire body shaking. She managed a smile when she saw Mackie. "Foot slipped."

He walked to the edge of the log to help her across. "You okay?"

"I'm fine," she said, taking his hand. She slide-stepped her way to the other side, never taking her feet off the log. "Not so much with the binoculars, though."

Mackie looked down into the ravine. Shattered glass sparkled like gemstones on the rock shards below. He turned back to Pham. "Aren't you supposed to be the one who's in shape for this kind of stuff?"

Pham dusted off her pants with still trembling hands.

"You sure you're okay?"

"I will be."

Mackie waited for her to compose herself. "There's a good view from up here." He guided her to the ledge where he'd left his camera. Keeping low, Mackie crept to the edge of the rock face. Pham eased into the position beside him.

The third car pulled to the side of a police cruiser and parked. Even though he and Pham had an unobstructed view of the driveway, Mackie removed the camera's lens cap and focused on the man climbing out of the third vehicle. He saw the boxy body with dark hair march up to one of the officers. Definitely Singh. He crossed the yard to the front door, unlocked it, and stepped inside. Moments later, he stepped back outside, shutting the door behind him. "Turning off the alarm?" Mackie asked, his nose still pressed to the viewfinder of the camera.

Pham squinted. "Probably."

Singh returned to the driveway. For the next few minutes, he spoke to both police officers, gesturing with his hands to the garage and the front of the house. The officers finally shook his hand and climbed back into their cruisers. A minute later, both were gone.

"No! That's not procedure, is it?" Mackie asked.

"Sure. Owner comes home, disables the alarm. Probably blames the cat. No reason for them to go inside."

"So much for Plan D," Mackie said.

He lifted himself from the rock, but Pham placed a hand on his arm before he could stand up. "Look over there."

Driving down the road, opposite the police officers, two more cars approached Singh's house. A black Suburban. And a desert-brown Humvee. Both turned into his driveway. Singh leaned against his car, arms crossed, obviously expecting them. The Humvee pulled in first, parking next to the BMW. The Suburban followed, turned around where the driveway fanned out before backing up to the garage door. Exactly as the cargo van had a half hour earlier. Two men in dark glasses and desert BDUs stepped out of the Humvee. They approached the black Suburban. Both car doors opened simultaneously. From the driver's side, out stepped Hank Stone. Mackie turned to Pham. "Look who's here." When he turned around to take one more look through the camera, he saw a thick-bodied man with silver hair step out of the passenger side. General Haywood Clark.

"And look who else," Mackie mumbled, handing the camera to Pham.

She edged closer to him. She tried to adjust the lens, but her elbow kept knocking into her holster. She unclipped her gun and handed it to Mackie. "Hold this for a second." Using the telephoto lens, she watched the men move about the property.

Mackie held the gun. He followed their movements, although he couldn't pinpoint individual details. He did recognize the principals from his position. Singh reached inside his car to press the garage door opener. The doors rolled up on their tracks. Mackie couldn't see the cardboard boxes from where he sat, but the other four men clearly could. Two soldiers from the Humvee walked behind their vehicle, obviously guarding the general and his interests. "What kind of guns are those?" he asked.

Pham adjusted the lens. "Military assault rifles."

With both guards in place, Singh led Hank and General Clark into the carport, all three disappearing from view.

Pham lowered the camera. "Help me walk through this scenario. Synthesis discovers the holy grail of blood substitutes when they learn how to make powdered H-BOC. They get a huge military contract, probably using Sarah as a go-between thanks to her earlier relationship with Clark during his time in Washington. She gets a fat payoff for her share of the patent and the General gets a finder's fee for greasing the deal with the military. One million dollars in cash."

Mackie faced Pham, resting the gun in front of him. "He brings big guys with guns to Atlanta to protect his investment. Plausible. Sarah's eventual murder doesn't make much sense to me, though."

"Sure it does. She sells patent rights to Synthesis—"

"Which should have terminated her relationship with the company."

Pham thought about this. "I see your point. She should be out of the picture by then."

"We assume Hank didn't killed her." Mackie glanced back at the house. None of the three had emerged from the garage yet. The guards stared at the road. "Hank had already planned to be in Nashville to ask Sarah to marry him. If she'd dead, he loses his bid on thirty million dollars."

Pham considered this. "So Singh did it?"

"Possibly, although he seems a bit small to inflict the kind of damage on her body." He repositioned himself, gazing at the armed men on Singh's property. "Clark could have killed her and then dispatched Singh to Nashville to take care of Reagan and me. If that's the case, someone screwed up the timing. Hank needed to be married first. Cold-hearted bastard."

Pham handed the camera to Mackie. "A tenuous connection. Too many assumptions to sit well with me. I still think we're missing something."

Mackie set the gun down and lifted the camera. Hank emerged from the garage carrying one of the Synthesis boxes. Singh followed close behind, opening the back of the Suburban for him. He began to load the boxes. Both guards went on alert when the loading began. Guns raised. Scanning their surroundings.

Mackie snapped several pictures of the guards, then a few more of Hank as he loaded a box. When he checked the screen, the digital images clearly showed several men in the driveway, but the resolution lacked precision. He would have to hope they could zoom in when he downloaded the pictures. He focused the lens once more. Singh carried a box, followed by Hank again. Clark emerged from carport, inspecting the process.

After a few more photographs, Pham tapped him on the arm. "My turn."

Mackie handed her the camera, picked up the handgun, and watched her fiddle with the dials. "You know what you're doing?"

"We've got one similar to this at work." She looked through the view finder, snapped a few shots, and then checked the images. "A little dark." She adjusted the settings once again.

Singh and Hank continued to disappear into the garage empty handed and to emerge with boxes of money.

"See if you can get a shot with all three of them in it." Mackie absentmindedly stroked the trigger while he watched.

Pham finished her adjustments and lifted the camera, cradling it in one hand while focusing the lens with the other. Clark stepped over to watch the final two boxes being loaded. Pham pressed the button on the camera. When she did, a flash of light assaulted Mackie's eyes. He jerked his hands, squeezing the trigger. Two quick shots rang out.

Pham jerked the camera away from her face. "What'd you just do?"

"I didn't mean to—"

Pham yanked the gun from him. "We're compromised. Scoot back. Now!"

In the moment it took Mackie to move, the guards raised their guns. Tree bark splintered on the hillside, followed almost immediately by a rifle report. Staccato bursts from the direction of Singh's house. Pham dropped the camera and rolled to her left. She pressed her back to the edge of a tree, optimizing cover without losing sight of the gunman. She pointed the gun at the house. More gunfire sounded from Singh's house. "I'm not going to hit a damn thing from this distance," Pham said, her voice tight with anxiety.

Bark rained down on Mackie. Immediately to his right, pine straw and dust kicked up.

"Move!" Pham yelled.

Mackie grabbed the camera. He scooted backward farther into the tree cover before pushing off the ground. He sprinted to the log.

Pham ran up behind him, holstering her gun. "Go, go, go!"

Another rifle shot cracked in the distance.

"Now." She pushed Mackie forward.

Slinging the camera over his back, he stepped onto the slick log. He glanced at the smashed binoculars as he balanced his way across the ravine. Two more shots. He reached the other side of the log. He turned to look at Pham, but she motioned him forward. Mackie stepped into the thick underbrush, cutting across the woods in the most direct route to the car. He couldn't see the road from his position, but he had a general idea of his destination. He picked up his pace.

Then, Pham screamed.

Mackie whirled around. "Libby?"

No answer.

He sprinted back, stumbling through the debris. When he broke free of the thicket, he heard her panting. Rapid. Panicked. He rushed to the ravine and saw her gripping the log on either side. She hung on from underneath, dangling. With one hand Pham grabbed for a better hold on the log, but the bark gave way.

"Shit," she groaned, her grip white-knuckled. "Can't grab it."

"Hold on." Mackie stepped onto the log. The tree groaned under their combined weight. Mackie squatted and then stretched out, reaching for her with his left hand. The camera dangled on his right, off-balancing him. He wrapped his legs around the wood to stabilize himself. "Give me your hand."

"I can't let go." Panic shimmered in her voice. She tried to swing her leg over the log, but only succeeded in kicking off more bark. Her fingers began to slide.

"Kick your leg toward me," Mackie said.

Pham clawed at the log, her grip slipping even more.

Mackie stretched out. He slid the camera off his shoulder and wrapped the strap around his wrist, a loop forming where the strap hung limp. "Kick again."

Pham flung her leg up. One hand slipped free of the log. Mackie looped the strap around her foot and yanked. He pinned her leg underneath the log, freezing her kick while reaching for her free hand. She groped for his hand, but her other one slipped off. Mackie lunged forward, slamming his chest into the log. He grabbed the top of her jacket, stopping her fall. With her ankle in one hand and and the back of her jacket in the other, Mackie leaned back, prying his stomach off the log, as he slowly lifted Pham.

She wrapped her arms around the log. With Mackie's help, she flipped herself atop it. As she gasped for breath, he freed her foot from the camera strap. They both inched backwards. His feet encountered solid ground, then his torso. He guided Pham to the edge, and she flopped onto the ground beside him.

"I almost dropped…" she managed, trying to catch her breath.

Mackie stood, dusted off, and reached for her. "We've got to get out of here."

Mackie blazed a path through the trees. Pham limped behind him. He plowed through the bramble. Minutes later, they burst into the clearing of the dirt road. Thirty yards away, their car sat on the side of the road. They sprinted for it.

"You okay to drive?" Mackie asked.

Pham collapsed into the driver's seat. "Just help me turn around."

Mackie looked out the back window. "No way. We've got to head in the opposite direction. They're going to follow the gun shot."

The engine roared to life when she turned the ignition. Mackie clicked his seatbelt as Pham put the car in gear and peeled off the shoulder. The tires spun on the pine straw, rocks ricocheting off the undercarriage. She took her foot off the accelerator, backed up a few feet, then slammed the gear into drive. When she stomped on the accelerator, the car rocketed forward down the dirt road.

Mackie steadied himself with a hand on the passenger door. "Road probably cuts across the top of the mountain. There's a good chance it connects up at the far end of the neighborhood street below."

Pham glanced at the clock on the dashboard. "Not much extra time. If this road dead ends, we're screwed." She continued to jam down on the accelerator. The rental car rocked between dirt furrows in the road.

Mackie looked behind him. No other cars he could see. The road cut a straight path across the mountain top, which should have made it easy to see any approaching cars. Then, something caught his attention.

Headlights bounced at the far end of the road where the hill flattened out. Easier to see with shadows of the tree canopy. A vehicle crested the hill. The Humvee. A half mile behind them. And closing.

"Speed up," Mackie said. "And don't tap your brakes. They're behind us." He unclipped his seatbelt to get a better view from the back window.

Headlights bobbed from the uneven road. The Humvee closed the distance. Relentless.

Pham glanced in the rearview mirror. "Half a mile back?"

"Less. They're more suited to driving on these roads."

Pham moved the car toward the shoulder, searching for more stable ground. Maintaining her speed, she avoided using the brakes. She checked the mirror again. "They're gaining on us."

The sound of the engine got louder.

Pham stepped on the accelerator. The car took off again, careening off the rocks and ruts in the road. For a moment, it appeared as if the approaching car had pulled back. But then the headlights came closer. Mackie faced forward, refastening his seatbelt, which tightened with each bounce of the car. Pham leaned against the steering wheel, gripping it with both hands. The road began to slope down hill. Toward the neighborhood.

They heard the vehicle getting closer.

When Mackie looked over his shoulder, Pham slammed on the brakes. He flew toward the dashboard. The seatbelt yanked him back. "What the hell are you doing?" he asked.

"Roadblock."

Ahead, three orange barricades crossed the road. "Drive around it to see what's there," Mackie said.

Pham eased onto the shoulder, pulling up to the cones. The road dipped downward, then dropped off into a gully. A dead end. The mossy turn around on the shoulder appeared flattened from previous use. Beyond it, another thicket of underbrush. Pham turned the car around. Because of the slope of the road, they couldn't see the approaching Humvee.

Mackie rolled down the passenger window. "Keep the car running but put it in park. Give me your gun."

"No. Too dangerous. For both of us."

Mackie persisted.

Pham said, "You think you can take on military assault rifles with a handgun?"

He released his seatbelt. "Roll down your window and push your seat all the way back." He grabbed the gun from Pham. Except for the earlier mishap that got them into this mess, it had been years since he'd fired one. He assumed the skills he needed now would return once he started firing. He helped Pham with her seat, then lowered the passenger window. They heard the Humvee slow, close enough to appreciate the sound of gravel crunching underneath its tires. "Put the car in low gear," he whispered. "When I tell you, I want you to step on the gas."

"I can't see a thing from down here," she said.

"Doesn't matter. Just drive straight. Hug the right side of the road. And don't hit their car."

Headlights peered over the top of the hill. The engine slowed.

"Damn it, Mackie, we can't just sit here and wait for them to see us." Pham shifted into gear.

"Get ready," he said. "On the count of three. One..."

She moved her left foot to the brake, sliding her right one to the accelerator.

The Humvee stopped. Its engine idled as a door opened.

"Two..."

Mackie heard two men talking. He didn't recognize either voice. He waited. When he saw the shadows of the men crossing in front of the headlights, his hand began to sweat beneath the grip of the gun. He wiped his palm on his pants, re-gripped the gun, and leaned out the passenger window.

"Three!" Mackie yelled.

Pham smashed the gas pedal to the floor. The car's back tires spun on the wet moss, searching for purchase. Mackie leaned out of his window, firing the handgun in the direction of the Humvee headlights. The rear wheels of the rental car finally bit into firm ground. The car rocketed forward. Pham crouched behind the steering wheel as Mackie continued to shoot. One man screamed. Pham didn't look up. She pressed her foot to the floorboard while she kept the steering wheel straight. The car bounced on the rutted road and flew past the Humvee.

Mackie ejected the spent magazine and slammed another into place. He sent three shots over Pham's head, through the driver's side window, then turned around and leaned out of the window. He emptied the remaining bullets into the back of the Humvee, taking out the rear left tire.

They raced forward. After a few seconds, he sat back. The back windshield suddenly shattered, glass showering over them. More gunshots. Mackie hunched forward. The car bounced until they reached gravel. Down the hill. Toward the paved road.

Slumped in his seat, he fastened his seatbelt, glanced at Pham, and smiled. "Good driving. You alright?"

"We need to get out of here." She glanced over her shoulder, but only saw the jagged remains of broken glass in the window and the shards littering the back seat. "You could have gotten us killed."

"We made out better than the car did," Mackie said.

Pham checked the dashboard clock. "We're screwed. Felonious assault, wrecked rental car, and our plane leaves in half an hour. No way we're gonna make it. We have to go to the local precinct. I need to make some calls."

"They don't know it was us."

"Of course they'll know it was us!"

"They may suspect it was us, but they won't know, at least for a couple of days. It gives us time to get home while we develop out next steps."

"I'm a cop, Mackie. We just shot at people. I have to report this. Even then I could still lose my job."

She pulled onto the main thoroughfare that led out of Singh's neighborhood. Traffic picked up.

Mackie glanced over at Pham. "I think you were right," he said. "We're going to need some backup."

Chapter Twenty-Six

MACKIE UNLOCKED THE motel door. He propped it open with his foot as he led Pham into the room. The afternoon sunlight in the parking lot sliced its way through the heavy curtains and into the darkness. The smell of stale cigarettes and exhaustion permeated the carpet. A dusty Bible sat atop the television. Mackie clicked on the nearest lamp and locked the door behind them. In the distance, he heard the retreating whine of a jet engine as a plane took off.

He kicked off his shoes and collapsed onto the double bed. His legs remained stiff from running through the woods. His ears still rang from the gun shots. His knuckles, still sore from gripping the car with one hand while firing the gun with the other, throbbed as he unlaced his shoes. Exhaustion from the day's activities sucked the energy out of him.

Pham crossed the room. She turned on the bathroom light, then disappeared behind the door.

Mackie's mind wrapped around the implications of the afternoon's event. The scam involving H-BOC and the U.S. Military topped anything he'd expected. More extensive. More dangerous. That Haywood Clark would pull armed guards with semi-automatic weapons from a post in Alabama to make a pick up in Atlanta meant that the General would go to any lengths to protect his million dollar investment. In part, Mackie supposed, because those payments would continue. More direct payments to Clark. More revenue for AFI. And all coming in the wake of more U.S. casualties.

But none of that explained Sarah's murder. Or who had killed her.

Mackie heard Pham turn on the shower. He surveyed himself. Dirt jammed underneath his fingernails. Mud caked on the sides of his shoe. Streaks of earth smeared across the front of his pants from when he'd crawled onto the ledge overlooking Singh's property. He leaned forward. Steam escaped from the bathroom. Mackie closed his eyes, massaging his temples with his fingertips. Suddenly, he heard Pham's muffled cry.

Mackie bolted for the bathroom.

She leaned halfway out of the shower, gripping the towel rod, dodging the flow of water. Pain streaked across her face.

"Water too hot?" Mackie asked.

Pham shook her head. "Glass. I think pieces of the windshield are still stuck to the back of my neck."

Mackie moved forward, stepping over her pile of clothes. A dirty footprint stained the bath mat. Mud swirls streaked the base of the tub. Mackie examined her back. A scrape coursed across her skin from the fall on the log, leaving a red abrasion atop an emerging bruise. Blood trickled from her neck. Mackie leaned over the toilet to grab a washcloth then placed his hand on Pham's shoulder. "I think I see it." He gently pressed her head forward.

"You're gonna get your clothes soaked," she said.

"They have to be washed before I get on the plane anyway."

She dipped her chin. "Be careful."

Using the tips of his fingernails, Mackie gripped the sliver of glass and pulled. It came out easily. He pivoted and flicked it into the open toilet.

"You get it all?" she asked.

"Hold still." Mackie turned back to her. Lathering the washcloth with the square of soap, he gently scrubbed her neck. He ran his free hand over her skin, not feeling any more debris. Clotted blood and dirt swirled with the soap, dribbling down his arm, cascading onto his shirt. He used the washcloth on her shoulders and back. When he was done, he uncapped the tube of shampoo, poured half of it into her hair, and worked up a rich lather with both hands. Her black hair contrasted with the white suds. Tension drained from her body. Mackie leaned forward to reach the top of her head, soaking his shirt in the process. His clothes clung to his upper body, too wet now to dry with a towel. He released Pham to rinse his own hands.

Pham's eyes remained closed as the water poured over her. "You done?" she asked.

Mackie stepped into the shower, still fully clothed. He lathered the washcloth once again. "Not quite."

Pham opened her eyes and turned to face him. "You're going to have a tough time getting through security like that."

Mackie steadied her with one hand on her hip while he washed the front of her body with the soaped cloth. "I'll take my chances."

He moved closer. The beat of the shower stung his face. He didn't stop to notice. Dirt and grime cascaded from his shirt, swirling in brown eddies near the drain. He worked the soapy cloth over Pham's breasts and flat belly. She relaxed with each advance, reaching up to peel away his own shirt. It landed in a heap at their feet, followed moments later by his trousers. Taking the washcloth, Pham repeated the process for him. She raked her fingers through his hair, massaging away the bits of the hillside still clinging to him.

It only took a few more minutes to clean up, but they held their embrace afterwards. Not wanting to release her, Mackie extended his foot to turn off the shower. He cradled Pham against his chest and carried her to the bed, dripping water on the bathroom tile and leaving a wet trail on the carpet. Neither paid attention to the mess. Mackie's hunger took over. Pham's body was hard, sculpted by exercise, but her legs felt soft against his. His hands explored her navel, her waist, her thighs. She quivered with each advance of his touch. By the time he moved atop of her, his body thrummed with anticipation.

Then, Pham rolled him over, positioning herself on top. His skin quivered as she ran her hands over his chest, investigating his body with her fingertips. She leaned into him when she kissed him, then wordlessly guided him into the heat of her body. Mackie relented, allowing her to lead. Her heels pressed against his calves, pulling the hair on his legs, intensifying the sensations and emotions. Their rhythm felt natural. Practiced. Patient.

Pham took her time. The intensity of the chase that afternoon seemed to blend with the pent up emotions of lost relationships. They reached a crescendo that simultaneously slammed into both of them. In a flood of emotions, Pham collapsed atop Mackie when they finished. They clung to one another afterwards, dozing on top of the comforter as the air conditioner chilled their bodies.

Mackie didn't know how long he slept. The covers were over him when he awoke alone in the bed. Turning over, he heard the muted whine of a hairdryer behind the closed bathroom door. Draped over a towel atop the television, Mackie saw his clothes.

The hairdryer stopped and the bathroom door opened. Pham walked into view, wrapped in a towel. She perched on the end of the bed. "You can go back to sleep. We don't leave for a few more hours."

"You've already rescheduled the flight?"

She nodded. "We're booked on the last flight to Nashville."

Mackie propped on one elbow and checked his cell phone on the nightstand.

"It rang once while you were asleep," Pham said.

"About Reagan?"

"I didn't recognize the number."

Mackie checked the caller ID. "Duel called. Twice."

"New information?" she asked.

Mackie set the phone down and leaned against the pillow. "God only knows. He didn't leave a message. I'll call him back in a bit."

Pham returned to the bathroom. A moment later, she brought out her clothes pressed between two towels. "It's not perfect, but it'll get us on the plane." She placed her damp, hand-washed clothes on top of the bureau. "A couple more hours, and they'll be ready to wear."

"And until then?"

Pham dropped her towel. The bathroom light backlit the curves and hollows of her body. "We'll just have to keep each other warm."

Smiling, Mackie made room for her. "For a detective, you're really cutting me a lot of slack in this investigation."

"Yes...don't abuse it." She crawled in beside him, pulling the covers over them both.

CHAPTER TWENTY-SEVEN

THEY MADE IT back in time for evening visiting hours in the ICU. Reagan slept through most of it, but this time breathing on her own and appearing comfortable. Mackie sat with her for an hour before being shooed away by a veteran night nurse in the unit. Satisfied with Reagan's progress, Mackie left her a note on the dry-erase board in her room and headed home to feed the dog. Pham, who remained in the waiting room during his hospital visit, gave Mackie a ride home. She informed him that a police contact in Atlanta had arranged for a search warrant to investigate the damaged truck in Singh's garage. She had also come clean with the local precinct about the shots from her gun. Mackie felt comfortable with the police's ability to handle the car accident. However, that still left the matter of AFI, which had prompted him to call his lawyer.

An hour later and well into the evening, Mackie sat on his sofa at home, waiting for Duel to finish reading the classified documents from the Department of Defense. "Thanks for coming over," Mackie said, trying to break the silence. And the tension.

Duel waved his hand, brushing off the comment. "What you stumbled upon in Atlanta needed to be addressed." He took a sip of his drink, making eye contact with Mackie. "It was stupid for you to go there in the first place. But since you've uncovered this shit, give me a minute more to review it."

Mackie sank back against the couch cushion, waiting.

Duel studied the final pages of the document. He glanced at the first page once more, then placed the documents on the coffee table. "This is a problem."

Mackie rubbed his neck. "What information in those documents is worth a million dollars cash to Synthesis?"

Duel slowly nodded. "That's the questions, isn't it?" He pulled a legal pad from his briefcase, balancing it on his knee. He wrote the date across the top in capital letters. "What made you suspect that swarthy little Indian, anyway?"

"I didn't, at least not initially," Mackie said. "I wanted to ask him about the accident. See if he knew anyone who drove a red truck at his company. Hank was such an asshole..."

Duel shrugged. "This is not a news flash."

"...I figured we'd try and catch Singh at home."

Duel continued to make notes. "And that's when you broke into his house?"

Mackie nodded. "His garage door was unlocked. I found the key to the back door."

Duel exhaled, the low rumble filling the room. "It's still trespassing."

"The truck that ran us off the road was parked in his garage."

"There are legal ways to obtain that information," Duel countered.

"I was with a cop."

"Who apparently let you run amuck without a search warrant."

Mackie sat up. "Whose side are you on, Duel?"

Duel shifted his girth, his body causing the leather chair to squeak in protest. "All I'm saying is, you need to be careful. Your ex-wife—God rest her soul—was not careful. Now, she's dead. We still don't know all the circumstances surrounding that event, and now you're taking your eye off the ball and chasing down red herrings in Atlanta."

Mackie slammed his fist on the coffee table. "I was almost killed by that truck. Your God-daughter was on a ventilator in the ICU because of that truck. How the hell is that taking my eye off the ball?"

Duel set down his pen. He took out a handkerchief to mop the sweat from his brow, folded it, then set it on the table. "Jesus. Take it easy. I'm offering some unemotional realism here. You and Sarah parted on bitter terms, and she wound up with a fortune. You stayed behind and got screwed. People can get bitter under those circumstances. Don't let that anger drive your investigation."

Mackie stood. "That anger is the only thing that's moving this investigation forward." He walked into the kitchen for a bottle of water, then returned. "Those documents demonstrate that Sarah was in over her head. She had no business distributing classified information. God only knows their true significance."

Duel glanced at the documents before changing the subject. "Reagan's still on the ventilator, you said. How's the rest of her?"

"She's off the vent now but she's got an epidural hematoma and a pulmonary fat embolus that almost killed her."

"Translate."

"A head bleed from the accident. And a glob of bone marrow blocking the vessels to her lungs like a blood clot. It can happen when you break your bones."

"Jesus."

"I should be spending more time there, instead of with your sorry ass, but the nurses keep telling me that won't speed along her recovery. The best thing I can do to protect her is help you and the police figure this stuff out." Mackie paced, too restless to sit back down. Thunder rumbled outside, heralding the returning rain. "The two are connected somehow, Duel. Sarah's death and the car accident. I can't tie it all together, but seeing Singh, Hank, and General Clark from AFI all at once convinced me."

Duel shrugged into his jacket, then gathered up his legal pad and briefcase. "Be careful drawing those conclusions. Sharing that information could get you into a lot of trouble."

Mackie scoffed. "What's going to happen? Is someone going to go after my family? Take my money? Shoot my dog? I don't have much more to lose, Duel."

"Just watch yourself." Duel paused at the front door, his tone somber when he asked, "What's your next step?"

"Follow up on what we saw in Atlanta," Mackie answered.

"You're going back?"

"Not if I can help it. I can't keep putting off Sarah's funeral arrangements. Reagan's going to be hospitalized for at least a few more days so I've got to deal with all that crap. I'm hoping they'll keep her body at the morgue until Reagan can attend the funeral."

Duel pulled opened the front door. "Watch yourself, Mackie. Like I said, you need to be more careful. I'm worried about you."

Mackie fixed himself a drink after Duel left, trying to unwind from the day. He opened the front door for Jonah, who scurried into the yard, trying to beat the storm. The dark air smelled of the promise of rain. The power flickered with each rumble of thunder as he waited on the dog. A few minutes later, Mackie retreated to the sofa with his drink. He picked up the classified documents and flipped through images of the Humvee and its fuel tank. Each page detailed precise measurements of the armor, the placement of each metal panel, and the composition of the metal itself. Mackie lingered over the specifics. This time, a notation about titanium caught his attention.

The composition of armor seemed familiar. Metal alloys. Ceramic polymers. Titanium and steel. Familiar because Mackie had spent a career working with various combinations of these materials in prosthetic joints. The very same ones Singh had displayed in his home. Sturdy metals. Incredibly durable. But not foolproof. In the early days of his career, it hadn't been uncommon for replacement joints to be removed because of infections that coated the joints like a membrane, eating away the integrity of the metal and the function of the prosthesis itself. Newer titanium alloys addressed many of those concerns. From the looks of the DOD documents, Armored Forces Industries had found similar benefit for their own uses.

The lights flickered in concert with the thunderclaps outside. Then, the power died.

Jonah ambled to the sofa, and Mackie scratched the dog's head. "Guess that means it's time for bed." As Mackie stood, he heard a thump outside the front door. Jonah cocked his head and growled. Mackie paused in the foyer to listen. Someone knocked on the door.

He walked to the door and checked the peephole. Too dark to see anyone without the porch lights. Mackie released the deadbolt to look. "Who—?" He never got the words out. The door burst open, slamming him against the wall.

Two shadowy figures charged into the foyer. Rain blew in on a gust of wind. Mackie slipped on the wet tile, tried to regain his balance, and fell. Bracing himself, he looked up. Before he could register the identity of either man, one of them crushed his foot down on Mackie's hand. He howled at the pain, curling up and rolling away from the intruders.

Mackie scrambled to the wall as one man closed the front door and the other one groped in the dark for him. He ducked, kicking at the intruder. He missed. The larger man grabbed Mackie by the shirt, lifted him up, and hurled him against the table in the foyer. Wood splintered, and Mackie toppled onto the floor.

Jonah barked and snapped at the men from the den.

Bolts of pain ripped through Mackie's back. In the dark foyer, he saw only one of the men. Facing the den, five feet ahead. Shadows concealed his identity. Mackie peeled himself off the floor, crouched low against the wall for a moment, and then lunged at the larger man's legs, smashing into his knees. He felt the joint give, bending backwards with a nauseating crack of splintering bone. The man screamed, crumpling to the floor. Mackie rolled to his right, jacked up on adrenaline. He came to rest at the base of the other wall. The man grunted in pain, struggling to stand. When he finally did, he charged Mackie, kicking at him. Mackie dodged it and grabbed the man's foot as it sailed past his head. When he crashed to the floor, Mackie pounced and pummeled him with his fists. The man clawed at Mackie and shouted for help. Mackie popped him in the mouth with the back of his elbow, feeling teeth crack. Then popped him again on the side of his skull. The man stopped moving.

Mackie trembled with anxiety. With anger. With fear. He pushed off the downed man and scanned the room for his companion. In the total darkness, Mackie didn't see the man walk up beside him. Didn't hear his approach over the thunder. Didn't even know he was right there until something crashed against his head. The first blow knocked him off-balance. The second one drew blood. Mackie tried to stay upright, but a starburst of lights showered his vision. The third blow sent Mackie to the floor.

Then, he blacked out.

CHAPTER TWENTY-EIGHT

MACKIE HEARD THE rain hammering against the front porch. Cool water pooled around his chin. The wind howled, blowing open the front door. Rain streamed into the foyer. When he rolled over, pain seared the back of his head and pierced his muddled brain. Something scratched him when he moved, rhythmic and warm, rough. Jonah. At least he wasn't alone.

Mackie crawled to the table in the foyer to get to his feet. Instead of smooth wood, he grabbed a handful of splinters. Only then did he remember being thrown against the furniture. God, his head hurt. A concussion for sure. He steadied himself, using the wall to pull himself up onto one knee. His head spun as he moved. Mackie felt ready to pass out again. He sat still for a moment, then pushed through the dizziness to stand. He felt the back of his head. Lumps of blood stuck to his skin, no longer sticky but not yet crusted. He slid his fingers across the coagulated mass and around the laceration. Large enough for stitches. When he felt the wound a second time, a trickle of blood seeped from the clot.

Mackie turned toward the sound of the rain. His front door swung open, bobbling with the breeze. Tree shadows undulated across the floor. He leaned forward and shut the door, locking the deadbolt. He stood motionless in the foyer, listening. No other sounds. Other than Jonah, he assumed he was now alone. He stumbled into the carpeted den, his feet squishing at the transition of hardwood to carpet. Darkness. Mackie inched his way forward, recalling the flashlight he kept in the den. Hell if he could find it in this mess. He'd stashed a second one in his bedside table, but after a few paces toward his room, his head pounded with intense pain and he abandoned the idea of going after it. The trickle of blood intensified with each exertion. Mackie leaned on the counter that led into to the kitchen. No idea what time it was. He swept his hand across the countertop, groping for his phone. He couldn't reconstruct what had happened, although the evidence around him told most of the story. He scrolled through recently dialed numbers until he found Pham's. She answered on the second ring.

"What's wrong?" she asked.

"I need your help." He paused, his breathing ragged. "Two guys broke in." Waves of nausea crashed around him each time he turned his head to the left. "My head's bleeding."

Rustling in the background at Pham's place. "Call 911."

"I'll wait for you."

"Bullshit. I'll call 911."

"Don't."

Pham paused on the other end of the line. "Sit down and stay there."

"Bring a flashlight," he said as he edged carefully to his sofa. "I'm at home. I'll wait for you."

The passage of time left him. It could have been hours, but was probably minutes, when he heard someone knock on the door. Just like before. Mackie opened his eyes, still recumbent on the sofa. He lifted his head, but the sofa fabric lifted with him, tugging on the back of his hair. Each pull against the couch ripped sparks of pain through his head. His wound had clotted again, this time to the back of the sofa. Mackie scanned the room. Power still out. Handkerchief on the table near him. Must have been Duel's. He reached out with his free hand and grabbed the cloth. He curled his fingers under the head wound, and using the handkerchief as a guide, slid it between his matted hair and the furniture fabric. He jerked his head forward, crying out as he freed himself.

More knocking. Then a frantic-sounding voice. "Are you okay? Mackie, open up."

Warm blood soaked the handkerchief. Mackie stumbled into the foyer, taking short steps and shallow breaths. Pham gave him a horrified look once he unlocked the door. Without asking any questions, she led Mackie into the den, propping him against the counter. She clicked on her flashlight, sweeping it across the destroyed room. Television busted and upended. CD's scattered across the carpet, their square cases reflecting the flashlight.

She turned the light on Mackie's head. "Christ Almighty, that looks horrible."

"Head wounds bleed a lot."

"I'll take you in my car."

Mackie focused on her. "We're staying here."

"You're going to tough it out at home and bleed to death so you don't have to answer any questions?"

"No. You're going to help me."

"Afraid your pride's going to be wounded if you go to the ER twice in one week."

Mackie managed a faint laugh. "Something like that. What would you do if you saw me in the ER like this?"

"Call the cops, then admit you."

Mackie shifted his weight against the counter. "Exactly. Which means I can't see Reagan for however long they think I need to stay."

Pham stepped back from the kitchen counter, crossing her arms while she studied Mackie's appearance. "I'm not buying it. There's another reason."

Unable to continue to lean against the counter, Mackie slid toward a kitchen chair. He felt better when he sat. "We're close, Libby. You can blow this case wide open in the next few days. But they're on to me, now. It's only a matter of time before they either destroy the evidence we have against them or take me out completely."

"You really believe that?"

"I believe that you can fix this damn head wound now and I'll be no worse off."

Pham shined her flashlight on the back of Mackie's scalp. "Your head's a mess."

"Get me to my bathroom, and I'll show you what to do."

Pham resisted. "Even if I knew how to sew, I'd leave a terrible scar."

Mackie steadied himself against her arm. "Trust me on this. Just help me to the bathroom."

"You're making a mistake," she said as she guided him across the den. They picked their way over the contents of his entertainment center. Shadows from the flashlight danced along the wall. She entered Mackie's bedroom and led him into the bathroom. Mackie sat on the closed toilet lid. From his perch, he turned on the hot water. "Check the cabinet next to the shower. Second shelf. Grab the black canvas bag, and give it to me."

Pham rummaged through the cabinet. "Two bags in here."

"Get them both. And the large green bottle."

"Chlorhexadine?"

"That's it." Mackie tested the water with his hand before levering himself upright. He leaned forward and dipped his head into the basin, diverting warm water from the faucet and allowing it to flow through his hair. Pain scraped across his skull, but Mackie gritted his teeth and held his position. In the dim illumination from the flashlight, he saw the swirling water in the sink turn from pink to dark red. Flecks of coagulated blood twisted in eddies near the drain before disappearing from sight. Mackie chewed on his tongue, tolerating the pain because he knew the consequences of ignoring the cut would double the discomfort he felt now. Several more minutes passed before the water cleared. Taking the green bottle of antiseptic, Mackie poured it on his head and carefully lathered his hair. More blood in the sink. He repeated the process twice more until he could scrub the wound without finding any more evidence of blood clots in the sink. He turned off the water and sank back on the lid of the toilet, out of breath, heart hammering in his chest. Pham handed him a towel. He massaged the wound before pulling back the hand towel. Light pink stained the fabric. Diluted. No active bleeding.

"How you doing?" she asked.

"My head hurts like hell, but at least it's clean. You ready to sew it up?"

"This is a bad idea," she said. "For both of us."

Mackie leaned back over the sink while Pham shone the light on the crown of his head. "What do you see?"

"A scar waiting to happen." She held the flashlight with one hand and parted his hair with the fingers of the other one, assessing the wound. "I've seen worse."

"That's the attitude I'm looking for," he encouraged. "Describe it for me?"

Pham separated a few more strands of hair. "A big cut. More of a slice, really."

The manipulation of the open wound nauseated Mackie. He

rested his forehead against the sink, finding solace on the cool porcelain. "How many?"

"One large one."

"Perfect." He took a few deep breaths then sat back up. "I've got a shaving mirror in the shower." Pham found it and handed it to him. Mackie steadied himself by gripping the counter and stood, his back to the bathroom mirror. He held the shaving mirror above his head. He peered at the reflection, confirming a two-inch long laceration across his scalp that extended to the top of his head. He reached for the wound. With the right amount of pressure, he could almost perfectly align the edges of the cut. "This will work," he said as he repositioned himself on the toilet. "Hand me the zippered canvas bag."

Pham grabbed the black bag and unzipped it, holding the flashlight up so that Mackie could inspect the contents. Capped needles and plastic syringes were tucked on one side of the bag. In the center, a dozen or more individually wrapped sutures sets. "Provided you don't lose your hair, I doubt anyone will ever see the scar," Pham said.

Mackie looked up and saw her smile. "I'll spare you the pressure." He reached into the bag and handed her a foil-wrapped container with a small plastic tube.

Pham inspected it. "DermaBond?"

"You're going to glue me back together." He took the flashlight from her. "Pinch the flaps of the laceration together with the fingers of one hand. With your other hand, squeeze the plastic tube to break the seal and then dab out the DermaBond glue and work it over the top of the cut."

"It's going to make a mess," she said as she quickly washed her hands.

"I guarantee you, it'll look better with a cop gluing it together than a doctor leaving it alone to heal up on its own."

Pham opened the foil wrapper in her teeth, pulling out a short plastic tube the size of a small crayon with a rounded sponge on the end of it. She crushed the sides of the tube, causing the sponge to moisten with the skin glue. Turning her attention to Mackie's scalp, Pham manipulated the edges of the laceration. When she had them aligned, she pinched the cut together and blotted the edges with the DermaBond.

Mackie shivered when the cool gel hit the open wound.

"Sit still," Pham said. "How much should I use?"

"Empty it."

Pham dabbed the remaining gel onto his scalp, held the cut in place, and counted to one hundred. She waited an additional minute before lifting her fingers from the wound. "How's it feel?"

Mackie reached to the top of his head, gently fingering the hardening gel, which gave slightly under the pressure but did not stick to his hands. "It'll hold." He steadied himself on the sink as he stood. The dizziness passed quicker than before, but his headache intensified.

She asked, "Any idea who broke in?"

"Yeah, I've got a real good idea," he muttered.

After hugging Pham in a wordless thank you, Mackie led the way out of the bathroom. He stopped at his bedside table and pulled out the flashlight he kept there for emergencies. He returned hers before easing his way to the den, using the wall to steady himself as he negotiated the rubble in the hallway. On the floor of the foyer, a metal candlestick holder lay in a shallow puddle of rainwater, the base covered with caked blood.

Pham gloved one hand before she bent down to pick it up. "You're lucky you don't have more significant injuries." She pulled a plastic baggie from her pocket and slid the candlestick holder inside. She scraped aside dozens of plastic CD cases with her foot, blazing a path through the den. Jonah stayed close by, whimpering at they stepped onto the carpet. Pham scratched him behind his ears, offering comfort.

Mackie paused at the entrance to the room. Amid the rubble, the couch remained untouched. One of the chairs had been upended, the other exactly still where it had been before the break-in and assault. And except for its position pressed back against the sofa, the coffee table appeared empty and ignored. "Libby, come here."

She hurried to his side. "What's wrong?"

Mackie gestured to the table and the bare carpet around it. "They took the documents."

She shined her light over the furniture. "AFI?"

Mackie nodded. "General Clark must have known all along."

CHAPTER TWENTY-NINE

EARLY THE NEXT morning, their car sped down the left lane of the interstate, twenty miles above the speed limit as they headed east. It had taken Pham all of fifteen minutes to arrange for transportation. Obtaining a search warrant took significantly longer, but her Chief assured her that the details would be worked out by the time they arrived. Pham drove the department-issued Crown Victoria, unmarked but still recognizable as a law enforcement vehicle. Mackie sat in the front seat, staring out at the blurred darkness. Ahead, the dawn emerged as a grey seam above the tree line.

Pham concentrated on the road, occasionally passing a semi but maintaining her silence. In the two hours since they'd left Nashville, neither of them had said much. Mackie dozed off and on. Tight throbbing had replaced the white-hot pain in his head, allowing him bouts of rest. He glanced at his watch. Five-forty a.m. At this rate, they would make it to Armored Forces Industries by sunrise. Whether they would make it in time was less clear.

Pham glanced at Mackie. "Who else knows about the documents?"

"The two of us, Duel, and Vern Philpot." Mackie rubbed his eyes, trying to clear his vision. "I'm sure Hank, Singh, and General Clark know, as well. And they also know that we have them."

Pham thought for a long moment. "Why are they so threatened by you, by this situation? You aren't on the receiving end of a major break-in and assault unless someone feels that your knowledge of those Humvee documents would risk their lives, livelihood, or reputation. What's your best guess about the documents?"

Mackie pinched the bridge of his nose. He'd wrestled with the connection between the documents and Sarah's murder for several days. Stumbling upon the military grade H–BOC and the pay–off for General Clark had resulted in both absurd accusations and fanciful conclusions. He hesitated, then pressed on with his suspicion. "The H–BOC is being sold to the U.S. military by Synthesis. Legitimately. General Clark helped to grease the negotiations. At least one million dollars for him, as we saw at Singh's home, but that probably wasn't the only delivery. I think he's also helping Singh and Hank divert the product overseas. Expanding their international market share."

"Though the military?"

Mackie nodded. "Exactly. Clark guarantees the increased need of H–BOC for U.S. troops by sending tainted vehicles into combat zones. In essence, he's attaching faulty armor on the back of the Humvees, like the ones we saw in the demonstration, to make them more vulnerable to a terrorist attack."

"That's ridiculous," Pham said.

"It's treason. And it connects the hole we saw ripped into the back of the Humvee during the field test to the structural details of the armored plates Clark sent to Sarah. For helping to facilitate the deal, Sarah is paid thirty million dollars."

"Then why would they murder her? She was complicit, if your theory is correct," Pham said. "What about the patents?"

"She knew too much," Mackie said. "Synthesis made a new product that didn't fall under the protection of our patents. No reason to kill Sarah for patent infringement. But she's the lawyer with total knowledge of the deal. General Clark and Hank both claimed national security as the reason they wouldn't discuss the product. I think the real national security issue is that no one else knew that market share for this product was generated by deliberately blowing up our own troops. But, in reality, it's a success story. Some kid gets maimed in an explosion, but he lives to tell the tale because he received H–BOC on the scene. And for every soldier that's killed in the explosions, the government vows to increase troop protection, funneling more money to AFI. Then, the cycle repeats itself."

Pham eased off the interstate toward Bridgeport, Alabama. "So who killed her?"

"I'm sure it wasn't Hank. Could've been Sigh but I'm guessing one of Clark's henchmen at AFI."

Their car rolled through the stop sign at the end of the exit ramp. They turned south toward AFI, passing an all-night mini-mart on their left before driving into the darkness. Off to one side, the grey rim of a new day disappeared behind the roadside trees. After another few miles, Pham eased the car to the shoulder, put it in park, and let the engine idle.

"We've not driven far enough," Mackie said.

"Exactly," Pham said. "We need some space to get ready. Unless you want to use the lobby bathroom at AFI to don your protective gear, I suggest we do this now." She stepped out of the car and opened the trunk.

Mackie sat in the front seat for a long moment before following her. He rubbed the sore on his head without wincing. He felt anxious about the upcoming encounter. He was ready for closure to this case. Ready to move on. And ready for some rest. He stepped out of the car and peered into the trunk, amazed by the contents. "My God, Libby. Who else is joining us?" Inside the trunk, a cache of weapons, ammunition, and various other supplies sat in orderly fashion. Pham slipped off her jacket, followed by her t-shirt and pants. Her skin rippled under the pre-dawn chill.

Mackie managed a smile as he stared at her body. "I think the back seat would be more comfortable for both of us."

Pham grinned as she stepped into a black body suit. "I'll make sure to clear off a spot for you for the drive back when your exposed ass gets shot." She pulled on the outfit and zipped the front. She then snapped on a pair of camouflage pants and a jacket. Reaching into the trunk, she found a similar black suit and tossed it to Mackie. "Put this on."

"I thought we had a search warrant coming," he said.

"We will, but the lobby doors don't open until seven. We still have little bit of time to look around. It's better if we're not seen doing that."

Following her lead, Mackie began to dress. The material slid over his skin like Spandex, leaving very few seams to catch on his surroundings. The camouflage pants and jacket were more tight than was comfortable, but when he walked with them on, he couldn't even hear the fabric rub together. "Does all of this come with the search warrant?"

"It all comes with the car. For emergency use. When I borrow this vehicle, I borrow everything that comes with it."

"And they just happened to have my size in the emergency kit?"

Pham smiled. "Lucky guess." She checked the handguns, then gave one to Mackie. Two assault rifles remained in their cases in the trunk. She grabbed a camouflage tarp before closing the trunk. She slid an extra clip of ammunition into Mackie's front pocket then slapped him on the butt.

"Ow."

She smiled. "Now you remember what happens when you disengage the safety, right?"

"You have to remind me every time?"

"Let's get going, soldier."

They climbed back into the car, and Pham pulled out onto the pavement. The dashboard clock read six a.m. Mackie had had a hard enough time finding the entrance when they'd driven here on Sunday. In the muted illumination of the dawn, it seemed impossible that they would find their way without a GPS, and he hadn't spotted one in the car. In the time it had taken them to dress, not a single car had passed them. In the distance, headlights appeared in the darkness. Pham slowed down, although she continued to drive.

"Business gets started early down here," she said.

"Keeping Busy Keeping Our Troops Safe," Mackie deadpanned.

Pham laughed.

As he spoke, the semi passed them, carrying two armored Humvee's chained to the bed of the truck.

Pham drove for another few miles before reaching the roadside clearing that indicated the entrance to AFI. A half mile ahead of them, headlights pierced the tree line, then turned in their direction.

"Don't turn in right here," Mackie said. "Let's check out that other entrance."

As they approached, they saw the truck pull out of the second entrance. More Humvees. The truck passed them, its tail lights receding toward the interstate. Pham eased forward, turning into what appeared to be the service entrance. Branches hung over the road and grew into the entrance, creating a tunnel and leaving just enough space for the trucks to pass through.

"We don't know where this ends up," Pham said. "Let's turn around and use the main entrance."

Mackie shook his head. "This has to connect to the rest of the facility. Besides, we're already dressed for snooping around. Let's see what's there."

She eased the car deeper into the tree canopy. After a hundred yards, the road widened. To their left, the shoulder flattened. A level turnabout led to a dirt path.

"Pull over," Mackie said as he pushed open his door and stepped out of the car. The headlight beams cast long shadows, blinding him to his surroundings. He motioned for Pham to kill the engine and cut off the lights. Once she did, his vision adjusted. He noticed that the path from the shoulder seemed wide enough for a car. Pham joined him. Like the main road, the path seemed carved from the dense overgrowth, intensifying the darkness the farther along they walked.

"How far back do you think this goes?" he asked.

Pham froze, gripping Mackie's arm. "Damn it." The rumble of the diesel engine hit them before they even saw the headlights. "I need to move the car."

In the time it took her to turn toward the Crown Victoria, headlights appeared on the road. "No time," Mackie said, grabbing her arm. "Come on." They stepped into the underbrush and squatted down, blending into the bramble. From where they waited, Mackie could see their vehicle. Looking like an abandoned car. Looking out of place. He held his breath and waited.

The truck lumbered down the road, its headlights intensifying. Accelerating. When the truck was almost upon them, something changed. The hiss of air brakes. The engine decelerating. The truck passed their position, then stopped. Ten yards ahead of their parked car. Mackie slipped his gun from its holster.

The driver opened the door of the semi and stepped out. The dome light from the cab illuminated the Crown Victoria. The driver walked to the car and peered in the window. He circled the car, pausing at the back license plate. He squatted near the trunk, studied the tag. Walking back to the driver's side, he pressed his hand against the glass, then walked back to his truck. Just before he climbed back into his truck, he turned in their direction.

"Shit," Pham whispered.

He returned to the Crown Victoria, placing the palm of his hand on the hood. He appeared to nod, pulled a cell phone from his belt, and dialed. Mackie heard the murmur of conversation, but not the exact words. The man nodded once more, walked behind the car, and read off the license plate number. He clipped his phone back onto his belt and climbed in the cab. Moments later, the truck accelerated, the silhouettes of Humvees fading into the darkness.

"We're screwed," Pham said as she pushed up onto one knee.

"Maybe," Mackie said. "Let's finish what we started."

Pham stood and walked toward the car. "Drive or walk?"

"Definitely drive." Mackie dusted off his camouflage. "When the guards arrive, they'll want to search the car. If it's missing, no search. Besides, if we run into trouble inside, it'll be nice to have transportation out of here."

"Plus a change of clothes." Pham pulled at her camouflage jacket. "I wasn't planning on wearing this when we served the warrant."

Pham started the engine and backed up a few feet. Cutting the steering wheel hard to the right, she pulled forward into the turnabout, then inched the car toward the dirt path. It just fit. Even with the rising sun, the canopy blocked any daylight, plunging them into a dark corridor when they most needed to see their surroundings. They drove for about a quarter mile before the underbrush receded. A parking space on either side of the narrow lane. And a wooden shed the size of a free-standing garage.

Mackie opened his door. "Cut the headlights and turn the car around. I want to be facing the right direction when we leave."

"I'll come with you."

Mackie shook his head. "I'm going to look inside. I won't be long."

He felt for the handgun on his belt then grabbed a flashlight from the car. A few chirping crickets quieted down as he walked to the building. Overhead, a light breeze rustled the branches. Other than that, silence. He paused halfway to the building and looked back. Too dark to spot the car. Mackie approached the back of the wooden shed. Vines snaked up the back wall. Uncut hedges surrounded this side. Only when the building was close enough to touch did Mackie see the rough-cut boards and windowless walls. Built for functionality, not form. He rounded the corner, heading to the front of the shed.

A flagstone path led away from the low-slung front porch of the building. Even in the dark, Mackie sensed that the trees parted nearby, perhaps giving way to a large pasture. Or a testing ground for armored vehicles. Mackie cut off the flashlight beam and stood on the flagstone path, allowing his eyes to adjust. Ahead, a low wall jutted up. Then the field, emerging into view in the grey tones of early dawn.

Mackie returned to the building. Two lawn chairs sat on the porch. No windows. A wooden door off-center. He walked to the door and pushed on the weathered boards. It opened easily. He stepped inside and closed the door, plunging himself into near total darkness once more. Mackie turned on his flashlight.

In the center of the room, he saw an overturned Humvee.

The vehicle filled the small building. Running his flashlight over the Humvee, Mackie realized that the undercarriage faced him. The Humvee had already been dismantled. Wheels removed, doors taken off their hinges. Soot singed the underside of the vehicle. Beyond the fuel tank, Mackie's spotted the far wall of the building, his flashlight beam passing through a gaping hole in the protective armor.

Mackie stared for a long moment, then turned his attention to the rest of the small building. Rows of improvised explosive devices stacked along a corner workbench. Above them hung rocket propelled grenades. Weapons of warfare used to test the AFI armor. If the Humvee in front of him was any indication, the weapons still held the advantage. Along the back wall, oversized double doors chained together with a padlock. Adjacent to them, amorphous pieces of metal hung like trophies. Armored panels, saved for analysis. Or posterity.

Mackie approached the Humvee. As he rounded the hood, he noticed the engine block had been removed as well as the interior seats. All that remained was the metal shell of the vehicle. Even the top of the car had been opened, offering an unobstructed view of the damage from the field test. Had a soldier been riding inside the Humvee, Mackie envisioned a quick death following an explosion beneath the vehicle. Best case scenario: the shrapnel would have maimed those riding in the front seat.

He stuck his head inside the vehicle for a closer look. That's when he heard the sound of two voices. Laughing. Getting closer.

Mackie cut off his flashlight and listened. The low murmur of conversation. He swung his head around, his eyes darting along the walls. No windows. No exits. No way out. He paused, heart racing. The voices drew even closer.

Mackie climbed into the shell of the Humvee. He sat exposed in the back, but still able to see the building's door. Still visible to anyone entering the area. He scrambled to the pillaged front seat, the vehicle rocking as he moved around inside. He squeezed into the front of the Humvee and pressed his back against the floorboard, which rose above him like a protective wall. Squatting there, he withdrew his gun and released the safety.

When the door opened, he heard both voices clearly—the deep voice of a man he didn't know, and the unmistakable sound of Hank Stone's laughter.

CHAPTER THIRTY

THE DOOR CREAKED open. Mackie glanced through the torn carcass of the truck bed. He waited and listened, a pulse loudly pounding in his ears. Hank entered first, talking to his companion, who laughed. Moments later, the overhead lights came on, blinding Mackie.

He held his breath while he squeezed shut his eyes. Slowly opening them, the room came into focus. Shards of metal in unrecognizable shapes hung along the back wall. Some appeared to be the size of a car's hood. Others, smaller than a soda can. Holes allowed each shard to be hung on hooks drilled into the wall, some marked with colored tape. Next to the collection, he saw the closed double doors used to admit the wrecked Humvees. Mackie concentrated on the back of the building as he listened to the men move around just a few feet beyond his location.

"Is this what you need?" Hank asked.

"It should be in the corner," the other man said.

Mackie heard metal objects clanging together on the workbench behind him.

"Got it." The other man again. "You ready to go?"

Mackie heard footsteps pause a few feet from the Humvee.

"Oh my God!" Hank gasped. "What the hell happened?"

"You haven't seen this before?" the other man asked as he joined Hank beside the Humvee.

Mackie crouched low on the thin metal flooring of the vehicle, listening to their exchange.

"Hell of a hole," Hank said.

"It's what you asked for."

"Impressive." Hank's footsteps moved left, closer to the bed of the truck. "How often do you guys do this? With the explosion?"

"Once a week or so. This one was done on Sunday."

Hank paused, resting his hands on the inside of the hole. Mackie saw the tips of his fingers, dirt under the nails.

"Come over here," the other man said.

Hank ran his fingers along the gash in the metal before disappearing. Mackie heard them make their way to the front of the vehicle, directly opposite his position.

"Pristine," Hank purred. "And that's with the armor in place?"

"Effective, isn't it? You're definitely getting your money's worth."

Hank laughed. "We damn well better be."

Mackie gripped his gun. Adrenalin surged through him. His hands trembled at the thought of confronting Hank with what he knew. If he waited, he would miss the best opportunity he'd ever have to insure justice. He squeezed the grip of his gun and took a deep breath, then he slowly exhaled. He still needed to deal with General Clark. And Singh. He forced his hand to relax. As much as he wanted to act, he let the moment pass. For now.

Mackie waited. Footsteps receded as both men exited the building. The overhead light went out. Total darkness. Mackie slumped against the back of the vehicle, tension draining from his body.

A few minutes later, he placed the gun back in his belt and unfolded himself from his crouched position. Sweat soaked the back of his shirt. His muscles stiffened when he stretched. His legs ached. Mackie held onto the doorframe of the Humvee to regain his balance, then stepped over to the back wall. Turning on his flashlight, he grabbed the smallest piece of metal hanging on the wall. Denser than a soda can. More sturdy. He couldn't even bend the thinning edges of the metal. He gripped it in the palm of one hand and headed for the door.

As he stepped outside, the testing field came into focus. For the first time since he'd entered the shed, enough sunlight had emerged to provide details of the clearing. The low wall at the end of the flagstone path was the same one that provided protection to the employees during a field test. In the distance, barely visible through the morning mist, he saw the observation deck. Behind it, the production facility for AFI.

Mackie crept around the corner of the shed. The return path to the car remained dark, the sun not yet able to penetrate the canopy of trees. He moved toward the woods. Suddenly, a twig snapped.

He dropped down, diving behind an overgrown hedge.

"Mackie?" Pham called out in an urgent whisper. "Are you back here?"

Exhaling his relief, he crawled out from under the protection of the bush. "Over here."

Pham stepped into view. "What kept you?"

"I'll show you."

They returned to the shed.

"I got worried about you when you didn't come right—" She paused when he opened the door to the shed. The armored plates on the undercarriage glinted off the flashlight. "My God."

Mackie shut the door behind her, flipping on the interior light. "I was snooping around inside here when Hank Stone and some other guy showed up."

"He's here?"

"He just left. I had to hide behind the Humvee."

"You could have been caught," she said.

"I could have been killed."

Pham walked around the vehicle, first trailing her finger through the blown out hole above the fuel tank, and then inspecting the hanging armor along the back wall. "What's Hank doing here?"

"Insuring his investment." Mackie walked over to the workbench. He stuffed the chunk of metal shrapnel into his pocket then began to gather up an armload of RPG's. When he couldn't carry any more, he turned toward the door and switched off the light with his elbow. "Let's go."

Pham frowned. "What are you doing?"

"Gathering evidence." Mackie nudged the door open with his foot. The sun, just emerging over the trees, illuminated the dirt clods and pockmarked red clay of AFI's simulated battlefield. Beyond the protection wall and across the clearing, Mackie spotted a shadow at the edge of the forest. He assumed that another shed lay in the dense growth of vegetation on that side of the property. Probably housing more evidence of faulty armor. He turned to Pham, who stood beside him on the porch. "Are you up for this?" he asked.

She shook her head. "Look, John Wayne, we need back-up."

Mackie scowled and headed for the car. Damned if he was going to wait any longer. He placed the weapons on the floor between the front and back seats. He was covering them with the camouflage tarp when Pham joined him. "There's no need to wait for back-up," Mackie said. "With your search warrant, we can enter the main building and do what we came here to do."

Pham resisted. "Your theory is playing out, Mackie. The evidence we need is in that shed, but this is bigger than the both of us. I can have a SWAT team here in under two hours. It's worth the wait."

Mackie stared at her for a moment, then began to remove his camouflage outerwear. He stripped down to his body suit, then pulled on his civilian clothes. Just in case. "Do what you have to do," he said. "but if you do it my way, I'll have answers before your SWAT team arrives. Hank is here. I'm sure General Clark is here, too. Probably sipping coffee in his office right now and counting his money. The longer we wait, the more likely it is that the people who have the answers we need won't be as accessible as they are right now." He closed the car door.

Pham crossed her arms. "I can't let you do that. We hand over the information we have and the legal process will unfold, as it should, so that these guys get nailed in a court of law. You have to trust the process."

"And watch Sarah's killer walk away?"

"You don't know that he's here," she said.

Mackie slammed his fist on the top of the car. "I know my daughter is in the ICU, because some asshole in a red truck ran us off the road. I know that I've been betrayed by a colleague and attacked for information that I'm not supposed to have. And I have every reason to expect that the answer to all of that is just a half a mile away in the admin offices of AFI." His head wound throbbed the angrier he became. He lowered his voice, measuring his breathing and willing his heart rate to slow down. "There wasn't much love lost when Sarah and I finally divorced, and none of what's happened to her changes that. But I owe it to my daughter—our daughter—to figure out what went wrong and why her mother was murdered. I'm the only parent she has left."

Pham listened, her arms crossed. "You're going to put your own safety at risk so that you can avenge your ex-wife's murder?"

Mackie looked into Pham's eyes, held her gaze for a moment,

then looked toward the path that led to the service road. "I'm going to go into AFI and confront General Clark with this information. If you can't do this with me, fine."

"Mackie..." she began.

He turned away, taking the narrow path to the service road. The tree-canopied path remained dark, but he could see well enough. He paused, looking to the right when he reached the service road. He imagined that it curved around the back of the clearing, looping to the other side of the field. At least a mile to the production facility from here. Maybe two. Too risky, though, to backtrack and cut across their field.

He walked down the center of the blacktop, no other semi-trucks in sight as he followed the road. Several minutes later, he heard a car's approach. Mackie darted for cover. The car slowed as he ducked behind a tree. He waited, then looked beyond the tree. Pham. Mackie smiled as he stepped into view. He wiped pine straw from his shirt as he hustled to the Crown Victoria.

She lowered the window. "You're going to get your outfit all dirty if you keep walking along the shoulder. Get in, damn it. I think you're deranged, but I can't abandon you now."

Mackie climbed into the front seat. "I thought you wouldn't come with me. Law enforcement code of conduct and all."

Pham kept her eyes on the road ahead as she sped up. "It's a long hike back to Nashville."

"Probably take almost a week on foot," Mackie said.

"We don't have that kind of time." Pham followed the one-way road in the opposite direction, the pavement narrowing on the turns with very little shoulder on either side of them. "What's your plan?"

"For starters, I want to see if there's another shed on this side of the field. If this road doesn't fork, we should be able to spot it on our right."

"I'm not sure how that's going to help us," Pham said. The farther they drove, the more apparent it became that this road had only one destination. No turnabouts. No intersecting roads. No driveways. Mackie could almost envision their position relative to the open field.

"The other structure must be where they store more evidence of faulty armor," he said.

Mackie finally spotted a possibility. "There." He pointed to a spot beyond his window.

Pham leaned forward over the steering wheel. "I don't see it."

"Pull over."

Pham edged the car to the side of the road and parked. The Crown Victoria still occupied most of the pavement. "This is only going to get us caught being in the wrong place."

"Just give me just a second." Mackie slipped out of the car and melted into the dense woods. Twenty yards later, he found an open pasture.

No shed. No storage area. He glanced back over his shoulder, no longer able to see the road. He walked a few yards more before he saw it. A structure positioned at the edge of the field. Nothing else to replicate a warehouse for bombed-out army vehicles.

Mackie moved closer, but he stayed near the tree line. Seeing nothing else of interest, he retraced his steps to the car. Halfway back, he heard the air horn of a semi.

Damn it. Pham was right. Again.

Mackie didn't hesitate. He raced down the path, tree branches whipping at his arms and face. He dodged a stump, rolling his ankle on a rock. He caught himself before he wound up on his face in the mud, his shirt front taking the worst of the mess. Mackie popped back up and surged forward. The truck's horn sounded once more. The engine idled nearby. Mackie burst into the open at the side of the road, his heart thundering and his head throbbing from the exertion.

The truck driver looked at Mackie as he emerged from the footpath, then back at Pham.

"Morning," Mackie said as he dusted the muck from his hands. "Looks like we blocked the road."

The driver stepped down from his truck. Clad in desert camouflage BDUs and a matching cap, he studied Mackie for a long moment. "This is restricted property, sir. You need to get in your car and leave the premises."

Mackie smiled. "Probably not the best place to take a piss, I'll admit, but after three cups of coffee and a hundred and twenty miles, I couldn't hold it any longer."

By the time Mackie reached the car, Pham had opened the driver's side door and craned her neck to see on either side. "Can we get by?" she asked.

The driver advised, "You'll need to go back to the beginning of this road, ma'am. It'll take you to the interstate." The driver reached into the truck cab for a walkie–talkie.

Mackie glanced at the two Humvees chained to the bed of the truck before looking at the driver. "How long does it take you to get to Fort Eustis?"

The soldier, still holding his radio, stiffened. "I beg your pardon, sir?"

Mackie pointed to the back of the truck. "The Humvees. They're headed to Virginia, aren't they? Before they're shipped overseas?"

"I can't discuss that, sir."

Mackie offered a reassuring smile. "It's okay, soldier. General Clark told me all about them. AFI's where these vehicles are readied for combat."

The soldier glanced at Pham, who leaned against the open car door. "Does General Clark know that you are here, sir? On the property?"

"Absolutely," Mackie said. "We have a meeting with him this morning." He glanced at his watch. "We're supposed to be in his office by seven."

"You may even want to radio ahead and alert them to the delay," Mackie said, his tone cheerfully innocent.

The soldier relaxed perceptibly, but still maintained a ready stance. "Forgive me, sir, but this is not the main entrance to the property. And the woods are not public restrooms. You're on a one–way service road that leads away from the production facility, which is why these roads are so narrow."

Mackie frowned. "We must have taken a wrong turn. It was so dark when we arrived, we obviously missed the main entrance."

"It can happen, sir," the soldier allowed.

Mackie walked in front of the semi, glancing to both sides of the road before he said, "Why don't we back up to the widest part of the shoulder and let you pass. We'll back up about ten yards then pull into the underbrush. That should give you just enough room to squeeze by, and we'll drive ahead to turn around. You said this road leads to the production facility?"

"A quarter mile ahead. It's the only building on this road." The soldier raised his radio. "I'm going to call ahead and let them know to expect you."

Mackie nodded, keeping his composure. "Good, good."

"Your name, sir?"

Pham stared at Mackie. Expectantly.

Mackie didn't hesitate. "Tell the General that Hank Stone from Synthesis Industries has arrived."

"Yes, sir."

The soldier climbed back into his cab, waiting while Pham backed up to the widest part of the shoulder. She stayed silent until the semi's brake lights disappeared from the rearview mirror. Finally, she turned to Mackie. "I can't decide whether that was ballsy or stupid."

"We're taking the offensive," Mackie said. "Having them look for Hank may buy us some time."

"A few minutes, tops."

"Might be all we need."

"Don't look so cheerful."

Pham pulled into the parking lot in front of the production facility. Like the administrative building in the distance, it also resembled a military airplane hangar, with its olive drab paint and corrugated metal construction. No company logos or signposts. Clearly an area unaccustomed to visitors. The parking lot was already half full, mostly with pick up trucks and SUV's. At the far end of the building, an open two-story metal door provided a gaping entrance to the facility. The hood of semi-truck poked out of the entrance to the loading bay. Another eighteen wheeler idled not far away, awaiting its cargo. Pham parked the car far from the semi trucks, perpendicular to the sidewalk. "I'm not waiting in the car this time," she said, killing the engine and pocketing the keys.

"Fair enough." Mackie stepped out of the vehicle, caught his reflection in the car's window and poked his head back inside to ask, "You have an extra shirt in the back? This one's trashed."

Pham nodded popped the trunk. "What happened back there? In the woods?"

"I heard the truck and started running back to you. Tripped on a rogue rock while avoiding a tree root."

She pulled out a navy blue t-shirt with NPD emblazoned in yellow on the back. "Probably not appropriate for the occasion." She tossed it back into the trunk and withdrew another option. "How about this?"

She held up a dark windbreaker with a logo for the Fraternal Order of Police over the breast pocket, but no markings on the back. "We can make this work." Mackie slipped on the jacket, zipped it halfway up to cover the dirt, then flipped the collar over the logo. Not perfect, but passable. Mackie unclipped his gun from his belt to check the magazine.

"What are you doing?" Pham asked.

"Taking a cue from the Boy Scouts…always be prepared."

Pham shook her head. "Don't even think about it. That's a registered weapon, and it's not registered to you. I'm the only one with a permit to carry a gun here. If they find that on you, they'll detain you first and ask questions later." She took the gun and placed it back in its case. "And the bullets from your pocket. Give 'em here."

Mackie fished them out of his pant's pocket and handed them over. Just as she was about to close the trunk, he reached into the other pocket and withdrew the metal shrapnel, which he dropped among the other items in the trunk. "No sense having to explain this, too."

Pham closed the trunk, picked up her cell phone, and pressed a pre-programmed number. "I'm double checking the search warrant. And asking for back up. Once we've been given the green light, we'll walk inside."

Mackie strolled along the sidewalk, studying the various cars and listening to the bustle of activity near the open metal doors of the hanger. He heard Pham's voice. She sounded and looked more animated than during the previous hours. Mackie continued down the sidewalk, noting the modest attempt to landscape the building.

Ten feet from the hanger opening, two men caught his attention. One wore BDUs, the other in civilian attire and holding a clipboard. A third man, heading to the nearby semi, glanced at Mackie, nodded, and continued on his way. Mackie nodded, turned around, and headed back to Pham, who was turned away, absorbed in her conversation.

"Excuse me, sir?"

Mackie paused in mid-stride.

"Sir? Can I help you?"

Mackie turned. "No, thanks. I'm okay. Just looking around. I have a seven o'clock meeting with General Clark."

The man closed the space separating them. "He's waiting for you, Dr. McKay."

Mackie froze.

"I can escort you, if you'd like," the man said.

"That won't be necessary. Just point the..."

He didn't finish his sentence. Something—a sudden burst of electricity—slammed into his chest and surged through his entire body. Seemingly paralyzed, Mackie dropped. No way to catch himself this time because his limbs wouldn't respond. Like a felled tree, he slammed full force onto the ground, his chest absorbing the fall. He lurched when he received another shock of the Taser.

CHAPTER THIRTY-ONE

MACKIE FELT LIKE he was watching a movie of himself. He saw the men approach his downed body and drag him into the warehouse. He heard their grunts as they strained against his dead weight. He listened to their plans when they strapped him to a chair. He couldn't, though, coordinate his body to move or fight back. The Taser had short circuited his brain's command to move his muscles, so for a brief moment he became a passive observer of his own capture. Unlike a movie, though, he felt every scrape. Every pull. Every slap.

Pressure pulled on Mackie's shoulders. Arms yanked back at an abnormal angle. Bones straining against their joints. The smallest movements intensified his pain. He heard voices. He blinked against the glare of the interior lights of the warehouse. Mackie closed his eyes, trying to calm his respirations. Each breath made his chest burn. The agony intensified when he inhaled, ripping the air out of him as he exhaled. He grunted, forcing his eyes to remain open.

They had pulled him into an office space. He saw a desk and three men. He heard their voices blending together. As he regained his wits, more distinct features emerged. Their conversation quieted as Mackie shifted, now able to relax his arms. The pain in his shoulders subsided, but did not cease.

"It stings, doesn't it, Dr. McKay?" A familiar voice. Graveled. Deep. Commanding. General Clark.

Mackie turned his head, searching for the bastard in the blinding light.

"It's okay. You're going to be just fine." Clark slapped Mackie on the back of the head as he stepped into view. "I wasn't expecting to see you so soon. At least, not here. I thought I had answered all of your questions during your first visit to AFI."

The fog in Mackie's head lifted. With increased consciousness, though, came increased pain. He took shallow breaths. He looked for Pham but didn't see her. He pressed his shoulder blades against the back of the metal folding chair, releasing some of the pressure on his arms.

Mackie concentrated on his surroundings. Inside an office at AFI. Mackie listened for the sound of others in the room. General Clark inhaled and exhaled just inches from his face. Two other people paced behind his chair.

"That Taser kind of sucks when you're on the receiving end." Clark sat on a stool directly in front of Mackie. "That burning you're feeling right now…it will get better. But watch out for that first shower. Stings like hell when the water hits you." He laughed, his fetid breath piercing the lingering confusion in Mackie's brain.

"Kiss my ass," Mackie muttered.

Clark smacked him, snapping his head back. "Watch your mouth."

Mackie tasted blood. Turning his head, he spat it out. "Is this how you treat all of your visitors? Welcome them back with a Taser?"

Clark smiled. "That was for your own protection." He leaned back on his stool, looking at the two other men behind Mackie. "Imagine what could happen if we allowed private citizens to trespass on our property. Someone could get hurt with all that live ammo we use. Think of the Taser as our way to protect you from yourself."

"And this?" Mackie strained against his bonds. "It this protecting me from myself?"

General Clark nodded to someone behind the chair. Mackie turned his head. The man looked vaguely familiar. Mackie remembered. One of the guards in the Humvee from Singh's house. The man didn't acknowledge Mackie.

Stepping closer, he used a knife to sever the duct tape binding Mackie's wrist. With one swift jerk, he yanked free the tape. Hair and skin clung to the adhesive. Mackie winced.

Clark shook his head. "I'm not sure what you're talking about. We brought you inside after your near accident. Unfortunately, we had to restrain you in the process. That's standard protocol, by the way. Once we've insured you're no longer a threat to yourself, you're free to leave. That is, of course, after we've determined your purpose in coming here." Clark lifted a sheet of paper from the desk behind him. "It's all in the incident report my employee filed. If you'd like, we'll send a copy to your lawyer. I think you'll find the report both accurate and unequivocal. And honestly, who will most people believe? A decorated Army general recently retired with honors or a washed-up orthopedic surgeon still under a cloud of suspicion for his ex-wife's mysterious death."

Clark walked over to a wet bar built into the office bookcase. Ice clinked against the bottom of a glass. He turned to Mackie. "Diet Coke?"

"Fuck off."

"I'll take that as a no." He fixed his own drink and returned to the stool in front of Mackie's chair. Taking a seat, he studied Mackie. "You've been snooping around where you don't belong. Twice in Atlanta. Once already at AFI, and now you're back. For Christ's sake, I got a call at six a.m. that you had parked an unmarked police car along the service road just inside our property. Does that mean Detective Pham is here again, too?"

Mackie remained silent. He absently massaged the raw spots on his wrist. He might be able to leave if he played his cards right. A caution light flashed in his mind. Say what they wanted to hear and then get the hell out. But, he wanted answers. Knowing that Pham was nearby emboldened him. He hoped she wasn't in an adjacent room and duct-taped to a folding chair. He waited for Clark to make the next move.

"I didn't think I needed to be so explicit last time," Clark finally said. "I figured you'd be more than capable of grasping innuendo and subtlety. Looks like I'm going to have to spell this out for you. Armored Forces Industries is a privately owned business engaged in contract work for the U.S. government. What we do on our own property, in conjunction with the military, is a private matter."

Mackie decided to speak the truth. "I'm here to follow up on a lead in my ex-wife's murder investigation."

"Which has nothing to do with AFI," Clark insisted.

"Except that much of what I've seen and learned does seem suspicious. The faulty armor over the fuel tank doesn't make sense. The secrecy surrounding a damn good H-BOC product doesn't make sense. That Sarah was involved with both situations provided a natural connection between AFI and Synthesis. That's what brought be me back to you." He lifted his depilated arms. "And this is how I'm greeted?"

"There is a legal process to obtain that information. If your lawyer sees fit to subpoena us in this case—which I seriously doubt—then we will cooperate to the fullest extent of the law."

A door opened behind Mackie. He couldn't see the man, but his voice sounded familiar. "We're ready, General."

Rage surged up inside Mackie. General Clark could and would act with impunity inside the walls of AFI. If he left the premises, it would be Clark's word versus Mackie's. Clark would do the same thing when the police back-up arrived, despite Pham's search warrant. Open his arms wide and smile, offering assistance before he ducked behind national security matters to obscure the truth. Mackie had made it this far, and he refused to go down without a fight. "What were you doing in Atlanta yesterday?" he finally asked.

Clark narrowed his eye. "If you keep your mouth shut, we'll both be better off right now." He stood in front of Mackie's chair, towering over him before he leaned down. "This never has been about Sarah, has it? Who else is working with you?"

"I don't know what you're talking about."

Clark straightened. One man walked behind him while the other one grabbed Mackie's arm.

Pain flashed in Mackie's shoulders.

"You look thirsty," Clark observed.

"I'm fine."

"We'll see about that."

Despite his efforts to wrench free, Mackie was hauled into the adjacent room. Clark marched behind them, shutting the office door behind him. Concrete floors replaced carpet. Bare walls instead of bookshelves. It looked as if a portion of the production floor had been walled off. No windows. The only light provided by a strip of fluorescent bulbs overhead. Ahead, two stacks of boxes, one taller than the other. A length of plywood situated across the top and positioned with an incline. A makeshift slide. On the floor, a pallet of bottled water.

"I think some water would do us all good," Clark said, nodding to the others.

The men restraining Mackie lifted him off the floor. Mackie scissored his legs and swung his arms. The more he resisted, the tighter the guards gripped him. The man who'd summoned them to the room stepped behind the plywood incline.

They hoisted him onto the board, head down, feet up. Mackie's pulse pounded in his ears, his head wound throbbing against the DermaBond.

"Careful with him. No other marks," Clark ordered.

Once positioned on the board, he was secured in place by narrow strips of fabric. He could barely draw a breath by the time they finished.

General Clark approached him. "Once more, doctor. Who are you working with? Who sent you here?"

Mackie met his cold gaze. "I'm here to find out about Sarah's murder."

Clark shook his head, disappointed. "Reputation is everything in this business. If we permit false accusations to circulate about AFI, our reputation could be stained. Lose that, and we lose the confidence of the government. Lost contracts translate into lost revenue. And so it goes, all because one man spread unsubstantiated rumors, desperately groping for information, and caring little about those he takes down in the process. It's all very dramatic, Dr. McKay, but I think it's all bullshit."

Panic welled up inside Mackie. He closed his eyes, determined to calm his breathing.

"You don't strike me as a man predisposed to drama, Dr. McKay. You do strike me, though, as an opportunist," Clark said. "Someone who might come here under the guise of a murder investigation, perhaps instructed to do so by another person…or another organization." He waited.

"You're crazy. You know why I called you Sunday." Pause. Breathe. His face flushed due to his position on the board. "I… wanted…answers."

Clark smiled. "Something we have in common. Wanting answers." He nodded to the man who stood to the right of the incline. He ripped a strip of clear plastic from a box. Saran wrap. The man forced the plastic wrap over Mackie's face.

Mackie thrashed his head, causing the man to press down harder, suffocating him. He bucked against the board, but the strips of cloth held. Finally, the man released the plastic wrap.

Mackie sucked in air. "Don't," he managed to gasp.

Clark's face came back into focus. He leaned over Mackie, enunciating each word. "You are disrupting a lucrative business, Doctor. You're also interfering with the government's war on terror. Who are you working for?"

Mackie couldn't think clearly. If he knew what Clark wanted to hear, he'd supply the answer.

Before he could speak, Clark nodded to the man with the cellophane. "Again."

The man ripped a fresh sheet from the roll. He folded it, pressing it over Mackie's mouth, his nose exposed. The guard from Singh's house handed General Clark a bottled water. Clark unscrewed the lid, took a sip, then dumped the remaining water on Mackie's face. Reflexively, Mackie breathed in, sucking more plastic than air. Desperate for air but with water on his face, Mackie felt like he was drowning. Each incomplete breath led to another. Each attempt more futile than the last. He tried to cough but lacked enough air to do it. Thoughts raced in his mind, one predominate among them—he was about to drown in a backwoods warehouse in Nowhere, Alabama.

His resistance weakened. Instead of gasping for breath, he exhaled through his nose, air escaping him like a punctured tire. He wouldn't survive much longer. Water continued to cascade across his face. Then, it stopped. The pressure released. He could breathe. The first rush of air caused his lungs to spasm. He gasped. Coughed. Gagged.

"Turn his head," Clark said.

The men tilted him sideways, still strapped to the board. He faced the ground. Mackie tried to turn his head when he vomited, but he couldn't coordinate his mind and his muscles. Stomach acid burned his throat. He opened his eyes, and he saw polished combat boots.

General Clark hooked the toe of his boot under Mackie's chin.

Mackie stared into his impassive eyes.

"Water boarding," Clark said. "It's not in the Army Field Manual, but it's an effective interrogation technique." He released Mackie's chin and ordered his men to flip him back so that he faced the ceiling again. He sat in the folding chair beside Mackie, their faces almost even. "Let me try this again. Who are you working for?"

"Sarathi Singh," Mackie blurted out in his mentally muddled state. "The money's been marked."

Clark shook his head, clearly disappointed. "Wrong answer."

Mackie struggled for calm. "If I die…" He took a deep breath. "…they'll find out anyway."

"Don't worry about that," Clark said. "We're not in the business of killing Americans. At least, not on U.S. soil. Was it Jefferson who said, 'The tree of liberty had to be fertilized with the blood of patriots'?"

"Refreshed," corrected the larger guard. "The tree of liberty has to be refreshed."

Clark smiled. "Either way. We're not refreshing today. Pruning, perhaps, but not refreshing."

Clark glanced at the man with the Saran Wrap. "I think we're ready for the syringe." Clark took it and waved it close to Mackie's face. "Versed. A highly effective anesthetic. Of course, you know more about that than I do, Doctor." He smirked. "Let's just say we sometimes use it for proscribed purposes, rather the prescribed. You'll forget the pain of what we're about to do. That's good for you. And with this dose, you'll forget the preceding hour. Retrograde amnesia, which is good for me."

"You're insane," Mackie said.

"It's all a mater of perspective." General Clark glanced at his watch, then addressed the other men in the room. "Could you give us just a moment alone? I'll let you know when I'm finished."

The men dutifully left the room. Like good little soldiers, Mackie though bitterly. After they departed, Clark settled onto the edge of the folding chair. "I've got another meeting in about fifteen minutes. We need to wrap things up." He set aside the syringe. Reaching to his belt for his hand gun, he pressed the cold metal to Mackie's forehead and clicked off the safety. "Once more. Who. Are. You. Working. For?"

Mackie expected to die. "Go to hell, General."

The roar of the gunshot was deafening.

Debris rained down on Mackie's face. At first, he couldn't tell if he had been shot. Deeper fear gripped him. He already felt so numb, new pain might not register. He could still see. His head pounded, and his ears rang. He smelled burning hair, then felt the muzzle of the gun singe his forehead. He could hardly hear the words when he spoke. "The police know I'm here." He caught his breath. Couldn't even form complete sentences. "A search warrant. A SWAT team is en route. They know Synthesis paid you."

Clark moved in. His calm expression replaced by rage. A blood vessel pulsated at his forehead. "If you really think that little gook can actually help you, then you're stupider than I thought. I'm wasting my time." Beads of sweat trickled down Clark's face. He stood and backhanded Mackie across the face. He tossed the gun onto the chair, knocking the syringe onto the floor beneath Mackie. Clark then grabbed two bottles of waters. He took the discarded Saran Wrap and shoved it into Mackie's mouth before he dumped the contents of both bottles onto his face.

Mackie couldn't prepare. Although he tried to suck air in through his nose, he was drowning once again. He thrashed his head, but the waterfall continued. His empty stomach heaved. The room began to spin. He felt consciousness slipping. Even as the water flowed over his face, he felt removed from the scene, as if it was all happening to someone else.

Random images of Reagan flashed before him. An infant. At the airport. High school graduation. Horseback riding for her birthday. And one recurring caption to each image. All for you, he thought. All for you.

An explosion suddenly rocked the building. Blasts of heat. Screams. Footsteps running across the concrete floor. General Clark yelled. More explosions. Discrete pops of gunfire. Mackie continued to fade. The scene unfolding around him reminded him of a movie. Part of the action, but also removed. He let go, slipping, falling. Darkness all around him, but punctuated by strobes of light. Then, something changed.

He could breath again. Air rushed into his lungs. His mind slowly cleared. He fell, feeling weightless until he slammed into the ground.

CHAPTER THIRTY-TWO

"MACKIE? COME ON. We need to get out of here."

Her voice reached him in the darkness, sounding frantic. He felt her beside him, but he couldn't see her until she leaned over him. He reached to steady himself, able to move his arms but not without great effort. He felt as if tendons had been cut and spliced back together. His arms could do their job, but nothing felt routine. Plastic burned nearby. The smell nauseated him. He dry heaved, then panicked when he felt a damp coolness slide across his forehead.

Libby Pham wiped his face with a wet cloth. "You gotta move. The car's waiting."

Flames danced across the black wall, cutting through the darkness. Pulsing waves of heat lapped at him, making him want to settle back and close his eyes, but the urgency in her voice told him he couldn't. He strained to remember what had happened, but his mind was blank. He forced himself up on one elbow, moving through the pain.

Pham slid her hand under his arm, helping him to his feet. She pressed a gun into the palm of his hand. "Don't use it unless you have to. Those bullets trace back to the Department."

"What happened?"

Pham pulled him toward the flames. "Later."

His strength returned as he stood there. Arms more solid. Legs supporting his own weight. His shirt stuck to his back, untucked and still damp. A slurry of dirt and mud caked across his abdomen. His blue jacket hung loosely across his waist, apparently ripped from him earlier. A constant sting nagged his arm. When he rubbed it, he knocked loose a syringe half-filled with fluid. A dot of blood stained the arm of his shirt. Nothing made sense to him right now.

Pham stood in the middle of the concrete floor. "Follow me. I know you're groggy, but you have to keep up."

Smoke began to fill the room. Mackie trailed behind her, stepping over strips of cloth and empty water bottles. Upended wooden crates and a metal folding chair blocked his path. He moved around them. Pham searched near the edge of the room for a way out. Mackie saw a rim of daylight beyond the flames. As he tried to stay near her, he tripped and fell. Rather than hitting hard concrete, he smacked into something softer. Someone face down in a puddle on the floor. "What the hell?" Mackie pushed off the body. He didn't recognize it. Smoke stung his eyes.

"You okay?" Pham called out.

"There's a body over here," Mackie said.

"Up here, too."

Mackie looked once again. Three people, or maybe four. In spite of concentrating, the details blurred in his head. He pushed himself to his feet, searching for Pham. Flames continued to lick the walls, blocking their path to the daylight. She turned to him, not even looking down as she spoke. "Another body's right behind me. Be careful."

He saw polished black combat boots. He knelt down, instinctively checking the carotid artery. Warm skin. No pulse.

"There's an open door over here," Pham said.

"Hold up. I'm right behind you," Mackie said as he stepped over the corpse of General Clark.

They entered the office. Images crept into Mackie's consciousness, still incomplete. He recognized the desk. Saw the folding chair, the discarded tape on the carpet. He didn't know how he'd gotten in here initially. Pham turned toward Mackie. "Which way out?"

"How about the way you came in?"

"Can't," she said. "An RPG detonated and blew a hole in the side of the building shortly after pops of gunfire came from inside. I rushed in to find you when I heard. I don't know what happened, but we've got to get out of here." She pointed to the closed second door in the office. "What's up here?"

Mackie cracked open the door. "A hallway."

"Recognize it?"

"No. I was out when they dragged me in here."

Pham opened the door all the way. "Come on. The car's parked outside the main entrance of the building."

The hallway extended another fifty feet or more. Closed office doors on one side. Windowless walls on the other. Pictures of military vehicles displayed along the corridor. Pham ran to the right, her footsteps muted by the carpet. Mackie followed her. At the end of the hallway, a wreath hung on a wooden door. Mackie stopped short, his memory returning in bits and pieces. Their first meeting with General Clark on Sunday. He took a moment to get his bearings. "Straight ahead is the lobby."

Pham pushed on the door at the end of the hallway. It wouldn't open. She pressed her shoulder against the door. Still no movement. "How else can we get out of here?"

"Move back," Mackie said. He pressed his ear to the door. No sound behind it. Pushing back, he raised the gun—

"Wait," Pham sputtered.

— and fired three rounds into the door handle. The force of the gunshots caused him to stumble back. The door creaked open.

"Shit." Pham knelt down and ran her hands over the floor. "There's a casing right by your foot," she said angrily as she collected two others. "They'll be coming now."

Mackie grabbed the third casing. They snuck through the doorway. No one else in the lobby. A steaming mug of coffee and a half eaten bagel sat on the desk. Crowd noise outside.

"Any other way to reach your car?"

"I think the two parking lots are connected." She looked at the rim of smoke already billowing in the sky. "We'll have to negotiate the crowds on the sidewalk."

Mackie approached the glass doors. Workers congregated, pointing at the fire. Dozens of employees filled the parking lot. He cracked open the door. Emergency horns blared. In the distance, sirens. They stepped outside.

Pulsing heat from the flames greeted them. Everyone in the parking lot appeared to be mesmerized by the conflagration. A fire engine pulled into the parking lot, then turned left toward the production facility. Two police cars raced in behind them, jerking to a stop at the end of the lot. Security personnel milled around the open hangar doors, barely visible from this distance. Mackie didn't see the Crown Victoria.

Pham pulled off her jacket, turning it inside out as she removed it. She handed it to Mackie. "Wear this and keep your head down." She stepped closer. "Follow me."

Mackie unzipped his own tattered jacket, but Pham placed her hand on his arm. "Just pull the jacket on over your own. We don't want to leave any more evidence than is necessary."

"You don't think we've left enough?" He struggled to add a third layer to the Spandex skin he still wore.

Pham nodded at the flames. "That's all done by their equipment. Come on, before someone makes it even harder for us to get out of here."

The heat of the inferno intensified as they approached the car. The crowd gathered near it appeared more interested in the fire damage than the vehicle. More rescue personnel arrived. Three ambulances parked along the edge of the pavement, back doors open, lights silently flashing. Two empty gurneys rolled toward the flames. A soldier pulled a charred body from the gaping hole in the side of the building.

They approached the scene, maintaining a steady pace. Mackie kept his head down. Their car was parked thirty feet away, facing outward, ready to drive away. Pham picked up her pace.

A young woman from the crowd turned as they walked past. "Dr. McKay?"

Mackie froze.

"My God, what's happened to you?"

Mackie recognized her face, but couldn't recall her name. Still fuzzy from the prick of the anesthetic needle, he couldn't fabricate a plausible explanation for his appearance or his presence at AFI.

Sensing his discomfort, the woman introduced herself. "I'm Barrett. We met on Sunday when you visited the general. Are you okay?"

"Have you seen General Clark?" Mackie asked.

"They're looking for him now," Barrett said. "That explosion went off right near where he was."

Mackie swallowed. "I was supposed to meet him today."

"I know. They told us at the front desk to notify him as soon as you arrived. He wanted to see you. He was waiting in his office, but someone called him down to the production facility. Something urgent, I heard." Tears formed in her eyes, and she said, "I think he might have been in the part of the building that exploded."

Through his peripheral vision, he saw Pham continue to their car. As she blended into the crowd, fragmented images of the previous hour returned to Mackie. "Hank Stone was to meet with us, too," he said. "Have you seen him?"

"Not yet." She began to sob.

Mackie turned toward the car. Pham had already unlocked the doors and stood by the driver's side, waiting. Another fire truck pulled into the lot, partially blocking the one-lane service road. A van marked with the logo of the local NBC affiliate inched through the crowd, looking for a place to park.

Pham opened the driver's side door as Mackie walked up. "Let's go."

Mackie circled the car and climbed into the passenger seat as Pham started the car. She carefully navigated the vehicle through the crowd of onlookers. AFI employees glanced at the car, but most remained riveted on the inferno. Mackie shed the jacket Pham had given him earlier and shoved it into the gym bag at his feet, his fingertips brushing against the metallic armor at the bottom of the bag. "RPG's?" he finally asked.

"Two of them." Pham cut her eyes to the scene in her rearview mirror, her hands trembling even as she gripped the steering wheel. "I wasn't going to go after you until I heard the gunfire and the explosion from inside. Now, I know how my husband must have felt that afternoon." She swiped at her eyes with the back of her hand, not making eye contact with him. "It's impossible to just stand by and wait."

Mackie slid his hand into hers as she drove.

She bit her lip, not speaking as she drove to the edge of the parking lot and turned down the main driveway. Several cars entered the complex. One car in front of them headed to the edge of the property. Pham swallowed the emotion lumped in her throat. "The SWAT team's on their way. They're probably an hour out, though."

"We'll be just about home by then."

She glanced at the bag at his feet. "Hide the gun."

Mackie wrapped his tattered jacket around the handgun, placed it in the bottom of his gym bag, and shifted the metal shrapnel to the top to conceal the weapon. Pham slowed as they approached the exit. Several cars backed up at the gate. One car pulled forward, waited a beat, then pulled onto the road. The process continued.

At the intersection of the main drive and the state road, a Humvee blocked the flow of traffic. Parked near the entrance, the military vehicle forced incoming cars to stop. An armed soldier stood near the front of the Humvee, inspecting each car before allowing it access to the property. The entering cars were forced to skirt the edge of the road and the shoulder to drive around the blockade. Outbound traffic was hindered, too. A second soldier monitored the departing vehicles. A third uniformed officer paced between the incoming and outgoing traffic, studying the passengers. "Shit," Pham said, drumming her fingers on the steering wheel. "Roadblock." A car pulled in behind them.

Mackie leaned forward in his seat. The car in front of them pulled forward. Pham took her foot off the brake. Their car rolled forward.

"Pull out your badge," Mackie said.

The soldier approached their car, dipped his chin and stared at them for a moment before turning to speak to his supervisor.

Pham gripped the steering wheel. "He recognized us."

All three uniformed guards looked up at the sound of the approaching siren.

"SWAT team?" Mackie cracked his window.

Pham shook her head. "Too soon."

The siren intensified. Moments later, an ambulance slammed on its brakes to avoid hitting the parked Humvee. All three soldiers froze. A uniformed officer stepped in front of the Humvee, directing the ambulance into the other lane in order to bypass the line of incoming cars. Red emergency lights pulsed atop the rescue vehicle, its siren now silent.

"We're blocking the entrance," Pham said.

"Pull forward when the cars part to let the ambulance in."

"I can't—"

"Just do it," he said.

Pham eased forward. A lane opened up between the roadblock and the main driveway to AFI. As the ambulance swung past the roadblock and turned onto the property, Pham cut the wheel left onto the shoulder of the state road, parallel to the incoming traffic.

"Don't wait," Mackie urged.

Pham pulled onto the road opposite the entrance. The Crown Victoria skated along the shoulder. Suddenly, the supervising soldier noticed.

"Halt!" he shouted at them.

Pham mashed the accelerator pedal. The car shot forward, rocketing past the Humvees. Twenty yards down the road, Mackie glanced back to see all three soldiers confused but mercifully remaining at their post.

Chapter Thirty-Three

SHOWERING HURT WORSE than he'd expected. Mackie squeezed the towel rack in the back of the shower in the doctor's lounge at Nashville Memorial, wincing each time he turned under the water's flow. At first the water sliced into his wound, expelling dirt and crusted blood. The longer he endured the cleaning, the more the pain turned into a low-intensity burn. By the time he finished, pink flesh stripped of hair glistened under the fluorescent lights of the bathroom. Wrapped in a towel, Mackie sat for several minutes and gathered his strength. When he could stand and walk, he searched for a fresh pair of scrubs in the lounge's laundry rack.

Pham had suggested that he clean up at home first, but Mackie would hear none of it. He hadn't seen Reagan in more than twenty-four hours. He was going back to the hospital. He had called the intensive care unit on the drive back, and learned that she was breathing on her own once again. But he couldn't walk into the ICU looking battered and bloody. Pham relented, dropping him off near the back entrance of the doctor's parking lot before she returned to police headquarters to complete a mound of paperwork and a meeting with her boss.

He threw his stained shirt into the garbage, then stuffed his trousers into his gym bag. He'd have the jacket and body suit cleaned and get them back to Pham. The other jacket was useless, but he couldn't throw it away here. As Pham would have said, too many questions if anyone looked for physical evidence of his presence at AFI. Of course, probably a dozen security cameras had already recorded his image that morning.

Mackie gulped down a cup of tepid coffee before he took the

elevator to the surgical ICU. After entering the double doors to the unit, he went directly to Reagan's bed. Monitors beeped and nurses scurried about the ward, but her cubical seemed largely ignored. A sure sign of stability, if not outright improvement. He stepped past the drawn curtain and paused at the glass doorway. With her hair combed and IV tubing tucked neatly under the covers, she slept peacefully. The sheet rose and fell with the metronomic precision of shallow breathing, which she was doing on her own this time. The ventilator sat beside her bed, tubes inert but ready for use if the need arose.

Mackie moved to the side of her bed and sat on the mattress, setting his bag at his feet.

Reagan opened her eyes.

He felt a thrill. "You look great."

She tried to smile, but her lips quivered instead. Tears welled up in the corners of her eyes. Too weak to sit up, she rolled her shoulders toward him. Mackie leaned over, awkwardly, and hugged her. The smell of antiseptic and shampoo permeated her bed. Her tiny body clung to his. After a moment, she eased back. "You're leaning on my stitches."

Mackie helped to reposition her. She looked exhausted from their brief embrace. The faded yellow bruises on her face added to her pallor.

"I don't feel so great," she murmured.

"Your stomach?"

She shook her head. "It's not that. I just feel tired. Like I could sleep for a week."

"That can be arranged," he said. "Your room is ready for you once you're discharged. You'll have plenty of time to get some rest once you're home."

She coughed, a phlegm-filled rattle that caused her to suck in her breath from the pain. "The nurse said I pulled out the breathing tube late last night. I don't remember doing it." She coughed again, more winded with every sentence. "I really don't remember much."

Mackie stroked her forehead with the back of his hand. "I'm glad you don't remember the wreck," he said.

She stared at the television bolted to the corner wall. "You know what's weird, though? The last thing I can remember is climbing into the front seat of the car. I remember you picking me up. And I remember seeing Mr. Richardson just before you arrived."

Mackie paused. "Duel?"

"He said you sent him to pick me up." She turned toward him. "I remember feeling so hurt that you'd send somebody else to pick me up after Mom..." She caught her breath. "After all that, you know, happened with mom."

"I didn't even consider it, Reagan." Mackie squeezed her hand. "Of course, I intended to be there. I was there. You think you're just remembering another time when you saw Duel?"

Reagan shook her head. "No, I remember very clearly. He came up to me on the sidewalk. Said you'd sent him to bring me home because something had come up with mom's funeral arrangements. It was, like, eleven o'clock at night, so I thought it was kind of weird. Especially since you'd told me you were on the way. "

"Didn't happen, Reagan. I left the house as soon as you called me."

Reagan stared at the television as she spoke. "It was kind of creepy. You know how he can be with his fancy clothes and cologne." She took a deep breath, then sighed. "He said you had gotten caught up in some deal with mom's boyfriend."

Mackie shook his head. "There's a lot we're still finding out... about the way she died."

Reagan began to cry. "I spoke to her Wednesday night. The day she died."

"How did she sound?" Mackie asked.

"Happy. Optimistic." Reagan sniffed, then cleared her throat. "Said she had a few surprises for me when I got home. The first one was that she'd upgraded me to first class for my return flight from Italy."

"She'd received a big payment that week," Mackie said carefully.

Reagan nodded. "That's what Mr. Richardson said, too."

Mackie straightened. Of course Sarah would be happy. She had just been bought out by Synthesis. Thirty million dollars would have made her ecstatic. But how could Duel have known, especially since he'd claimed ignorance about the money? And why had Duel been at the airport? Why involve Reagan? Unless he'd known the truth all along. A cold sweat prickled Mackie's spine, causing him to shiver with the horrible realization of Duel's potential involvement.

Mackie thought about the time since Sarah's murder. Duel had been the first to tell Mackie about the autopsy results, the first to arrive at the scene of the car accident that next morning, and he'd deflected Mackie's attention away from his own investigation into what had happened. Mackie's heart sprinted into a gallop as he considered the implications. None of it made sense.

"Dad?" Reagan interrupted. "You okay?"

He forced a smile. "Don't worry about it, sweetie. I just need to talk to Duel." He stood, grabbing his things from the floor. "The nurses are going to fuss at me for spending too much time in here outside of visiting hours. You need to get some rest, anyway."

"Can you come back tonight? Hang out for a little bit?"

"Count on it." He squeezed her fingers before releasing her hand.

Someone pulled back the curtain, and in walked a team of nurses. The lead nurse paused when she saw him standing at Reagan's bed. Mackie didn't recognize any of the nurses. Most were students, but the lead nurse was older. Probably new to the hospital.

"It's time for your bath, Miss McKay." Turning her attention to Mackie, the head nurse asked, "And you are...?"

"Cooper McKay. I'm Reagan's dad."

The nurse glanced at the clock on the side wall. "It's not visiting hours. Even for family members. It is time, however, for us to care for your daughter. I'm sure you'll understand we need to respect her privacy. You can wait in the visitor's lounge with the other families until we re-open the unit for visitors.

Mackie ground his teeth. Almost thirty years of working at the same hospital and in a week he had become just another worried parent. He turned his back on the nurse, and leaned down to kiss Reagan's cheek. "Hang in there, kiddo. I'll see you tonight."

He brushed past the nurses, searching for the nearest phone.

* * *

"You've got to turn yourself in," Duel said on the other end of the phone line. "AFI is pressing charges against you. Something about trespassing and vandalism."

"That's ridiculous," Mackie said.

"Might be, but that's what I'm told," Duel said. "I can't help you if you keep pulling this crap."

Mackie paced in the waiting room of the surgical ICU. An elderly woman sat in a cracked vinyl chair in the corner, reading a magazine. A cable news channel played on the muted corner television. Otherwise, the room was empty. Mackie pulled the coil of the phone cord back from the counter, keeping his voice low. "For Christ's sake, Duel, they zapped me with a Taser, then they shot me up with an anesthetic so I'd forget what they'd done. Torture's no joke. File a counter-suit against the bastards."

"Uh-huh," Duel wheezed on the other end of the line. "I came into my office this morning and found a fax on my desk. An incident report of some kind. Jesus, pal."

Mackie heard him rattling papers on his desk.

"This says you walked into the production floor unannounced after being caught trespassing on their property, you assaulted one of the guards when he asked you to leave, you used a private service road instead of the main entrance to gain illegal access, and to top it off, it appears you took a piss on the side of their driveway."

"Not true!" Mackie slapped the countertop. Blood pounded in his head. The palm of his hand stung. The woman in the corner of the waiting room looked up. Mackie stepped away from the counter, pulling the phone cord tight as he prowled back and forth. How had AFI even known to send the paperwork to Duel in the first place?

"Where do you want to do this?" Duel asked. "We've got to get this taken care of."

"What were you doing at the airport on the night Reagan arrived home?"

Duel paused. "There are some things you need to know, Mackie. Things about Sarah."

Mackie heard him breathing, obviously measuring his words.

"Things I'd rather tell you in person," Duel said.

"You've had plenty of opportunity to tell me, but you wait until I start asking questions to bring it up? How'd you know about the crash site, Duel? Who told you about the H-BOC in Sarah's body? The autopsy report hadn't even been released yet."

"I can explain all of this to you, but not on the phone," Duel said. "What time can you come by?"

Mackie raked his fingers through his hair. He had another few hours before evening family visiting hours. If he left now, he could make it back in time. But he had one other stop to make first. "I'll meet you at your house in an hour." He slammed down the receiver and stormed out of the waiting room, heading for the elevators.

CHAPTER THIRTY-FOUR

MACKIE WALKED ALONG the linoleum floors of the basement hallway. The mid-afternoon pace of business in the morgue seemed similar to the two other times he'd been down here in the last week. Windowless corridors betrayed the actual time of day. Fluorescent lights hummed overhead. The elderly clerk looked up from his newspaper, smiling at Mackie. Halfway to Vern Philpot's office, Mackie stopped. He looked through the observation widow. An overhead light spotlighted a charred body on the metal table. Vern worked on the far side of the gurney, facing the observation window. He wore a blue gown and a mask with a plastic face shield. His autopsy assistant stood nearby, holding a handful of stainless steel instruments smeared with blood. Mackie tapped on the window.

Vern's eyes smiled behind his face shield when he recognized Mackie. He lifted a gloved hand from the body, motioning him into the room.

Mackie entered the autopsy suite. The smell of singed flesh accosted him. He stayed near the doors, not moving any closer to the autopsy table. The assistant, gowned and gloved like Vern, lifted a hose to rinse debris from the edge of the table.

"Hey, man," Vern said, his voice muffled behind the mask. "Wanna see what your liver looks like after being roasted at nine hundred degrees in a house fire?" He held up a piece of purple flesh on the end of a clamp, the sample looking more like grape jelly than human viscera.

Mackie remained against the wall. "No, thanks." He lifted his gym bag. "I came to talk to you about some metals."

"That anal trophy still on your mind?"

"Not exactly."

Vern directed his attention back to the burned carcass before him. "There was a house fire downtown by the stadium earlier this morning. An elderly couple. The man woke up to the smell of smoke. Stumbled outside to the neighbor's house to call for help. Tried to go back inside to find his wife, but it was too late then." He pointed to the body before him. "A horrible way to go. Not much revealing on autopsy, either, but these kinds of things are always a coroner's case. Got to do the autopsy just to make sure there's no funny business."

Metal clinked as he removed several more organ samples, which the assistant placed inside glass containers, affixing a label on each one.

"You about done?" Mackie asked.

Vern nodded. "If I can't persuade you to keep me company with my patients, then I guess we'll have to chat in my office. Give me a few more minutes, and I'll be done in here. Can't guarantee the smell will be gone from my hands, though." He cleared his throat. "You never really get used to burned flesh."

Mackie stepped out the room and made his way to Vern's office. He sat in the chair next to the desk and stared at the familiar clutter of journals scattered about the floor. Stacks of papers covered the top of his desk. A Sponge Bob cartoon screensaver danced across the computer screen. Beethoven's sixth symphony played from a speaker on the bookshelf. Mackie placed his bag beside his chair and waited.

It took more than a few minutes for Vern to join him. He adjusted his ponytail beneath his scrub cap as he walked through the door. "To what do I owe this pleasure, Mackie?"

"I want you to take a look at something." Mackie unzipped his bag and pulled out the soda-can sized armor shrapnel from AFI.

Vern took the metallic disk from him and turned it over in his hand. He ran his finger through the center hole. Tried to bend the edges. Even held the piece under the light, inspecting the marks etched on it. "This is a titanium alloy. Some kind of a high-carbon laminate mixed in. Where'd you get this?"

"Scrap metal from a friend who works for the military," Mackie said. "I was curious about what would cause it to melt like that."

Vern flipped the disk over once more then returned it to Mackie. "Probably impurities."

"What do you mean?"

"A fly in the ointment at the manufacturing plant." He leaned back in his chair, stretching his arms above his head. "These metal alloys are designed to withstand amazing forces. But if an impurity gets into the production line, it throws off the specifications of the metal. I'm sure you've seen that with prosthetic joints. Remember the Jonestown nursing home fire?"

Mackie nodded as he sat back. "That was—what?—fifteen years ago?"

"Something like that." Vern rolled his chair toward the bank of filing cabinets. He studied the unmarked doors for a moment before he leaned forward to open a bottom drawer. He ran his fingers along the manila folder tabs, shaking his head. He closed the drawer and opened the one just above it. "There it is." He pulled out an accordion folder.

"I would've thought you had all this digitized by now," Mackie said.

Vern reached inside the folder and produced a piece of metal the size of a quarter. "You can't digitize the physical evidence. A few images might give you an idea of what you saw on autopsy, but nothing takes the place of being able to personally inspect these treasures."

"I was on call the night of the Jonestown fire," Mackie said. "We filled up the burn unit with those nursing home residents. Worst burns I think I've ever seen. It was a nightmare for those people. Wasn't it some kind of an electrical fire?"

"Lightning struck the transformer near the nursing home," Vern said. "The explosion killed a few people outright, but it was the fire that did the most damage. I think we had twenty-one bodies that night. Most burned beyond recognition. Awful."

Mackie nodded toward the metallic coin. "Did that happen in the fire?"

"This, my friend, came from a prosthetic hip." He held up the misshaped coin. "One of the victims of the fire. She'd had a hip replacement. When we went to perform the autopsy, she had almost a dozen of these stippled along her hip. At first I thought maybe she'd rolled onto her change purse or something. But it's pretty hard to melt nickels and quarters in a house fire. We looked a little closer, and it turned out her prosthetic hip had melted in the heat. Just split open and oozed out like the yolk of a soft-boiled egg. After the fire, the material cooled into these metallic coins."

Mackie leaned closer. "That doesn't sound right. Titanium alloys can withstand extremes of weight and heat." He examined the coin. Like the metallic disk he had taken from AFI, this coin had a durability to it that seemed unexpected given its density.

"That low melting point confused me at first," Vern said. "Bionic hips should be able to just laugh off a little old house fire. But this one didn't." He pulled several pages of handwritten notes from the accordion folder. "It turns out the company that made these replacement hips overlooked a key aspect in their research and development. Notches in the metal ended up weakening the product."

"That's not all that unusual, though, to notch the metal," Mackie said.

"I wouldn't want to pay God knows how many thousands of dollars to you to put a new hip in me with holes in it."

"You'd want to sue me if I didn't," Mackie said. "Otherwise, the hip's not going to stick to the native bone."

"I don't follow you."

"Most companies these days notch the metal with tiny pores so that the bone cement sticks to the prosthesis. I used to tell my patients that a prosthetic hip is like a scoop of cream on a sugar cone. If you grab an ice cream cone from the scoop end, the paper wrapper slides off the bottom of the cone."

Vern sat back and smiled. "That's why most of us grab the cone first."

"Of course. Otherwise, the ice cream sticks to the palm of your hand, just like the ball of the new joint sticks to the original socket of the bone. Nothing's sticking the cone to the paper, though. The stem of the prosthetic joint replacement—your cone—is going to slide out of the leg bone—your paper wrapper—unless you glue it in place. There're enough imperfections in the bumpy sugar cone to stick to the paper if you coat in with glue. Same thing with the metal joints. If they're too smooth, they won't hold the sticky bone cement."

Vern nodded as he stroked his goatee. "That's brilliant. So I'll take the hole-y hip. Only one problem, though. The company that made the prosthesis from the Jonestown fire used the wrong metals. The cobalt-chrome metals, and even the older ceramic used in traditional joint replacements, could withstand the scratches on it. This company switched to a stronger titanium alloy, but that metal was too notch sensitive. Once the heat reached the joint, those notches undermined the metal's integrity. At least, in this case. And to continue your analogy, the joint melted like ice cream in August."

Mackie studied the coin once more before returning it to Vern. "What happened to the prosthesis company? Seems like I would have heard if the FDA pulled a synthetic joint from the market."

Vern filed the coin back in its folder. "That was the interesting thing. The prosthesis never had FDA approval to begin with. It was a product in development that had passed biologic safety in animals and was in the early phase of human studies. This nursing home resident was part of a small group of patients who received the hip. Presumably it did just fine until she found herself in a thousand degree inferno."

"The metal in the earlier generation of joints would have held up just fine in those conditions," Mackie said. "Newer ones, too, for that matter."

Vern laughed. "I can see that discussion going well, telling the family the good news is grandma's hip survived the fire; the bad news is that's all that's left of her." He held up his notes from the autopsy folder. "This was probably just one of many concerns with that company. Frankly, I'm surprised you didn't hear more about this incident when it happened. The lady's joint was replaced by a team at Nashville Memorial working on this experimental product."

"Which company?" Mackie asked.

"It was a start-up company…" Vern glanced at his notes, "… named New Horizon Prosthetics."

Mackie's mouth turned dry as the realization dawned on him. "The same one Sarathi Singh worked on," he said, more to himself than to Vern.

"Who?"

Mackie looked up. "A former resident of mine." Pieces of the mystery of Sarah's death unfolded before him. Hank's vision to grow Synthesis Industries. Singh's understanding of the failed metals. Clark's ability to exploit the flaws in his own armored vehicles. All brought together by Sarah. But where did Duel fit in? Surely his willingness to run interference with Reagan at the airport was motivated by more than just money. And why would he be motivated to turn against Mackie at all? Unless Duel had been in on New Horizon from the beginning.

"Dude, you look like something just spooked you," Vern said.

Mackie refocused on Vern. "What did Duel say to you on the morning of Sarah's autopsy?"

"Who?"

"Duel Richardson. My attorney. What did he tell you when you talked to him about finding the H-BOC in Sarah."

Vern shook his head as he placed the notes from the melted coins back in their folder. "I don't know what you mean. Before you came to see me that day, only three other people knew about the H-BOC: my assistant plus Nashville PD's Detective Libby Pham. That's why I was so surprised when you brought it up. I've never even heard of this Duel guy."

"Then how did he—" Mackie stopped short. The potential reality of the situation slammed into him, and he sank back in his chair. Either Sarah's killer had told Duel about the H-BOC. Or Duel had murdered Sarah.

In less than one hour, Mackie would find out for himself.

CHAPTER THIRTY-FIVE

MACKIE LEFT THE morgue in Vern's car. The pathologist let him borrow it for the afternoon under the auspices of driving home for a shower and a change of clothes. Mackie reassured him he'd have it back in a couple of hours. As he left the hospital, Mackie called Pham, hoping she would accompany him to his final stop. Over the last few days, they'd located crumbs of evidence, offering a taste of what might have happened to Sarah. But with what Vern had shown him, Mackie thought he would find a load of convicting evidence in Sarah's copied emails. Unequivocal proof of why she had died. And who was involved. With the connections of New Horizon Prosthetics, Mackie formed a convincing thesis of the events surrounding her murder. Now, Duel would be called into account. But Pham didn't answer her phone. When he tried her at home, her voicemail clicked on. He called police headquarters. Detective Pennington came onto the line, instead. Mackie explained just enough to obtain his cooperation, then waited while Pennington looked for Pham.

"She's not done yet," Pennington said when he returned. "Whatever y'all did down in Alabama, it pissed off the Chief. Detective Pham said she'll call you when she's done."

Mackie cradled the phone between his ear and his shoulder, shifting gears in Vern's car. "When's that going to be?"

"Whenever the Chief is done," Pennington said. "Based on what I just saw, I'd say you're out of luck for a few hours."

Mackie glanced at the clock on the dashboard. He didn't have time to wait for Pham. "Have her call me," he finally said.

"What for?"

"She'll know." The phone slipped off his shoulder when he turned the steering wheel. Mackie braked in the middle of the road as he leaned down to pick up the phone. The drivers behind him blared their horns while he grabbed it.

Mackie hung up and tossed the phone onto the passenger seat. He drove home too fast, blasting through yellow lights and running a red one. He whipped into the driveway, jerking on the emergency brake as he parked.

Mackie burst through his front door. Jonah, sprawled out on the kitchen floor, perked up his ears when Mackie tore through the house to his study.

He'd not spent much time returning the study back to its original immaculate condition. One more thing for him to do, but not today. Mackie pulled up a chair as he woke up the screen saver. The folder containing her emails remained open on the desktop. He scrolled through the Inbox folder, scanning for any mention of New Horizon Prosthetics. Nothing obvious. He moved down to the "Sent" documents. Near the bottom of the list, three document headings appeared, obviously overlooked in his scanning of her emails before. A fourth document with the same title of NHP, had been sent as a spreadsheet. Mackie opened the first of three emails he encountered.

Scrolling through several pages, he skimmed over legalese of small business incorporation and company organization, but he saw no mention of the metals used in the prostheses or the names of the individuals involved. Wherever Sarah might have mentioned the name of the prosthesis, she had simply inserted "The Product" and then written descriptions of how it would fit into New Horizon's business plan. Mackie skipped to the next email. More legal language, specifically detailing the venture capitalists and financial arrangements for the company. No closer to what he hoped to find, he moved to the final document listed under NHP.

That's where he found it.

Sent on now-defunct letterhead for the small company, Sarah had attached a letter she had written to the Food and Drug Administration. In two paragraphs, she explained that, due to a manufacturing concern with the product, the company was withdrawing their titanium-alloy prosthetic hip from consideration by the FDA advisory committee. No mention of the tainted metal.

No reference to the lower melting point. Simply a letter stating the product's withdrawal from testing in human subjects.

He would need more than that to convince Duel of what he knew.

Mackie turned his attention to the spreadsheet sent in the fourth document. Entitled "NHP Finances", the spreadsheet enumerated various payments related to the prosthetic hip, all arranged chronologically. The ledger dated back over fifteen years. Only Sarah would hang onto such antiquated information, he thought. The ledger for New Horizon specified date and recipient. He searched for recognizable names.

Mackie glanced at his watch. He'd already taken twice as long as he'd expected, and still didn't have the exact information he needed. Sweat slicked his palms as he moved the mouse through the financial listings.

Time was running out.

Mackie's hand slipped on the mouse. He wiped his palm over his trouser legs, acknowledging his own nervousness as he strained to pick out a recognizable name in the list.

Then, he saw it.

Mackie printed the entire email, ledger and all.

Buried among the dozens of payments, he found a five thousand dollar check payable to Duel Richardson.

Chapter Thirty-Six

THE DRIVE TO DUEL'S house took more than twenty minutes. He had left a detailed message on Pham's cell phone, figuring that was the smart thing to do. What began as a spattering of raindrops turned into a downpour. Mackie turned on his headlights in the premature twilight, squinting through the windshield at the reflections of other cars. He drove into the pastoral neighborhoods of Nashville's suburbs, hunched over the steering wheel of Vern's car as he peered through the rain. The house was harder to find in the bad weather, but the rusted construction dumpster in the front yard helped him locate it. Mackie pulled into the unpaved driveway, splashing through the potholes. No sign of Pham's car. He wondered if she'd gotten the message he'd left with Pennington. Maybe she wasn't even finished with her meeting with the Chief yet. Mackie parked next to the blue tarp that covered stacks of lumber.

He could wait for her, but Duel would notice him sitting in the driveway. Instead, Mackie grabbed the gym bag with the printed pages of the New Horizon ledger, which also contained Libby Pham's handgun—still wrapped in the torn police jacket.

Rain soaked his shirt as he ran to the front door. Mackie stood under the small awning, but the cascading water from the gutters soaked his shoes. His hospital scrubs stuck to the back of his legs. He rang the doorbell.

Duel answered almost immediately. "Well, Jesus H. Christ, look at you," Duel said, standing in the open doorway.

Mackie brushed past him. His shoes made puddles on the hardwood floors of the foyer. The smell of peanut oil still hung in the air from the last time he was here.

Duel shut the door. "Go stand in the study on the rug. You're about to leave a stain on the hardwoods." He walked down the hallway to the kitchen while Mackie stepped into the carpeted study. Moments later, Duel returned from the kitchen with an armload of towels. "You hungry? I was just heating up the fryer for dinner." He tossed them on the floor and rubbed them around with his foot. "What the hell did you get yourself into down in Atlanta?"

Mackie paused a beat. "I was in Alabama."

"Whatever. Judging from this incident report, you'd think you drove down there looking for revenge."

Mackie gripped his bag. He placed it next to him on the sofa as he sat down. "How did you get the fax to begin with? I never told them you were my lawyer."

Duel approached the fireplace and added a log to the embers. The wood immediately caught fire, cracking in the silence of the house. He leaned back against the credenza, smiling. "I've known Haywood Clark for years, and Hank Stone called earlier to fill me in on the crap you've been up to in his neck of the woods."

His stomach sank. Duel had known all along. "That's what I want to talk to you about," Mackie said.

"Hold that thought." Duel reached behind him and picked up a remote control. "Let me show you something first." On the flat screen television embedded in the bookshelves, aerial images of a burning building appeared. A ticker across the bottom of the screen proclaimed "Breaking News", identifying the scene as Bridgeport, Alabama. Smoke billowed from the building. Rescue vehicles fanned out across the bottom of the screen. The recorded program cut to an interview with an employee, tearfully explaining the explosion.

"You recorded this?" Mackie asked.

"Thought you'd find it interesting. You probably didn't have as good of an overall view from where you were located." Duel turned to Mackie, the images still playing on the muted screen. "Three people died in the fire. Including General Clark."

Mackie glanced at the screen once more before looking at Duel. "Armored Forces Industries has been producing tainted military armor in exchange for kickbacks from Synthesis Industries. Remember them, Duel?" he asked sarcastically.

Duel crossed his arms. "Why would they do that?"

"You tell me. Why would someone knowingly sabotage armored protection for American soldiers? Not for ideological reasons. At this point, a few dead GI's is not going to change either the conflict overseas or public opinion at home." Mackie settled into the couch, steadying himself. He moved the gym bag closer.

"And you think I had something to do with that?"

Mackie ignored his question. "I'm still trying to put my finger on your motive. Surely not for personal revenge. It's virtually impossible to predict which soldier is going to end up in a tainted vehicle. Harder still to know if that vehicle is going to be the victim of a roadside bomb." Mackie unzipped his bag. "So the only reason I can think of that someone would do this is for their own financial gain."

"You really bought into that theory," Duel scoffed. "Desperate overtures from a guilty man, fabricating stories to deflect attention away from himself."

Mackie glared at Duel. "Are you talking about my situation or yours?"

A clap of thunder rocked the house, causing the lights to flicker. The television blinked. A blue screen replaced the images from AFI as it searched for a signal. Mackie reached into his bag and grabbed the print-out from Sarah's computer files. "What do you remember about New Horizon Prosthetics?"

Duel paused. He stared at Mackie but he didn't answer the question.

Mackie flipped through the pages. "Not ringing a bell? How about this? Almost twenty years ago, Sarah invited you to help her with legal work for a start-up company called New Horizon Prosthetics. A promising new joint replacement company that ultimately got pulled from FDA consideration due to a design flaw in the metal." Mackie looked up. "Sound familiar at all?"

"How'd you get that?"

"You sent it to me on your fancy computer. It's all in Sarah's emails. Remember?" Mackie tossed the pages onto the coffee table in front of him. "Sarah paid you five thousand dollars when the company folded. Split her payment fifty-fifty with you. I assume that's when you met Sarathi Singh. Where Hank Stone fits in, I can only guess."

"Maybe you can ask him," Duel said as he glanced at his watch.

"I hadn't made the connection when I last saw him." Mackie slid his hand into the bag, resting it on the jacket-wrapped handgun. "After New Horizon folded, it was a few more years before Singh figured out how to reformulate H–BOC into a powdered form. By then, you were established in your Nashville legal practice and Sarah had met General Clark. Within a few more years, America's military involvement in the Middle East gave you guys just the outlet you needed to land a governmental contract for the new H–BOC. And General Clark gave you the mechanism to ensure a steady return on your investment."

Duel reached for the printed ledger on the coffee table. "That's absurd." He flipped through the print–out.

"It's actually quite clever, if it weren't so preposterous," Mackie said. "You ever see what happens to a body hit by shrapnel? Anytime an RPG slams into one of AFI's Humvees, the false armor surrounding the gas tank shears off, puncturing the fuel tank and acting as an accelerant. The soldier riding in the back isn't your target audience. He's dead before he even hears the explosion. It's the guys up front. Lots of blood loss when hot metal explodes in a closed space. It's only a few vehicles. Just enough to not arouse suspicion. But you knew the Pentagon would pour money into a product that could bring those soldiers home in anything other than a body bag."

Duel studied the pages of the ledger before looking up. "No one's going to believe this shit." He walked to the fireplace and tossed the pages into the flames. The pages ignited immediately, then curled into cinders. "That's the beauty of the entire scheme. It's so outrageous that unless you have hard evidence to convince someone, no one would believe you."

Mackie watched the pages disintegrate. "It's not going away that easily, Duel. There's more documentation. Other people know about this."

"There's not a jury in the world who would convict someone with the information you've shown me. Look around you, Mackie." Duel spread his arms out, emphasizing the opulence of the study. "This didn't come to me by accident. It came from hard work. Honest work. None of this so–called evidence you're talking about will undermine what I've accomplished. But I can guarantee you one thing: this is not a battle you want to pick with me, because it is not a battle you're going to win."

Mackie shifted forward on the sofa. "How did Hank convince you to go along with the scheme? Come on, Duel. What could be so damned important that you'd come after me, of all people? Trying to frame me for a murder you know I didn't commit. What does Hank have on you that you'd go to those lengths?"

Mackie glanced out the window of the study. Still no sign of Pham.

Duel ignored Mackie's question. He strode to the foyer and opened the front door. The sound of rain splattering on the front stoop echoed off the hardwood entrance floor. He stood for a moment. Curious, Mackie stood and cautiously followed him. Duel closed the front door when he heard Mackie behind him, a faint smile spreading across his face. Raindrops spotted his leather shoes. "Right on time."

"For what?"

"For you." He laughed to himself. "Your timing's impeccable, Mackie. I'm sure you came out with more than just printed check registers as your justification for making these allegations."

"I came out here to get some answers," Mackie said. "I came here because you're the one who said AFI would press charges. Said the police were looking for me. But it's all a bunch of crap, isn't it? The only person looking to find out what I know is you. You never had any intention of defending me, did you? Even though you know good and well that I didn't murder my wife."

"Ex-wife, Mackie. Don't forget that. She left you for someone else."

The doorbell rang.

Mackie's heart accelerated. Had Pham parked where he couldn't see her through the window?

Duel smiled, unaffected by the doorbell. "Here's your chance. You can explain your little tale of greed and corruption. Of this plot for businessmen in Atlanta to kill American soldiers abroad. I'm sure he'll get a kick out of your story, too."

Mackie moved back from the door, suddenly losing confidence in his plan. "What are you talking about?"

Duel opened the door. And in walked Hank Stone.

CHAPTER THIRTY-SEVEN

"WHAT IN THE hell is he doing here?" Hank demanded as he stared at Mackie.

"You were supposed to arrive first," Duel said. He locked the door and removed the key from the deadbolt.

Not good, Mackie thought. Knowing he was in over his head and likely trapped, his mind raced to plan his exit strategy. He couldn't wait for Pham.

"Anyone else here?" Hank asked.

Duel shook his head. "Not yet."

Hank walked inside, water pooling on the wooden floors in his wake. He took off his overcoat and tossed it on the bannister at the bottom of the staircase. Without saying a word, he turned around and punched Mackie in the jaw. Mackie stumbled from the unexpected blow, sprawling onto the foyer floor.

"Son of a bitch," Hank said. "You just couldn't leave well enough alone, could you?"

Blood flooded Mackie's mouth. He wiped his lip with the back of one hand while steadying himself with the other.

"Jesus, you two, don't go messing up the floor" Duel kicked a wad of wet towels toward Mackie.

"What does he know?" Hank demanded.

"Most of it. It's circumstantial, though. A few things in writing that don't prove shit."

Mackie pushed himself off the floor, keeping his back toward the door and his gaze on Hank, who looked possessed. Wet strands of hair hung over his face. Mud adorned his trousers and shoes. Hank angrily paced the foyer.

"You had Sarah killed," Mackie said as he edged toward the study. "And you tried to frame me for the murder."

"Fucking idiot." Hank spat on the floor. "You think I'd actually kill a woman then stand around with my dick in my hands at the Parthenon on the day I planned to ask her to marry me?"

Mackie stood when he reached the foyer threshold and backed slowly into the study, moving to the gym bag on the sofa. "You were in Nashville on the night of the murder."

Duel followed Mackie. "You guys need to cool off." He strode to the credenza, opened a drawer, and pulled out a pistol. "I don't trust either one of you not to do something stupid."

Both Hank and Mackie glanced at one other, giving a knowing glance of a situation spiraling out of control.

The lights flickered once more after a thunderclap as Duel picked up a poker and stirred the fire's embers. "You came here for answers, Mackie," he said, still facing the fire. "Let's start by dispensing one of your myths. Hank didn't kill Sarah last week." He paused, restored the poker to the fireplace implement stand, and turned around, a demonic grin on his face. "I did."

A stunned Mackie stared at Duel. Hank abruptly halted in the hallway. The two men glanced at one another before turning back to Duel.

"Why?" Mackie asked.

Duel checked the gun, then ran his thumb over the top of it. "Hank paid her thirty million dollars. Sarah kept it all for herself, even though we had a deal. An agreement dating back to the New Horizons contract. Even splits for collaborative projects. She screwed me out of my share."

Mackie slumped down onto the sofa, the gym bag wedged against his hip. He felt the barrel of the hand gun. "You murdered Sarah for fifteen million dollars? Look around you, Duel. You're not exactly hurting for money."

"You fucking asshole," Hank shouted as he charged into the study.

Duel never flinched. He raised the gun and unloaded the magazine. The sound deafened Mackie. Hank crumpled to the floor. Duel took two steps forward, firing into Hank's limp body at his feet.

Mackie sat paralyzed at first, shocked into immobility by Duel's actions. Duel was insane, Mackie realized. Beyond reason. Mackie knew that he would be next. No way Duel would allow him to witness a cold blooded murder and then leave on his own. He had to get out of the house. With the key to the front door deadbolt in Duel's pocket, Mackie had to go out the back. Or through the construction zone.

The gun clicked when Duel ran out of bullets. The hollow sound prompted Mackie to lunge at Duel. With no time to extract the weapon from the gym bag, he swung the weighted bag with all the strength he possessed, nailing Duel in the side of the head. Duel stumbled back, but he didn't go down. Mackie slammed Duel with his shoulder, knocking them both off balance. Duel grabbed at Mackie as he fell, and they both tumbled onto the coffee table.

Mackie felt a sharp pain as he hit the edge of the table, causing him to drop the bag. Pushing past the pain, Mackie kicked out at Duel, catching him beneath his chin. Both struggled to stand as a flash of lightning lit up the window. A harsh-sounding thunderclap followed, and the lights died. The embers of the fire cast a distorting glow across the upended furniture. Mackie groped around for a means of self-defense. Where the hell was his gym bag? Or Duel's gun. Mackie rolled to the fireplace and wrestled the poker off its hanger.

Duel sat up on the floor, then seized Mackie's ankle. Blindly swinging the poker, Mackie felt something crack as the poker smashed into Duel, who immediately released his leg.

Mackie scrambled to his feet, still gripping the metal rod. He stumbled toward the foyer, but he tripped over Hank's body. The poker flew across the entrance way, disappearing into the darkness. Mackie limped to the front door. He desperately yanked on the handle, but he couldn't open the locked door. Mackie heard movement in the study.

"Damn you, Mackie!" Duel yelled.

Mackie turned, spotting Duel backlit by the smoldering fire. He doubted Duel could see him given the near total darkness of the house.

Duel made it to his feet, leaned down to collect something from the floor, and then used the bookshelf for support to stay upright.

Mackie turned toward the kitchen but slipped in the wet foyer, uncertain if Duel had figured out his location. He bumped against the banisters and Hank's jacket slid off its perch, landing at his feet. Mackie found himself retreating toward the closest exit as he backed up the first two stairs. He could still see Duel's backlit shadow.

Duel paused at Hank's body. "What are you gonna do now, Mackie?" he called out in a predatory tone Mackie had never heard before. "The house is boarded up and locked."

Mackie slowly backed up the stairs. When he reached the halfway point, he saw Duel's body move into the foyer. Rain hammered the house. Mackie reached the top of the stairs. He paused.

Duel swept the gun in an arch, searching the darkness for Mackie. "You may put up more of a fight than Sarah did…" He breathed raggedly. "…but I'd doubt you'll squeal as much as she did before she died."

Mackie squatted on the landing, watching Duel. He remained silent, his gaze taking in the painter's tarp atop the hardwoods at his feet. Mackie slid along the landing until he reached the base of the plywood barricade. He stood, registering the padlock that secured the entrance to the construction zone of Duel's master suite.

Duel stood in the center of the foyer, peering down the hallway to the kitchen. "You're a dead man, Mackie." He turned the corner, out of view.

Mackie desperately searched for a key. Nothing tacked to the side of the door jamb. He heard Duel directly below him on the first floor. Mackie reached up to the lip above the door frame. His fingers slid over the key, knocking it to the floor. The key landed on the wooden transition at the base of the door, the metallic clink of impact like a cannon shot. He froze, then glanced over his shoulder to the foyer.

A cone of light emerged from the hallway. Duel swept the beam across the entrance. Front door. Study entrance. Stairway.

Mackie stepped back to unlock the door, the floor creaking beneath his feet. He froze again, checking to see if Duel heard him move.

The sweep of the flashlight beam stopped.

Mackie didn't breathe. Duel stood at the bottom of the stairs. Mackie leaned toward the door, careful not to shift his feet. He gripped the padlock, fumbling to unlock it.

Duel aimed the flashlight up the stairs.

Mackie yanked the lock open, then pulled out the key. Each noise announced his presence like a bell. He still needed to remove the padlock, but he was out of time. He squatted down, just avoiding the flashlight beam, which danced above his head. He didn't move as Duel stepped onto the bottom stair, pausing to listen for Mackie before he took another step.

Mackie steadied himself. The floor creaked beneath his feet. The flashlight stopped again. He heard Duel wheeze near the bottom of the stairwell. Then, the air exploded in a barrage of bullets. Wood splinters and drywall rained down on Mackie.

In the silence that followed, Mackie tossed the key over the bannister. The echo of the key off the wooden floors in the foyer wasn't loud, but it was enough.

The flashlight beam streaked across the ceiling as Duel turned to locate the noise. In the brief moment that followed, Mackie stood and removed the padlock. He pushed open the door and stepped through the plywood barricade.

The noise from the rain intensified when he opened the door. Lightning flashed, back lighting Mackie before he could shut the door.

"You're a dead man, Mackie," Duel shouted, sounding truly insane.

Two more bullets whizzed past Mackie, smashing into the plywood around the door. He slammed the door, but it creaked back open. No way to lock out Duel, he realized. He rushed into the darkness, stumbling over the floor joists. Mackie picked his way across the planks on the exposed floor. With each flash of lightning, he saw more of the construction zone. Stacks of lumber to one side. Opened boxes of tile squares on the other. A translucent tarp tacked to a wooden barricade of the unframed wall. Mackie turned toward the tile boxes. His foot slipped off the plank, scraping his shin across wood. He dropped to his knees, crawled to the stack, and searched for a way out. Or a place to hide.

The door burst open, slamming against the plywood wall. Three gunshots ripped holes in the plastic tarp. Rainwater and twilight seeped through. Mackie crouched behind the stacks of tile, the frame of the existing wall pressing into his spine as he shrank back.

Duel's flashlight danced around the room. "Come out, come out, wherever you are," Duel mocked. He stood in the doorway, his bulky frame silhouetted by the faint flicker of the downstairs fire.

Mackie held his breath. No escape. No windows or doors along the existing walls. A two-story drop off beyond the tarp.

Duel, gripping the flashlight, then moved forward. With each advancing step, he methodically swept the beam from side to side. Left, center, right. Step. Left, center, right. Step. Each sweep moved him deeper into the room. And closer to Mackie.

Ten feet away from Duel, Mackie seized a length of broken tile. The sharp edges pinched his palm as he gripped the tile shard.

Left, center, right. Duel progressed forward.

Mackie strained to see his surroundings. A tool box sat across the room, near the lumber. Too far to reach without completely exposing himself.

Left, center, right. Duel moved even closer.

Mackie glanced at the tarp, almost within arm's reach.

Left, center, right. The plywood walkway creaked. Duel's labored breathing broke the silence. Less than five feet from his position.

Mackie gripped the tile shard. His heart slammed in his chest. He tensed his body, readying himself to attack.

Duel swept the flashlight left, exposing the position directly across the room from Mackie's hiding place. The light shone in the center, piercing the bullet holes in the tarp. In Duel's other hand, the gun's metal reflected the light.

Mackie held his breath. He lobbed the shard of tile across the room. It crashed onto the stack of lumber even as he closed his hand around another jagged length of tile. The flashlight beam rocketed to the stack of lumber, followed by three quick blasts of Duel's gun.

Mackie lunged at Duel, slashing at him with the tile shard. He slammed into the bigger man with such force, both of them crashed to the floor. Duel's gun spun across the floor, stopping at the edge of the tacked-down tarp ten feet away.

Duel rolled over, flailing for gun. Mackie struggled to get to his feet. Duel caught Mackie's leg, tripping him up. He fell toward Duel.

"Goddamn you!" Duel howled.

Mackie kicked Duel in the gut. He twisted free his foot, then crawled toward the tarp, looking for the gun. Scrambling forward, he crashed against the wooden barricade. The plastic ripped under his weight.

Rain poured into the room. Mackie scrambled through the

opening, his hands slipping on the new decking. Water dripped into his eyes. Duel grabbed his ankle before he could pull free. Cocking his other leg, Mackie thrust it through the opening and smashed Duel's face with his foot. Duel's grip eased, and Mackie pulled himself through the opening and into the rain.

Instead of a functional deck, Mackie discovered he was perched on a ledge. Large four–by–fours intended to support the new deck rose out of the ground. A twenty foot frame expanded in front of him, none of the planks installed. Rainwater slashed at the small ledge, loosening Mackie's grip. Below him, he saw a muddy patio enclosure, metal rebar jutting up from the ground. Mackie knew he'd impale himself if he tried to jump off the ledge.

Lightning flashed. The ripped tarp billowed in the rain, its jagged edge resembling a scar on the side of the house. He groped along the edge of the planks, searching for a secure hand–hold. Hoping to find scaffolding he could climb down.

Duel punched a fist through the flap, then his other fist. Mackie, with no place to hide, frantically glanced around. Nothing. Duel spotted Mackie perched on the exposed boards. He smiled a disturbing grin. "You're fucked, buddy."

Mackie pressed his body against a two–by–four nailed to the edge of the house. His foot slipped. He clung to a wooden barricade intended to secure a tarp not support a grown man.

Duel stood at the entrance to the room where a window and a wall would one day be. He said, "This all would have worked out if you'd let me do my job." Each breath seemed more labored than before. Duel looked possessed. "I had it all worked out. You were protected! I staged the H–BOC resuscitation in Sarah and faked the break–in at your house. If you'd have sat back and let me steer the investigation, you probably would have received most of Sarah's fortune. At least until Reagan reached inheritance age. Minus my substantial legal fees, of course." Duel shifted forward, one foot on the deck and the other still positioned inside the house.

Mackie couldn't move. His hand slipped each time he tried to reposition it on the flimsy wooden barricade. He knew he couldn't remain crouched in place much longer. Without a firm purchase with his feet, his only option was to edge forward. Toward the house. Toward Duel.

"You know the saddest part of all this," Duel said. "Besides the fucking mess you've created in my house. The saddest part is your precious little Reagan is going to end up just like her mommy and daddy, her abandoned body found in a ditch somewhere with no one to identify her except dear old Uncle Duel." He grinned, standing tall and clearly savoring the moment. "At least then the money will come to me, where it should have gone all along. Before Sarah started sleeping around and screwing us both out of what we most wanted."

The thought of Duel harming Reagan caused a surge of rage inside Mackie.

Lightning suddenly flashed, exposing Duel's gun jammed against the wooden planks. Both men saw it at the same time. Less than five feet from Mackie's body. And directly below Duel's foot.

When Duel leaned down to pick it up, Mackie lunged toward him. He grabbed Duel.

Duel tumbled forward, slamming onto the wet deck. The gun slipped from his grip, spinning to the deck ledge. Duel flailed, then seized one of Mackie's legs. Both men fought for a grip on the slick boards. Duel's momentum and weight jerked Mackie back toward the edge of the deck.

Mackie grabbed at anything he could find, landing his grip on the protective railing beneath the tarp. He heard the wood groan under the force of their combined weight.

Mackie spotted the gun near the edge of the deck.

Duel saw it too. He pulled harder on Mackie's leg, teetering on the edge of the boards. Duel freed one hand to reach for the weapon.

When he did, Mackie used his free leg to kick Duel in the face.

"You little prick!" Duel screamed as he floundered, fingers clawing at the wet lumber.

Mackie kicked again, driving his heels forward. He connected with Duel's forehead.

Duel screamed. His body tumbled forward, past the gun, as he slipped over the edge of the deck.

Mackie rolled away from him, across the threshold and under the cover of the roof. The rain streamed into the opening. He flipped onto his stomach, belly-crawling back across the threshold. With his feet firmly hooked along the floor joist, Mackie reached for the edge of the unfinished deck.

Darkness below. Rain splattered his face and dripped off his nose. As his eyes adjusted, he made out the shape of Duel's body. Fifteen feet below. Lightning streaked across the sky, exposing Duel's horrified facial expression. Eyes and mouth open. Metal spikes punching though his chest and neck.

CHAPTER THIRTY-EIGHT

MACKIE PUSHED BACK from the edge of the deck. The rain continued to pummel the side of the house, saturating everything. Mackie struggled to his feet, his respirations uneven. Even stepping back inside the house did not stop the rainfall. The plastic tarp lay crumpled at his feet, draped over the splintered guardrail. Rain gusted. Above him, the upper portion of the tarp flapped in the wind. When he turned around, he noticed Duel's flashlight. It cast an odd glow in the far corner of the room. He walked over and picked it up.

Using the beam, he surveyed the room. Broken tiles. Water-stained drywall. Upended lumber. Mackie picked his way through the debris.

The door in the plywood barricade opened easily. He stepped onto the landing at the top of the stairs. The smell of burning cooking oil greeted him, more intense than it had been when he arrived. Light flickered in the study below, casting long shadows across Hank's body. Mackie descended the stairs. Halfway down, he heard a phone ring.

He paused. The muffled ringing came from the bottom of the stairs. Mackie scanned the flashlight ahead of him, seeing Hank's discarded coat at the foot of the banister. By the time he reached the bottom steps, the ringing had stopped. He tapped the jacket with his foot. Cell phone. Mackie ignored it. He turned toward the study. Hank's body blocked the doorway. A pool of coagulated blood surrounded him, the two bullet holes in his head oozing a dark trickle onto the carpet. He stepped over Hank's body and moved into the study. Even in this surreal state, he knew he had to get his bag. Beneath the rubble of the crushed table, Mackie saw it. He checked for Pham's gun, finding it nestled inside. No way he was leaving that behind. He'd already left enough fingerprints.

Another phone rang. He jumped, startled. The sound seemed amplified in the ominous quiet. Duel's mobile on the credenza rang again. Mackie approached it. The phone rang twice more before it stopped. He slipped his hand inside the tail of his shirt then picked up the phone. A missed call from Sarathi Singh. Mackie wiped off any prints before he set it down. He approached the hearth, collected two pieces of firewood, and tossed them onto the glowing embers. The fire roared to life. He inspected the study as he warmed himself. He knew he had to leave, and quickly, but he needed a minute to figure out what to do next.

Dozen of books, mostly legal texts, lined the upper bookcase. Along the lower shelves sat the three-ring binders Mackie had seen on his earlier visit. In contrast to the damaged coffee table and blood-stained carpet, the bookcase appeared immaculate. Hardbacks neatly aligned to the edge of the shelves. Binders alphabetized. Mackie stepped closer. One hand-labeled binder read: Collins-McKay. Another had been labeled SI and AFI. Mackie pulled them both from the shelf. He tucked the binder under his arm and moved to the sofa across the room.

He sat on the couch. His inner voice urged him to get out of the house but his morbid curiosity about Sarah's murder anchored him in place. Using light from both the flashlight beam and the fire, he opened the binder and read. What he found shocked him. Documents detailing each step of the conspiracy had been collated, categorized, and listed in chronological order. Beginning with the ledger for New Horizon Prosthetics, Duel had kept a paper timeline of the plan. Damn idiot. Right in plain sight. He was a gifted attorney in some ways, but in others just plain stupid. In one section, descriptions of the metallic concerns with the prosthetic pulled from the market. In another, details of the powdered H-BOC. Near the back, Mackie found the same nineteen-page classified document describing the Humvee's fuel tank and surrounding armor. The same one embedded in the holiday picture of Mickey Mouse. That someone would even hatch this scheme still astounded Mackie. Even more astounding was Duel's impulse to keep it so readily available.

Mackie closed the binder. As he did, an envelope slipped out of the back pocket. He reached down to the carpet and pick it up. The flashlight beam revealed Duel's name written on the outside in a familiar script. He nearly dropped the envelope when he saw Sarah's handwriting.

Mackie turned it over and pulled out a sheet of stationery. Unfolding it, he saw Sarah Collins imprinted across the top. The letter below was dated from a year ago. Just before their divorce. Not long after she'd revealed her relationship with Hank to Mackie. His hands trembled as he read the note.

Dearest Duel,

It pains me to write these words to you, but I feel that I must be as honest with you as I would be with my own husband (although we both know that may not be the best example of honesty!) I will soon be leaving Cooper as I have fallen in love with another man. As painful as it is for me to write this, that man is not you. I treasure our relationship, both personally and professionally, but I have to follow my heart. This new person speaks to my heart in a way that I never thought possible. Although it seems like I am giving up everything to follow my emotions, I am overwhelmed by the thrill of it. Of course, this means the end of our own trysts, ones that I will continue to smile over even as I remember them. Cooper would kill us both if he only knew!

We always said ours was a relationship of convenience, and one that would never last. I just didn't expect it would end with my falling for another man. Know that I will always treasure the time we've had together. Though it may be awkward, we have more than enough financial incentive to maintain a healthy professional relationship.

With all my devotion and appreciation.

Love,

Sarah

Mackie leaned back on the sofa, taking shallow breaths. He reread the letter once more. He marveled at his own naïveté, believing Sarah in the final years of their marriage when she repeatedly blamed work for her late-night arrivals at home. Never suspecting Duel, his long-time friend, of infidelity and the ultimate act of betrayal. Physical pain gripped his chest, making each breath he took an effort of will.

Embarrassed at being the cuckold and enraged at not recognizing it, Mackie crumpled the stationery. He tossed Sarah's letter in the fireplace. Black cinders formed on the edge of the paper as the page began to curl. He stared transfixed as Duel's name, written in Sarah's flowery script, slowly transformed to black ash.

Duel's cell phone rang again.

Mackie stared at the blue glow from the phone as it illuminated the credenza. He stood and moved to the bookshelves, lifted the phone with his bare hands, and answered it on the third ring. He waited for someone to respond on the other end.

"Duel? Where the hell—I've been calling you for ten minutes." Singh's voice carried notes of irritation and and concern. "Hello? Come on, Duel. How in God's name do I get to your house? Once I reach the traffic light—"

Mackie pressed the disconnect button and tossed the phone in the fireplace. The plastic popped, the glass faceplate snapped, then the device sizzled. The smell of burning electronics permeated the room.

Singh was coming.

Mackie was running out of time.

He stared at the fire for a long moment before walking back to the bookshelves. White hot anger caused Mackie to snap. He swept his arm across the nearest shelf, knocking other binders onto the floor. Some careened off the shelves and slid across the floor. Others popped open when they hit the carpet, the pages scattering like confetti. Books tumbled from the shelf like dominoes, bouncing off the desk, dislodging the television. Rage fueled his outburst as he emptied two more shelves onto the carpet.

He stood in the center of the study, panting as the tantrum passed. As cathartic as trashing the study was, it didn't blind him from the pressing reality of the situation. Two men were dead and a third was on the way there. Regathering his wits, Mackie scooped up the SI and AFI binder from the sofa. He cradled the documents against this chest as he stepped over the rubble.

As he walked past the locked front door, Hank's phone began its muffled alert from his jacket. Mackie ignored it. He walked around the bloody slick in the foyer. Toward the kitchen. The stink of used peanut oil in the turkey fryer nauseated him. A five gallon reserve jug of fresh oil sat on the floor nearby. In the corner of the kitchen, exactly where Mackie had seen it last week, the turkey fryer simmered. Duel had left it on. Neglected for the last hour, the oil had begun to burn. Mackie walked passed the shimmering pot, pressing the back of his hand against his nose as he passed.

Mackie opened the back door then wiped off his prints. With the binder in one hand and the flashlight in the other, he nearly lost his balance when he stepped ankle-deep into the mud outside. He shone the beam across the unfinished backyard. Metal rebar reflected the light. Ten feet ahead of him, he saw Duel's impaled body, awash in mud. Mackie held the flashlight steady for a long moment before he picked his way across the yard.

Hank had parked beside Vern Philpot's car, but he hadn't blocked it. Mackie sank into the driver's seat, shut the door, and slumped back. He needed to go home and clean up before he saw Reagan again. If he hurried, he could make it back to the hospital with time to spare. He glanced out the car window. The neighborhood remained dark, a stark contrast to the flickering glow inside Duel's study.

Mackie reached across the seat, grabbed his cell phone, and dialed the number from memory. He closed his eyes as he waited for her to answer.

"Pham," she said in a clipped voice.

"I need a favor, Libby?"

"Mackie? What's wrong?"

He exhaled, debating how much she needed to know right now. He gripped the SI and AFI binders, which rested in his lap. She would find out soon enough.

He looked out the windshield. Exhaustion threatened to overtake him. "Singh's in Nashville, meeting Duel tonight. Can you send a couple of cops out to Duel's house to question him?"

"Question, maybe. But to bring him in, I'm going to need more than a grudge as a reason," she said.

Mackie stretched the stiffness out of his neck as he shifted the binder into the passenger seat. He started the car, then backed out of the driveway. "Trust me. I've got more than enough to go on."

"Explain."

"Soon enough."

Mackie hung up and turned onto the main road. He accelerated as he pulled out of the neighborhood, settling in for the long drive back.

CHAPTER THIRTY-NINE

THREE DAYS LATER, Mackie stood in the doorway to Reagan's hospital room, waiting on the nurse. He had partially completed the removal of dozens of cards and well wishes adorning the wall of her room. They lay in a stack at the foot of her bed. With Doctor Greenfield having already signed her discharge papers, Mackie was eager to get Reagan back home. He had called in a favor from Hollie Blanton's cleaning crew and now had a clean house for them to return to. Even the study was reassembled.

A half dozen balloons bobbed above the mailbox. Pham's idea, coming twenty-four hours after she had officially cleared Mackie's name as a suspect in the murder investigation.

Mackie rubbed his hand across his scalp, feeling the stubble of the skin glue. He knew better than to remove the adhesive, but he was tired of waiting.

"Dad?"

Mackie's heart skipped a beat. After the turmoil of the last two weeks, he felt happy just to hear her voice. He turned from the door, finding Reagan waking up.

"You're here early," she said through a yawn.

Mackie left his lookout at the door. He sat on the edge of her bed, careful not to topple the tower of cards. Her skin glistened pink with a fine sheen of ointment over healing scrapes. The last visible reminders of the accident. The blood clots now being treated would take longer to resolve, but kids were resilient, Mackie reminded himself.

"We're going home, sweetie, just as soon as I pack up and we get your paperwork."

Reagan stretched her arms, glancing as the clock on the wall. "Seven o'clock," she said. "It's morning shift change. Just be patient, dad. I'm not in any hurry."

They heard a knock on the partially opened door.

Pham entered the room. She held a large balloon in one hand and carried a container with two cups of coffee plus snacks in the other hand. "Not many breakfast options at this hour," she said.

"Dad's not planning on being here that long," Reagan responded.

Pham set the box of coffee cups and snack packs on the bedside table then tied the balloon to the bedrail. "Have you seen today's newspaper, yet?" she asked Mackie. "A front page story about the murder–suicide of a local lawyer at his house."

"Is that the official version?" Mackie asked.

"Doctor Philpot hasn't concluded his autopsy report." Pham handed Mackie one of the cups of coffee. "The first body they found in the foyer was so badly burned from the fire that they had trouble initially determining the cause of death."

Mackie could tell she was choosing her words carefully in front of Reagan. She didn't need to bother, though. Reagan was already checking messages on her phone and sending status updates, tuning out the adult conversation.

"Yesterday the newspaper floated the idea of arson but no mention of the cause of death," Mackie said.

Pham blew on her coffee and shook her head. "The fire chief's already disproven that theory. They now claim the turkey fryer in the kitchen was the source and the jugs of cooking oil were the accelerant. Who operates a deep fryer inside the house?"

"You'd be surprised," Mackie said.

With Singh's arrest two days ago and the surviving documentation Duel left behind, the Nashville Police Department has more than enough information to build a case against Duel as the ringleader of a treasonous scam of epic proportions. How far the feds would run with this information, though, Mackie had no idea. What was even less clear was the hard evidence tracing Duel back to Sarah's murder. Mackie heard the confession but had no proof. The other key witnesses were dead. In spite of Duel's meticulous record keeping, he had not left much of a trail of evidence leading from his involvement in Sarah's murder. Earlier, Pham had reassured Mackie that she had a top notch team in the Nashville PD interrogating what was left of Duel's computer hard drive.

Pham interrupted Mackie's thoughts. "Hungry?" She reached into the carton that had held the coffee and snacks. "The vending machines don't have much to offer for breakfast. Hope you like junk food."

She offered him a cellophane-wrapped snack cake.

Mackie stared at the Twinkie.

"What?" she asked, looking offended. "You have a problem with cream-filled cakes? You know some people down here even fry these things?"

"I think I've lost my taste for those." Mackie wrapped both hands around his coffee and took a sip. If he never saw another Twinkie it would be fine with him. "You have it."

"I've already eaten."

"Then save it," he said as he resumed removing cards of well wishers from the wall. "I hear those things are timeless."

~The End~

Dr. Cooper McKay Returns in

COMMAND AND CONTROL

CHAPTER ONE

THIRTY-FIVE THOUSAND feet above the Atlantic Ocean and half an hour from Washington, D.C., a first class passenger on an inbound flight from London began to sweat. Subtle at first; almost imperceptible. A fine sheen on his forehead followed by a trickle down his cheek. The young man shifted in his seat. He zipped up his jacket. His sweating intensified. He gripped the arm rests and began to mumble to himself. Silent words spoken in a foreign language. The passenger across the aisle didn't recognize the words. They sounded Arabic to Dr. Cooper McKay, but he couldn't be sure. Success in Dr. McKay's medical specialty hinged on close observation, and on this early morning flight, he recognized that something was wrong.

He looked closer at the distressed passenger. Early twenties. Well-groomed. Middle Eastern descent. Probably a student. Dr. McKay set aside his iPhone and leaned across the aisle.

"Can I help you?" he asked.

The passenger stiffened. He continued to stare, trancelike, at the seat in front of him. His mumbling intensified. Repeating a cadence, as if reciting a prayer. The young man never averted his gaze. He began to rock in his seat to the rhythm of his words.

Dr. McKay glanced around the half-empty first class cabin. A lone flight attendant, obviously overworked, cleared breakfast trays from the front row. She didn't notice the distressed man across from McKay. The nearest passenger sat two rows ahead, headphones firmly fixed over her ears. Behind McKay, three empty rows. A curtain sequestered the first class passengers from the rest of the plane.

McKay reached across the aisle. He touched the rocking passenger's hand. Cold fingers. Clammy palms. Racing heartbeat. He recognized the signs. This man was sick. Probably infected. "Let me get you some help," he said.

The passenger didn't even pause to shrug off the intrusion. He continued to pray. McKay withdrew his hand, unclipped his seatbelt, and depressed the call button for the flight attendant. She didn't acknowledge it. McKay stepped into the aisle to summon her. He hustled toward the front of the aircraft, brushing past the woman with the headphones. Past the remaining half-dozen passengers in first class. A bearded man sitting in the first row noticed his approach. The flight attendant looked up at him from her station. Her weary eyes betrayed her smile.

"Excuse me," McKay said. "A sick passenger's sitting across from me. Young male. Uncomfortable. Probably febrile." He lapsed back into the clipped speech of medical summaries etched into his subconsciousness from thirty years of patient presentations. "I need your First Aid Kit."

The flight attendant straightened. "And you are..."

"Dr. Cooper McKay."

She ignored his outstretched hand, obviously annoyed by his intrusion. "Please take your seat, sir. I'll be with you in a moment."

He scanned the bulkhead behind her. Piles of refuse stacked from the overnight flight. Steam rising from the carafe of the coffee maker. No visible First Aid Kit. McKay persisted. "I need your medical kit. This kid can't wait until we reach Nashville. He needs help now."

"You can help me, sir, by returning to your seat. I'll be right there."

McKay paused. He wasn't being an alarmist. Although still adjusting to his recent retirement, he didn't think he was over reacting. He did relish the opportunity, though, to get back involved. Not his medical specialty, but he knew he could help him. He retraced his steps down the aisle, keeping an eye on the sick passenger. He left his seatbelt unbuckled when he sat down. Just in case.

The young passenger continued to rock.

Continued to sweat.

And continued to pray.

The flight attendant completed her work. Only then did she leave her post. She checked with the passenger in the front row. The bearded man in a blazer spoke to her, but she shook her head. The man leaned into the aisle to take a look as the flight attendant approached McKay, empty handed. Two rows away from them, she finally looked at the rocking passenger.

She stopped short.

She glanced at his ski parka. Saw his trance. Heard his mumbling. She turned and strode back to the bulkhead. Spoke into a phone near her station. Signaled to the bearded man in the blazer. The man stepped into the aisle. The flight attendant trailed after him.

The bearded man carried himself with the self-importance of a surgeon. McKay knew the type. A sense of purpose emanated from the man, as if he finally had a chance to enact his training. Like he'd been waiting for such an occasion. His blazer billowed as he marched toward the ailing passenger, stopped one aisle away, and bent toward the passenger. McKay saw the butt of a harnessed SIG SAUR pistol beneath his blazer. Without bothering to touch the passenger, the bearded man announced, "Federal Air Marshal. Unzip your jacket and stand up."

McKay rose from his seat. "This man is sick."

"The pilot's notifying MedAssist," the flight attendant said to him from behind the Federal Air Marshal. "One of their doctors will be in radio contact shortly. If we need them."

The Marshal tensed at McKay's movement, but he didn't turn around. "Sit down, sir. I don't need your help." He stepped closer to the passenger, forcing McKay back into his seat. He landed on the arm rest as he fell back into his chair. He felt the faceplate of his phone crack from the impact.

The Federal Air Marshal fingered his weapon. He kept one hand on the gun while he grabbed the passenger's jacket with the other. He jerked him up from the seat. The passenger didn't resist. His head rolled back. His eyes glazed over. He stopped his prayer. He then proceeded to vomit. Even the Marshal's wide body couldn't block the splatter from reaching McKay. The Federal Air Marshal recoiled, releasing his grip on the man's jacket.

The sick man slumped between the seats. McKay heard the passenger gurgling. Struggling to breathe. Asphyxiating.

Dr. McKay had had enough. He shoved the Marshal out of his

way. "Get me the First Aid Kit," he called to the flight attendant. "Now!"

He dragged the ill passenger by his ankles into the aisle and knelt beside him. When he flopped him onto his side to clear his airway, he heard the high-pitched wheeze of sucking secretions. He pounded on his back. To no avail. His airway remained clogged.

The flight attendant returned, carrying a cordless headset, a blood pressure cuff, and a bright orange medical kit no bigger than a purse. "Put this on," she instructed, handing McKay the headset. "A doctor from MedAssist is on the line."

McKay grabbed the headset. He explained the predicament to the stateside physician. Following the physician's instructions, he situated the cuff on the passenger's arm. Moments later, the physician of MedAssist had the vital signs radioed to him.

"Open the medical kit the stewardess will give you and find the oropharyngeal airway," the doctor on the phone instructed. "This is a curved plastic device—"

"I'm an orthopedic surgeon," McKay snapped. "I know what an O.P.A. is. That's not going to help. He's suffering from laryngeal spasm."

McKay sat back on his heels to grab the orange medical kit. The cracked glass on his phone pinched him. He removed his damaged iPhone from his hip pocket and tossed it onto the seat cushion. He snatched the orange purse from the stewardess and opened the First Aid Kit, dumping the contents onto his vacated seat. Band-aids, gauze pads, and alcohol swabs scattered on the cushion. A blue rubber bulb of an artificial resuscitator tumbled from the orange bag. He recognized the Ambu bag and its two accompanying face masks. Finally, he found the plastic shepherds crook of the O.P.A. He shoved the plastic airway stabilizer into the passenger's mouth. No response.

"It's not working," he said.

"Stay calm," the absentee physician coached. "Try to reposition the O.P.A."

The passenger continued to gasp for air, each breath more shallow than the last. McKay rolled him onto his back. His eyes rolled back in a lifeless retreat. "There's no time for this," McKay said. He ripped off the headset and tossed it back to the stewardess. His advanced cardiac life support training kicked in. He ripped open the young man's jacket, then his shirt. The passenger's pale brown chest appeared recently shaved, his skin slick and rubbery to the touch. His heart thrummed beneath his hands.

"What's his name?" McKay asked the flight attendant.

She bent to pick up the headset at her feet. "Sir, you need to follow the instructions of MedAssist."

"Find out this passenger's name," he barked.

The flight attendant stared at the scene unfolding before her. Clearly out of her element. She made eye contact with McKay. A terrified gaze eclipsed her annoyance. Without answering, she fled to the front of the cabin. The Federal Air Marshal, still soaked in vomit, stepped over Dr. McKay and the prostrate passenger. He dialed his cellphone.

The airplane began its descent.

Gripping the back of one hand with the other, McKay jammed his fists into the soft spot of the passenger's stomach just beneath the rib cage. The young man's body lurched.

The airway didn't clear.

McKay grabbed the blue bulb of the Ambu bag and snapped the face mask on the end. He jammed the resuscitator against the passenger's mouth. Cupping his hand around it, he created a seal. He began artificial respirations. With each squeeze of the bulb, the passenger's cheeks ballooned before air leaked out from the seal around his mouth. His chest wall remained motionless.

McKay recognized the situation for what it was. Spasm of the muscles of the larynx. The O.P.A. would not reach far enough to solve the problem. With the top of the airway blocked, the diaphragm and all of the supporting muscles of the chest wall could not suck air into the lungs. Suffocation resulted. The young passenger was drowning in his own secretions.

The flight attendant returned. "Omar," she said. "His name is Omar Shahani."

Dr. McKay began chest compressions. "Hang on, Omar," he said, searching for any signs of life in the passenger. "Mackie's going to take care of you."

"Mackie?" the flight attendant said.

"Mackie McKay. It's what I go by."

The flight attendant scoffed. "I'm sure he can't hear you."

Mackie cut his eyes at her, never losing the pace of his chest compressions. "We'll see." He returned his attention to Omar. "We've got to get him to a hospital."

"The pilots know," she said. "We're making an emergency landing."

"Dulles airport?" Mackie asked.

She didn't respond.

With chest compressions ineffective and the Ambu bag unable to force air into Omar's lungs, Mackie reexamined the medical supplies. Still straddled over Omar Shahani's legs, he fanned through the contents of the bag on the seat, bumping his hand against his cracked iPhone. Meager supplies at best. He needed a scalpel. Something sharp to relieve the blockage. His eyes darted from the scattered contents to Omar's dwindling condition and back. His gaze snagged on his phone once more. It might work, he thought. Not standard of care, but better than a body bag. He performed a dozen more chest compressions before reaching for his phone.

In the corner of the device he saw a fractured web of glass at the site of impact. A transverse crack extended from it, scarring the faceplate. Mackie gently lifted the phone. He pressed his thumb into the web of broken glass. Selective pressure over the weakest part of the screen. The glass collapsed. He set the phone down on top of the other supplies.

"You have a cappuccino maker on board?" he asked the flight attendant as he resumed chest compressions.

She blinked in surprise. "Two of them."

"Unscrew the heating wand and bring it to me." Mackie repositioned his hands to ease the fatigue settling into his arms. "I also need some chewing gum—as much as you can get—and a roll of tape."

"I hardly think this is the time..." the flight attendant began.

"Just do it!" He snapped on a pair of rubber gloves and reached for his supplies.

Ripping into a stack of alcohol pledgets, he swabbed Omar's neck. With two fingers, he pressed into the ridge to the side of Omar's trachea. The pulse continued its frantic dance, but weaker now. Omar's blood pressure was dropping. The plane wouldn't land in time for emergency personnel to intervene.

Mackie offered the only lifeline.

He interrupted the compressions long enough to retrieve the phone. Pressing once again on the corner, he forced up the transverse crack. The faceplate popped free, lifting up along the casing of the phone. He positioned a gloved finger along the edge of the split glass and pried loose a sharp sliver of glass almost four inches long. The cabin lights overhead winked off the cut edge of the glass faceplate.

Mackie steadied his breathing, as he'd done countless times in a medical crisis, and gripped the makeshift scalpel. He heard the flight attendant return down the aisle. She carried a fistful of supplies. The sun streaming through the cabin window glinted off the metal cappuccino wand. Behind her, the cockpit door opened. Mackie saw the Federal Air Marshal relaying information to the crew, gesturing toward Mackie with one hand while cradling his cell phone with the other.

The flight attendant placed the supplies on the seat close to Mackie. Two packs of bubble gum. A sleeve of breath-freshening chiclets in a blister pack. Two slender silver wands, unscrewed from their moorings. Crusted milk clouded one end. He saw a roll of duct tape. And a spool of cellophane adhesive.

Mackie lifted the first cappuccino wand and handed it back to the flight attendant. "Unscrew the end of this. Remove the outer casing. Then wipe it down." He handed her a stack of alcohol swabs.

He shucked two wads of bubble gum from their wrappers and popped them into his mouth. He positioned his thumb and fingers around the sharp edge of the glass faceplate. With a steady hand and a sure stroke, he pressed the impromptu blade firmly into Omar's neck, aiming for the skin just below his Adam's apple. The neck split open.

The inch-long incision oozed blood. Nothing more than a trickle. Mackie pressed a wad of sterile gauze over the wound. He placed the glass sliver on the seat atop a mound of more gauze. He held out his hand, palm up. The stewardess-turned-scrub-nurse offered the sparkling metal tube.

"Pull off three lengths of duct tape, six inches each," Mackie ordered. "Tear each length halfway down the center to look like legs on a pair of pants."

He transferred the makeshift endotracheal tube to the gauze next to the sharp glass. With his gloved hands, he pried open the incision, probing his way to the thick band of tissue separating Omar's airway from the spasmed muscles above. The crycothyroid membrane. Identifying it with his fingers, Mackie positioned his fingertips against it. With his other hand, he lifted the sliver of glass, the shard poised above his finger. With surgical precision, he nicked the membrane with the tip of the glass. Air rushed into the neck. Omar's chest heaved. Mackie immediately fed the metal tube through the tiny opening.

Air flooded the tube, causing a high-pitched wheeze like the sound of air sucked through a straw. Needing to secure the airway, Mackie reached for the duct tape. He pressed the top edge of the tape along the tube near the skin, as if straddling it with a six-inch pair of pants, and then wrapped the legs in opposite directions. One leg folded around the tube then stuck to the neck, then the other. He reinforced the anchor with a second strip of tape.

"Hand me the Ambu bag," Mackie said.

The flight attendant bent to grab the blue bulb, but the plane banked hard right, dipping into its descent. Mackie's shoulder smacked into the armrest of his own seat. His hand slipped from the taped tube. The bulb of the artificial resuscitator rolled under the seat.

The flight attendant gripped a nearby seat cushion to steady herself. Overhead, the captain's voice spoke from the intercom to prepare the cabin for an emergency landing.

Mackie pinched his free fingers around the E.T. tube. He leaned his chest across Omar and reached for the Ambu bag. At full extension, his arm could just touch it, but it rolled away with the next bank of the plane. He heard nervous murmurs as other passengers in the first class cabin leaned into the aisle to watch. Seeing the blue plastic bulb rolling nearby, the lady with the earphones unclipped her seatbelt and knelt in the aisle. She reached for the Ambu bag, then turned to hand it to Mackie. Obviously horrified by the scene, she turned her head as she held out the mask.

Mackie repositioned Omar on his back. He adjusted his own position atop him to anchor his legs. "Tape," Mackie said.

The flight attendant, now back on her feet, clutched a wadded strip of tape. Useless. Mackie grabbed the roll, ripped two lengths off with his teeth, and stuck them to the tray table. He removed the face mask from the resuscitator, exposing the nub of plastic tubing almost twice as large in diameter as the metal E.T. tube. Mackie wrapped a length of tape around the cappuccino wand now extending from Omar's neck. Once he judged it to be thick enough, he positioned the tube from the respirator over the newly taped end.

A close fit, but not perfect.

Mackie worked the chewing gum into the front of his mouth. Ripping off his latex gloves with his teeth, he grabbed the gum and began to work it around the tube connection, creating a seal. He gave two squeezes of the bulb. Omar's chest wall rose with each compression of the Ambu bag. Tiny bubbles formed in the gum seal. Mackie used the last piece of duct tape to cover the seal between the two tubes.

The flight attendant, bracing herself against the plane's descent, worked her way back to the bulkhead. She spoke to the Federal Air Marshal first, then to the pilots. Moments later, the cockpit door closed.

What should have been an easy task of depressing the Ambu bag became that much harder as the plane descended. Mackie pressed his knees against Omar's chest as he wedged his shoulders against the arm rest. Once he secured his own position, he squeezed the Ambu bag again. Omar's chest rose with each artificial respiration. Mackie felt for his carotid artery. He found a steady pulse, slam dancing against his fingers. Improved blood pressure, Mackie thought. Omar's eyes remained closed. His skin still felt clammy. Every five seconds, Mackie squeezed the Ambu bag. Twelve times a minute. Normal respirations.

The flight attendant's voice came over the intercom.

"Ladies and gentlemen, due to a medical emergency in the first class cabin, we will soon make an emergency landing."

Mackie unwrapped one more piece of bubble gum. He began to chew, preparing for landing.

He continued to squeeze the Ambu bag. Every five seconds. Twelve times a minute. Breathing for Omar.

Command and Control will be available summer 2014.

CPSIA information can be obtained
at www.ICGtesting.com
Printed in the USA
LVOW11s0056210317
527886LV00001BB/54/P